THE JUNGLE

The Uncensored Original Edition

by

Upton Sinclair

See Sharp Press ◆ Tucson, AZ ◆ 2003

Sinclair, Upton, 1878-1968.
    [Jungle]
    The jungle : the uncensored original edition / Upton Sinclair ; with an
introduction by Kathleen De Grave. — Tucson, AZ : See Sharp Press, c2003.
    ISBN 1-884365-30-2
    Summary: The horrifying conditions in the meatpacking industry in the early 1900's
are revealed through the experiences of immigrants as they try to make a living working in
the Chicago stockyards.

    1. Packing-houses — Corrupt practices — Illinois — Chicago — Fiction.
2. Immigrants — Illinois — Chicago — Fiction. 3. Beef industry — Corrupt practices —
Illinois — Chicago — Fiction. 4. Chicago (Ill.) — Fiction. I. Title.

PS3537.I85 J85 2003
813.52

CONTENTS

FOREWORD

Despite nearly a century of neglect, Upton Sinclair's classic novel *The Jungle* has survived the efforts of censors to subvert its political message. The story of how *The Jungle* found its way into print in 1906 is a strange one. How the original, uncut version found its way, briefly, into print in 1988 is even stranger.

Those familiar with this classic know that it shocked America when it was first published in book form in 1906. The novel's graphic description of unsanitary conditions in the Chicago meatpacking industry and the brutal treatment of immigrant laborers came as a revelation to most Americans. The resulting outcry soon became so great that President Teddy Roosevelt and Congress were forced to pass the first Pure Food and Drug laws in this country. Some years later, Sinclair wrote about the amazing popularity of his book, saying, "I aimed at the public's heart, and by accident I hit it in the stomach."

Less well known is how the book came into existence. In 1904, the editors of the Socialist newspaper, *The Appeal to Reason*, published in Girard, Kansas, gave Upton Sinclair $500 and sent him to Chicago to do research on the meatpacking industry. When Sinclair began his investigation, he discovered that the unsanitary practices of the meatpacking industry were far more horrible than anyone could have imagined. Sinclair began writing his novel, using the plot of John Bunyan's classic, *Pilgrim's Progress,* as a model. The main character, Jurgis Rudkos,[1] became an immigrant pilgrim in the sinful city of Chicago.

The editors at *The Appeal* planned to run Sinclair's novel in serialized form in their weekly newspaper. But after about two thirds of the novel had been published, the newspaper's socialist readers began clamoring for more news and less fiction. The editors stopped running the novel.

Shortly after signing a deal with *The Appeal* for the serial rights, Sinclair found a book publisher for *The Jungle*. He got a contract with Macmillan (which had published his earlier book, *Manassas*), promising to write a book that described the "breaking of human hearts by a system which exploits the labor of men and women." The publishers recognized that *The Jungle* had the potential to become a bestseller, but they were troubled by the graphic descriptions in the book. After the first half of the novel arrived at their

---

1. The last name of this character was changed to "Rudkus" in the abbreviated, commercial edition of the novel published in 1906 by Doubleday, Page and Company.

office, they became hesitant about publishing *The Jungle* and expressed their concerns about the book to Sinclair, giving him a long list of suggested changes. By September 13, 1905, an exhausted Sinclair was trying to convince the editors at Macmillan to go ahead and publish the first half of the novel, as is. He wanted them to allow him to completely rewrite the second half of the novel as a sequel, to be called *The Story of Jurgis,* which would focus on crime in Chicago. On September 19th, Macmillan was still negotiating with *The Appeal*, but by the 21st they reversed course and withdrew the deal.

Instead of publishing *The Jungle* as is, the editors at Macmillan decided to cancel their contract with Sinclair. The editors at Macmillan had been ready to publish a sanitized version of the book, but something happened to change their minds. Given later events, there may be some question about whether the editors were truly unhappy with the book or whether they were "persuaded" to drop publication because of pressure from the meatpacking industry.

Sinclair began looking for a new publisher, and for a while even considered self-publishing, but he discovered that the expense would be crippling. Sinclair then approached and soon got a contract with the Doubleday, Page publishing company. Sinclair had numerous discussions with Frank Doubleday and his staff about the form a Doubleday, Page edition of the book would take. Clearly Doubleday wanted a muckraking novel about the corrupt meatpacking industry, and Sinclair saw this as his last chance to get *The Jungle* published.

Using the directions given him earlier by the editors at Macmillan, Sinclair cut numerous scenes from the book. For example, he cut the scene where a woman gives birth on the factory floor and places her baby on a meat cart. While she tries to clean herself, the meat cart carries the newborn toward a conveyor belt that empties into a sausage vat. Only at the very last second are the baby's cries heard and the workers rush to rescue it. This and many other scenes were deemed too graphic for the American reading public. The editors also insisted that Sinclair tone down the book's language. For example, throughout the novel Sinclair eliminated the word "blood." Many scenes of immigrant life deemed too "ethnic" for middle-class readers were also deleted. In its final form, the novel was cut in length by over a third, and many disturbing scenes and descriptions were removed, along with much of the graphic language.

Sinclair's expurgated version of *The Jungle* was soon ready for publication. But the efforts to suppress the novel were only beginning. As editor Frank Doubleday describes it in his autobiography, *Memoirs of a Publisher*:

We notified Armour & Company that we were going to publish the book, and they replied that they would at once institute a suit for libel for half a million dollars, to which we replied that if they could find half a million dollars around the building and could beat us in a suit they would be welcome to it.

The Armour company never sued. After the book came out in 1906, Upton Sinclair sent a copy to President Theodore Roosevelt. Roosevelt's response was to write a scathing letter to F. N. Doubleday asking why he would "publish such an obnoxious book as *The Jungle.*" Roosevelt's response was based on a report from the Agriculture Department that the meatpacking industry was perfectly safe. Based on this report, there was no problem with rotten meat being canned and sold to consumers.

Frank Doubleday responded that the book was accurate in its description of the squalid conditions in the meatpacking industry. Teddy Roosevelt then sent for Doubleday, because he wanted to see the evidence for himself. It soon became clear to Roosevelt that government inspectors had been bribed to give the meatpackers a clean bill of health. One inspector had accepted a measly $125 to write a false report. When Roosevelt discovered this, he became furious and launched his own investigation, this time through the Bureau of Commerce and Labor.

The book's popularity continued to grow, and news of the bribery scandal sent *The Jungle* on its way to becoming a bestseller. However, the efforts to suppress *The Jungle* continued. As Doubleday relates:

But they did not give up easily. One day a man came into my office . . . and said that he was Mr. Armour's personal attorney . . . and they would give us a three-page contract for each of our magazines and resume friendly relations.

Doubleday went "into a fury" at such an obvious attempt at bribery. He had just received a telegram from Europe and was struggling with the idea of allowing the book to be published in England and, in so doing, "wash our dirty linen" in the capitals of Europe. He recalls that "this chap made me so angry, particularly when he offered me some canned meat, that I showed him this telegram and told him we would give permission to have the book reprinted in Europe."

In the months after *The Jungle* was published, it began to attract attention worldwide. Upton Sinclair became famous, and his novel helped push the federal government to pass its first comprehensive Pure Food and Drug laws. But virtually no one was aware of how Sinclair had changed *The Jungle* in order to get it published by a large commercial publisher. In later years, Sinclair insisted that the novel was essentially unchanged from when the early chapters were first published in *The Appeal*. It may have been that Sinclair made this claim to protect himself from being accused of self-censorship. Or it may be that Sinclair found a middle-class audience for his books, and as a famous writer he became a prisoner of his own success. After *The Jungle*, Sinclair went on to a remarkable career as an author, and in later years he even ran for governor of California and was only narrowly defeated in a nasty, turbulent election in 1934.

75 years later . . .

In 1980, a young man showed up on the loading dock of the library at Pittsburg State University with a pickup truck full of papers he had found in an old cellar near Girard, Kansas. He had realized that these papers and manuscripts might be important, and he decided to try to find a home for them. So, he wanted to show the papers to Gene DeGruson, Curator of Special Collections at Pittsburg State.

The papers were water damaged, and some of them had an exotic purple mold growing on them, but DeGruson dived into them anyway. As he looked through them, he realized that they had come from the old *Appeal to Reason* office. They turned out to be letters and other papers from some of the most famous people of the early 20th century, including Eugene V. Debs and Helen Keller.

DeGruson enlisted the help of his many friends in sorting through the material. Much of it had to be cleaned, and torn pieces had to be put together like a jigsaw puzzle. When it was finally done, he had a cigar box filled with bits of paper that could not be matched to anything else. Based on what he found, DeGruson began to investigate the history of *The Jungle* and how it was first published, in part, in *The Appeal*.

After years of work, DeGruson put together a manuscript of the original uncut version of *The Jungle* and began contacting publishers. He quickly got an offer from St. Lukes Press, a small publisher in Memphis, and signed a contract with them. After St. Lukes announced publication of the original, uncensored version of *The Jungle*, the book began to get a lot of attention —both good and bad.

St. Lukes Press was soon approached by the mid-sized company, Peach-tree Publishers (offices, at the time, located on Armour Circle in Atlanta). St. Lukes and Peachtree soon agreed that the larger Peachtree Publishers would be better able to handle advertising and distribution of the novel. DeGruson's contract with St. Lukes Press specified that he would get 50% of the money from any resale of the rights. Whether this had anything to do with St.Lukes and Peachtree deciding to merge, rather than St. Lukes selling the rights to Peachtree, we don't know. In any event, St. Lukes Press became, briefly, an imprint of Peachtree Publishers.

A few months later, Peachtree/St. Lukes brought out the uncut version of *The Jungle*. For such an important book, the cover art was very disappointing (a black and white photo of Sinclair surrounded by green leaves) and the choice of typeface for the lengthy text was highly unusual—Korinna, an advertising face which tends to fatigue the eye when used in extended passages. (The Peachtree/St. Lukes version of *The Jungle* is the only book we have ever seen typeset in Korinna.) To make matters worse, the text for this large-format (6"X9") book was not only set in that strange face, but it was set in 10-point type, which is a small type size for such a large book. (This is 10-point Korinna.) In spite of all this, the new *Jungle* was getting a lot of attention. DeGruson was contacted by NBC's *Today Show* and appeared on it to promote the book. The White House also contacted DeGruson and asked him to send a copy of *The Jungle*. Given that in 1988 the Bush Administration was trying to "streamline" the federal meat inspection process, it's not hard to see why the White House was concerned about this book.

Although St. Lukes had already gotten the book pre-catalogued by the Library of Congress, using the title *Upton Sinclair's The Jungle: the lost first edition,* Peachtree decided to change the title to *The Lost First Edition of Upton Sinclair's The Jungle*. This caused a great deal of confusion for bookstores and individuals who tried to buy the book. It was listed in the reference source, *Books in Print,* as *Upton Sinclair's The Jungle*, and there was no listing under *The Jungle*, under *The Lost First Edition*, or even under Upton Sinclair's name as the author. To further confuse things, the University of Illinois Press (offices located in Chicago) brought out a reprint of the old 1906 Doubleday, Page edition at the same time. There is no way of knowing how many people bought the University of Illinois reprint thinking that it was the new, uncut *Jungle*.

In spite of this, after DeGruson's appearance on *The Today Show*, several other television programs, including *Oprah* and *Donahue*, contacted him about appearing on their shows to promote his book. DeGruson contacted Peachtree as these phone calls came in and waited for them to make the arrangements. It turned into a long wait. DeGruson was preoccupied with his duties as Faculty Senate President and his position as Curator of Special Collections, along with his extensive involvements in community theater, historic preservation, and local history projects, and did not realize—until too late—that someone had dropped the ball in promoting *The Jungle*.

This was just the beginning of a long series of disappointments, including a rather surreal attempt by the publisher to auction off the paperback rights to *The Jungle*. Peachtree arranged to auction the rights, and then, (according to DeGruson) after getting an offer approaching six figures, dramatically canceled the auction and announced that Peachtree/St. Lukes would bring the book out in paperback themselves.

Over the next few months, interest in *The Jungle* slowly died out, and the novel was not issued in paperback. Some time later, Peachtree bundled their contract rights to *The Jungle* together with some cookbooks and sold the rights to a cookbook publisher in Kentucky. This new publisher listed a paperback edition of *The Jungle* in its catalog, but never published it, and the book went quietly out of print.

In 1997, Gene DeGruson died suddenly from a brain aneurism. Today, he is remembered fondly by his many friends in Southeast Kansas, and his portrait now hangs in the lobby of the historic Stilwell Hotel, which he had helped to renovate. Like this newly restored hotel, the bringing to light of the lost, original edition of Upton Sinclair's classic novel is part of Gene DeGruson's legacy.

The importance of Gene's work is slowly being recognized, and literary scholars are beginning to look closely at the original *Jungle*. This edition has also influenced other writers. In 1990, the Lookingglass Theater Company produced an adaptation of *The Jungle* which was written and directed by David Schwimmer (who went on to star in the television series, *Friends*). This play was actively promoted by Studs Terkel and included many surreal images, including men hanging from straps and meat hooks in the packing-house. This shift in emphasis from bad food to the sufferings of the workers was clearly inspired by the original edition of the novel.

Nearly a century after its suppression and, following its rediscovery, a bizarre saga of missed opportunities, the original version of *The Jungle* is once again available.[2]

—Earl Lee

(Earl Lee is a librarian and the author of *Libraries in the Age of Mediocrity* and the novel *Drakulya*.)

---

2. The present edition varies slightly from Gene DeGruson's edition. DeGruson's version was taken from the mass-circulation socialist newspaper, *Appeal to Reason*, whereas the present, very similar edition is taken from the smaller-circulation socialist periodical, *One-Hoss Philosophy*.

INTRODUCTION

I. In 1905 Upton Sinclair wrote a powerful book, full of impassioned rhetoric against the excesses of capitalism, deeply empathizing with the immigrant worker, and boldly naming the perpetrators of crime. In 1906 a lesser book was published—one that certainly rocked the nation in its gruesome detail about meat processing, but that skirted the realities of disease and death among the poor, apologized to the rich and powerful by its silences, and pictured the immigrant worker as responsible in large part for his own degradation. Both of these books are called *The Jungle*. The 1906 version has been taught in the schools, sits on library shelves, and is easily available at the bookstore in the local mall. The original, 1905, version came out piecemeal in a socialist newspaper and a quarterly magazine at the time Sinclair wrote it, but essentially disappeared until 1988, when it was re-printed as a hardback book. That edition quickly went out of print under odd circumstances (see Foreword). Now, in 2003, the true first version of *The Jungle* comes to us again. Can we handle the truth this time?

Both versions of *The Jungle* feature the story of Jurgis Rudkos and his wife Ona, Lithuanians who have come to Chicago to pursue the American dream. They work hard and try to make the best of bad living conditions, but they are beaten down relentlessly. Both versions show disturbing details of the turn-of-the-century meatpacking industry: meat processed amid blood and dirt, diseased animals cut up for food, inspectors letting rotten meat go by. At the same time, it is clear that there is a major difference between the two versions of the novel. The 1906 novel has 31 chapters, whereas the original has 36. In all, the newer version is about one-third shorter than the original (DeGruson xxvii). Of course, cutting text often happens when a writer revises a work, to tighten the style and eliminate redundancy of scene and character. Usually the second, more artful version is the one that gets published, and this is considered the official, final text. However, if a revision is not driven by a desire for artistic economy but is instead produced under coercion, directly or indirectly, for political or economic reasons, we must question which version should be the final and definitive text. In the case of *The Jungle*, two versions were published: one in 1905 as a serial by *The Appeal to Reason*, a socialist newspaper (and again in several issues of the quarterly *One-Hoss Philosophy*), and the second version in 1906 by Doubleday, Page and Company. Cut from the 1905 version are passages that create sympathy for the immigrant worker; grimly detailed descriptions of disease and death;

the reasons for alcoholism and prostitution among the workers; stories of cheating and lying by businessmen; indictments of the rich, of the police, of the press; a rhetoric of excess that overwhelms by its sheer accumulation and by its high tone; and references to and data on the deaths of children. If these cuts were made for artistic reasons, then the later, 1906, version should stand. If, however, the cuts were made under coercion, even if indirect, then the earlier version will be closer to Sinclair's true vision.

We have evidence that Sinclair didn't want to revise the novel, even though he is the one who made the cuts—Doubleday, Page didn't specifically demand them. When Sinclair began his project in October of 1904—going to the Chicago meatpacking district for seven weeks, living with the immigrant working people, talking with social workers, slipping into the meatpacking plants by picking up a lunch pail and fading in with the workingmen to see firsthand what the workers' lives were like—his trip was subsidized by the socialist newspaper, *The Appeal to Reason*. But a newspaper serial does not reach as wide an audience as a novel can if it is published by a major publisher, nor can a newspaper serial have as enduring an impact, so Sinclair presented his idea to the Macmillan publishing house, publisher of some of his earlier work. Macmillan was very interested, and, based on an outline of the story, advanced Sinclair $500 (equivalent to approximately $10,000 today). However, once the novel was completed, Macmillan gave Sinclair a list of what had to be changed if that company were to publish his book. Sinclair refused: "They told me that they could not publish it as it stood, and would have to require omissions and alterations that would ruin the book for the purpose for which I had written it" (quoted in DeGruson xxi). That purpose, the purpose for which he had written the book, was to argue for workers' rights and the Socialist vision.

Macmillan had paid for a muckraking book on the meatpacking industry; Sinclair wrote a book about the exploitation and systematic "grinding up" of immigrant workers. He wrote the book the socialists wanted, the book that spoke the truth as Sinclair saw it. Macmillan pulled out—rejecting the manuscript and canceling the contract with Sinclair. The precise reasons for Macmillan saying "yes" one moment then suddenly saying "no" are unclear. Some speculate that the details about meatpacking were too coarse; others say it was the socialist message. At any rate, Sinclair no longer had a publisher for his novel.

The problem was that the socialists didn't have enough money to publish the book and adequately promote and distribute it. Sinclair tried other capitalist publishers, but again and again he was turned down. He asked for contributions from the socialist readers of *The Appeal to Reason*, but the amount of money that came in would have barely covered printing costs (but not the costs of advertising, promotion, and distribution) and certainly would not have gotten the novel out to the general public (DeGruson xxiii). He would have to give in.

Sinclair must have agonized over the revisions he made. They went against what he believed in, and what he'd seen for himself. But the book would be worth nothing if it wasn't read, so he knew what he had to do. He censored himself. In Chapter 34 of his original version—Chapter 30 of the book that was published in 1906—the state organizer of the socialist party and owner of the hotel Jurgis lives and works in, Billy Hinds, speaks of a book that took on the Standard Oil Company: "the book was bought up and allowed to die, and you can hardly get a copy of it" (303; all page numbers refer to this present text unless otherwise specified). In the 1906 version, the statement reads, "the book was allowed to die, and you hardly ever hear of it" (Barrett 1988 edition, page 312; all future references to this edition will be noted as *B*. It is instructive to see what the 1906 version leaves in and what it omits—sometimes whole pages. For this reason, I will sometimes refer to the places in Barrett where a passage should be, but isn't. These missing passages will be marked as *Bm.*). This is what Sinclair feared if he gave the book as it was first written into the hands of a non-socialist publisher: that the publisher, allied to capitalist interests, could buy control of his book, publish it feebly, and let it die.

In a letter to "My Comrades of the Movement," published in *The Appeal to Reason* on November 18, 1905, before he revised the manuscript, Sinclair explained his reasons for not wanting to work with a big publisher. He said first that a "capitalist concern" would make the book too costly for the general reader. "And more important than this," he added, "a publisher may completely suppress a book if he sees fit. . . . I may be mistaken, but I believe I know where I could get a good sum of money to withhold 'The Jungle' from the public; and I do not believe the book would be out a month before its publishers would receive mysterious offers for its copyright" (quoted in DeGruson xxi). But since the socialists could not raise the revenue to adequately publish, promote, and distribute his book, the only alternative was to revise the novel in such a way that a capitalist publisher would accept it.

Using the suggestions for revisions Macmillan had given him, Sinclair made the cuts that he believed would allow his book to live (DeGruson xxiii–iv). But how far did he gut the book in the process? Once the revised novel came out, it was wildly popular: "Within six weeks of its publication in early 1906, the novel had become an international favorite, selling more than 25,000 copies" (Barrett xii). People rushed to buy the book that told them just how bad the processed meat they were eating really was. The 1906 version of *The Jungle* resulted in the Pure Food and Drug Act of that same year. It was a powerful work. But Sinclair was disappointed: "I aimed at the public's heart, and by accident I hit it in the stomach" (quoted in Barrett xiii).

Maybe his bad aim resulted from his successful revisions: Sinclair had "ruined" his book in order to save it.

In 1905 Sinclair had written a dangerous novel. The original version of *The Jungle* is a novel that sees beyond a particular abuse in society to something much bigger. Sinclair did not mean to write a reformist book, but a revolutionary one. In a long monologue late in the book by an old Polish socialist, Comrade Ostrinski, we can hear the purpose of Sinclair's novel. Sinclair argues, as Ostrinski does, for "the great purpose . . . the organizing of the working-class for the revolution," not "to beguile the American workingman with futilities like free silver, municipal ownership, and 'reform'"—or futilities like pure food laws (295; *Bm* 304—in Barrett the section ends with the reference to revolution. The quarter page following, which discusses the "futility" of making "an alliance with the capitalists" is gone .). The focus on the working class is in large part what disappears from *The Jungle* in the "expurgated" version (see DeGruson xiii and xxvii on the origin of that term). By eliminating a compassionate adjective, a gut-wrenching scene, or an explanation, Sinclair missed the reader's heart. He had been courageous in his desire to write the truth about the condition of the working class in a time when capitalists had a free hand. But that courageous book was not the one published in 1906. Now we have a chance to read that original attempt at truth again, without all the "omissions and alterations." And the truth Sinclair told in 1905 still has resonance for us. For although America has implemented many socialist ideas since 1906—workers' unions have a certain amount of power; workers have some protection under the law—these are reforms only and serious abuses continue, especially in the treatment of immigrant labor. The worker in the meatpacking plant is no longer Lithuanian but Mexican. Workers in the sweatshops of New York and L.A. come not from the Balkans but from Asia. Perhaps reading about the plight of the immigrant worker at the beginning of the twentieth century will help us to understand the plight of workers today, in our even more diverse, multicultural society. This is the book we have before us—a novel with a strong socialist vision that does not back away from the truth.

II. When I sat down to write this introduction, I decided to see for myself what all the fuss was about. Why did we need a new edition of *The Jungle*? In 1988, James R. Barrett came out with a comprehensive scholarly edition of *The Jungle*, widely acknowledged to be the standard edition for academic and classroom use. In that same year, Gene DeGruson, a library archivist in southeast Kansas, published the "unexpurgated edition" of the novel based on papers found in Girard, Kansas, home of *The Appeal to Reason*. DeGruson's edition is now out of print. The *Appeal* serial, although it was re-run once or twice after 1905, never sold more than 11,000 copies after the Doubleday, Page edition came out. This current edition is based on the *One-Hoss Philosophy* version, which DeGruson says has "little difference" from the *Appeal* serial (see DeGruson xviii–iv and xxvii–xxxi for details on this publication history). Although Sinclair scholars since 1988 routinely make mention of the DeGruson edition, the Barrett edition is the focus of interpretation. I determined to find out whether it made any difference which version one read.

DeGruson made the search easy. As an appendix to his edition of *The Jungle*, he gives every word, phrase, paragraph, and page Sinclair cut from the 1905 version. By comparing these passages to the Barrett edition, I saw that DeGruson was accurate in most of his identifications of "omissions." Of particular interest are those cuts that encompass several whole pages, a circumstance that occurs reasonably often—I'll discuss some of those cuts below. It is also illuminating to see which specific words and phrases Sinclair cut. One thing the DeGruson appendix does not do is give the words that Sinclair adds, to make his sentences work smoothly once something is cut out. The appendix also does not show other additions or alterations. For instance, in reducing the overall number of chapters, Sinclair moved whole scenes and speeches at the end of the novel, preserving the material, but putting it in a different order.

My discussion here will be limited to what I found in following DeGruson's appendix; but that will be enough to make clear the essence of what Sinclair lost in making his revisions. I do not try to evaluate the artistry of the two versions of any passage, since the cuts I focus on seem clearly to deal more with content than style.

As regards style, we should remember that in 1906, with modernism in the offing, the new idea would be to make the narrator as impersonal as possible and to focus on form rather than political content. So it's understandable that much of the dissatisfaction with Sinclair's style has come because of his overtly political, critical stance. If the political rhetoric and narrative intrusions of the 1906 version bother readers, the style of the 1905 version will be even more abrasive. My argument is that Sinclair meant to abrade; for him, politics was personal.

Many of the changes Sinclair made would be hard to defend on any stylistic grounds, however. An example of such an alteration (which also involves a cut) occurs early in the book in the discussion of Jurgis and Ona's wedding. DeGruson's appendix indicates the loss of the word "panei" on page 22. On searching the original text for that word, I discovered that the word is used twice on that page, once alone, and once as part of a name: "Panei Aniele Juknos." In the Barrett edition, the single word "panei" is indeed missing, but in addition, "Panei Aniele Juknos" has become "Mrs.

Jukniene" (*B* 27). Although DeGruson's appendix doesn't note the change, it is an important one: it's an example of how Sinclair systematically reduced the ethnic voice he had created in the original, undermining the power of that voice. Sinclair substitutes the American "Mrs." for "Panei," eliminates the Lithuanian first name, and makes the last name less Slavic by adding the Romance-language ending. This strikes me as a telling alteration, showing how purposeful Sinclair's revisions were—certainly not because weakening the ethnic flavor produces better art, but because not stressing the ethnicity of the characters reduces disturbing social implications.[1]

The excisions Sinclair made fall into certain categories. It is clear that he had a plan in making the cuts he did in his effort to make his book publishable by a capitalist press. Most of the time, if I was surprised, as a reader of the original text, by the forthrightness of a passage in its condemnation of the labor system, I discovered that the passage had been cut from the 1906 version. Eventually I was able to predict with some consistency which scenes or commentary would be eliminated. But, provocatively enough, my anticipation was sometimes proven false: a passage that should by all rights have gone, according to the system Sinclair seems to have constructed, ended up remaining.

The following discussion explains the categories of cuts Sinclair made and offers an interpretation of his rationale. It also presents some of the major inconsistencies in his cutting system to show how Sinclair tried to retain as much of his socialist statement as he could.

III. Some of the most significant types of cuts Sinclair made are passages that develop empathy for the worker. DeGruson calls these cuts "curious," pointing out that the passages that disappear would have made the "immigrant workers more empathetic or less alien to the reader" (xxv). However, the cuts are not so much "curious" as to be expected in an expurgated version of the novel that would downplay class oppression. If we do not empathize with the people being crushed by the system, we will be less likely to want to change that system. The Pure Food and Drug laws are not system changes; they deal with adulteration of edible products, not with the inhumane treatment of the workers who process the products. For instance, in the original, in the same passage where Panei Aniele Juknos becomes Mrs. Jukniene, we are told that she was "a wizened-up little woman, with a wrinkled and heart-sick face" (22). In the 1906 version, she is still wizened, but "with a wrinkled face" only (*B* 27). What had been a psychological profile becomes straight description. Sinclair leaves in the immediately following statement: "Her home was unthinkably filthy." Without the "heart-sick," we don't wonder why the house is filthy, but take the statement as data. In both versions we find out that the house is "filthy" because the old woman raises chickens and they have free reign. We also learn that she is "under pressure of an attack of rheumatism" that began two months before, leaving her "doubled up in one corner of her room for over a week," and in both versions that information creates a sense of empathy (23; *B* 27). But only the original explains that her boarders "had decamped" even though they were "heavily in her debt." (The 1906 version has them merely "try their chances" in Kansas City while in her debt, without the direct implication that they would not try to repay her [23; *B* 27–28].) Only in the original do we get the following sentence to end the description of Panei Aniele Juknos (Mrs. Jukniene) and her plight—it is deleted entirely from the 1906 version: "Meantime, as the widow Juknos had been trying for over a year to pay for her furniture, and was in debt to her landlord besides, she was, perhaps, not to blame for concluding to give up, and let ruin come when it would" (23).

Eliminating the final sentence is a typical cut that Sinclair made. In the original version he would draw conclusions from the data, such as "It was enough to make anybody sick, to think that people had to eat such meat as this" or "the place which is here called the Jungle is not Packingtown, nor is it Chicago, nor is it Illinois, nor is it the United States—it is Civilization" (89, 116). These kinds of conclusions are not drawn in the 1906 version (*Bm* 94, 121).[2] The result is a novel with much less impact than the original. It seems to be telling the story of a local problem, not a worldwide disease, and the people who are hurt seem distant from us, undeserving of our empathy as they live like animals in their "filthy" houses.

As to Panei Juknos, in the 1905 version the narrator has already set her up as a good and giving woman, by saying that she has given more than she could to help pay for Jurgis and Ona's wedding—she is a woman of the old tradition trying to shame the young men who eat the food and drink the alcohol at the wedding but donate nothing. In the 1905 version she is a role model: "Panei Aniele had given three dollars—and that meant that she had saved the entire profit of her chickens this year," and spent those savings to help the family out (13). For the 1906 version, Sinclair altered the line to read "Aniele had given the entire profit of her chickens for several months" (*B* 17). By eliminating the fact that profits from those chickens (that a few pages later will result in the loss of her boarders) is a mere three dollars a year, Sinclair makes Panei Juknos not only less generous but also less needy. We see her as more of an entrepreneur in the 1906 version, making the later "filthy house" seem to be her fault—bad business sense.

The placing of blame is a big difference between the two versions of this novel. In the original, Sinclair offers explanations for why men drink and why women become prostitutes. In the later version, he retains the data on drinking and prostitution, but his silence on motivation implies that these people are derelicts, not worthy of our sympathy.

In fact, Sinclair did some very precise cutting in the section that explains why the workers go to the saloons. In the original we see that they go to saloons in winter for survival—to escape the cold that literally freezes them "to death" and to have a warm place to sit and eat. The 1905 version shows "the lords of Packingtown" in their "private dining-room" eating "as good food as can be had in the city at cost," whereas for the men "they have not provided even so much as a bench to sit down on!" (72). This discussion disappears in the later version, as does the fact that Jurgis has to eat "standing upon the killing-floor, amid the stench" or that "he might go and sit on the stairs, where it was colder yet; or he might sit outside, where it was probably below zero, and snowing" (72). The 1906 version tells us that Jurgis had to eat "amid the stench in which he worked," but that's all (*B* 79). The stench is an inconvenience; the cold can kill. The 1906 version eliminates that direct motivation.

In both versions, Jurgis has an alternative when he eats: "he might rush out, as did all his companions, to any one of the hundreds of saloons which stretched out their arms to him" (72; *B* 79—in Barrett the "saloons" here become "liquor stores"). However, the original explains that although there are two hundred saloons in the area, there is "not another store or shop of any sort whatever" where the men can warm themselves. The later version drops that bit of information. Sinclair's cuts are meticulous. He cuts saloon names like "The Glory" and "The Vision," but leaves "Love's Delights" (71; *B* 79). The result is a much less sympathetic view of the causes of alcoholism among the workers. Rather than laying the blame directly on the owners' doorstep, the novel now makes the men seem to choose their fate through weakness.

The same may be said for prostitution. Although the disturbing story of why Ona becomes her boss's mistress remains in the 1906 version, prostitutes in general are not allowed to tell their tales. Most references to prostitution (e.g., being forced to go "downtown") disappear (as do many sexual innuendoes and references to swearing, miscegenation, and syphilis), although Marija in the second half of the book works in a bordello in both versions and has a long section where she talks to Jurgis about her situation (269–77; *B* 279–88). This is an example of Sinclair leaving some of the disturbing images in but taking much out. He leaves in the quick story of the girl who came to Chicago to work in a factory but was doped and "ruined." She started having "crazy fits" and jumped out a window (275; *B* 286). He leaves in that "French girls" and "Japanese women" are brought in (276; *B* 286), but eliminates that girls are also brought down from New York (276). He leaves in—but with alterations from the original—that Marija considers the women in the bordello "pretty decent" and her comment that she "used to think they did it because they liked to" but that she realizes now that no woman would like "selling herself to every kind of man that comes, old or young, black or white" (B 286). However, he cuts in half her repeated exclamation that "it's misery, always misery!" (276; B 286). In both versions, Marija's empathy for her companions is a strong statement against the stereotype of the debauched prostitute who deserves what happens to her. Still, the original statement was even stronger. In the 1905 version, Marija says, "I used to think that such women must be fiends," but she realizes the absurdity of imagining any woman wanting to "sell herself to ten or a dozen men in a day—every kind of man . . ." etc. The rhetoric is much higher in the original, and the fact of having sex with ten or twelve men in a day is an overwhelming statement of just what the prostitutes' "misery" consists of (276).

In the original version, this discussion of prostitutes' motivation ends in a long story of one woman—Alena Jasaitis—whose story is entirely eliminated in the 1906 edition. Alena was a beautiful young woman who came down with a toothache. The dentist "told her that all her teeth were decaying and that if she didn't have them taken care of at once, she would lose them all." She doesn't have the fifty dollars to fix them, but the dentist says he can pull them all and order false teeth for fourteen dollars. "Poor Alena nearly cried her eyes out. . . . It would have disfigured her for life, you see." She raises the money by becoming her boss's mistress and eventually ends up on the street, and then at a house of prostitution, like Marija (276–77). This is an oddly affecting story—such a personal motive for turning to prostitution. It breaks the stereotype of the prostitute as "fiend" or debauchee and presents her as Alena, the young woman who was terrified of losing her good looks. I presume that this is why Sinclair cut the story from the 1906 version. It's self-gratifying to shake one's head at poor French girls sold into prostitution; it's another thing altogether to realize the mundane and pathetic irony of a girl who sells herself to save her teeth.

Much of the empathy with the workers that Sinclair establishes in his original novel comes through descriptions of illness and death. In the 1906 version, again and again those descriptions are cut or severely toned down. One easy example is the story of the boy whose ears were so frostbitten that when his boss roughly rubs his ears to get the circulation back, the ears fall off. Sinclair leaves the bare fact in both versions: "as they were frozen stiff, it took only two or three rubs to break them short off" (71; B 78). The data, no more. In the original, the sentence continues, "and then the little fellow lay down and rolled on the floor in his agony." We feel more for the "little fellow," the child, who reacts to the pain than we do when we are left to imagine the ears simply breaking.

The 1906 version of *The Jungle* lacks a powerful image that is in the original of how many children had died in the Packingtown district, because of the "stinking green water" with its "swarms of flies . . . literally blackening the air, and the strange, fetid odor . . . a ghastly odor, of all the dead things of the universe." The description of the bad water remains in the later version, but in the original, the narrator ends the section by saying that a young man "made a map of the district, and in each block he put a black dot for every child who had died there in the past year; [and] when he finished you would have said that his map had been made with a pepper cruet" (24; *Bm* 29—in Barrett the section ends, "Was it not unhealthful? The stranger would ask; and the residents would answer, "Perhaps; but there is no telling."). Sinclair routinely cuts descriptions of infection, pollution, and consumption (tuberculosis). He takes out the image of a man's finger being cut off as a result of a speed-up, and the description of Ona curled on the floor in the corner at work when she swooned from being ill—the implication being that the boss refused to let sick women go home (82, 67; *Bm* 88; 74). He cut this image: a woman "crept away at last into a dark passage and gave birth to a baby boy; and not knowing what to do with him, and in terror of losing her place, she crept up to the floor above and dropped him into one of the carts full of beef, that was all ready for the cooking-vats. It was by the merest chance that some one heard the baby cry, just as the cart was in the act of being dumped" (97; *Bm* 104). In the 1906 version we do not see "the man . . . mashed right in half" by the elevator or the man who "had one of his feet cut off" by it; we do not hear about the children crippled by malnutrition and exposure living in "unventilated and filthy homes," doing "dangerous and exhausting work"—children who are "not human beings at all, but simply parts of a machine for producing wealth" (111, 118; *Bm* 117, 123). We don't get the full impact of Jurgis working in the fertilizer works. The word "suffocating" is deleted once, as is the fact that in "November, 1900, there was one week when one hundred and twenty-six men were employed and only six were able to continue." In the original, but not in the revised version, Sinclair's narrator says, "Every man who worked in the fertilizer plant was dying slowly of deadly diseases; but so long as the process was slow enough, it did not trouble them much—the men outside were dying more rapidly still" (119–21; *Bm* 124, 126, 127).

It is possible that Sinclair cut out or toned down the references to disease, accident, and dying because he did not want the publisher to be worried about being sued for libel. William Bloodworth, in his biography of Upton Sinclair, says that "after Macmillan decided that many of [*The Jungle's*] scenes—especially those in the packing plants—were possibly libelous," Doubleday, Page decided to "confirm Sinclair's facts by sending investigators to Chicago" (57). Doubleday, Page was satisfied that Sinclair's allegations were justified. (See Barrett's notes for references to historical documents that support Sinclair's facts.) From the beginning of the 1906 version of the novel to the end, Sinclair eliminates references to deliberate crime. Negligence and cruelty he leaves in, but if there seems to be a law broken, the reference disappears. First of all, he changes the names of the meat companies from alliterative aliases in the original (Anderson is Armour, Smith is Swift, and Morton is Morris) to names that have no sound association at all in the new version (Anderson now is Durham, Smith is Brown, and Morris is Jones) (see DeGruson xxiv). He eliminates bribery of meat inspectors, but keeps that bad meat goes through because of neglect (31; *B* 37); he eliminates references to cheating ("they cheated constantly and systematically . . . they cheated anywhere and anyhow. . . . To lie and to cheat are an essential part of that fundamental privilege of a business men [sic] to manage his own business in his own way" (79; *Bm* 86), including cheating the widow of the man "mashed" by the elevator out of her death benefits (111; *Bm* 117), and he cuts details about stealing (150; *Bm* 159). Any direct reference to being outside the law goes, although the activity itself sometimes stays in. For instance, both versions refer to "prize fights every now and then, and cockfights, and even dog-fights" run by the War-whoop League, but only the original adds that "all these were against the law" and the police belonging to the league "was also against the law" (86; *Bm* 91).

Sometimes Sinclair alters the discussion of crime rather than deleting it altogether. The result is a less forceful image of the criminal intricacies of meatpacking in Chicago. A good example is the discussion of water mains. The original tells us that "the packers had secret mains, it was said, and were stealing the city water by the millions of gallons every year. That meant hundreds of thousands of dollars in their pockets; and make believe that Cassidy [the 'democratic boss'] was not coming in for a piece of that pie!" (87). It then goes into detail on how this was done. The narrator comments, "The great advantage that the packers enjoy in these things is that they are so big that people will not believe they can be dishonest; they are a national institution, and it is absurd to suppose that they would stoop to things like this" (87). The 1906 version reads, "The packers had secret mains, through which they stole billions of gallons of the city's water. The newspapers had been full of this scandal—once there had even been an investigation, and an actual uncovering of the pipes; but nobody had been punished and the thing went right on" (*B* 92–93). That's it. No comment on how much money this netted anyone, no names named, and no socialist conclusion drawn about the façade of honesty big corporations have.

The novel Sinclair envisioned was a socialist novel with a scope wide enough to comment on the injustices and fraudulent promises of capitalism anywhere in the world. The meatpacking industry in Chicago, Illinois was just a case in point. The novel that was finally published by Doubleday, Page was much more narrow. Sinclair systematically cut references that widened the purposes of the book, realizing that if he wanted the novel published at all, he would have to appear to restrict the problem to Chicago and meatpacking. So he cut references to the wider capitalist problem (13; *Bm* 16), cut references to injustices in other businesses like saloons (65; *Bm* 73), real estate (60, 75–76; *Bm* 69, 82), plumbing (75; *Bm* 82), trolley cars (112; *Bm* 118), and universities (231, 311; *Bm* 244, 320), cut discussions of unfairness and distortions in the press, and cut descriptions of police brutality.

Many critics have noticed the removal of the strong socialist statement given early in the original book in which Sinclair compares his project to Harriet Beecher Stowe's:

> [Stowe] had many things in her favor which cannot be counted on by him who would paint the life of the modern slave—the slave of the factory, the sweat-shop and the mine. The lash which drives the latter cannot either be seen or heard; most people do not believe that it exists—it is the cant of the philanthropist and the political convention that it does not exist. This slave is never hunted by bloodhounds. . . . [T]he hounds that hunt him are disease and accident, and the villain who murders him is merely the prevailing rate of wages. And who can thrill the reader with the tale of a man-hunt in which the hunted is a lousy and ignorant foreigner, and the hunters are the germs of consumption, diphtheria and typhoid? Who can make a romance out of the story of a man whose one life adventure is the scratching of a finger by an infected butcher knife, with a pine box and a pauper's grave as the denouement? (68–69; *Bm* 76)[3]

This passage is a great example of socialist rhetoric, coming early to help the reader see the wider point being made. Eugene Debs says of *The Jungle*, making reference to the slavery metaphor, "In this fearful story the horrors of industrial slavery are as vividly drawn as if by lightning. It marks an epoch in revolutionary literature."[4] Debs was, of course, referring to the uncut version of the novel.

This socialist statement lays out the problem of the working man in an almost unfettered capitalist system. It also lays out the main realities facing the immigrant worker that will be cut from the book: disease, accident, death. Matthew Maris, in "The Two Lives of Jurgis Rudkus," says that because Sinclair is not proletarian himself we see "traces of the detachment of its author and readers from the working class [that the novel] purports to help" (51). But that sense of detachment is often a direct result of the heavy cuts Sinclair had to make to be published at all. The original version has passion and commitment, as the excised "wage slavery" passage demonstrates.

By eliminating problems with businesses other than meatpacking, some of the most affecting details of Jurgis's family life disappear. One example is the opening of Chapter 8, when the water pipes freeze and break in the family home: "[W]hen, in their ignorance they thawed [the pipes] out, they had a terrible flood in their house. It happened while the men were away, and poor Teta Elzbieta rushed out into the street screaming for help, for she did not even know whether the flood could be stopped, or whether they were ruined for life" (75; *Bm* 82). That passage—which helps close the distance between reader and characters—presumably had to go because the discussion immediately following shows the plumbers overcharging the family and making them buy unneeded materials. In the same paragraph in the original, again we get a personal view of the family, this time dealing with a real estate agent: "When they went to pay their January installment on the house, the agent terrified them by asking them if they had had the insurance attended to yet." This new cost would be about a week's wages for Jurgis. "Poor Teta Elzbieta, upon whom again fell the blow, demanded how much it would cost them. Seven dollars, the man said; and that night came Jurgis, grim and determined, requesting that the agent would be good enough to inform him, once and for all, as to all the expenses they were liable for" (75). This Teta Elzbieta comes very close to us. This Jurgis shows intelligence in his grim sarcasm. But they exist only in the original where Sinclair did not limit his social criticism. (In place of this plumbing and real estate section, Sinclair adds a love story in the 1906 version! Marija falls happily in love with a violinist and ecstatically gets engaged. [*B* 82])[5] In an ironic comment on the wealthy men who owned the street cars and were directly responsible for Ona's illness because of the exorbitant prices they charged for transfers, even in the freezing rain, the narrator in the first version says that the owners believed it was "the elemental right of business men to manage their own business in their own way" (66; *Bm* 74). If business men do have this right, then Sinclair had better not question it. The comment was deleted from the 1906 version.

One of the most passionate outcries in the original novel comes in the section where Jurgis is frantically trying to protect his weak wife from the jungle she and he are caught in. It is an outcry that does not make it into the 1906 version, and thereby severely limits both the reader's empathy for Jurgis and his family, and the reader's understanding of the vast problem the novel and socialism were trying to confront. The narrator, here speaking as if from Jurgis's point of view, draws the following intense and ironic conclusion:

> The whole country was a lie; its freedom was a lie, a snare for pauper working-men; its prosperity was a lie of rich employers, its justice was a lie of grafting politicians. And so no matter where you went in it, or for what purpose—to buy a house, for instance—you did not pay any attention to all the fine speeches and you were not taken in by politeness; you were polite yourself, as long as it suited you, but you understood that you were dealing with a knave, and you were ready to flash out in anger and defiance at the least occasion. (66; *Bm* 73–74)

If the 1906 versions seems distant, it is perhaps because Sinclair did not believe that his publisher would let him get this close.

Certain discussions are simply off limits in the book that was published in 1906. Any reference to the culpability of the rich in general had to go. Those children's deaths, as plentiful as from a pepper cruet, were in part caused by "the neighboring district, a 'swell' part of the city, whence came all this garbage to be dumped" (24; *Bm* 29). That entire passage disappears. Such odd bits as that the rich have to deal with vermin too could not remain (68; *Bm* 75), or that they hire old immigrant women like Teta Elzbieta to be "kitchen-wench[es]." (The story of Teta Elzbieta being hired by a family in "the swell district near the lake front" to do "the dirty work of the kitchen" arises three times and is cut all three times [112–13, 122, and 156; *Bm* 118–19, 127, 165]). The 1906 version can talk about prostitution vaguely, but not the reasons for prostitution, about alcoholism, but not the reasons for alcoholism; so, the onus is on the worker rather than the system.

Apparently, criticizing the meatpacking industry itself was acceptable, but not criticizing capitalism in general, except in formalized speeches confined to the second half of the book. If a socialist radical says something, the effect on the reader is much less than if the commentary runs through the book, as an integral part of the action. All the way through the revised version of the novel, Sinclair lowers the rhetoric and as a result his socialist message becomes muffled.

Eliminating the jungle metaphor was one consistent lowering of rhetoric. Right from the beginning the metaphor seems too dangerous to keep:

> To the strangers it seemed like a wilderness, a very jungle—a jungle of houses. It was a jungle, too, ruled by strange powers, about which they did not understand, full of creatures which preyed upon each other—that were hunting you without rest, tracking you in the daytime and watching in your path by night. The only difference was that they sought, not your life-blood, but your money—and when you had been caught by them once or twice, you came to understand that this difference was no difference at all. (20; *Bm* 25)

This is a denunciation of capitalist business as it was run at the turn of the century. Businessmen are compared to beasts of prey, so of course the comparison had to go. In a discussion of the excessive prices of the saloon-keepers—those "devourer[s] of the poor"—the narrator defends the saloon-keepers because they themselves are caught in the throes of competition and are in debt to the brewers, who take over their businesses when the saloon owners can't pay. The 1906 version does not have the conclusion the narrator draws: "Thus again were the strong devouring the weak, according to the law which prevails in the jungle" (65; *Bm 73*).

Often the jungle comparison comes in the midst of a longer piece of rhetoric, at a climactic moment. Page 116 is a case in point: almost an entire page disappears from the 1906 version, a page in which Sinclair's narrator creates a gruesome scenario of the workers' struggle—"the ups and downs of [which] might have been shown in a chart":

> The most striking single fact about Packingtown is the large number of the children, and the next most striking fact is the small number of the old people. This is in accordance with two well-known laws of nature, the first that those creatures whose order is the lowest and whose existence is the most precarious, cast out into the world the largest number of offspring; and the other—which has been mentioned before—that the creatures of the jungle never die a natural death. . . . [T]he vast majority had given up in despair, and either were living upon others, or dying of starvation and exposure, and the diseases to which these made them liable. Or else they had wandered off to beg for work in some other place; or had gone down into the heart of the city and become prostitutes and beggars and criminals; or had gone out into the country and became [sic] tramps and vagrants—all of them certain to perish in the end, of the same cold, the same hunger, and the same diseases, as if they had stayed at home.

This tour de force ends with the ringing line previously quoted, that "The Jungle is not Packingtown," nor Chicago, nor Illinois, but "it is Civilization" (116; *Bm 121*).[6]

This is the rhetoric of excess. Sinclair seems to have eliminated it not just because of the reference to the "jungle," but because it is straightforward about death, disease, prostitution, crime—all the ideas he had to avoid if he wanted to be published. He had to downplay the "struggle going on between the unions and the packers" (81; *Bm* 88—an entire page is gone) and down-play the reasons for it. Some of the most potent rhetoric of the original occurs in this passage that was cut in 1906, a discussion that speaks directly to the obstructions the unions were confronting. The narrator explains that "editors," "statesmen," and "other pillars of things as they are" controlled the media coverage of the union demands, giving the public a skewed view of the problems in Packingtown: "Lazy workingmen presuming to get together and say to their employers how much work they would do for their wages! Trying to restrict the productive capacity of the factories, and bring ruin upon this great country!" But "charity compels" us, the narrator says, to believe these leaders of the community didn't know the truth:

> that what the unions were really trying to do was to put a stop to murder. For murder it was that went on there upon the killing-floor, systematic, deliberate and hideous murder— . . . They were slaughtering men there, just as certainly as they were slaughtering the cattle; they were grinding the bodies and souls of them, and turning them into dollars and cents.

This was the effect of "speeding-up." In the sausage rooms, men would lose a finger in the machine "and when that happened they would stop the machine, but only for a minute or so; if they could not find the finger they would let it go and call it sausage. And that was grinding up men; as anyone will admit" (all on 82; all missing from *Bm* 88).

Why Sinclair made the cuts that he had previously claimed would "ruin the book" can perhaps be explained by Jack London's take on the publishing situation at the time. In a letter written for *The Appeal to Reason*, asking for contributions to help publish Sinclair's original novel (quoted by Sinclair in 1920), London says:

> *The Jungle* is written for the proletarian. It is to be published by a proletarian publishing house. It is to be read by the proletarian. And depend upon it, if it is not circulated by the proletarian it will not be circulated at all. . . . Remember, this book must go out in the face of the enemy. It will be laughed at—some; jeered at—some; abused—some; but most of all, worst of all, the most dangerous treatment it will receive is that of silence. For that is the way of capitalism. . . . the conspiracy of silence.[7]

Sinclair did what was necessary to get published. At the same time, amid all the crucial cuts he made, he did manage to salvage much important material. The gruesome deaths of Ona and the child Antanas remain. The long socialist speeches at the end stay, as do such statements as that marriage is a form of prostitution (312; *B* 322), although with numerous excisions, and with a disclaimer at the beginning.[8] In fact, it is intriguing to see just what Sinclair felt safe leaving in. For instance, he cuts an old woman buying Jurgis a meal (263–64; *B* 274), but retains Stanislovas, the boy who was terrified of the cold, being eaten alive by rats (270; *B* 280). He keeps in Ona as her boss's mistress, drawing her in such a way as to make the reader quail for her and for Jurgis's reaction to the news (126–41; *B* 132–51), but takes out from the midst of this that "everyone laugh[s] at" this common fate (143; *Bm* 151). He systematically eliminates suggestions that workers have to work on Saturday or Sunday (77, 117; *Bm* 86, 123), but has Jurgis remember, as he sits in his cell after trying to kill Ona's violator, that "Last Christmas Eve and all Christmas day [he] had toiled on the killing-floor, and Ona at wrapping hams" (146; *B* 154). He removes the sarcasm about child labor "in this glorious land of freedom," but keeps the fact (63; *Bm* 71).

The section on child labor is a good example of how Sinclair reworked certain passages, keeping what he could. In the original, as printed in *The Appeal to Reason*, "little Stanislovas" goes out to find work and when questioned about his age answers that he is "fortin" (fourteen) (DeGruson 60). Teta Elzbieta "had gotten a certificate to the effect that he was a year older than he was," meaning he was really thirteen (DeGruson 59). We see him in the "stench of the warm lard" in the summertime, but "in winter the cans would all but freeze to his naked little fingers," all for three dollars a week, five cents an hour, "just about exactly his proper share of the total earnings of the million and three-quarters of children under fifteen years of age who are now engaged in earning their livings in this glorious land of freedom" (63; DeGruson 60). The 1906 version has Stanislaus (note the spelling change) answer "sixtin" (*B* 71; this age change is also in the *One-Hoss* version, here page 62). Now Teta Elzbieta's certificate shows him two years older than he was, making him fourteen (*B* 70; in *One-Hoss,* the certificate makes him three years older, so he remains thirteen). He still endures the stench and the freezing cans on naked fingers, and he still takes home three dollars a week, five cents an hour, but now the passage ends, "just about his proper share of the total earnings of the million and three-quarters of children who are now engaged in earning their livings in the United States" (*B* 71). Even though we lose the piercing sarcasm of "in this glorious land of freedom" and lose the reference to the million and three-quarters children being under fifteen, and even though the company can no longer be to blame since Stanislaus "proves" he's sixteen, we keep the naked fingers, the poor pay, the exploitation. It is a compromise, and such compromises are made from the beginning to the end of the 1906 edition.

The strongest socialist statements Sinclair retains are the speeches at the end, and the 1906 version still gives us a lot. But the compromises occur here too. He cuts strong pro-union statements and references to class warfare (80, 210–11; *Bm* 88, 225). He cuts four pages of the race prejudice of the Democrats and the idea that Democrats and Republicans are the same (326–31; *Bm* 332—this same section, deleted from the 1906 version, has Jurgis speaking out in a meeting in "ardor" [330]). He tones down the idea that when workers see through Democratic lies, they will vote Socialist (331; *B* 334). And he omits both a long, clear debate (306–09; *Bm* 314) between Hinds and a clergyman on the evils of capitalism, and a forthright argument that socialism works (292; *Bm* 304) and that capitalism will inevitably fail (325; *Bm* 316).

Still, the thrilling speech of a man clearly meant to be Eugene V. Debs remains (281–88; *B* 290–97), with just a few cuts, as does Ostrinski's monologue (similarly altered). Sinclair obviously did what he could to be true to his socialist purpose within strict bounds. Matthew Maris sees a "subtext of censorship and revision" running through the second half of the novel, the persistent prison scenes a metaphor, in part, for the "hostile publishing climate" and anti-socialist feelings (64, 62). According to Maris, Sinclair sees himself as caged (63).

Sinclair had an intriguing mind. He was an impassioned socialist with a solid understanding and linguistic fervor, and the facts to back them up. But he was also a realist who ruthlessly eliminated some of his favorite ideas and most heartfelt scenes in order to get his book into print.

The re-publication of Upton Sinclair's original vision of *The Jungle* is long past due. We can now read what he wrote the first time around and experience the novel he wanted us to. Upton Sinclair scholars will find a rich field for study in looking at the alterations Sinclair made from the first version to the second. His choices illuminate his mind and shed light on the fears and secrets of his time. The everyday reader will simply marvel at a book so bold, so fervent, and a story so well told.

—Kathleen De Grave

(Kathleen De Grave is a professor of American Literature at Pittsburg State University in Pittsburg, Kansas. She is the author of *Swinder, Spy, Rebel: the Confidence Woman in 19th Century America* and the anti-corporate, feminist novel, *Company Woman*.)

Works Cited

Barrett, James R. Introduction. *Upton Sinclair: The Jungle*, by Upton Sinclair. Urbana, IL: University of Illinois Press, 1988. xi–xxxiii.

Bloodworth, William A., Jr. *Upton Sinclair*. Boston: Twayne, 1977.

DeGruson, Gene. Introduction. *The Lost First Edition of Upton Sinclair's The Jungle*, by Upton Sinclair. Memphis: Peachtree Publications, 1988. xiii–xxxi.

Derrick, Scott. "What a Beating Feels Like: Authorship, Dissolution, and Masculinity in Sinclair's *The Jungle.*" *Studies in American Fiction*. 23.1 (Spring 1995): 85-100.

Maris, Matthew J. "The Two Lives of Jurgis Rudkus." *American Literary Realism 1870–1910*. 29.2 (1997): 50-67.

A New Edition of The Jungle by Upton Sinclair. Pasadena, CA: Upton Sinclair, 1920. (pamphlet, including London's "Circulate *The Jungle*" and the quote from Eugene V. Debs on the back cover of this book)

Sinclair, Upton. *The Lost First Edition of Upton Sinclair's The Jungle*. Ed. Gene DeGruson. Memphis: Peachtree Publications, 1988.

Upton Sinclair: The Jungle. Ed. James R. Barrett. Urbana, IL: University of Illinois Press, 1988.

Tavernier-Courbin, Jacqueline. "*Call of the Wild* and *The Jungle*: Jack London and Upton Sinclair's Animal and Human Jungles." *The Cambridge Companion to American Realism and Naturalism: Howells to London*. Ed. Donald Pizer. Cambridge: Cambridge University Press, 1995. 236-62.

Notes

1. DeGruson's appendix includes a few oversights, such as this one, but such oversights do not occur often. (For each major cut that DeGruson notes, I double checked the accuracy with the Barrett edition.) Likewise, some of DeGruson's page number references are off by a few lines. (The page numbers here are correct for this edition; the pagination in this edition and in DeGruson's is close to the same, but not exact. His source was *The Appeal to Reason*; the source for this edition is *One-Hoss Philosophy*; as well, the page layouts and fonts used are different in the two editions.) The significance of these discrepancies for my interpretation is slight, because the sheer number of overall cuts and alterations of similar types allows an interpretation to hold even if a couple of examples slip by. What is needed is a comprehensive annotated edition of *The Jungle*, giving both versions of every passage that has been changed. Only then could one make a full interpretation of Sinclair's revision theory. DeGruson discusses name changes in general on xxiv.

2. Jacqueline Tavernier-Courbin, in her comparison of Jack London and Upton Sinclair, explains that drawing conclusions goes against the naturalist dictum of objectivity: "Indeed, both Zola and London believed that the novel should neither preach nor satirize but only dramatize life objectively, never drawing conclusions, because the conclusions are implicit in the material" (239). Her article gives a clear statement of the prevailing criticism against Sinclair's rhetorical style, implying that Sinclair's message, unlike London's, is "an assault on the reader." This reading of *The Jungle* would favor the second, toned-down version of the book. Ironically, the fact that often London's social "message gets lost" is, from this point of view, an "unwitting tribute to his talent" because the characters overwhelm the social point (237). In contrast, I read the high rhetorical passages in *The Jungle* as an intensification of the reader's feelings about the workers' situation, so that character and message go hand in hand.

3. Matthew Maris says of this passage that "its excision improves the novel" because Sinclair is reducing Stowe's achievement to the sensational, not giving her credit for her "inventiveness" (56). I agree that Stowe's book discusses the effects of slavery on a much more sophisticated basis than a series of whippings and chases by bloodhounds. But I disagree about the importance of the passage itself. Sinclair's purpose is not to critique Stowe but to raise the reader's consciousness of the physical and psychological depredations of what Sinclair and the socialists call "wage slavery."

4. This quotation comes from a pamphlet, *A New Edition of* The Jungle *by Upton Sinclair*, created and marketed by Sinclair in 1920. In four pages, he quotes Debs, Charlotte Perkins Gilman, and Jack London among numerous others.

5. A corollary result of toning down the social critique is the loss of a sense of Jurgis's intelligence, as in this passage. Many of the statements of disillusionment early in the book seem to come from Jurgis's point of view (see 20; *Bm* 25, the jungle metaphor that is lost, and 83; *Bm* 89 where the 1905 version has Jurgis "come to understand" that "every man has rights," thereby giving him "a standard by which to judge the larger state, the country in which he lived, in which the laws were not enforced, and in which a man, as a man, was nothing"), but these do not make it into the later version. The loss of this intelligent insight increases our sense of distance from him. Tavernier-Courbin criticizes Jurgis's sudden social conscience in the second half of the book (258), but we would have been better prepared for this had his earlier understandings not been cut.

6. James Barrett notes how accurate Sinclair's generalizations are about the lives of the poor in Packingtown. See his excellent introduction to the 1988 edition of the 1906 version of *The Jungle* and his notes.

7. Again from Sinclair's 1920 pamphlet, although London had written the letter addressed "Dear Comrades" and signed "Yours for the Revolution" for the original version of the novel while Sinclair was trying to get it published by the socialist press.

8. Although the first half of the original novel clearly supports socialist ideas about the working class, and clearly the revised version backs off from these ideas, the second half of the novel in both versions is more problematic. The socialist speeches and monologues that Sinclair allowed to remain in the revised edition are sometimes prefaced in both versions by ambiguous language, allowing readers to discount the ideas if they wish. For example, Nicholas Schliemann, a socialist who appears near the end of the novel, states some radical socialist ideas in both versions—the marriage-as-prostitution concept is just one of them. But the narrator tells us that Schliemann blew "human institutions about like soap-bubbles" and that "it was amazing that so much destructiveness could be contained in one human mind" (311; B 322). The original actually takes the commentary a step further, saying that Schliemann's "words were like a stream of burning acid, which frizzled to nothingness everywhere they touched." How these lines are read depends on the viewpoint of the reader: they shift in the same way some trick sketches do—if you expect to see a beautiful young woman, you do; if you expect a hag, that's what you find. The ambiguity in Sinclair's narrative voice allows us to read the language straight—Schliemann's ideas are destructive—if we are uneasy with socialist ideas, or allows us to "bond" with Schliemann as Jurgis does and see that institutions that undermine the human spirit should be destroyed and should be shown to be the airy bubbles they are. It is easier to read the commentary in a positive manner if we already see Jurgis as an intelligent, responsive person. If we doubt Jurgis' perception, as we are more likely to do in the 1906 version, we will probably read the "destructiveness" as a condemnation of certain elements of socialist theory.

Likewise, Sinclair's racism and misogyny are problematic. At times they seem to go directly against the socialist cause. In the description of the Beef Strike (245–59), the narrator uses extreme language to talk about the blacks brought in as scabs:

> a howling throng of three or four thousand surged about, men and women, young white girls from the country rubbing elbows with big buck negroes with daggers in their boots, while rows of wooly heads peered down from every window of the surrounding factories. The ancestors of these black people had been savages in Africa. . . . Now for the first time they were free—free to gratify every passion—free to wreck themselves. They were wanted to break a strike, and when it was broken they would be shipped away. . . . So whiskey and women were brought in by the car-load and sold to them, and hell was let loose in the yards (254; B 264–65).

In this quotation we hear both racial prejudice and some understanding of how the blacks were being used by the packing companies. Sinclair's "innocent" bigotry is a sign of just how bad race relations were at the time.

Scott Derrick, in his study of masculinity in *The Jungle*, argues that there is a similar unconscious misogyny in the book, despite its strong female characters. He says that the novel demonstrates "not just a hatred of social injustice, poverty, and suffering, but an aversion to the body and all its fluids, smells, and processes" (87). In his reading, capitalism is allied with the jungle, which is both nature and the fertile female, and socialism will clean it all up. He calls the novel "gynophobic." In any event, whether or not one agrees with Derrick, how Sinclair deals with race and gender needs a closer look.

PUBLISHER'S NOTE

The alert reader will notice a large number of grammar, spelling, capitalization, and, especially, punctuation errors and inconsistencies in this book. These errors and inconsistent usages—for example, sometimes Lithuanian terms are italicized, sometimes they aren't—were present in the original edition of this work as published in *One-Hoss Philosophy*, and we have chosen not to correct them; instead, we have corrected only the most obvious typographical errors, replacing, for instance, "mihgt" with "might" and putting in missing periods at the ends of sentences. We made approximately 40 to 50 such corrections, and when there was even the slightest doubt about whether an error was in Sinclair's original text or was the result of typographical error, we let it stand. There are two reasons for this.

1) This text is of historical significance, and scholars will want to compare it with the heavily edited commercial edition published by Doubleday, Page (and subsequently by many other publishers) and be confident that they are consulting the original text exactly as published (minus obvious typos).

2) The number of errors is so high—well in excess of 1,000—that it would have been impractical to have corrected them and to have included a list of emendations.

IT WAS four o'clock when the ceremony was over and the carriages began to arrive. There had been a crowd following all the way, owing to the exuberance of Marija Biarczynskas. The occasion rested heavily upon Marija's broad shoulders—it was her task to see that all things went in due form, and after the best home traditions; and, flying wildly hither and thither, bowling everyone out of the way, and scolding and exhorting all day with her tremendous voice, Marija was too eager to see that others conformed to the proprieties to consider them herself. She had left the church last of all, and, desiring to arrive first at the hall, had issued orders to the coachman to drive faster. When that personage had developed a will of his own in the matter, Marija had flung up the window of the carriage, and, leaning out, proceeded to tell him her opinion of him, first in Lithuanian, which he did not understand, and then in Polish, which he did. Having the advantage of her in altitude, the driver had stood his ground and even ventured to attempt to speak; and the result had been a furious altercation, which, continuing all the way down Ashland avenue, had added a new swarm of urchins to the cortege at each side street for half a mile.

This was unfortunate, for already there was a throng before the door. The music had started up, and half a block away you could hear the dull "broom, broom" of a 'cello, with the squeaking of two fiddles which vied with each other in intricate and altitudinous gymnastics. Seeing the throng, Marija abandoned precipitately the debate concerning the ancestors of her coachman, and, springing from the moving carriage, plunged in and proceeded to clear a way to the hall. Once within, she turned and began to push the other way, roaring, meantime, "*Eik! Eik Uzdarekdurys!*" in tones which made the orchestral uproar sound like fairy music.

"Z. Grajczunas, Pasilinksminimams darzas. Vynas. Sznapsas. Wines and Liquors. Union Headquarters"—that was the way the signs ran. The reader, who perhaps has never held much converse in the language of far-off Lithuania, will be glad for the explanation that the place was the rear room of a saloon in that part of Chicago known as "back of the yards." This information is definite and suited to the matter of fact—but how pitifully inadequate it would have seemed to one who understood that it was also the hour and place of the apotheosis of one of God's gentlest creatures, of the wedding feast and the joy-transfiguration of little Ona Lukoszis!

She stood in the doorway, shepherded by Cousin Marija, breathless from pushing through the crowd, and in her happiness painful to look upon. There was a light of wonder in her eyes and her lids trembled, and her otherwise wan little face was flushed. She wore a muslin dress, conspicuously white, and a stiff little veil coming to her shoulders. There were five pink paper roses twisted in the veil, and eleven bright green rose-leaves. There were new white cotton gloves upon her hands, and as she stood staring about her she twisted them together feverishly. It was almost too much for her—you could see the pain of too great emotion in her face, and all the tremor of her form. She was so young—not quite sixteen—and small for her age, a mere child; and she had just been married—and married to Jurgis, of all men, to Jurgis Rudkos, he with the white flower in the button-hole of his new black suit, he with the mighty shoulders and the giant hands.

Ona was blue-eyed and fair, while Jurgis had great black eyes, with beetling brows and thick black hair that curled in waves about his ears—in short, they were one of those incongruous and impossible married couples with which Mother Nature so often wills to confound all prophets, before and after. Jurgis could take up a two hundred and fifty pound quarter of beef and carry it into a car without a stagger, or even a thought; and now he stood in a far corner, frightened as a hunted animal, and obliged to moisten his lips with his tongue each time before he could answer the congratulations of his friends.

Gradually there was effected a separation between the spectators and the guests—a separation at least sufficiently complete for working purposes. There was no time during the festivities which ensued when there were not groups of onlookers in the doorways and the corners; and if any one of these onlookers came sufficiently close, or looked sufficiently hungry, a chair was offered him and he was invited to the feast. It was one of the laws of the *veselija* that no one goes hungry; and, while a rule made in the forests of Lithuania is hard to apply in the stock-yards district of Chicago, with its quarter of a million inhabitants, still they did their best, and the children who ran in from the street, and even the dogs, went out again happier. A charming informality was one of the characteristics of this celebration. The men wore their hats, or, if they wished they took them off, and their coats with them; they ate when and where they pleased, and moved as often as they pleased. There were to be speeches and singing, but no one had to listen who did not care to; if he wished, meantime, to speak or sing himself, he was perfectly free. The resulting medley of sound distracted no one, save possibly alone the babies, of which there were present a number equal to the total possessed by all the guests invited. There was no place for the babies to be, and so part of the preparations for the evening consisted of a collection of cribs and carriages in one corner. In these the babies slept three or four together—or wakened together, as the case might be. Those which were still older and could reach the tables, marched about munching contentedly at meat-bones, and bologna sausages.

The room is about thirty feet square, with white-washed walls, bare save for a calendar, a picture of a race-horse, and a family tree in a gilded frame. To the right there is a door from the saloon, with a few loafers in the doorway, and in the corner beyond it a bar, with a presiding genius clad in soiled white, with waxed black mustaches and a carefully oiled curl plastered against one side of his forehead. In the opposite corner are two tables, filling a third of the room and laden with dishes and cold viands, which a few of the hungrier guests are already munching. At the head, where sits the bride, is a snow-white cake, with an Eiffel tower of constructed decorations, with sugar roses and two angels upon it, and a generous sprinkling of pink and green and yellow candles. Beyond opens a door into the kitchen, where there is a glimpse to be had of a range with much steam ascending from it, and many women, old and young, rushing hither and thither. In the corner to the left are the three musicians, upon a little platform, toiling heroically to make some impression upon the hubbub; also the babies, similarly occupied, and an open window whence the populace imbibes the sights and sounds and odors.

Suddenly some of the steam begins to advance, and peering through it you discern Aunt Elizabeth, Ona's stepmother—Teta Elzbieta, as they call her—bearing aloft a great platter of stewed duck. Behind her is little Kotrina, one of Ona's unnumbered step-sisters, staggering beneath a similar burden; and half a minute later there appears old Grandmother Majauszkis, with a big yellow bowl of smoking potatoes, nearly as fat and as round as herself. So, bit by bit, the feast takes form—there a ham and a dish of sauerkraut, boiled rice, macaroni, bologna sausages, great piles of penny buns, bowls of milk, and foaming pitchers of beer. There is also, not six feet from your back, the bar, where you may order all you please and do not have to pay for it. "Eiksz! Graicziau!" screams Marija Biarczynskas, and falls to work herself—for there is more upon the stove inside that will be spoiled if it be not eaten.

So, with laughter and shouts and endless badinage and merriment, the guests take their places. The young men, who for the most part have been huddled near the door, summon their resolution and advance, and the shrinking Jurgis is poked and scolded by the old folks until he consents to seat himself at the right hand of the bride. The two bridesmaids, whose insignia of office are paper wreaths, come next, and after them the rest of the guests, old and young, boys and girls. The spirit of the occasion takes hold of the stately bartender, who condescends to a plate of stewed duck; even the fat policeman—whose duty it will be, later in the evening, to break up the fights—draws up a chair to the foot of the table. And the children shout and the babies yell, and everyone laughs and sings and chatters—while above all the deafening clamor Counsin Marija shouts orders to the musicians.

The musicians—how shall one begin to describe them? All this time they have been there, playing in a mad frenzy—all of this scene must be read, or said, or sung, to music. It is the music which makes it what it is—it is the music which changes the place from the rear room of a saloon in back of the yards to a fairy place, a wonderland, a little corner of the high mansions of the sky.

The little person who leads this trio is an inspired man. His fiddle is out of tune, and there is no rosin on his bow, but still he is an inspired man—the hands of the muses have been laid upon him. He plays like one possessed by a demon, by a whole horde of demons. You can feel them in the air round about him, capering frenetically; with their invisible feet they set the pace, and the hair of the leader of the orchestra rises on end, and his eyeballs start from their sockets, as he toils to keep up with them.

Tamoszius Kuszlejka is his name, and he has taught himself to play the violin by practicing all night, after working all day on the killing-floor. He is in his shirt-sleeves, with a vest figured with faded gold horse-shoes, and a pink-striped shirt, suggestive of peppermint candy. A pair of military trousers, light blue with yellow stripe, serve to give that suggestion of authority proper to the leader of a band. He is only about five feet high, but even so these trousers are about eight inches short of the ground. You wonder where he can have gotten them—or rather you would wonder, if the excitement of being in his presence left you time to think of such things.

For he is an inspired man. Every inch of him is inspired—you might almost say inspired separately. He stamps with his feet, he tosses his head, he sways and swings to and fro; he has a wizened-up little face, irresistibly comical; and, when he executes a turn or a flourish, his brows knit and his lips work and his eyelids wink—the very ends of his necktie bristle out. And every now and then he turns upon his companions, nodding, signaling, beckoning frantically—with every inch of him appealing, imploring, in behalf of the muses and their call.

For they are hardly worthy of Tamoszius, the other two members of the orchestra. The second violin is a Slovak, a tall, gaunt man with black-rimmed spectacles and the mute and patient look of an overdriven mule; he responds to the whip but feebly, and then always falls back into his old rut. The third man is very fat, with a round, red, sentimental nose, and he plays with his eyes turned up to the sky and a look of infinite yearning. He is playing a bass part upon his 'cello, and so the excitement is nothing to him; no matter what happens in the treble, it is his task to saw out one long-drawn and lugubrious note after another, from four o'clock in the afternoon until nearly the same hour next morning, for his third of the total income of one dollar per hour.

Before the feast has been five minutes under way, Tamoszius Kuszlejka has risen in his excitement; a minute or two more and you see that he is beginning to edge over towards the tables. His nostrils are dilated and his breath comes fast—his demons are driving him. He nods and shakes his head at his companions, jerking at them with his violin—until at last the long form of the second violinist also rises up. In the end all three of them begin advancing, step by step, upon the banqueters, Valentynaicza, the 'cellist, bumping along with his instrument between notes. Finally all three are gathered at the foot of the tables, and there Tamoszius mounts upon a stool.

Now he is in his glory, dominating the scene. Some of the people are eating, some are laughing and talking—but you will make a great mistake if you think there is one of them who does not hear him. His notes are never true, and his fiddle buzzes on the low ones and squeaks and scratches on the high; but these things they heed no more than they heed the dirt and noise and squalor about them—it is out of this material that they have to build their lives, and with it that they have to utter their souls. And this is their utterance; merry and boisterous, or mournful and wailing, or passionate and rebellious, this music is their music, music of home. It stretches out its arms to them, they have only to give themselves up. Chicago and its saloons and its slums fade away—there are green meadows and sunlit rivers, mighty forests and snow-clad hills. They behold home-landscapes and childhood scenes returning; old loves and friendships begin to waken, old joys and griefs to laugh and weep. Some fall back and close their eyes, some beat upon the table. Now and them one leaps up with a cry and calls for this song or that; and then the fire leaps brighter in Tamoszius' eyes, and he flings up his fiddle and shouts to his companions, and away they go in mad career. The company take up the choruses, and men and women shout like all possessed; some leap to their feet and stamp upon the floor, lifting their glasses and pledging each other. Before long it occurs to some one to demand an old wedding song, which celebrates the beauty of the bride and the joys of love. In the excitement of this masterpiece Tamoszius Kuszlejka begins to edge in between the tables, making his way towards the head, where sits the bride. There is not a foot of space between the chairs of the guests, and Tamoszius is so short that he pokes them with his bow whenever he reaches over for the low notes; but still he presses in, and insists relentlessly that his companions must follow. During their progress, needless to say, the sounds of the 'cello are pretty well extinguished—but at last the three are at the head, and Tamoszius takes his station at the right hand of the bride and begins to pour out his soul in melting strains.

Little Ona is too excited to eat. Once in a while she tastes a little something, when Cousin Marija pinches her elbow and reminds her; but for the most part she sits gazing, with the same fearful eyes of wonder. Teta Elzbieta is all in a flutter, like a humming-bird; her sisters, too, keep running up behind her, whispering, breathless. But Ona seems scarcely to hear them—the music keeps calling, and the far-off look comes back, and she sits with her hands pressed together over her heart. Then the tears begin to come into her eyes; and as she is ashamed to wipe them away, and ashamed to let them run down her cheeks, she turns and shakes her head a little, and then flushes red when she sees that Jurgis is watching her. When in the end Tamoszius Kuszlejika has reached her side, and is waving his magic wand above her, Ona's cheeks are scarlet, and she looks as if she would have to get up and run away. In this crisis, however, she is saved by Marija Biarczynskas, whom the muses suddenly visit. Marija is fond of a song, a song of lovers' parting; she wishes to hear it, and as the musicians do not know it she has risen and is proceeding to teach them. Marija is short, but powerful in build. She works in Smith's canning factory, and all day long she handles cans of beef that weigh fourteen pounds. She has a broad Slavic face, with prominent red cheeks. When she opens her mouth it is tragical, but you cannot help thinking of a horse. She wears a blue flannel shirt-waist, which is now rolled up at the sleeves, disclosing her brawny arms; she has a carving-fork in her hand with which she pounds on the table to mark the time. As she roars her song, in a voice of which it is enough to say that it leaves no portion of the room vacant, the three musicians follow her, laboriously and note by note, but averaging one note behind; thus they toil through stanza after stanza of a lovesick swain's lamentation:

"Sudiev' kvietkeli, tu brongiausis;
Sudiev' ir laime, man biednam,
Matau—paskyre teip Aukszcziausis,
Jog vargt ant svieto reik vienam!"

When the song is over it is time for the speech, and old Diedas Antanas rises to his feet. Grandfather Anthony, Jurgis's father, is not more than sixty years of age, but you would think that he was eighty. He has been only six months in America, and the change has not done him good. In his manhood he worked in a cotton mill, but then a coughing fell upon him, and he had to leave; out in the country the trouble disappeared, but he has been working in the pickle-room at Anderson's and the breathing of the cold, damp air all day has brought it back. Now as he rises he is seized with a coughing fit, and holds himself by his chair and turns away his wan and battered face until it passes.

Generally it is the custom for the speech at a veselija to be taken out of one of the books and learned by heart; but in his youthful days Diedas Antanas used to be a scholar, and really made up all the love-letters of his friends. Now it is understood that he has composed an original speech of congratulation and benediction, and this is one of the events of the day. Even the boys, who are romping about the room, draw near and listen, and some of the women sob and wipe their aprons in their eyes. It is very solemn, for

Antanas Rudkos has become possessed of the idea that he has not much longer to stay with his children. His speech leaves them all so tearful that one of the guests, Jokubas Szadwilas, who keeps a delicatessen-store on Halsted street, and is fat and hearty, is moved to rise and say that things may not be as bad as that, and then to go on and make a little speech of his own, in which he showers congratulations and prophesies of happiness upon the bride and groom, proceeding to particulars which greatly delight the young men, but which cause Ona to blush more furiously than ever. Jokubas possesses what his wife complacently describes as "poetiszka vaidintuve"—a poetical imagination.

Now a good many of the guests have finished, and, since there is no pretense of ceremony, the banquet begins to break up. Some of the men gather about the bar; some wander about, laughing and singing—here and there will be a little group, chanting merrily, and in sublime indifference to the others and to the orchestra as well. Everybody is more or less restless—one would guess that something is on their minds. And so it proves; the last tardy diners are scarcely given time to finish before the tables and the debris are shoved into the corner, and the chairs and the babies piled out of the way, and the real celebration of the evening begins. Then Tamoszius Kuszlejka, after replenishing himself with a pot of beer, returns to his platform, and, standing up, reviews the scene, then taps authoritatively upon the side of his violin, then tucks it carefully under his chin, then waves his bow in an elaborate flourish—and finally smites the sounding strings and closes his eyes and floats away in spirit upon the wings of a dreamy waltz. His companion follows, but with his eyes open, watching where he treads, so to speak; and finally Valentynaicza, after waiting for a little and beating with his foot to get the time, casts up his eyes to the ceiling and begins to saw—"Broom! broom! broom!"

The company pairs off quickly, and the whole room is soon in motion. Apparently nobody knows how to waltz, but that is nothing of any consequence—there is music, and they dance, each as he pleases, just as before they sang. Most of them prefer the "two-step," especially the young, with whom it is the fashion. The older people have dances from home, strange and complicated steps which they execute with grave solemnity. Some do not dance anything at all, but simply hold each other's hands and allow the undisciplined joy of motion to express itself with their feet. Among these are Jokubas Szadwilas and his wife, Lucija, who, together, keep the delicatessen-store and consume nearly as much as they sell; they are too fat to dance, but they stand in the middle of the floor, holding each other fast in their arms, rocking slowly from side to side and grinning seraphically, a picture of toothless and perspiring ecstasy.

Of these older people many wear clothing reminiscent in some detail of home—an embroidered waistcoat or stomacher, or a gaily-colored handker-chief, or a coat with large cuffs and fancy buttons. All these things are carefully avoided by the young, most of whom have learned to speak English and to affect the latest style of clothing. The girls wear ready-made dresses or shirt-waists, and some of them look quite pretty. Some of the young men you would take to be Americans, of the type of clerks, but for the fact that they wear their hats in the room. Each of these younger couples affects a style of its own in dancing. Some hold each other tightly, some at a cautious distance. Some hold their arms out stiffly, some drop them loosely at their sides. Some dance springily, some glide softly, some move with grave dignity. There are boisterous couples, who tear wildly about the room, knocking everyone out of their way. There are nervous couples, whom these frighten, and who cry, "Mustok! Kas ira?" at them as they pass. Each couple is paired for the evening—you will never see them change about. There is Alena Jasaitis, for instance, who has danced unending hours with Juozas Roczis, with whom she is engaged. Alena is the beauty of the evening, and she would be really beautiful if she were not so proud. She wears a white shirt-waist, which represents, perhaps, half a week's labor painting cans. She holds her skirt with her hand as she dances, with stately precision, after the manner of the *grandes dames*. Juozas is driving one of Anderson's wagons, and is making big wages. He affects a "tough" aspect, wearing his hat on one side and keeping a cigarette in his mouth all the evening. Then, there is Jadviga Marciukus, who is also beautiful, but humble. Jadviga likewise paints cans, but, then, she has an invalid mother and three little sisters to support by it, and so she does not spend her wages for shirt-waists. Jadviga is small and delicate, with jet black eyes and hair, the latter twisted into a little knot and tied on the top of her head. She wears an old white dress which she has made herself and worn to parties for the past five years; it is high-waisted—almost under her arms, and not very becoming—but that does not trouble Jadviga, who is dancing with her Mikolas. She is small, while he is big and powerful; she nestles in his arms as if she would hide herself from view, and leans her head upon his shoulder. He in turn has clasped his arms tightly around her, as if he would carry her away; and so she dances, and will dance the entire evening, and would dance forever, in ecstasy of bliss. You would smile, perhaps, to see them—but you would not smile if you knew all the story. This is the fifth year, now, that Jadviga has been engaged to Mikolas, and her heart is sick. They would have been married in the beginning, only Mikolas has a father who is drunk all day, and he is the only other man in a large family. Even so, they might have managed it (for Mikolas is a skilled man), but for cruel accidents which have almost taken the heart out of them. He is a beef-boner, and that is a dangerous trade, especially when you are on piece-work and trying to earn a bride. Your hands are slippery, and your knife is slippery, and you are toiling like mad, when somebody happens to speak to you or you strike a bone. Then your hand slips up on the blade, and there is a fearful gash. And that would not be so bad, only for the deadly contagion. The cut may heal, but you never can tell. Twice, now, within the last three years, Mikolas has been lying at home with blood-poisoning—once for three months and once for nearly seven. The last time, too, he lost his job, and that meant six weeks more of standing at the doors of the packing-houses, at six o'clock on bitter winter mornings, with a foot of snow on the ground and more in the air. There are learned people who can tell you out of the statistics that beef-boners make forty cents an hour, but, perhaps, these people have never looked into a beef-boner's hands.

When Tamoszius and his companions stop for a rest, as perforce they must, now and then, the dancers halt where they are and wait patiently. They never seem to tire; and there is no place for them to sit down if they did. It is only for a minute, anyway, for the leader starts up again, in spite of all the protests of the other two. This time it is another sort of a dance, a Lithuanian dance. Those who prefer to, go on with the two-step, but the majority go through an intricate series of motions, resembling more fancy skating than a dance. The climax of it is a furious *prestissimo*, at which the couples seize hands and begin a mad whirling. This is quite irresistible, and everyone in the room joins in, until the place becomes a maze of flying skirts and bodies, quite dazzling to look upon. But the sight of sights at this moment is Tamoszius Kuszlejka. The old fiddle squeaks and shrieks in protest, but Tamoszius has no mercy. The sweat starts out on his forehead, and he bends over like a cyclist on the last lap of a race. His body shakes and throbs like a runaway steam-engine, and the ear cannot follow the flying showers of notes—there is a pale blue mist where you look to see his bowing arm. With a most wonderful rush he comes to the end of the tune, and flings up his hands and staggers back exhausted; and with a final shout of delight the dancers fly apart, reeling here and there, bringing up against the walls of the room.

After this there is beer for everyone, the musicians included, and the revellers take a long breath and prepare for the great event of the evening, which is the *aczaviuas*. The *aczavuas* is a ceremony which, once begun, will continue for three or four hours, and it involves one uninterrupted dance. The guests form a great ring, locking hands, and, when the music starts up, begin to move around in a circle. In the center stands the bride, and one by one the men step into the enclosure and dance with her. Each dances for several minutes—as long as he pleases; it is a very merry proceeding, with laughter and singing, and when the guest has finished he finds himself face to face with Teta Elzbieta, who holds the hat. Into it he drops a sum of money—a dollar, or, perhaps, five dollars, according to his power, and his estimate of the value of the privilege. The guests are expected to pay for this entertainment—if they be proper guests they will see that there is a neat sum left over for the bride and bridegroom to start life upon.

Most fearful they are to contemplate, the expenses of this entertainment. They will certainly be over two hundred dollars, and may be three hundred; and three hundred dollars is more than the year's income of many a person in this room. There are able-bodied men here who work from early morning until late at night, in ice-cold cellars with a quarter of an inch of water on the floor—men who for six or seven months in the year never see the sunlight from Sunday afternoon till the next Sunday morning—and who cannot earn three hundred dollars in a year. There are little children here, scarce in their teens, who can hardly see the top of the work benches—whose parents have lied to get them their places—and who do not make the half of three hundred dollars a year, and perhaps not even the third of it. And then to spend such a sum, all in a single day of your life, at a wedding-feast!—for obviously it is the same thing, whether you spend it at once for your own wedding, or in a long time, at the weddings of all your friends.

It is very imprudent, it is tragic—but, ah, it is so beautiful! Bit by bit these poor people have given up everything else, but to this they cling with all the power of their souls—they cannot give up the *veselija!* To do that would mean, not merely to be defeated, but to acknowledge defeat—and the difference between these two things is what keeps the world going. The *veselija* has come down to them from a far-off time, a time when money was made for man and not man for money—when the fruits of the earth belonged to the person who tilled it, and when plenty and to spare was the reward of honest toil. And the meaning of it was that one might dwell within the cave and gaze upon shadows, provided only that once in his lifetime he might break his chains, and feel his wings, and behold the sun; provided that once in his lifetime he might testify to the fact that life, with all its cares and its terrors, is no such great thing after all, but merely a bubble upon the surface of a river, a thing that one may toss about and play with, as a juggler tosses his golden balls, a thing that one may quaff, like a goblet of rare red wine. Thus, having known himself for the master of things, a man could go back to his toil and live upon the memory all his days.

Endlessly the dancers swung round and round—when they were dizzy they swung the other way; and meantime Ona welcomed all who came, suiting herself with gentle timidity to the manner and gait of each. There were young men with starched shirts and high, stiff collars, and old men with gay-colored handkerchiefs; there were benevolent old ladies, and frightened little girls who had begged a few pennies to pay for a turn. Hour after hour this continued—the darkness had fallen and the room was dim from the light of two smoky oil lamps. The musicians had spent all their fine frenzy by this time, and now played only one tune, wearily, ploddingly. There were twenty bars or so of it, and when they came to the end they began again. Once every ten minutes or so they would fail to begin again, but instead would sink back exhausted; a circumstance which invariably brought on a painful and terrifying scene that made the fat policeman stir uneasily in his sleeping-place behind the door.

It was all Marija Biarczynskas. Marija was one of those hungry souls who cling with desperation to the skirts of the retreating muse. All day long she had been in a state of wonderful exaltation; and now it was leaving—and she would not let it go. Her soul cried out in the words of Faust, "Stay, thou art fair!" Whether it was by beer, or by shouting, or by music, or by motion, she meant that it should not go. And she would go back to the chase of it—and no sooner be fairly started than her chariot would be thrown off the track, so to speak, by the stupidity of those thrice-accursed musicians. Each time, Marija would emit a howl and fly at them, shaking her fists in their faces, stamping upon the floor, purple and incoherent with rage. In vain the frightened Tamoszius would attempt to speak, to plead the limitations of the flesh; in vain would the puffing and breathless Panas Jokubas insist, in vain would Teta Elzbieta implore "Szalin!" Marija would scream, "Palauk! isz kelio! What are you paid for, children of hell!" And so, in sheer terror, the orchestra would strike up again, and Marija would return to her place and take up her task.

She bore all the burden of the festivities now. Ona was kept up by her excitement, but all of the women and most of the men were tired—the soul of Marija was alone unconquered. She drove on the dancers—what had once been the ring had now the shape of a pear, with Marija at the stem, pulling one way and pushing the other, shouting, stamping, singing, a very volcano of energy. Now and then some one coming in or out would leave the door open, and the night air was chill; Marija as she passed would stretch out her foot and kick the door-knob, and slam would go the door! Once this procedure was the cause of a calamity of which Sebastijonas Szadwilas was the hapless victim. Little Sebastijonas, aged three, had been wandering about oblivious to all things, holding turned up over his mouth a bottle of liquid known as "pop," pink-colored, ice-cold, and delicious. Passing through the doorway the door smote him full, and the shriek which followed brought the dancing to a halt. Marija, who threatened horrid murder a hundred times a day, and would weep over the injury of a fly, seized little Sebastijonas in her arms and bid fair to smother him with kisses. There was a long rest for the orchestra, and plenty of refreshments, while Marija was making her peace with her victim, seating him upon the bar, and standing beside him and holding to his lips a foaming schooner of beer.

In the meantime there was going on in another corner of the room an anxious and frightened conference between Teta Elzbieta and Diedas Antanas, and a few of the more intimate friends of the family. A trouble was come upon them—a terrible trouble. It could not precisely be called a new one; it was becoming cruelly common—but it was something in which no one could believe until he had actually experienced it, from which with blind confidence they had felt certain of escape. It was so hard for the old people—it was something which meant the collapse of all the world which they knew, of all faith and religion, all decency and honor. Old Diedas Antanas was all a-tremble at the lips, and Ona's step-mother wrung her hands together wailing, "Ai! skausmas! What times are come upon us—what vipers are we cherishing." For the *veselija* is a compact, a compact not expressed, but therefore only the more binding upon all, and one which no man in all Lithuania would ever have dreamed of violating. Everyone's share was different—and yet everyone knew perfectly well what his share was and strove to give a little more. Now, however, since they had come to the new country, all this was changing; and it was just like feeling the ground failing under your feet. It seemed as if there must be some subtle poison in the air that one breathed here—it was affecting all the young men at once. They no longer cared about the laws of the *veselija*, or about any laws; they no longer cared about the good opinion of men—they cared only about themselves. They did not believe in faith and honor, but made fun of such things; it was the fashion, and they thought that it was smart. They would be no simple-minded victims, not they; they had learned the rules of the game. There was common among them a witticism which they had picked up somewhere, and which they never tired of laughing over: "Do unto others as they would do unto you, but do it first." And this meant in practice that instead of caring for their old people, their little brothers and sisters, and being true to their sweethearts, they spent all their money upon shoddy clothing and vanities and went downtown after women so dreadful that one could not speak of them. It meant that when there was a *veselija* they came in crowds and filled themselves with a fine dinner and then sneaked off. One would throw another's hat out of the window, and both would go out to get it, and neither would be seen again. Or now and then half a dozen of them would get together and march out openly, staring at you, and making fun of you to your face. Still others, worse yet, would crowd about the bar, and at the expense of the host drink themselves sodden, paying not the least attention to anyone, and leaving it to be thought that either they had danced with the bride already, or meant to later on. Now and then one of these might be shamed into going forward, but when he did so the amount of his contribution would be an insult.

All these things were going on now, and the family was helpless with dismay. So long they had toiled, and such an outlay they had made—and now it was all gone and ruin staring them in the face. Ona stood by, her eyes wide with terror; for the tale lost nothing in its telling by the old women, and this in its turn was magnified by the imagination of the child. Those frightful bills—how they had haunted her, each item gnawing at her soul all day and spoiling her rest at night. How often she had named them over one by one and figured on them as she went to work—fifteen dollars for the hall, twenty-two dollars and a quarter for the ducks, twelve dollars for the musicians, five dollars at the church, and a blessing of the Virgin besides—and so on without an end! Worst of all was the frightful bill that was still to come from Grajczunas for the beer and liquor that might be consumed. One could never get in advance more than a guess as to this from a saloon-keeper—and then, when the time came he always came to you scratching his head and saying that he had guessed too low, but that he had done his best—your guests had gotten so very drunk. By him you were sure to be cheated unmercifully, and that even though you thought yourself the dearest of the hundreds of friends he had. He would begin to serve your guests out of a keg that was half full, and finish with one that was half empty, and then you would be charged for two kegs of beer. He would agree to serve a certain quality at a certain price, and when the time came you and your friends would be drinking some horrible poison that could not be described. You might complain, but you would get nothing for your pains but a ruined evening; while, as for going to law about it, you might as well go to heaven at once. The saloon-keeper stood in with all the big politics men in the district—and in the city, and in the nation, so far as any poor man's eye could reach; and when you had once found out what it meant to get into trouble with such people, you would know enough to pay what you were told to pay and shut up.

What made all this the more painful was that it was so hard on the few that had really done their best. Some tried to do still more, hoping to turn the tide and to shame the recreant. There was poor old panas Jokubas, for instance—he had already given five dollars, and recently poeni Lucija had danced also and given two more; and did not everyone know that Jokubas Szadwilas had just mortgaged his delicatessen-store for two hundred dollars to meet several months' overdue rent? And then there was withered old panei Aniele—who was a widow and had three children, and the rheumatism besides, and did washing for the tradespeople on Halsted street at prices it would break your heart to hear named. Panei Aniele had given three dollars—and that meant that she had saved the entire profit of her chickens this year. Eight of them she owned, and she kept them in a little place fenced around on her back stairs. All day long the children of panei Aniele were raking in the dump for food for these chickens; and sometimes, when the competition there was too fierce, you might see them on Halsted street, walking close to the gutters, and with their mother following to see that no one robbed them of their finds. Money could not tell the value of these chickens to old Mrs. Juknos—she valued them differently, for she had a feeling that she was getting something for nothing by means of them—that with them she was getting the better of a world that was getting the better of her in so many other ways. So she watched them every hour of the day, and had learned to see like an owl at night to watch them then. One of them had been stolen long ago, and not a month passed that some one did not try to steal another. As the frustrating of this one attempt involved a score of false alarms, it will be understood what a tribute old Mrs. Juknos brought, just because Teta Elzbieta had once loaned her some money for a few days and saved her from being turned out of her house.

More and more friends gathered round while the lamentations about these things was going on. Some drew nearer, hoping to overhear the conversation, who were themselves among the guilty—and surely that was a thing to try the patience of a saint. Finally there came Jurgis, urged by some one, and the story was retold to him. Jurgis listened in silence, with his great black eyebrows knitted. Now and then there would come a gleam underneath them and he would glance about the room. Perhaps he would have liked to go at some of those fellows with his big clenched fists; but then, doubtless, he realized how little good it would do him. No bill would be any less for turning out any one at this time; and then there would be the scandal—and Jurgis wanted nothing except to get away with Ona and to let the world go on its way. So his hands relaxed and he merely said quietly: "It is done, and there is no use in weeping, Teta Elzbieta." Then his look turned toward Ona, who stood close to his side, and he saw the wide look of terror in her eves. "Little one," he said, in a low voice, "do not worry—it will not matter to us. We will pay them all somehow. I will work harder." That was always what Jurgis said. Ona had grown used to it as the solution of all difficulties— "I will work harder!" He had said that in Lithuania when one official had taken his passport from him and another had arrested him for being without it, and the two had divided a third of his belongings. He had said it again in New York, when the smooth-spoken agent had taken them in hand and made them pay such high prices, and almost prevented their leaving his place, in spite of their paying. Now he said it a third time, and Ona drew a deep breath; it was so wonderful to have a husband, just like a grown girl—and a husband who could solve all problems, and who was so big and strong!

The last sob of little Sebastijonas has been stifled, and the orchestra has once more been reminded of its duty. The ceremony begins again—but there are few now left to dance with, and so very soon the collection is over and promiscuous dances once more begin. It is now after midnight, however, and things are not as they were before. The dancers are dull and heavy—most of them have been drinking hard, and have long ago passed the stage of exhilaration. They dance in monotonous measure, round after round, hour after hour, with eyes fixed upon vacancy, as if they were only half conscious, in a constantly growing stupor. The men grasp the women very tightly, but there will be half an hour together when neither will see the other's face. Some do not care to dance, and have retired to the corners, where they sit with their arms enlaced. Others, who have been drinking still more, wander about the room, bumping into everything; some are in groups of two or three, singing, each group its own song. As time goes on there is a variety of drunkenness, among the younger men especially. Some stagger about in each other's arms, whispering maudlin words—others start quarrels upon the slightest pretext and come to blows and have to be pulled apart. Now the fat policeman wakens definitely, and feels of his club to see that it is ready for business. He has to be prompt—for these two-o'clock-in-the-morning fights, if they once get out of hand, are like a forest fire, and may mean the whole reserves at the station. The thing to do is to crack every fighting head that you see, before there are so many fighting heads that you cannot crack any of them. There is but scant account kept of cracked heads in back of the yards, for men who have to crack the heads of animals all day seem to get into the habit, and to practice on their friends, and even on their families, between times. This makes it a cause for congratulation that by modern methods a very few men can do the painfully necessary work of head-cracking for the whole of the cultured world.

There is no fight that night—perhaps because Jurgis, too, is watchful— even more so than the policeman. Jurgis has drunk a good deal, as any man naturally would on an occasion when it all has to be paid for, whether it is drunk or not; but he is a very steady man, and does not easily lose his temper. Only once there is a tight shave—and that is the fault of Marija Biarczynskas. Marija has apparently concluded about two hours ago that if the altar in the corner, with the deity in soiled white, be not the true home of the muses, it is, at any rate, the nearest substitute on earth attainable. And Marija is just fighting drunk, when there comes to her ears the facts about the villains who have not paid that night. Marija goes on the warpath straight off, without even the preliminary of a good cursing, and when she is pulled off it is with the coat collars of two villains in her hands. Fortunately the policeman is disposed to be reasonable, and so it is not Marija who is flung out of the place.

All this interrupts the music for not more than a minute or two. Then again the merciless tune begins—the tune that has been played for the last three hours without one single change. It is an American tune this time, one which they have picked up on the streets; all seem to know the words of it—or, at any rate, the first line of it, which they hum to themselves, over and over again without rest: "In the good old summer time—in the good old summer time! In the good old summer time—in the good old summer time." There seems to be something hypnotic about this, with its endlessly-recurring dominant. It has put a stupor upon everyone who hears it, as well as upon the men who are playing it. No one can get away from it, or even think of getting away from it; it is three o'clock in the morning, and they have danced out all their joy, and danced out all their strength, and all the strength that unlimited drink can lend them—and still there is no one among them who has the power to think of stopping. Promptly at seven o'clock this same Monday morning they will every one of them have to be in their places at Anderson's or Smith's or Morton's, each in his working clothes. If one of them be a minute late he will be docked half a day's pay, and if he be many minutes late he will be apt to find his brass check turned to the wall, which will send him out to join the hungry mob that waits every morning at the gates of the packing houses, from six o'clock until nearly half past eight. There is no exception to this rule, not even little Ona—who has asked for a holiday the day after her wedding day, a holiday without pay, and been refused. While there are so many who are anxious to work as you wish, there is no occasion for incommoding yourself with those who must work otherwise.

Little Ona is nearly ready to faint—and half in a stupor herself, because of the heavy scent in the room. She has not taken a drop herself, but everyone else there is literally burning alcohol, as the lamps are burning oil; some of the men who are sound asleep in their chairs or on the floor, are reeking of it so that you cannot go near them. Now and then Jurgis gazes at her hungrily —he has long since forgotten his shyness; but then the crowd is there, and he still waits and watches the door, where a carriage is supposed to come. It does not, and finally he will wait no longer, but comes up to Ona, who turns white and trembles. He puts her shawl about her and then his own coat. They live only two blocks away, and Jurgis does not care about the carriage.

There is almost no farewell—the dancers do not notice them, and all of the children and many of the old folks have fallen asleep of sheer exhaustion. Diedas Antanas is asleep, and so are the Szadwilases, husband and wife, the former snoring in octaves. There is Teta Elzbieta, and Marija, sobbing loudly—and then there is only the silent night, with the stars beginning to pale a little in the east. Jurgis, without a word, lifts Ona in his arms, and strides out with her, and she sinks her head upon his shoulder with a moan. When he reaches home he is not sure whether she has fainted or is asleep, but when he has to hold her with one hand while he unlocks the door he sees that she has opened her eyes.

"You shall not go to Smith's today, little one," he whispers, as he climbs the stairs; and she catches his arm in terror, gasping: "No! No! I dare not! It will ruin us!"

But he answers her again: "Leave it to me; leave it to me. I will earn more money—I will work harder."

JURGIS talked lightly about work, because he was young. They told him stories about the breaking down of men, there in the stockyards of Chicago, and of what had happened to them afterwards—stories to make your flesh creep, but Jurgis would only laugh. He had only been there four months, and he was young, and a giant besides. There was too much health in him. He could not even imagine how it would feel to be beaten. "That is well enough for men like you," he would say "szilpnas, puny fellows—but my back is broad."

Jurgis was like a boy, a boy from the country. He was the sort of man the bosses like to get hold of, the sort they make it a grievance they cannot get hold of. When he was told to go to a certain place he would go there on the run. When he had nothing to do for the moment he would stand round fidgeting, dancing, with the overflow of energy that was in him. If he were working in a line of men the line always moved too slowly for him, and you could pick him out by his impatience and restlessness. That was why he had been picked out on one important occasion; for Jurgis had stood outside of Smith and Company's "General Time Station" not more than half an hour, the second day of his arrival in Chicago, before he had been beckoned by one of the bosses. Of this he was very proud, and it made him more disposed than ever to laugh at the pessimists. In vain would they all tell him that there were men in that crowd from which he had been chosen who had stood there a month—yes, many months—and not been chosen yet. "Yes," he would say, "but what sort of men? broken-down tramps and good-for-nothings, fellows who have spent all their money drinking, and want to get more for it. Do not tell me, there is always work for a man! Do you want me to believe that with these arms"—and he would clench his fists and hold them up in the air, so that you might see the rolling muscles—"that with these arms people will ever let me starve?"

"It is plain," they would answer to this, "that you have come from the country, and from very far in the country." And this was the fact, for Jurgis had never seen a city, and scarcely even a fair-sized town, until he had set out to make his fortune in the world and earn his right to Ona. His father, and his father's father before him, and as many ancestors back as legend could go, had lived in that part of Lithuania known as Bialowicza, the Imperial Forest. This was a great tract of a hundred thousand acres, which from time immemorial has been a hunting preserve of the nobility. There are a very few peasants settled in it, holding title from ancient times; and one of these was

Antanas Rudkos, who had been reared himself, and had reared his children in turn, upon half a dozen acres of cleared land in the midst of a wilderness. There had been one son besides Jurgis, and one sister. The former had been drafted into the army; that had been over ten years ago, but since that day nothing had ever been heard of him. The sister was married, and her husband had bought the place when old Antanas had decided to go with his son.

It was nearly a year and a half ago that Jurgis had met Ona, at a horse-fair a hundred miles from home. Jurgis had never expected to get married—he had laughed at it as a foolish trap for a man to walk into; but here, without ever having spoken a word to her, with no more than the exchange of half a dozen smiles, he found himself, purple in the face with embarrassment and terror, asking her parents to sell her to him for his wife—and offering his father's two horses he had been sent to the fair to sell. But Ona's father proved as a rock—the girl was yet a child, and he was a rich man, and his daughter was not to be had in that way. So Jurgis went home with a heavy heart, and that spring and summer toiled and tried hard to forget. In the fall, after the harvest was over, he saw that it would not do, and tramped the full fortnight's journey that lay between him and Ona.

He found an unexpected state of affairs—for the girl's father had died, and his estate was tied up with creditors; Jurgis's heart leaped as he realized that now the prize was within his reach. There was panei Elzbieta Lukoszig, Teta, or Aunt, as they called her, Ona's stepmother, and there were her six children, of all ages. There was also her brother Jonas, a dried up little man who had worked upon the farm. They were people of great consequence, as it seemed to Jurgis, fresh out of the woods; Ona knew how to read, and knew many other things that he did not know; and now the farm had been sold, and the whole family was adrift—all they owned in the world being about seven hundred roubles, which is half as many dollars. They would have had three times that, but it had gone to court, and the judge had decided against them, and it had cost the balance to get him to change his decision.

Ona might have married and left them, but she would not, for she loved Teta Elzbieta. It was Jonas who suggested that they all go to America, where a friend of his had gotten rich. He would work, for his part, and the women would work, and some of the children, doubtless—they would live some-how. Jurgis, too, had heard of America. That was a country where, they said, a man might earn three roubles a day; and Jurgis figured what three roubles a day would mean, with prices as they were where he lived, and decided forthwith that he would go to America and marry, and be a rich man in the bargain.

So it was arranged that they should leave the following spring, and meantime Jurgis hired himself as an obiezyzasy, a sort of peon laborer. He sold himself to a contractor for a certain time, and he tramped nearly four hundred miles from home with a gang of men to work upon a railroad in Smolensk. This was a fearful experience, with filth and bad food and cruelty and over-work; but Jurgis stood it and came out in fine trim, and with eighty roubles sewed up in his coat. No amount of work made any difference to Jurgis, and with men he had a way of his own. He did not drink or fight, because he was thinking all the time of Ona; and for the rest, he was a quiet, steady man, who did what he was told to, did not lose his temper often, and when he did lose it made the offender anxious that he should not lose it again. When they paid him off he dodged the company gamblers and dramshops, and so they tried to kill him, but he escaped, and tramped it home, working at odd jobs and sleeping always with one eye open.

So in the summer they had all set out for America. At the last moment there joined them Marija Biarczynskas, who was a cousin of Ona's. Marija was an orphan, and had worked since childhood for a rich farmer of Vilna, who beat her regularly. It was only at the age of twenty that it had occurred to Marija to try her strength, when she had risen up and nearly murdered the man, and then came away.

There were twelve in all in the party, five adults and six children—and Ona, who was a little of both. They had a hard time of the passage; there was an agent who helped them, but he proved a scoundrel, and got them into a trap with some officials, and cost them a good deal of their precious money, which they clung to with such horrible fear. This happened to them again in New York—for, of course, they knew nothing about the country, and had no one to tell them, and it was easy for a man in a blue uniform to lead them away, and to take them to a hotel and keep them there, and make them pay enormous charges to get away. The law says that the rate card shall be on the door of a hotel, but it does not say that it shall be in Lithuanian.

It was in the stockyards that Jonas' friend had gotten rich, and so to Chicago the party was bound. They knew that one word—Chicago—and that was all they needed to know, at least, until they reached the city. Then, tumbled out of the cars without ceremony, they were no better off than before; they stood staring down the vista of Dearborn street, with its big, black buildings towering in the distance, unable to realize that they had arrived, and why, when they said "Chicago," people no longer pointed in some direction, but instead looked perplexed, or laughed, or went on without paying any attention. They were pitiable in their helplessness; above all things they stood in deadly terror of any sort of person in official uniform, and so, whenever they saw a policeman they would cross the street and hurry by. For the whole of the first day they wandered about in the midst of deafening confusion, utterly lost; and it was only at night that, cowering in the doorway of a house, they were finally discovered and taken by a policeman to the station. In the morning an interpreter was found, and they were taken and put upon a car and taught a new word—"stockyards." Their delight at discovering that they were to get out of this adventure without losing another share of their possessions it would not be possible to describe.

They sat and stared out of the window. They were on a street which seemed to run on forever, mile after mile—thirty-four of them, if they had known it—and each side of it one uninterrupted row of wretched little two-story frame buildings. Down every side street they could see, it was the same—never a hill and never a hollow, but always the same endless vista of ugly and dirty little wooden buildings. Here and there would be a bridge crossing a filthy creek, with hard-baked mud shores and dingy sheds and docks along it; here and there would be a railroad crossing, with a tangle of switches, and locomotives puffing and rattling freight cars filing by; here and there would be a great factory, a dingy building with innumerable windows in it, and immense volumes of smoke pouring from the chimneys, darkening the air above and making filthy the earth beneath. But after each of these interruptions, the desolate procession would begin again—the procession of dreary little buildings. To the strangers it seemed like a wilderness, a very jungle—a jungle of houses. It was a jungle, too, ruled by strange powers, about which they did not understand, full of creatures which preyed upon each other—that were hunting you without rest, tracking you in the daytime and watching in your path by night. The only difference was that they sought, not your life-blood, but your money—and when you had been caught by them once or twice, you came to understand that this difference was no difference at all.

A full hour before the party reached the city they had begun to note the perplexing changes in the atmosphere. It grew darker all the time, and upon the earth the grass seemed to grow less green. Every minute, as the train sped on, the colors of things grew dingier; the fields were grown parched and yellow, the landscape hideous and bare. And along with the thickening smoke they began to notice another circumstance, a strange, pungent odor. They were not sure that it was unpleasant, this odor; some might have called it sickening, but their taste in odors was not developed, and they were only sure that it was curious. Now—sitting in the trolley car—they realized that they were on their way to the home of it—that they had traveled all the way from Lithuania to it. It was now no longer something far-off and faint, that you caught in whiffs; you could literally taste it, as well as smell it—you could take hold of it, almost, and examine it at your leisure. They were divided in their opinions about it. It was an elemental odor, raw and crude; it was rich, almost rancid, sensual and strong. There were some who drank it in as if it were an intoxicant; there were others who turned pale and put their handkerchiefs to their faces. The new emigrants were still tasting it, lost in wonder, when suddenly the car came to a halt, and the door was flung open, and a voice shouted—"Stockyards!"

They were left standing upon the corner, staring; down a side street there were two rows of brick houses, and between them a vista: half a dozen chimneys, tall as the tallest of buildings, touching the very sky—and leaping from them half a dozen columns of smoke, thick, oily and black as night. It might have come from the center of the world, this smoke, where the fires of the ages still smoulder. It came as if self-impelled, driving all before it, a perpetual explosion. It was inexhaustible; one stared, waiting to see it stop —but still the great streams rolled out. They spread in vast clouds overhead, writhing, curling; then uniting in one giant river, they streamed away down the sky, stretching a black pall as far as the eye could reach.

Then the party became aware of another strange thing. This, too, like the odor, was a thing elemental; it was a sound, a sound made up of ten thousand little sounds. One scarcely noticed it at first—it sunk into one's consciousness, a vague disturbance, a trouble. It was like the murmuring of the bees in the spring, the whisperings of the forest; it suggested endless activity, the rumblings of a world in motion; it was only by an effort that one could realize that it was made by animals, that it was the distant lowing of ten thousand cattle, the distant grunting of ten thousand swine.

They would have liked to follow it up, but, alas, they had no time for adventures just then. The policeman on the corner was beginning to watch them; and so, as usual, they started up the street. Scarcely had they gone a block, however, before Jonas was heard to give a cry, and began pointing excitedly across the street. Before they could gather the meaning of his breathless ejaculations he had bounded away, and they saw him enter a shop over which was a sign: "J. Szadwilas, Delicatessen." When he came out again it was in company with a very stout gentleman in shirt sleeves and an apron, clasping Jonas by both hands and laughing hilariously. Then Teta Elzbieta recollected suddenly that Szadwilas had been the name of the mythical friend who had made his fortune in America. To find that he had been making it in the delicatessen business was an extraordinary piece of good fortune in this juncture. Though it was well on in the morning they had not breakfasted, and the children were beginning to whimper.

Thus was the happy ending of a woeful voyage. The two families literally fell upon each other's necks—for it had been years since Jokubas Szadwilas had met a man from his part of Lithuania. Before half the day they were lifelong friends. Jokubas understood all the pitfalls of this new world, and could explain all its mysteries; he could tell them the things they ought to have done in the different emergencies—and what was still more to the point, he could tell them what to do now. He would take them to panei Aniele, who kept a boarding house the other side of the yards; old Mrs. Juknos, he explained, had not what one would call choice accommodations, but they might do for the moment. To this Teta Elzbieta hastened to respond that nothing could be too cheap to suit them just then; for they were quite terrified over the sums they had had to expend. A very few days of practical experience in this land of high wages had been sufficient to make clear to them the cruel fact that it was also a land of high prices, and that in it the poor man was just exactly as poor as in any other corner of the earth; and so there vanished in a night all the wonderful dreams of wealth that had been haunting Jurgis. What had made the discovery all the more painful was that they were expending at American prices money which they had earned at home rates of wages—and so were really being cheated by the world. The last two days they had all but starved themselves—it made them quite sick to pay the prices that the railroad people asked them for food.

Yet, when they saw the home of the Widow Juknos they could not but recoil, even so. In all their journey they had seen nothing so bad as this. Panei Aniele had a four-room flat in that wilderness of two-story frame tenements that lie in "back of the yards." There were four such flats in each building and each of the four was a "boarding house" for the occupancy of foreigners—Lithuanians, Poles, Slovaks, or Bohemians. Some of these places were kept by private persons, some were co-operative. There would be an average of half a dozen boarders to each room—sometimes there were thirteen or fourteen to one room, fifty or sixty to a flat. Each one of the occupants furnished his own accommodations—that is, a mattress and some bedding. The mattresses would be spread upon the floor in rows—and there would be nothing else in the place except a stove. Sometimes the boarders would hire a woman to cook for them, sometimes they would do their own cooking; in a few rare cases the landlady would furnish the food and prepare it for all. It was by no means unusual for two men to own the same mattress in common, one working by day and using it by night, and the other working at night and using it in the daytime. Very frequently a lodging-house keeper would rent the same beds to double shifts of men. This had not been the custom, but it was getting to be, owing to the system upon which the packing-houses were now being run. It was said to be owing to the increasing insubordination of the labor unions that the packers were employing so many men and giving each of them such a small amount of work to do. This kept wages low and the district crowded—a sure preventive of trouble.

Panei Aniele Juknos was a wizened-up little woman, with a wrinkled and heart-sick face. Her home was unthinkably filthy; you could not enter by the front door at all, owing to the mattresses, and when you tried to go up the back stairs you found that she had walled up most of the porch with old boards to make a place to keep her chickens. It was a standing jest of the boarders that panei Aniele cleaned house by letting the chickens loose in the rooms. Undoubtedly this did keep down the vermin, but it seems probable, in view of all the circumstances, that the old lady regarded it rather as feeding the chickens than as cleaning the rooms. The truth was that she had definitely given up the idea of cleaning the rooms nearly two months ago, under pressure of an attack of rheumatism, which had kept her doubled up in one corner of her room for over a week. During this time eleven of her boarders, heavily in her debt, had concluded to try their chances of employment in Kansas City, and had decamped. This was July, and the fields were green; one never saw the fields, nor any green thing whatever, in Packingtown—but one could go out on the road and "hobo it," as the men phrased it, and see the country, and have a long rest, and an easy time riding on the freight cars. Meantime, as the widow Juknos had been trying for over a year to pay for her furniture, and was in debt to her landlord besides, she was, perhaps, not to blame for concluding to give up, and let ruin come when it would.

Such was the home to which the new arrivals were welcomed. There was nothing better to be had—they might not do so well by looking further, for Mrs. Juknos had at least kept one room for herself and her three little children, and now offered to share this with the women and the girls of the party. They could get bedding at a second-hand store, she explained; and they would not need any while the weather was so hot—doubtless they would all sleep on the sidewalk, such nights as this, as did nearly all of her guests. "Tomorrow," Jurgis said with quiet confidence, when they were left alone, "tomorrow I will get a job; and perhaps Jonas will get one also; and then we can get a place of our own."

Later that afternoon he and Ona went out to take a walk and look about them to see more of this district which was to be their home. In back of the yards the dreary two-story frame houses were spread out farther than in most of Chicago they had seen; there were great spaces bare—that seemingly had been overlooked by the great sore of a city as it spread itself over the surface of the prairie. These bare places were grown up with dingy, yellow weeds, hiding innumerable tomato cans; innumerable children played upon them, chasing one another here and there, screaming and fighting. The most uncanny thing about this neighborhood was the number of the children; you thought there must be a school just out, and it was only after long acquaintance that you were able to realize that there was no school, but that these were the children of the neighborhood—that there were so many children to the block in Packingtown that nowhere on its streets could a horse and buggy move faster than a walk!

It could not move faster anyhow, of course—on account of the state of the streets. Those through which Jurgis and Ona were walking resembled streets less than they did a miniature topographical map of a continent. The roadway was commonly several feet lower than the level of the houses, which were sometimes joined by high board walks; there were no pavements—there were mountains and valleys and rivers, gullies and ditches, and great hollows full of stinking green water. In these pools the children played, and rolled about in the mud of the streets; here and there one noticed them digging in it, after trophies which they had stumbled on. One wondered about this, as also about the swarms of flies which hung about the scene, literally blackening the air, and the strange, fetid odor which assailed one's nostrils, a ghastly odor, of all the dead things of the universe. It impelled the visitor to questions—and then the residents would explain, quietly, that all this was "made" land—and that it had been "made" by using it as a dumping-ground for the city garbage. After a few years the unpleasant effect of this would pass away, it was said; but meantime, in hot weather—and especially when it rained—the flies were apt to be annoying. Was it not unhealthy? the stranger would ask, and the residents would answer: "Perhaps, but there is no telling." Yet there chanced one day to be passing a young man who thought that there might be telling, and who set to work to count the deaths of the children in back of the yards. He found that they were five times as numerous as in the neighboring district, a "swell" part of the city, whence came all this garbage to be dumped. Then, also, he made a map of the district, and in each block he put a black dot for every child who had died there in the past year; when he finished you would have said that his map had been made with a pepper cruet.

A little way further on, and Jurgis and Ona, staring open-eyed and wondering, came to the place where this "made" ground was in process of making. Here was a great hole, perhaps two city blocks square, and with long files of garbage wagons creeping into it. The place had an odor for which there are no polite words; and it was literally black with children, who raked in it from dawn till dark. Sometimes visitors from the packing-houses would wander out to see this "dump," and they would stand by and debate as to whether the children were eating the food they got, or merely collecting it for the chickens at home. Apparently none of them ever went down to find out.

Beyond this dump there stood a great brickyard, with smoking chimneys. First they took out the soil to make bricks, and then they filled it up again with garbage, which seemed to Jurgis and Ona a felicitous arrangement, characteristic of an enterprising country like America. A little way beyond was another great hole, which they had emptied and not yet filled up. This held water, and all summer it stood there, with the nearby soil draining into it, festering and stewing in the sun; and then, when winter came, somebody cut the ice on it, and sold it to the people of Packingtown. This, too, seemed to the newcomers an economical arrangement; for they did not read the newspapers, and their heads were not full of troublesome thoughts about germs.

They stood there while the sun went down upon this scene; the sky in the west turned blood-red, and the tops of the houses shone like fire. Jurgis and Ona were not thinking of the sunset, however—their backs were turned to it, and all their thoughts were of Packingtown, which they could see so plainly in the distance. The line of the buildings stood clear-cut and black against the sky; here and there out of the mass rose the great chimneys, with the river of smoke streaming away to the end of the world. It was a study in colors now, this smoke; in the sunset light it was black and brown and grey and purple. All the sordid suggestions of the place were gone—in the twilight it was a vision of power. To the two who stood watching while the darkness swallowed it up it seemed a land of wonder, with its tale of human energy, of things being done, of employment for thousands upon thousands of men, of opportunity and freedom, of life and love and joy. When they came away, arm in arm, Jurgis was saying, "Tomorrow I shall go there and get a job!"

3

IN HIS capacity as delicatessen vendor, Jokubas Szadwilas had many acquaintances. Among these was one of the special policemen employed by Anderson, whose duty it frequently was to pick out men for employment. Jokubas had never tried it, but he expressed a certainty that he could get some of his friends a job through this man. It was agreed, after consultation, that he should make the effort with old Antanas and with Jonas. Jurgis was confident of his ability to get work for himself, unassisted by any one.

As we have said before, in this he was not mistaken. He had gone to Smith's and stood there not more than half an hour before one of the bosses noticed his form towering above the rest, and signalled to him. The colloquy which followed was brief and to the point:

"Speak English?"

"No; Lit-uanian." (Jurgis had studied this word carefully.)

"Job?" "Je." (A nod.)

"Worked here before?" "No 'stand."

Signals and gesticulations on the part of the boss. (Vigorous shakes of the head by Jurgis.) "Shovel guts?"

"No 'stand." (More shakes of the head.)

"Zarmos. Pagaikstis. Sziouti!" (Imitative motions.) "Je."

"See door. Durys?" (Pointing.) "Je."

"To-morrow, seven o'clock. Understand? Rytoj! Priespietys! Septyni!"

"Dekui, tamistai!" (Thank you, sir)—and that was all. Jurgis turned away; and then in a sudden rush the full realization of his triumph swept over him, and he gave a yell and a jump, and started off on a run. He had a job! He had a job! And he went all the way home as if upon wings, and burst into the house like a cyclone, to the rage of the numerous lodgers who had just turned in for their daily sleep.

Meantime Jokubas had been to see his friend, the policeman, and received encouragement, so it was a happy party. There being no more to be done that day, the shop was left under the care of panei Lucija, and her husband sallied forth to show his friends the sights of Packingtown. Jokubas did this with the air of a country gentleman escorting a party of visitors over his estate; Jokubas was an old-time resident, and all these wonders had grown up under his eyes, and he had a personal pride in them. The packers might own the land, but he claimed the landscape, and there was no one to say nay to this.

They passed down the busy street that led to the yards. It was still early morning, and everything at its high tide of activity. A steady stream of employees was pouring through the gate—employees of the higher sort, at this hour, clerks and stenographers and such. For the women there were waiting big, two-horse wagons, which set off at a gallop as fast as they were filled. In the distance there was heard again the lowing of the cattle, a sound as of a far-off ocean calling. They followed it, this time, as eager as children in sight of a circus menagerie—which, indeed, the scene a good deal resembled. They crossed the railroad tracks, and then on each side of the street were the pens full of cattle; they would have stopped to look, but Jokubas hurried them on, to where there was a stairway and a raised gallery, from which everything could be seen. Here they stood, staring, breathless with wonder.

There is over a square mile of space in the yards, and more than half of it is occupied by cattle-pens; north and south as far as the eye could reach there stretched before it a sea of pens. And they were all filled—so many cattle no one had ever dreamed existed in the world. Red cattle, black, white and yellow cattle; old cattle and young cattle; great bellowing bulls and little calves not an hour born, meek-eyed milch-cows, and fierce, long-horned Texas steers. The sound of them here was as of all the barnyards of the universe; and as for counting them—it would have taken all day simply to count the pens. Here and there ran long alleys, blocked at intervals by gates; and Jokubas told them that the number of these gates was twenty-five thousand. Jokubas had recently been reading a newspaper article, which was full of statistics such as that, and he was very proud as he repeated them, and made his guests cry out with wonder. Jurgis, too, had a little of this sense of pride. Had he not just gotten a job, and become a sharer in all this activity, a cog in this marvellous machine?

Here and there about the alleys galloped men upon horseback, booted, and carrying long whips; they were very busy, calling to each other, and to men who were driving the cattle. They were drovers and stock raisers, who had come from far states, and brokers and commission merchants, and buyers for all the big packing-houses. Here and there they would stop to inspect a bunch of cattle, and there would be a parley, brief and business-like. The buyer would nod or drop his whip, and that would mean a bargain; and he would note it in his little book, along with hundreds of others he had made that morning. Then Jokubas pointed out the place where the cattle were driven to be weighed, upon a great scale that would weigh a hundred thousand pounds at once and record it automatically. It was near to the east entrance that they stood, and all along this east side of the yards ran the railroad tracks, into which the cars were run, loaded with cattle. All night long this had been going on, and now the pens were full; by to-night they would all be empty, and the same thing would be done again.

"And what will become of all these creatures?" cried Teta Elzbieta.

"By to-night," Jokubas answered, "they will all be killed and cut up; and over there on the other side of the packing-houses are more railroad tracks, where the cars come to take the products away."

There were two hundred and fifty miles of track within the yards, their guide went on to inform them. They brought about ten thousand head of cattle every day, and as many hogs, and half as many sheep—which meant some eight or ten million live creatures turned into food every year. One stood and watched, and little by little caught the drift of the tide, as it set in the direction of the packing-houses. There were groups of cattle being driven to the chutes, which were roadways about fifteen feet wide, raised high above the pens. In these chutes the stream of animals was continuous; it was quite uncanny to watch them, pressing on to their fate, all unsuspicious—a very river of death. Our friends were not poetical, and the sight suggested to them no metaphors of human destiny; they thought only of the wonderful efficiency of it all. The chutes into which the pigs went climbed high up—to the very top of the distant buildings; and Jokubas explained that with refinement of cynicism they made the pigs literally clean and dress themselves. They went up by the power of their own legs, and then their own weight carried them back through all the processes necessary to make them into pork.

"They don't waste anything here," said the guide; and then he laughed and added a witticism, which he was pleased that his unsophisticated friends should take to be his own: "They use everything about the pig except the squeal." In front of Smith's General Office building there grows a tiny plot of grass, and this, you may learn, is the only bit of green thing in Packingtown; likewise this jest about the pig and his squeal, the stock in trade of all the guides, is the one gleam of humor that you will find there.

After they had seen enough of the pens, the party went up the street, to the mass of buildings which occupy the center of the yards. These buildings, made of brick, and stained with innumerable layers of Packingtown smoke, were painted all over with advertising signs, from which the visitor realized suddenly that he had come to the home of many of the torments of his life. It was here that they made those products with the wonders of which they pestered him so—by placards that defaced the landscape when he traveled, and staring advertisements in the newspapers and magazines—by silly little jingles that he could not get out of his mind, and gaudy pictures that lurked for him around every street-corner. Here was where they made Smith's Imperial Hams and Bacon, Smith's Dressed Beef, Smith's Excelsior Sausages! Here was the headquarters of Anderson's Pure Leaf Lard, Anderson's Breakfast Bacon, Anderson's Canned Beef, Potted Ham, Devilled Chicken, Peerless Fertilizer. "But they might as well save the paint they waste around here," observed Jokubas Szadwilas; "they can't fool anybody that has worked here."

This was a remark which caused Jurgis to look at the speaker in perplexity.

"How do you mean?" he asked. "Aren't the things all right?"

"Tai jukai!" Jokubas laughed. "Wait till you have been in here a while. I wouldn't put a piece of their canned beef into my mouth to save my grandmother's soul from purgatory!"

Entering one of the Anderson buildings, they found a number of other visitors waiting; and before long there came a guide, to escort them through the place. They make a great feature of showing strangers through the packing-plants, for it is a good advertisement. But panas Jokubas whispered maliciously that the visitors did not see any more than the packers wanted them to.

They climbed a long series of stairways outside of the building, to the top of its five or six stories. Here was the chute, with its river of pigs, all patiently toiling upwards; there was a place for them to rest to cool off, and then through another passageway they went into a room, from which there is no returning for pigs.

It was a long, narrow room, with a gallery along it for visitors. At the head there was a great iron wheel, about twenty feet in circumference, with rings here and there along its edge. Upon both sides of this wheel there was a narrow space, into which came the pigs at the end of their journey; in the midst of them stood a great burly negro, bare-armed and bare-chested. He was resting for a moment, for the wheel had stopped while men were cleaning up. In a minute or two, however, it began slowly to revolve, and then the men upon each side of it sprang to work. They had chains which they fastened about the leg of the nearest pig, and the other end of the chain they hooked into one of the rings upon the wheel. So, as the wheel turned, a pig was suddenly jerked off his feet and borne aloft.

At the same instant the ear was assailed by a most terrifying shriek; the visitor started in alarm, the women turned pale and shrank back. The shriek was followed by another, louder and yet more agonizing—for once started upon that journey, the pig never came back; at the top of the wheel he was shunted off upon a trolley, and went sailing down the room. And meantime another was swung up, and then another, and another—until there was a double line of them, each dangling by a foot and kicking in frenzy—and squealing. The uproar was appalling, perilous to the ear-drums; one feared there was too much sound for the room to hold—that the walls must give way, or the ceiling crack. There were high squeals and low squeals, grunts, and wails of agony; there would come a momentary lull, and then a fresh outburst, louder than ever, surging up to a deafening climax. It was too much for some of the visitors—the men would look at each other, laughing nervously, and the women would stand with hands clenched, and the blood rushing to their faces, and the tears starting in their eyes.

Meantime, heedless of all these things, the men upon the floor were going about their work. Neither squeals of pigs nor tears of visitors made any difference to them; but one by one they hooked up the pigs, and one by one with a swift stroke they slit their throats. There was a long line of pigs, with squeals and life-blood ebbing away together; until at last each started again, and vanished with a splash into a huge vat of boiling water.

It was all so very business-like that one watched it fascinated. It was pork-making by machinery, pork-making reduced to mathematics. And yet somehow the most matter-of-fact person could not help thinking of the pigs; they were so innocent, they came so very trustingly and they were so very human in their protests—and so perfectly within their rights! They had done nothing to deserve it; and it was adding insult to injury as the thing was done here—swinging them up in this cold-blooded, impersonal way, without a pretense at apology, without the homage of a tear. Now and then a visitor wept, to be sure; but this slaughtering-machine ran on, visitors or no visitors. It was like some horrible crime committed in a dungeon, all unseen and unheeded, buried out of sight and memory.

One could not stand and watch very long without becoming philosophical, without beginning to deal in symbols and similes, and to hear the pig-squeal of the universe. Was it permitted to believe that there was nowhere upon the earth, or above the earth, a heaven for pigs, where they were requited for all this suffering? Each one of these pigs was a separate creature. Some were white pigs, some were black; some were brown, some were spotted; some were old, some were young; some were long and lean, some were monstrous. And each of them had an individuality of his own, a will of his own, a hope and a heart's desire; each was full of self-confidence, of self-importance, and a sense of dignity. And trusting and strong in faith he had gone about his business, the while a black shadow hung over him, and a horrid Fate waited in his pathway. Now suddenly it had swooped upon him, and had seized him by the leg. Relentless, remorseless, it was; all his protests, his screams, were nothing to it. It did its cruel will with him, as if his wishes, his feelings, had simply no existence at all; it cut his throat and watched him gasp out his life. And now was one to believe that there was nowhere a god of pigs, to whom this pig personality was precious, to whom these pig-squeals and agonies had a meaning? Who would take this pig into his arms and comfort him, reward him for his work well done, and show him the meaning of his sacrifice? For all the while there was a meaning—if only the poor pig could have known it. Perhaps if he had, he would not have squealed at all, but died happy! If only he had known that he was to figure in the bank-account of some great captain of industry, and perhaps help to found a university, or endow a handful of libraries, when the captain of industry died! It is one of the crimes of commercialism that it thus cruelly leaves its victims to grope in darkness; that delicate women and little children, who toil and groan in factories and mines and sweatshops and die of starvation and loathsome diseases, are not taught and consoled by the reflection that they are adding to the wealth of society, and to the power and greatness of some eminent philanthropist. Perhaps some glimmering of this truth was in the thoughts of our humble-minded Jurgis, as he turned to go on with the rest of the party, and muttered: "Diewes—but I'm glad I'm not a pig!"

The carcass of the pig was scooped out of the vat by machinery, and then it fell to the second floor, passing on the way through a wonderful machine with numerous scrapers, which adjusted themselves to the size and shape of the animal, and sent it out at the other end with nearly all of its bristles removed.

It was then again strung up by machinery, and sent upon another trolley ride; this time passing between two lines of men, who sat upon a raised platform, each doing a certain single thing to the carcass as it came to him. One scraped the outside of a leg; another scraped the inside of the same leg. One with a swift stroke cut the throat; another with two swift strokes severed the head, which fell to the floor and vanished through a hole. Another made a slit down the body; a second opened the body wider; a third with a saw cut the breast-bone; a fourth loosened the entrails; a fifth pulled them out—and they also slid through a hole in the floor. There were men to scrape each side and men to scrape the back; there were men to clean the carcass inside, to trim it and wash it. Looking down this room one saw, creeping slowly, a line of dangling pigs a hundred yards in length; and for every yard there was a man, working as if a demon were after him. At the end of this pig's progress every inch of the carcass had been gone over several times, and the pig was a work of art; then it was rolled into the chilling room, where it stayed for twenty-four hours, and where a stranger might lose himself in a boundless forest of freezing hogs.

Before the carcass was admitted here, however, it had to pass a government inspector, who sat in the doorway and felt of the glands in the neck for tuberculosis. This government inspector did not have the manner of a man who was worked to death; he was apparently not haunted by a fear that the pig might get by him before he had finished his testing. If you were a sociable person, he was quite willing to enter into conversation with you, and to explain to you the deadly nature of the ptomaines which are found in tuberculous pork; while he was talking with you you could hardly be so tactless as to notice that a dozen carcasses were passing him untouched. This inspector wore a blue uniform, with highly ornamental brass buttons, and he gave an atmosphere of authority to the scene, and as it were, put the stamp of official approval upon the things which were done in Anderson's. For this reason the firm was very grateful to him; it appointed no bosses and no spies to see that he did his work thoroughly and it kept no record of his going and coming. It was the law that no employe might carry meat out of Anderson and Company's houses under any circumstance whatever; not even a boss might break this rule, not even one of the mighty superintendents; and many a poor workingman had been caught taking home a link of sausages in his dinner-pail, and been sent to the county jail for thirty days and never after been employed by any firm in Packingtown. The government inspectors alone were graciously excepted from this—they might carry away all the meat they chose, and they did carry it; any day you might see them going home with great roasts of beef wrapped in paper and tucked under their arms.

These were things that Jurgis was to learn in time; at present he was as innocent as a child, and went down the line with the rest of the visitors, staring open-mouthed, lost in wonder. Jurgis had dressed pigs himself, in the forest of Lithuania; but he had never expected to live to see one pig dressed by several hundred men. It was like a wonderful poem to him, and he took it all in guilelessly—even to the conspicuous signs demanding immaculate cleanliness of the employees. Jurgis was vexed when the cynical Jokubas translated these signs with sarcastic comments, offering to take them to the secret rooms where the spoiled meats went to be doctored.

The party descended to the next floor, where the various waste materials were treated. Here came the entrails, to be scraped and washed clean for sausage casings; men and women worked here in the midst of a sickening stench, which caused the visitors to hasten by, gasping. To another room came all the scraps to be "tanked," which meant boiling and pumping off the grease to make soap and lard; as it was all done in open vats, this, too, was a region in which the visitors did not linger. In still other places men were engaged in cutting up the carcasses that had been through the chilling-rooms. First there were the "splitters," the most expert workmen in the plant, who earned as high as 50 cents an hour, and did not a thing all day except chop hogs down the middle. Then there were "cleaver-men," great giants with muscles of iron; each had two men to attend to him—to slide the half carcass in front of him on the table, and hold it while he chopped it, and then turn each piece so that he might chop it once more. His cleaver had a blade about two feet long, and he never made but one cut; he made it so neatly, too, that his implement did not smite through and dull itself—there was just enough force for a perfect cut, and no more. So through various yawning holes there slipped to the floor below—to one room hams, to another forequarters, to another sides of pork. One might go down to this floor and see the pickling-rooms, where the hams were put into vats, and the great smoke-rooms, with their air-tight iron doors. In other rooms they prepared salt pork—there were whole cellars full of it, built up in great towers to the ceiling. In yet other rooms they were putting up meat in boxes and barrels, and wrapping hams and bacon in oiled paper, sealing and labeling and sewing them. From the doors of these rooms went men with loaded trucks, to the platform where freight cars were waiting to be filled; and one went out there and realized with a start that he had come at last to the ground-floor of this enormous building.

Then the party went across the street to where they did the killing of beef —where every hour they turned four or five hundred cattle into meat. Unlike the place they had left, all this work was done on one floor; and instead of there being one line of carcasses which moved to the workmen, there were fifteen or twenty lines, and the men moved from one to another of these. This made a scene of intense activity, a picture of human power wonderful to watch. It was all in one great room, like a circus amphitheatre, with a gallery for visitors running over the center.

Along one side of the room ran a narrow gallery, a few feet from the floor; into this gallery the cattle were driven by men with goads which gave them electric shocks. Once crowded into here the creatures were prisoned, each in a separate pen, by gates that shut, leaving them no room to turn around; while they stood bellowing and plunging, over the top of the pen there leaned one of the "knockers," armed with a sledge hammer, and watching for a chance to deal a blow. The room echoed with the thuds in quick succession, and the stamping and kicking of the steers. The instant the animal had fallen the "knocker" passed on to another; while a second man raised a lever, and the side of the pen was raised, and the animal still kicking and struggling, slid out to the "killing-floor." Here a man put shackles about one leg, and pressed another lever, and the body was jerked up into the air. There were fifteen or twenty such pens, and it was a matter of only a couple of minutes to knock fifteen or twenty cattle and roll them out. Then once more the gates were opened, and another lot rushed in; and so out of each pen there rolled a steady stream of carcasses, which the men upon the killing-floor had to get out of the way.

The way in which they did this was a sight to be seen and never forgotten; they worked with furious intensity, literally upon the run—at a pace with which there is nothing to be compared except a football game. It was all highly specialized labor, each man having his task to do; generally this would consist of only two or three specific cuts, and he would pass down the line of fifteen or twenty carcasses, making these cuts upon each. First there came the "butcher," to bleed them; this meant one swift stroke, so swift that you could not see it—only the flash of the knife; before you could realize it, the man had darted on to the next line, and a stream of bright red blood was pouring out upon the floor. This floor was half an inch deep with blood, in spite of the best efforts of men who kept shoveling it through holes; it must have made the floor slippery, but no one could have guessed this by watching the men at work.

The carcass hung for a few minutes to bleed; there was no time lost, however, for there were several hanging in each line, and one was always ready. It was let down to the ground, and there came the "headsman," whose task it was to sever the head, with two or three swift strokes. Then came the "floorman," to make the first cut in the skin; and then another to finish ripping the skin down the center; and then half a dozen more in swift succession, to finish the skinning. After they were through, the carcass was again swung up. While a man with a stick examined the skin, to make sure that it had not been cut, and another rolled it up and tumbled it through one of the inevitable holes in the floor, the carcass proceeded on its journey; there were men to cut it, and men to split it, and men to gut it and scrape it clean inside. There were some with hoses which threw jets of boiling water upon it, and others who removed the feet and added the final touches. In the end, as with the hogs, the finished beef was run into the chilling-room, to hang its appointed time. The visitors were taken there and shown them, all neatly hung in rows, labeled conspicuously with the tags of the government inspectors—and some, which had been killed by a special process, marked with the sign of the "kosher" rabbi, certifying that it was fit for sale to the orthodox. And then they were taken to the other parts of the building, to see what became of each particle of the waste material that had vanished through the floor; and to the pickling-rooms, and the salting-rooms, the canning-rooms and the packing-rooms, where choice meat was prepared for shipping in refrigerators, destined to be eaten in all the four corners of civilization. Afterwards they went outside, wandering about among the mazes of buildings in which was done the work auxiliary to this great industry. There was not a thing needed in the business that Anderson and Company did not make for themselves. There was a great steam-power plant, and an electricity plant. There was a barrel factory, and a boiler-repair shop. There was a building to which the grease was piped, and made into soap and lard; and then there was a factory for making lard-cans, and another for making soapboxes. There was a building in which the bristles were cleaned and dried, for the making of hair cushions and such things; there was a building where the skins were dried and tanned, there was another where heads and feet were made into glue, and another where bones were made into fertilizer. No tiniest particle of organic matter was wasted in Anderson's. Out of the horns of the cattle they made combs, buttons, hairpins and imitation ivory; out of the shin-bones and other big bones they cut knife and tooth-brush handles, and mouth-pieces for pipes; out of the hoofs they cut hairpins and buttons, before they made the rest into glue. From such things as feet, knuckles, hide-clippings and sinews, came such strange and unlikely products as gelatin, isinglass and phosphorous, bone-black, shoe-blacking and bone oil. They had curled-hair workers for the cattle tails, and a "wool-pullery" for the sheepskins; they made pepsin from the stomachs of the pigs, and albumen from the blood, and violin strings from ill-smelling entrails. When there was nothing else to be done with a thing, they first put it into a tank and got out of it all the tallow and grease, and then they made it into fertilizer. All these industries were gathered in buildings nearby, connected by galleries and railroads with the main establishment; and it was estimated that they had handled nearly a quarter of a billion of animals since the founding of the plant by old man Anderson, the self-made merchant, a generation and more ago. If you counted with it the other big plants—and they were now really all one—it was, so Jokubas informed them, the greatest aggregation of labor and capital ever gathered in one place. It employed thirty thousand men; it supported directly two hundred and fifty thousand people in its neighborhood, and indirectly it supported half a million. It sent its products to every country in the civilized world; and it furnished the food for no less than thirty million people!

To all of these things our friends would listen, open-mouthed—it seemed to them impossible of belief that anything so stupendous could have been devised by mortal man. That was why to Jurgis it seemed almost profanity to speak about the place as did Jokubas, skeptically; it was a thing as tremendous as the universe—the laws and ways of its working no more than the universe to be questioned or understood. All that a mere man could do, it seemed to Jurgis, was to take a thing like this as he found it, and do as he was told; to be given a place in it, and a share in its wonderful activities, was a blessing to be grateful for as one was grateful for the sunshine and the rain. Jurgis was even glad that he had not seen the place before meeting with his triumph—for he felt that the size of it would have overwhelmed him. But now he had been admitted—he was a part of it all! He had the feeling that this whole huge establishment had taken him under its protection, and had become responsible for his welfare. So guileless was he, and ignorant of the nature of business, that he did not even realize that he had become an employe of Smith's; and that Smith and Anderson were supposed by all the world to be deadly rivals—and were even required to be deadly rivals by the law of the land, and compelled to cut each other's throats under penalty of fine and imprisonment!

4

PROMPTLY at seven the next morning Jurgis reported for work. He came to the door that had been pointed out to him, and there he waited, for nearly two hours. The boss had meant for him to enter, but he had not said this, and so it was only when on his way out to hire another man that he came upon Jurgis. He gave him a good cursing, but as Jurgis did not understand a word of it this did him no harm. He followed the boss, who showed him where to put his street-clothes, and waited while he donned the working-clothes which he had brought with him in a bundle; then he led him to the "killing-floor." The work which Jurgis was to do here was very simple, and it took him but a few minutes to learn it. He was provided with a stiff besom, such as is used by street-sweepers, and it was his place to follow down the line the man who drew out the smoking entrails from the carcass of the steer; this mass was to be swept into a trap, which was then closed, so that no one might slip into it. As Jurgis came in, the first cattle of the morning were then just making their appearance; and so, with scarcely time to look about him, and none to speak to anyone, he fell to work. It was a sweltering day in July, and the place ran with steaming hot blood—one waded in it on the floor. The stench was almost overpowering, but to Jurgis it was nothing. His whole soul was dancing with joy—he was at work at last. He was at work and earning money! All day long he was figuring to himself. He was paid the fabulous sum of seventeen-and a half cents an hour, and as it proved a rush day and he worked until nearly seven o'clock in the evening, he went home to the family with the tidings that he had earned more than a dollar and a half in a single day!

At home, also, there was more good news; so much of it at once that there was quite a celebration in panei Aniele's hall bedroom. Jonas had been to have an interview with the special policeman to whom Szadwilas had introduced him, and had been taken to see several of the bosses, with the result that one had promised him a job the beginning of the next week. And then there was Marija Biarczynskas, who, fired with jealousy by the success of Jurgis, had set out upon her own responsibility to get a place. Marija had nothing to take with her save her two brawny arms and the word "job," laboriously learned; but with these she had marched about Packingtown all day, entering every door where were signs of activity. Out of some she had been ordered with curses; but Marija was not afraid of man or devil, and asked every one she saw—visitors and strangers, or work-people like herself, and once or twice even high and lofty office personages, who stared at her as if they thought she was crazy. In the end she had reaped her reward. In one of the smaller plants she had stumbled upon a room where scores of women and girls were sitting at long tables preparing smoked beef in cans; and wandering through room after room, Marija came at last to the place where the sealed cans were being painted and labeled, and here she had the good fortune to encounter the "forelady." Marija did not understand then, as she was destined to understand later, what there was attractive to a "forelady" about the combination of a face full of boundless good-nature and the muscles of a dray horse; but the woman had told her to come the next day and she would perhaps give her a chance to learn the trade of painting cans. The painting of cans being skilled piece-work, and paying as much as two dollars a day, Marija burst in upon the family with a yell of a Comanche Indian, and fell to capering about the room so as to frighten the baby almost into convulsions.

Better luck than all this could hardly have been hoped for; there was only one of them left to seek a place, Jurgis was determined that Teta Elzbieta should stay at home to keep house, and that Ona should help her. He would not have Ona working—he was not that sort of a man, he said, and she was not that sort of woman. It would be a strange thing if a man like him could not support the family, with the help of the board of Jonas and Marija. He would not even hear of letting the children go to work—there were schools here in America for children, Jurgis had heard, to which they could go for nothing, and he made up his mind that the children of Teta Elzbieta should have as fair a chance as any other children. The oldest of them, little Stanislovas, was but thirteen, and small for his age at that; and while the oldest son of Szadwilas was only twelve, and had worked for over a year at Morton's, Jurgis would have it that Stanislovas should learn to speak English, and grow up to be a skilled man.

So there was only old Diedas Antanas; Jurgis would have had him rest too, but he was forced to acknowledge that this was not possible, and besides, the old man would not hear it spoken of—it was his whim to insist that he was as lively as any boy. He had come to America as full of hope as the best of them; and now he was the chief problem that worried his son. For every one that Jurgis spoke to assured him that it was a waste of time to seek employment for the old man in Packingtown. Szadwilas told him that the packers did not even keep the men who had grown old in their own service—to say nothing of taking on new ones. And not only was it the rule here, it was the rule everywhere, so far as he knew; an old man might just as well get off the earth at the start, for nobody would have anything to do with him. To satisfy Jurgis he had asked the policeman, and brought back the message that the thing was not to be thought of. They had not told this to old Anthony, who had consequently spent the two days wandering about from one part of the yards to another, and had now come home to hear about the triumph of the others, smiling bravely and saying that it would be his turn another day.

Their good luck, they felt, had given them the right to think about a home; and sitting out on the doorstep that summer evening they held consultation about it, and Jurgis took occasion to broach a weighty subject. Passing down the avenue to work that morning he had seen two boys leaving an advertisement from house to house; seeing that there were pictures upon it, Jurgis had asked for one, and had rolled it up and tucked it into his shirt. At noon-time a man with whom he had been talking had read it to him, and told him a little about it, with the result that Jurgis had conceived a wild idea.

He brought out the placard, which was quite a work of art. It was nearly two feet long, printed on calendered paper, with a selection of colors so bright that they shone even in the moonlight. The center of the placard was occupied by a house, brilliantly painted, new and dazzling. The roof of it was a purple hue, and trimmed with gold; the house itself was silvery, and the doors and windows red. It was a two-story building with a porch in front, and a very fancy scroll-work around the edges; it was complete in every tiniest detail, even the door-knob, and there was a hammock on the porch, and white lace curtains in the windows. Underneath this, in one corner, was a picture of a husband and wife in loving embrace; in the opposite corner was a cradle, with fluffy curtains drawn over it, and a smiling cherub hovering upon silver-colored wings. For fear that the significance of all this should be lost, there was a label, in Polish, Bohemian, Lithuanian and English—"Namai. Home." "Why pay rent?" The linguistic circular went on to demand: "Why not own your own home? Do you know that you can buy one for less than your rent? We have built thousands of homes which are now occupied by happy families"—and then the poster became eloquent, picturing the blissfulness of married life in a house with nothing to pay. It even quoted "Home, Sweet Home," and made bold to translate it into Polish—though for some reason it omitted the Lithuanian of this, perhaps because Lithuanian is not hospitable to poets. Most persons would admit that it might prove a difficult matter to be sentimental in a language in which a sob is known as a "gukeziojimas," and a smile as a "nusiszypsojimas."

Over this document the family pored long, while Ona spelled out its contents. It appeared that this house contained four rooms, besides a basement, and that it might be bought for fifteen hundred dollars, the lot and all. Of this only three hundred dollars had to be paid down, the balance being paid at the rate of twelve dollars a month. These were frightful sums, but then they were in America, where people talked about such sums without fear. They had learned that they would have to pay a rent of nine dollars a month for a flat, and there was no way of doing better, unless the family of twelve was to exist in one or two rooms, as at present. If they paid rent, of course they might pay forever, and be no better off; whereas, if they could only meet the extra expense in the beginning, there would at last come a time when they would not have any rent to pay for the rest of their lives.

They figured it up. There, was a little left of the money belonging to Teta Elzbieta, and there was a little left to Jurgis. Marija had about fifty dollars pinned up somewhere in her stockings, and Grandfather Anthony had part of the money he had gotten for his farm. If they all combined they would have enough to make the first payment; and if they had employment, so that they could be sure of the future, it might really prove the best plan. It was, of course, not a thing even to be talked of lightly; it was a thing they would have to sift to the bottom. And yet, on the other hand, if they were going to make the venture, the sooner they did it the better; for were they not paying rent all the time, and living in a most horrible way besides? Jurgis was used to dirt—there was nothing could scare a man who had been with a railroad gang, where one could gather up the fleas off the floor of the sleeping-room by the handful; but that sort of thing would not do for Ona. They must have a better place of some sort very soon—Jurgis said it with all the assurance of a man who had just made a dollar and fifty-seven cents in a single day. Jurgis was at a loss to understand why, with wages as they were, so many of the people of this district should live the way they did.

The next day Marija went to see her "forelady," and was told to report the first of the week, and learn the business of can-painter. Marija went home singing out loud all the way; and was just in time to join Ona and her stepmother as they were setting out to go and make inquiry concerning the house. That evening the three made their report to the men—the thing was altogether as represented in the circular, or at any rate so the agent they had seen had told them. The houses lay to the south, about a mile and a half from the yards; the gentleman would go at any time to show them. The houses were wonderful bargains, he had assured them personally—and for their own good. He could do this, so he explained to them, for the reason that he had himself no interest in their sale—he was merely the agent for a company that had built them. These were the last, and the company was going out of business, so if anyone wished to take advantage of this wonderful no-rent plan he would have to be very quick. As a matter of fact there was just a little uncertainty as to whether there was a single house left; for the agent had taken so many people to see them, and for all he knew the company might have parted with the last. Seeing Teta Elzbieta's evident grief at this news, he had added, after some hesitation, that if they really intended to make a purchase he would send a telephone message at his own expense, and have one of the houses kept. So it had finally been arranged—and they were to go and make an inspection the following Sunday morning.

That was Thursday; and all the rest of the week the killing-gang at Smith's worked at full pressure, and Jurgis cleared a dollar seventy-five every day. That was at the rate of $10.50 a week, and forty-five a month; Jurgis was not able to figure, except it was a very simple sum, but Ona was like lightning at such things, and she worked out the problem for the family. Marija and Jonas were each to pay sixteen dollars a month board, and the old man insisted that he could do the same as soon as he got a place—which might be any day now. That would make ninety-three dollars. Then Marija and Jonas were between them to take a third share in the house, which would leave only eight dollars a month for Jurgis to contribute to the payment. So they would have eighty-five dollars a month—or, supposing that Diedas Antanas did not get work at once, seventy dollars a month—which ought surely to be sufficient for the support of a family of twelve.

An hour before the time on Sunday morning the entire party set out. They had the address written on a piece of paper, which they showed to someone now and then. It proved to be a long mile and a half, but they walked it, and half an hour or so later the agent put in appearance. He was a smooth and florid personage, elegantly dressed, and he spoke their language freely, which gave him a great advantage in dealing with them. He escorted them to the house, which was one of a long row of the typical frame dwellings of the neighborhood, where architecture is a luxury that is dispensed with. Ona's heart sank, for the house was not as it was shown in the picture; the color-scheme was different, for one thing, and then the house did not seem quite so big. Still, it was freshly painted, and made a considerable show. It was all brand new, so the agent told them, but he talked so incessantly that they were quite confused, and did not have time to ask many questions. There were all sorts of things they had made up their minds to inquire about, but when the time came they either forgot them or lacked the courage. The other houses in the row did not seem to be new, and few of them seemed to be occupied. When they ventured to hint at this the agent's reply was that the purchasers would be moving in shortly. To press the matter would have seemed to be doubting his word, and never in their lives had any one of them ever spoken to a person of the class called "gentlemen" except with deference and humility.

The house had a basement, about two feet below the street line, and a single story, about six feet above it, reached by a flight of steps. In addition there was an attic, made by the peak of the roof, and having one small window in each end. The street in front of the house was unpaved and unlighted, and the view from it consisted of a few exactly similar houses, scattered here and there upon lots grown up with dingy brown weeds. (Of other verdure there is none in all the stockyards district, for nothing will grow in the smoke.) The house inside contained four rooms, plastered white; the basement was but a frame, the walls being unplastered and the floor not laid. The agent explained that the houses were built that way, as the purchasers generally preferred to finish the basements to suit their own taste. The attic was also unfinished—the family had been figuring that in case of an emergency they could rent this attic, but they found that there was not even a floor, nothing but joists, and beneath them the lath and plaster of the ceiling below. All of this, however, did not chill their ardor as much as might have been expected, because of the volubility of the agent. There was no end to the advantages of the house, as he set them forth, and he was not silent for an instant; he showed them everything, down to the locks on the doors and the catches on the windows, and how to work them. He showed them the sink in the kitchen, with running water and a faucet, something which Teta Elzbieta had never in her wildest dreams hoped to possess. After a discovery such as that it would have seemed ungrateful to find any fault, and so they tried to shut their eyes to other defects.

Still, they were peasant people, and they hung on to their money by instinct; it was quite in vain that the agent hinted at promptness—they would see, they would see, they told him; they could not decide until they had had more time. And so they went home again, and all day and evening there was figuring and debating. It was an agony to them to have to make up their minds in a matter such as this. They never could agree all together; there were so many arguments upon each side, and one would be obstinate, and no sooner would the rest have convinced him than it would transpire that his arguments had caused another to waver. Once, in the evening, when they were all in harmony, and the house was as good as bought, Szadwilas came in and upset them again. Szadwilas had no use for property-owning. He told them cruel stories of people who had been done to death in this "buying a home" swindle. They would be almost sure to get into a tight place and lose all their money; and there was no end of expense that one could never foresee; and the house might be good for nothing from top to bottom—how was a poor man to know? Then, too, they would swindle you with the contract—and how was a poor man to understand anything about a contract? It was all nothing but robbery, and there was no safety but in keeping out of it. And pay rent? asked Jurgis. Ah yes, to be sure, the other answered, that too was robbery. It was all robbery, for a poor man. The rich people not only had all the money, they had all the chance to get more; they had all the knowledge and the power, and so the poor man was down, and he had to stay down. After half an hour of this depressing conversation they had their minds quite made up that they had been saved at the brink of a precipice; but then Szadwilas went away, and Jonas, who was a sharp little man, reminded them that the delicatessen business was a failure, according to its proprietor, and that this might account for his pessimistic views. Which, of course, reopened the subject!

The controlling factor was that they could not stay where they were—they had to go somewhere. And when they gave up the house plan and decided to rent, the prospect of paying out nine dollars a month forever they found just as hard to face. The world is divided into those who have and those who have not, and all the stars in their course fight against the latter; the little family had been stung by the thought that by one great effort they might spring into the winning class. All day and all night for nearly a whole week they wrestled with the problem.

In the end it was Jurgis who took the responsibility. Brother Jonas had gotten his job, and was pushing a truck in Anderson's; and the killing-gang at Smith's continued to work early and late so that Jurgis grew more confident every hour, more certain of his power. It was the kind of thing the man of the family had to decide and carry through, he told himself. Others might have failed at it, but he was not the failing kind—he would show them how to do it. He would work all day, and all night, too, if need be; he would never rest until the house was paid for and his people had a home. So he told them, and so in the end the decision was made.

They had talked about looking at more houses, before they made the purchase; but then they did not know where any more were, and they did not know any way of finding out. The one they had seen held the sway in their thought; and, whenever they thought of themselves in a house, it was this house that they thought of. And so they went and told the agent that they were ready to make the agreement. They knew, as an abstract proposition, that in matters of business all men are to be accounted liars; but they could not but have been influenced by all they had heard from the eloquent agent, and they were quite persuaded that the house was something they had run a risk of losing by their delay. They drew a deep breath when he told them that they were still in time.

They were to come on the morrow, and he would have the papers all drawn up. This matter of papers was one in which Jurgis understood to the full the need of caution; yet he could not go himself—everyone told him that he could not get a holiday, and that he might lose his job by asking. So there was nothing to be done but to trust it to the women, with Szadwilas, who promised to go with them. Jurgis spent a whole evening impressing upon them the seriousness of the occasion—and then finally, out of innumerable hiding-places about their persons and in their baggage, came forth the precious wads of money, to be done up tightly in a little bag and sewed fast in the lining of Teta Elzbieta's dress.

Early in the morning they sallied forth. Jurgis had given them so many instructions, and warned them against so many perils, that the women were quite pale with fright, and even the imperturbable delicatessen-vender, who prided himself upon being a business man, was ill at ease. The agent had the deed all ready, and invited them to sit down and read it; this Szadwilas proceeded to do—a painful and laborious process, during which the agent drummed upon the desk. Teta Elzbieta was so embarrassed that the perspiration came out upon her forehead in beads; for was not this reading as much as to say plainly to the gentleman's face that they doubted his honesty? Yet Jokubas Szadwilas read on and on; and presently there developed that he had good reason for doing so. For a horrible suspicion had begun dawning in his mind; he knitted his brows more and more as he read. This was not a deed of sale at all, so far as he could see—it provided only for the renting of the property! It was hard to tell with all this strange legal jargon, words he had never heard before; but was not this plain—"the party of the first part hereby covenants and agrees to 'rent' to the said party of the second part!" And then again—"a monthly 'rental' of twelve dollars, for a period of eight years and four months!" Then Szadwilas took off his spectacles, and looked at the agent, and stammered a question.

The agent was most polite, and explained that that was the usual formula; that it was always arranged that the property should be merely rented. He kept trying to show them something in the next paragraph; but Szadwilas could not get by the word "rental"—and when he translated it to Teta Elzbieta, she too was thrown into a fright. They would not own the home at all, then, for nearly nine years! The agent, with infinite patience, began to explain again; but no explanation would do now. Teta had firmly fixed in her mind the last solemn warning of Jurgis: "If there is anything wrong, do not give him the money, but go out and get a lawyer." It was an agonizing moment, but she sat in the chair, her hands clenched like death, and made a fearful effort, summoning all her powers, and gasped out her purpose.

Jokubas translated her words. She expected the agent to fly into a passion, but he was, to her bewilderment, as ever imperturbable; he even offered to go and get a lawyer for her, but she declined this. They went a long way, on purpose to find a man who would not be a confederate. Then let anyone imagine their dismay, when, after half an hour, they came in with a lawyer, and heard him greet the agent by his first name!

They felt that all was lost; they sat like prisoners summoned to hear the reading of their death warrant. There was nothing more that they could do—they were trapped! The lawyer read over the deed, and when he had read it he informed Szadwilas that it was all perfectly regular, that the deed was a blank deed such as was often used in these sales. And was the price as agreed? the old man asked—three hundred dollars down, and the balance at twelve dollars a month, till the total of fifteen hundred dollars had been paid? Yes, that was correct. And it was for the sale of such and such a house—the house and lot and everything? Yes—and the lawyer showed him where that was all written. And it was all perfectly regular—there were no tricks about it of any sort? They were poor people, and this was all they had in the world, and if there was anything wrong they would be ruined. And so Szadwilas went on, asking one trembling question after another, while the eyes of the women folks were fixed upon him in mute agony. They could not understand what he was saying, but they knew that upon it their fate depended. And when at last he had questioned until there was no more questioning to be done, and the time came for them to make up their minds, and either close the bargain or reject it—it was all that poor Teta Elzbieta could do to keep from bursting into tears. Jokubas had asked her if she wished to sign; he had asked her twice—and what could she say? How did she know if this lawyer were telling the truth—that he was not in the conspiracy? And yet, how could she say so—what excuse could she give? The eyes of everyone in the room were upon her, awaiting her decision; and at last, half blind with her tears, she began fumbling in her jacket, where she had pinned the precious money. And she brought it out and unwrapped it before the men. All of this Ona sat watching, from a corner of the room, twisting her hands together, meantime, in a fever of fright. Ona longed to cry out and tell her step-mother to stop, that it was all a trap; but there seemed to be something clutching her by the throat, and she could not make a sound. And so Teta Elzbieta laid the money on the table, and the agent picked it up and counted it, and then wrote them a receipt for it and passed them the deed. Then he gave a sigh of satisfaction, and rose and shook hands with them all, still as smooth and polite as at the beginning. Ona had a dim recollection of the lawyer telling Szadwilas that his charge was a dollar, which occasioned some debate, and more agony; and then, after they had paid that, too, they went out into the street, her step-mother clutching the deed in her hand. They were so weak from fright that they could not walk, but had to sit down on the way.

So they went home, with a deadly terror gnawing at their souls; and that evening Jurgis came home and heard their story, and that was the end. Jurgis was sure that they had been swindled, and were ruined; and he tore his hair and cursed like a madman, swearing that he would kill the agent that very night. In the end he seized the paper and rushed out ot the house, and all the way across the yards to Halsted street. He dragged Szadwilas out from his supper, and together they rushed to consult another lawyer. When they entered his office the lawyer sprang up, for Jurgis looked like a crazy person, with flying hair and bloodshot eyes. His companion explained the situation; and the lawyer took the paper and began to read it, while Jurgis stood clutching the desk with knotted hands, trembling in every nerve.

Once or twice the lawyer looked up and asked a question of Szadwilas; the other did not know a word that he was saying, but his eyes were fixed upon the lawyer's face, striving in an agony of dread to read his mind. He saw the man look up and laugh, and he gave a gasp; the man said something to Szadwilas, and Jurgis turned upon him, his heart almost stopping.

"Well?" he panted.

"He says it is all right," said Szadwilas.

"All right!"

"Yes, he says it is just as it should be." And Jurgis, in his relief, sank down into a chair.

"Are you sure of it?" he gasped, and made Szadwilas translate question after question. He could not hear it often enough; he could not ask with enough variations. Yes, they had bought the house, they had really bought it. It belonged to them, they had only to pay the money and it would be all right. Then Jurgis covered his face with his hands, for there were tears in his eyes, and he felt like a fool. But he had had such a horrible fright; strong man as he was, it left him almost too weak to stand up.

The lawyer explained that the rental was a form—the property was said to be merely rented until the last payment had been made, the purpose being to make it easier to turn the party out if he did not make the payments. So long as they paid, however, they had nothing to fear, the house was all theirs. Jurgis was so grateful that he paid the half dollar the lawyer asked without winking an eyelash, and then rushed home to tell the news to the family. He found Ona in a faint and the babies screaming, and the whole house in an uproar—for it had been believed by all that he had gone to murder the agent. It was hours before the excitement could be calmed; and all through that cruel night Jurgis would wake up now and then and hear Ona and her stepmother in the next room, sobbing softly to themselves.

THEY HAD bought their home. It was hard for them to realize that the wonderful house was theirs to move into whenever they chose. They spent all their time thinking about it, and what they were going to put into it. As their week with panei Aniele was up in three days, they lost no time in getting ready. They had to make some shift to furnish it, and every instant of their leisure was given to discussing this.

A person who had such a task before him would not need to look very far in Packingtown—he had only to walk up the avenue and read the signs, or get into a street car, to obtain full information as to pretty much everything a human creature could need. It was quite touching, the zeal of people to see his health and happiness were provided for. Did the person wish to smoke? There was a little discourse about cigars, showing him exactly why the Thomas Jefferson Five-Cent Perfecto was the only cigar worthy of the name. Had he, on the other hand, smoked too much? Here was a remedy for the smoking habit, twenty-five doses for a quarter, and a cure absolutely guaranteed in ten doses. Here also was the beverage which would make him think he was still drinking his usual coffee poison, while in reality he was having his body all made new by a marvelous concentrated health food. In innumerable ways such as this, the traveler found that somebody had been busied to make smooth his paths through the world, and to let him know what had been done for him. In Packingtown the advertisements had a style all of their own, adapted to the peculiar population. One would be tenderly solicitous. "Is your wife pale?" it would inquire. "Is she discouraged, does she drag herself about the house and find fault with everything? Why do you not tell her to try Dr. Lanahan's Life Preservers?" Another would be jocular in tone, slapping you on the back, so to speak. "Don't be a chump!" it would exclaim. "Go and get the Goliath Bunion Cure." "Get a move on you!" would chime in another. "It's easy, if you wear the Eureka Two-fifty Shoe."

Among these importunate signs was one that had caught the attention of the family by its pictures. It showed two very pretty little birds building themselves a home; and Marija had asked an acquaintance to read to her, and told them that it related to the furnishing of a house. "Feather your nest," it ran—and went on to say that it could furnish all the necessary feathers for a four-room nest for the ludicrously small sum of seventy-five dollars. The particularly important thing about this offer was that only a small part of the money need be had at once—the rest one might pay a few dollars every month. Our friends had to have some furniture, there was no getting away from that; but their little fund of money had sunk so low that they could hardly get to sleep at night, and so they fled to this as their deliverance. There was more agony, and another paper for Teta Elzbieta to sign, and then one night when Jurgis came home he was told the breathless tidings that the furniture had arrived and was safely stowed in the house—a parlor set of four pieces, a bedroom set of three pieces, a dining-room table and four chairs, a toilet-set with beautiful pink roses painted all over it, an assortment of crockery, also with pink roses—and so on. One of the plates in the set had been found broken when they unpacked it, and Ona was going to the store the first thing in the morning to make them change it; also they had promised three sauce-pans, and there had only two come, and did Jurgis think that they were trying to cheat them?

The next day they went to the house; and when the men came from work they ate a few hurried mouthfuls at panei Aniele's, and then set to work at the task of carrying their belongings to their new home. The distance was in reality over two miles, but Jurgis made two trips that night, each time with a huge pile of mattresses and bedding on his head, with bundles of clothing and bags and things tied up inside. Anywhere else in Chicago he would have stood a good chance of being arrested; but the policemen in Packingtown were apparently used to these informal movings, and contented themselves with a cursory examination now and then. It was quite wonderful to see how fine the house looked, with all the things in it, even by the dim light of a lamp; it was really home, and almost as exciting as the placard had described it. Ona was fairly dancing, and she and Cousin Marija took Jurgis by the arm and escorted him from room to room, sitting in each chair by turns, and then insisting that he should do the same. One chair squeaked with his great weight, and they screamed with fright, and woke the baby and brought everybody running. Altogether it was a great day; and tired as they were, Jurgis and Ona sat up late, contented simply to hold each other and gaze in rapture about the room. They were going to be married as soon as they could get everything settled, and a little spare money put by; and this was to be their home—that little room yonder would be theirs!

It was in truth a never-ending delight, the fixing up of this house. They had no money to spend for the pleasure of spending, but there were a few absolutely necessary things, and the buying of these was a perpetual adventure for Ona. It must always be done at night, so that Jurgis could go along; and even if it were only a pepper-cruet, or half a dozen glasses for ten cents, that was enough for an expedition. On Saturday night they came home with a great basketful of things, and spread them out on the table, while everyone stood round, and the children climbed up on the chairs, or howled to be lifted up to see. There was sugar and salt, and tea, and crackers, and a can of lard and a milk-pail, and a scrubbing-brush and a pair of shoes for the second oldest boy, and a can of oil and a tack-hammer and a pound of nails. These last were to be driven in the walls of the kitchen and the bedrooms, to hang things on; and there was a family discussion as to the place where each one was to be driven. Then Jurgis would try to hammer, and hit his fingers because the hammer was too small, and get mad because Ona had refused to let him pay fifteen cents more and get a bigger hammer; and Ona would be invited to try it herself, and hurt her thumb, and cry out, which necessitated the thumb being kissed by Jurgis. Finally after every one else had had a try, the nails would be driven, and something hung up. Jurgis had come home with a big packing-box on his head, and he sent Jonas to get another that he had bought. He meant to take one side out of these tomorrow, and put shelves in them, and make them into bureaus and places to keep things for the bedrooms. The nest which had been advertised had not included feathers for quite so many birds as there were in this family.

They had, of course, put their dining-table in the kitchen, and the dining-room was used as the bedroom of Teta Elzbieta and five of her children. She and the two youngest slept in the only bed, and the other three had a mattress on the floor. Ona and her cousin dragged a mattress into the parlor and slept at night, and the three men and the oldest boy slept in the other room, having nothing but the very level floor to rest on for the present. Even so, however, they slept soundly—it was necessary for Teta Elzbieta to pound more than once on the door at a quarter past five every morning. She would have ready a great pot full of steaming black coffee, and oatmeal and bread and smoked sausages; and then she would fix them their dinner pails with more thick slices of bread with lard between them—they could not afford butter—and some onions and a piece of cheese, and so they would tramp away to work.

This was the first time in his life that he had ever really worked, it seemed to Jurgis; it was the first time that he had ever had anything to do which took all he had in him. Jurgis had stood with the rest up in the gallery and watched the men on the killing-floor, marveling at their speed and power as if they had been wonderful machines; it somehow never occurred to one to think of the flesh and blood side of it there—not until he actually got down into the pit and took off his coat. Then he saw things in a different light, he got at the inside of them. The pace they set here, it was one that called for every faculty of a man—from the instant the first steer fell till the sounding of the noon whistle, and again from half past twelve till Heaven only knew what hour in the late afternoon or evening, there was never one instant's rest for a man, for his hand or his eyes or his brain. Jurgis saw how they managed it; there were portions of the work which determined the pace of the rest, and for these they had picked men whom they paid high wages, and whom they changed frequently. You might easily pick out these pace-makers, for they worked under the eye of the bosses, and they worked like men possessed. This was called "speeding up the gang," and if any man could not keep up with the pace, there were hundreds outside begging to try.

Yet Jurgis did not mind it, he rather enjoyed it. It saved him the necessity of flinging his arms about and fidgeting as he did in most work. He would laugh to himself as he ran down the line, darting a glance now and then at the man ahead of him. It was not the pleasantest work one could think of, but it was necessary work; and what more had a man the right to ask, than a chance to do something useful, and to get good pay for doing it?

So Jurgis thought, and so he spoke, in his bold, free way; very much to his surprise, he found that it had a tendency to get him into trouble. For most of the men here took a fearfully different view of the thing. He was quite dismayed when he first began to find it out—that most of the men hated their work. It seemed strange—it was even terrible, when you came to find out the universality of the sentiment; but it was certainly the fact—they hated their work. They hated the bosses, and they hated the owners; they hated the whole place, the whole neighborhood—even the whole city, with an all-inclusive hatred, bitter and fierce. Women and little children would fall to cursing about it; it was rotten, rotten as hell—everything was rotten. When Jurgis would ask them what they meant, they would begin to get suspicious, and content themselves with saying—"Never mind, you stay here and see for yourself."

One of the first problems that Jurgis ran upon was that of the unions. He had had no experience with unions, and he had to have it explained to him that the men were banded together for the purpose of fighting for their rights. Jurgis asked them what they meant by their rights, a question in which he was quite sincere, for he had not any idea of any rights that he had, except the right to hunt for a job, and do as he was told when he got it. Generally, however, this harmless question would only make his fellow workingmen lose their tempers and call him a fool. There was a delegate of the butcher-helpers' union who came to see Jurgis to enroll him; and when Jurgis found that this meant that he would have to part with some of his money, he froze up directly, and the delegate, who was an Irishman and only knew a few words of Lithuanian, lost his temper and began to threaten him. In the end Jurgis got into a fine rage, and made it sufficiently plain that it would take more than one Irishman to scare him into a union. Little by little he gathered that the main thing the men wanted was to put a stop to the habit of "speeding up;" they were trying their best to force a lessening of the pace, for there were some, they said, who could not keep up with it, whom it was killing. But Jurgis had no sympathy with such ideas as this—he could do the work himself, and so could the rest of them, he declared, if they were good for anything. If they couldn't do it, let them go somewhere else. Jurgis had not studied the books, and he would not have known how to pronounce "laissez-faire;" but he had been round the world enough to know that a man has to shift for himself in it, and that if he gets the worst of it, there is nobody to listen to him holler.

Yet there have been known to be philosophers and plain men who swore by Malthus in the books, and would, nevertheless, subscribe to a relief fund in time of a famine. It was the same with Jurgis, who consigned the unfit to destruction, while going about all day sick at heart because of his poor old father, who was wandering somewhere in the yards begging for a chance to earn his bread. Old Antanas had been a worker ever since he was a child; he had run away from home when he was twelve, because his father beat him for trying to learn to read. And he was a faithful man too, he was a man you might leave alone for a month, if only you had made him understand what you wanted him to do in the meantime. And now here he was, worn out in soul and body, and with no more place in the world than a sick dog. He had his home, as it happened, and some one who would care for him if he never got a job; but his son could not help thinking, suppose this had not been the case. Antanas Rudkos had been into every building in Packingtown by this time, and into nearly every room; he had stood mornings among the crowd of applicants till the very policemen had come to know his face and to tell him to go home and give it up. He had been likewise to all the stores and saloons for a mile about, begging for some little thing to do; and everywhere they had ordered him out, sometimes with curses, and not once even stopping to ask him a question.

So after all there was a crack in the fine structure of Jurgis' faith in things as they are. The crack was wide while Diedas Antanas was hunting a job —and it was yet wider when he finally got it. For one evening the old man came home in a great state of excitement, with the tale that he had been approached by a man in one of the corridors of the pickle-rooms of Anderson's and asked what he would pay to get a job. He had not known what to make of this at first; but the man had gone on with matter-of-fact frankness to say that he could get him a job, provided that he were willing to pay one-third of his wages for it. Was he a boss? Antanas had asked; to which the man had replied that that was nobody's business, but that he could do what he said.

Jurgis had made some friends by this time, and he sought one of them and asked what this meant. The friend, who was named Tamoszius Kuszlejka, was a sharp little man who folded skins on the killing-floor, and he listened to what Jurgis had to say, without seeming at all surprised. They were common enough, he said, such cases of petty graft. It was simply some boss who proposed to add a little to his income. After Jurgis had been there awhile he would know that the plants were simply honey-combed with rottenness of that sort—the bosses grafted off the men, and they grafted off each other; and some day the superintendent would find out about the boss, and then he would graft off the boss. Warming to the subject, Tamoszius went on to explain the situation; here was Anderson's, owned by a man who was trying to make as much money out of it as he could, and did not care in the least how he did it; and underneath him, ranged in ranks and grades like an army, were managers and superintendents and foremen, each one driving the man next below him and trying to squeeze out of him as much work as possible. And all the men of the same rank were pitted against each other; the accounts of each were kept separately, and every man lived in terror of losing his job, if another made a better record than he. So from top to bottom the place was simply a seething cauldron of jealousies and hatreds; there was no loyalty or decency anywhere about it; there was no place in it where a man counted for anything against a dollar. And worse than there being no decency, there was not even any honesty. The reason for that? Who could say? It must have been old Anderson in the beginning, it was a heritage he had left to his son, along with his millions; for there had been no more thoroughly dishonest man in all Chicago than old man Anderson, the self-made merchant. Since he had died they had dropped the custom of giving two pounds short in every forty; but they still did ten thousand things every day that would have landed them in state's prison if they had not been able to buy up the law of the land. What were these things? Oh, Jurgis would find them out for himself, if he stayed there long enough. It was the men who had to do all the dirty jobs, and so there was no deceiving them; and they caught the spirit of the place, and did like all the rest. Jurgis had come there, and thought he was going to make himself useful, and rise and become a skilled man; but he would soon find out his error—for nobody rose in Packingtown by doing true work of any sort. You could lay that down for a rule—if you met a man who was rising in Packingtown, you met a knave. That man who had been sent to Jurgis' father by the boss, he would rise; the man who told tales and spied upon his fellows would rise; but the man who minded his own business and did his work—why, they would "speed him up" till they had worn him out, and then they would simply throw him into the gutter.

Jurgis went home with his head buzzing. Yet he could not bring himself to believe such things—no, it could not be so. Tamoszius was simply another of the grumblers. He was a man who spent all his time fiddling; and he would go to parties at night and not get home till sunrise, and so, of course, he did not feel like work. Then, too, he was a puny little chap; and so he had been left behind in the race, and that was why he was sore. And yet so many strange things kept coming to Jurgis' notice every day!

He tried to persuade his father to have nothing to do with the offer, but old Antanas had begged about until he was worn out, and all his courage was gone; he wanted a job, any sort of a job. So the next day he went and found the man who had spoken to him, and promised to bring him a third of all he earned; and that same day was put to work in Anderson's cellars. He found that his wages were to be a dollar twenty-five a day, and so he would have five dollars each week as the result of his toil. Every cent of it he brought home to his family for his board—he would not hear of anything else; he had no need of money, he told them; he did not care for beer, and they would give him all he wanted to eat. Yet, as it proved, he had to break his resolution at the very beginning; for they had put him in a place where there was never a dry spot to stand upon, and so he had to take more than half of his first week's earnings to buy him a pair of heavy-soled boots. Antanas was a "squeedgie" man; he worked in one of the "pickle-rooms," going about all day with a long-handled mop, swabbing up the floor. Except that it was damp, it was not an unpleasant job, in summer; nor was it very hard work—if only he had been allowed to sit down for an instant or two now and then.

Now, Antanas Rudkos was the meekest man that God ever put on earth; and so Jurgis found it a striking confirmation of what the men all said, that his father had been at work only two days before he came home as bitter as any of them, and cursing Anderson's with all the power of his soul. For they had set him to cleaning out the traps; and the family sat around and listened in wonder while he told them what that meant. It seemed that he was working in the room where the men prepared the beef for canning, and the beef had lain in vats full of chemicals, and men with great forks speared it out and dumped it into trucks, to be taken to the canning-room. When they had speared out all they could reach, they emptied the vat on the floor, and then with shovels scraped up the balance and dumped it into the truck; this floor was filthy with manure tracked in from the streets, and with spit, and the accumulated dirt of years; yet they set Antanas with his mop slopping the "pickle" into a hole that connected with a sink, where it was caught and used over again forever; and if that were not enough, there was a trap in the pipe, where all the scraps of meat and odds and ends of refuse were caught, and every few days it was the old man's task to clean these out, and shovel them into one of the trucks with the rest!

This was the experience of Antanas; and then there came also Jonas and Marija with tales to tell. Marija was working for one of the independent packers, and was quite beside herself and outrageous with triumph over the sums of money she was making as a painter of cans. But one day she walked home with a pale-faced little woman who worked opposite to her, Jadwiga Marciukus by name, and Jadwiga told her how she, Marija, had chanced to get her job. She had taken the place of an Irish woman who had been working in that factory ever since any one could remember, for over fifteen years, so she declared. Mary Dennis was her name, and a long time ago she had been seduced, and had a little boy; he was a cripple, and an epileptic, but still he was all that she had in the world to love, and they had lived in a little room alone somewhere back of Halsted street, where the Irish were. Mary had had consumption, and all day long you might hear her coughing as she worked; of late she had been going all to pieces, and when Marija came, the "forelady" had suddenly decided to turn her off. The forelady had to come up to a certain standard herself, and could not stop for sick people, Jadwiga explained. The fact that Mary had been there so long had not made any difference to her; it was doubtful if she even knew that, for both the forelady and the superintendent were new people, had only been there two or three years themselves. The poor creature had burst into tears when the forelady told her that same afternoon; and Jadwiga did not know what had become of her. Somebody said that she had given up trying to get another place in the yards, and had gone downtown and disappeared. Jadwiga would have gone to see her, but had been sick herself; she had pains in her back all the time, she explained, and feared that she had womb trouble. It was not fit work for a woman, handling fourteen-pound cans all day.

It was a striking circumstance that each member of the family had gotten his job by the misfortune of some other person; Jurgis found upon inquiry that on the very morning the boss had chosen him, a man had been carried out to his death not ten minutes earlier. One of the cattle butchers had been drunk the night before, and been in a fight; meeting his enemy on the floor, he had hurled his knife at him, and, missing him, slashed open the abdomen of an inoffensive Polack, who had been shoveling guts with the same implement that Jurgis was now using. The cut had refused to heal (every wound that a man gets on the killing-floor is an infected one), and the man had died the third day.

And it was the same with Jonas. Jonas pushed a truck loaded with hams from the smoke-rooms onto an elevator, and thence to the packing-rooms. The trucks were all of iron, and heavy, and they put about three-score hams on each of them, a load of more than a quarter of a ton. On the uneven floor it was a task for a man to start one of these trucks, unless he was a giant; and when it was once started he naturally tried his best to keep it going. There was always the boss prowling about, and if there was a second's delay he would fall to cursing; Lithuanians and Slovaks and such, who could not understand what was said to them, the bosses were wont to kick about the place like so many dogs. Therefore, these trucks went for the most part on the run, and there was need to look sharp for them; Jonas's predecessor had been jammed against the wall by one, and crushed in a horrible and nameless manner.

All of these were sinister incidents; but none of them were so bad as some that Jurgis saw with his own eyes before long. One curious thing he had noticed, the very first day in his profession of shoveler of guts; which was the sharp trick of the floor bosses whenever there chanced to come a "slunk" calf. Any man who knows anything about butchering knows that the flesh of a cow that is about to calve, or has just calved, is not fit for food. A good many of these came every day to the packing-houses—and, of course, if they had chosen, it would have been an easy matter for the packers to keep them till they were fit for food. But for the saving of time and fodder, it was the law that cows of that sort came along with the others, and whoever noticed it would tell the boss, and the boss would start up a conversation with the government inspector, and the two would stroll away. So in a trice the carcass of the cow would be cleaned out, and the entrails have vanished; it was Jurgis's task to slide them into the trap, calves and all, and on the floor below they took out these "slunk" calves, and used even the skins of them. Sometimes, when they were cut out, the calves would stand up and start to walk away and have to be butchered all over.

Yet this was a minor matter compared with what came after two or three weeks. One day a man slipped and hurt his leg; and that afternoon, when the last of the cattle had been disposed of and the men were leaving, Jurgis was ordered to remain and do some special work which this injured man had usually done; and so for the first time in his life Jurgis was the participant in a crime. It was late, almost dark, and the government inspectors had all gone, and there were only a dozen or two of men on the floor. That day they had killed about four thousand cattle, and these cattle had come in freight trains, from far states, and some of them had got hurt. There were some with broken legs and some with gored sides; there were some that had died, from what cause no one could say; and they were all to be disposed of here in darkness and silence. "Downers" the men called them; and Anderson and Company had a special elevator upon which they were raised to the killing-floor, where the gang proceeded to handle them with an air of business-like nonchalance which said plainer than any words that it was a matter of every-day routine. It took a couple of hours to get them out of the way, and in the end Jurgis saw them go into the chilling-rooms with the rest of the meat. For this work he was paid double time, and understood full well what that meant.

When he came home that night he was in a very somber mood; having begun to see at last how those might be right who had laughed at him for his faith in the packers, and in America, telling him that he was in the employ, not of honest merchants, but of knaves and public enemies.

6

JURGIS and Ona were very much in love; they had waited a long time—it was now well into the second year, and Jurgis judged everything by the criterion of its helping or hindering their union. All his thoughts were there; he accepted the family because it was a part of Ona, and he was interested in the house because it was to be Ona's home. Even the tricks and cruelties he saw at Anderson's had little meaning for him just then, save as they might happen to affect his future with Ona.

The marriage would have been at once if they had had their way; but this would mean that they would have to do without any wedding-feast, and when they suggested this they came into conflict with the old people. To Teta Elzbieta especially the very suggestion was an affliction. What! she would cry. To be married on the roadside like a parcel of beggars! No! No! Teta Elzbieta had some traditions behind her; she had been a person of importance in her girlhood—had lived on a big estate and had servants, and might have married well and been a lady but for the fact that there had been nine daughters and no sons in the family. Even so, however, she knew what was decent, and clung to her traditions with desperation. They were not going to lose all caste, even if they had come to be unskilled laborers in Packingtown; and that Ona had even talked of omitting a *veselija* was enough to keep her stepmother lying awake all night. It was in vain for them to say that they had so few friends; they were bound to have friends in time, and then the friends would talk about it. They must not give up what was right for a little money—if they did, the money would never do them any good, they could depend upon that. And Teta Elzbieta would call upon Diedas Antanas to support her; there was a fear in the souls of these two lest this journey to a new country might somehow undermine the old home virtues of their children. The very first Sunday they had all been taken to mass; and, poor as they were, Elzbieta had felt it advisable to invest a little of her resources in a representation of the babe of Bethlehem, made in plaster, and painted in brilliant colors. Though it was only a foot high, there was a shrine with four snow-white steeples, and the Virgin standing with her child in her arms, and the kings and shepherds and wise men bowing down before him. It had cost fifty cents; but Teta Elzbieta had a feeling that money spent for such things was not to be counted too closely; it would come back in hidden ways. The piece was beautiful on the parlor mantel, and one could not have a home without some sort of ornament.

The cost of the wedding-feast would, of course, be returned to them; but the problem was to raise it even temporarily. They had been in the neighborhood so short a time that they could not get much credit, and there was no one except Szadwilas from whom they could borrow even a little. Evening after evening Jurgis and Ona would sit and figure the expenses, calculating the term of their separation. They could not possibly manage it decently for less than two hundred dollars, and even though they were welcomed to count in the whole of the earnings of Marija and Jonas, as a loan, they could not hope to raise this sum in less than four or five months. So Ona began thinking of seeking employment herself, saying that if she had even ordinarily good luck, she might be able to take two months off the time. They were just beginning to adjust themselves to this necessity, when out of the clear sky there fell a thunderbolt upon them—a calamity that scattered all their hopes to the four winds.

About a block away from them there lived another Lithuanian family, consisting of an elderly widow and one grown son. Their name was Majauszkis, and our friends struck up an acquaintance with them before long. One evening they came over for a visit, and naturally the first subject upon which the conversation turned was the neighborhood and its history; and then Grandmother Majauszkis, as the old lady was called, proceeded to recite to them a string of horrors that fairly froze their blood. She was a wrinkled up and wizened personage—she must have been eighty—and as she mumbled the grim story through her toothless gums she seemed a very old witch to them. Grandmother Majauszkis had lived in the midst of misfortune so long that it had come to be her element, and she talked about starvation, sickness and death as other people might about weddings and holidays.

The details came gradually. In the first place, as to the house they had bought, it was not new at all, as they had supposed; it was about fifteen years old, and there was nothing new upon it but the paint, which was so bad that it needed to be put on new every year or two. The house was one of a whole row that was built by a company which existed to make money by swindling poor people. They had paid fifteen hundred dollars for it; it had not cost the builders five hundred, when it was new—Grandmother Majauszkis knew that because her son belonged to a political organization with a contractor who put up exactly such houses. They used the very flimsiest and cheapest material; they built the houses a dozen at a time, and they cared about nothing at all except the outside shine. The family could take her word as to the trouble they would have, for she had been through with it all—she and her son had bought their house in exactly the same way. They had fooled the company, however, for her son was a skilled man, who made as high as a hundred dollars a month, and as he had had sense enough not to marry, they had been able to pay for the house.

Grandmother Majauszkis saw that her friends were puzzled at this remark;

they did not quite see how that was "fooling the company." Evidently they were very inexperienced. Cheap as the houses were, they were sold with the idea that the people who bought them would not be able to pay for them. When they failed—if it were only by a single month—they would lose the house and all that they had paid on it, and then the company would sell it over again. And did they often get a chance to do that? *Diewes!* (Grandmother Majauszkis raised her hands.) They did it—how often no one could say, but certainly more than half of the time. They might ask any one who knew anything at all about Packingtown as to that; they would find that the family that was able to carry out its contract to the end and come into full ownership of a house was an exception. And if the family was large or its workers not skilled—God help them, that was all! Why was that? Well, they would see. There was the irregularity of the work, and there was sickness, and accidents—they would find it all out in time. They might take the case of this one house for an example. Grandmother Majauszkis had been living here ever since the house was built, and she could tell them all about it. And had this house ever been sold before? *Susimilkis!* Why, since it had been built no less than six families that their informant could name had tried to buy it and failed. She would tell them a little about it.

The first family had been Germans. It was a curious thing, but the families had all been of different nationalities—there had been one representative of each of the races that had displaced each other in the stock-yards. Grandmother Majauszkis had come to America with her son at a time when, so far as she knew, there was only one other Lithuanian family in this district. They had all been Germans then—skilled cattle-butchers that the packers had brought from abroad to start the business. Afterwards, as cheaper labor had come, these Germans had moved away. The next were the Irish—there had been six or eight years when Packingtown had been a regular Irish city. There were a few colonies of them still here, enough to run all the unions and the police force and get all the graft; but the most of those who were working in the packing-houses had gone away at the very next drop in wages—after the last big strike. The Bohemians had come then, and after them the Poles. People said that old man Anderson himself was responsible for these immigrations. He had sworn that, by God, he would fix the people of Packingtown so that they would never again call a strike on him; and so he had sent his agents into every city and town and village in Europe to spread the tale of the chances of work and high wages at the stock-yards. The people had come in hordes; and old Anderson had squeezed them tighter and tighter, speeding them up and grinding them to pieces, and sending for new ones. The Poles, who had come by tens of thousands, had been driven to the wall by the Lithuanians; and now the Lithuanians were giving way to the Slovaks. Who there was poorer and more miserable than the Slovaks, Grandmother

Majauszkis had no idea, but Old Anderson's son, who ran things now, would find them, never fear. It was easy to bring them, for wages were really much higher, and it was only when it was too late that the poor people found out that everything else was higher, too. They were exactly as badly off here as at home, said the old woman; did they know any city in old Lithuania where workingmen lived as they did in the boarding-houses, a dozen sleeping in one room, and a shift day and night? To be sure, many of these were single men, who were trying to save a little to go back home; but then if things were so much better, why did they want to go home? They were like rats in a trap, that was the truth; and more of them were piling in every day. By and by they would have their revenge, though—for the thing was getting beyond human endurance, and the people would rise and murder the packers. Grandmother Majauszkis was a Socialist, or some such strange thing; another son of hers was working in the mines of Siberia, and the old lady herself had made speeches in her time—which made her seem all the more terrible to her present auditors.

They called her back to the story of the house. The German family had been a good sort. To be sure, there had been a great many of them, which was a common failing in Packingtown; but they had worked hard, and the father had been a steady man, and they had a good deal more than half paid for the house. But he had been killed in an elevator accident in Anderson's; and before he died the company lawyers had tricked him into signing away his damage claims for twenty-five dollars; and so the family had not held out very long. What had become of them? Nobody could say as to that; they had gone the way of those who fail in Packingtown. Then there had come the Irish, and there had been lots of them, too; the husband drank and beat the children—the neighbors could hear them shrieking any night. They were behind with their rent all the time, but the company was good to them; there was some politics back of that, Grandmother Majauszkia could not say just what, but the Laffertys had belonged to the Warwhoop League, which was a sort of political club of all the thugs and rowdies in the district; and if you belonged to that you could never be arrested for anything. Once upon a time old Lafferty had been caught with a gang that had stolen cows from several of the poor people of the neighborhood, and butchered them in an old shanty back of the yards and sold them. He had been in jail only three days for it, and had come out laughing, and had not even lost his place in the packing-house. He had gone all to ruin with the drink, however, and lost his power; one of his sons, who was a good man, had kept him and the family up for a year or two, but then they too had been turned out, and had disappeared.

Then there were the Bohemians, the families of two brothers. They had stood no chance at all; they had no right to make the attempt, for they had no money to start on. The company agent had been patient with them, too—in those days the company would wait until they had gotten a good part of the money; of late they did not do this, for there was more demand for houses anywhere near the yards, and they could find a new purchaser at once. One of these brothers had got consumption—and that was another thing. Grandmother Majauszkis interrupted herself—this house was unlucky. Every family that lived in it, some one was sure to get consumption in a year or so, and die of it in three or four. Nobody could tell why that was; there must be something about a house, or the way it was built—some folks said it was because the building had been begun in the dark of the moon. There were dozens of houses that way in Packingtown. Sometimes there would be a particular room that you could point out—if anybody slept in that room he was just as good as dead. With this house it had been the Irish first, one of the children had died; and one of the Bohemians had been on the point of death when the family had lost the house. For that matter, most of his children had been just as bad with it, but it was hard to tell just what was the matter with children who worked in the yards. In those days there had been no law about the age of children—the packers had worked all but the babies. At this remark the family looked puzzled, and Grandmother Majauszkis again had to make an explanation—that it was against the law for children to work before they were sixteen. What was the sense of that? they asked. They had been thinking of letting little Stanislovas go to work. Well, there was no need to worry about it, Grandmother Majauszkis said. The law made no difference except that it forced people to lie about the ages of their children. One would like to know what the lawmakers expected them to do; there were families that had no possible means of support except the children, and the law provided them no other way of getting a living. If they begged or stole they would be put in jail—it would be very interesting to know what the rich people meant. Very often a man could get no work in Packingtown for months, while a child could go and get a place easily; there was always some new machine by which the packers could get as much work out of a child as out of a man, and for a third of the pay.

To come back to the house again, it was the woman of the next family that had died. That was after they had been there nearly four years, and this woman had had twins regularly every year—and there had been more than you could count when they moved in. After she died the man would go to work all day and leave them to shift for themselves—the neighbors would help them now and then, for they would almost freeze to death. At the end there were three days that they were alone before it was found out that the father was dead. He was a "floorsman" at Morton's, and a wounded steer had broken loose and mashed him against a pillar. Then the children had been taken away, and the company had sold the house that very same week to a party of immigrants.

So this grim old woman went on with her tale of horrors. How much of it was exaggeration—who could tell? It was only too plausible. There was that about consumption, for instance. They knew nothing about consumption whatever, except that it made people cough; and for two weeks they had been worrying about a coughing-spell of Diedas Antanas. It seemed to shake him all over, and it never stopped; you could see a red stain wherever he had spit upon the floor.

And yet all these things were as nothing to what came a little later. They had begun to question the old lady as to why one family had been unable to pay, trying to show her by figures that it ought to have been possible; and Grandmother Majauszkis had disputed their figures—"You say twelve dollars a month; but that does not include the interest."

Then they stared at her. "Interest!" they cried.

"Interest on the money you still owe," she answered.

"But we don't have to pay any interest!" they exclaimed, three or four at once. "We only have to pay twelve dollars each month."

And for this she laughed at them. "You are like all the rest," she said; "they trick you, and eat you alive. They never sell the houses without interest. Get your deed and see."

Then, with a horrible sinking of the heart, Teta Elzbieta unlocked her bureau and brought out the paper that had already caused them so many agonies. Now they sat around, scarcely breathing, while the old lady, who could read English, ran over it. "Yes," she said, finally, "here it is, of course: 'With interest thereon monthly, at the rate of seven per cent per annum.'" And there followed a dead silence.

"What does that mean!" asked Jurgis, finally, almost in a whisper.

"That means," replied the other, "that you have to pay them seven dollars interest next month, as well as the twelve dollars."

Then again there was not a sound. It was sickening, like a nightmare, in which suddenly something gives way beneath you, and you feel yourself sinking, sinking down into bottomless abysses. As if in a flash of lightning they saw themselves—victims of a relentless fate, cornered, trapped, in the grip of destruction. All the fair structure of their hopes came crashing about their ears. And all the time the old woman was going on talking. "Of course, you do not have to pay as much as seven dollars all the time," she said; "you will owe them less and less—after a year you will only have to pay them six dollars, and so on." But they did not hear her; they wished that she would be still; her voice sounded like the croaking of some dismal raven. Jurgis sat with his hands clenched, and beads of perspiration on his forehead, and there was a great lump in Ona's throat, choking her. Then suddenly Teta Elzbieta broke the silence with a wail, and Marija began to wring her hands and sob, "Ai! Ai! Beda man!"

All their outcry did them no good, of course. There sat Grandmother Majauazkis, unrelenting, typifying fate. No, of course it was not fair, but, then, fairness had nothing to do with anything in Packingtown. And, of course, they had not known it. They had not been intended to know it. But it was in the deed, and that was all that was necessary, as they would find when the time came.

Somehow or other they got rid of their guest, and then they passed a night of lamentation. The children woke up and found out that something was wrong, and they wailed and would not be comforted. In the morning, of course, most of them had to go to work, the packinghouses would not stop for their sorrows; but by seven o'clock Ona and her stepmother was standing at the door of the office of the agent. Yes, he told them, when he came, it was quite true that they would have to pay interest. And then Teta Elzbieta broke forth into protestations and reproaches, so that the people outside stopped and peered in at the window. The agent was as bland as ever. He was deeply pained, he said. He had not told them, simply because he had supposed they would understand that they had to pay interest upon their debt, as a matter of course. That was the law, he said, and he had nothing to do with it himself. If he had sold them the house without any interest he would have been liable to be put in jail, and would Mrs. Lukoszis have liked that? No, Teta Elzbieta did not want anybody to go to jail; but it seemed a shame that life was so very hard for poor people—there was no way they could keep alive in the world. They had gotten a lawyer, and paid him a dollar, which heaven knew they could not spare; and he ought to have told them about the interest. If they had known that they had to pay it they would never have taken the house. To this the agent replied that they had not asked the lawyer about interest, and that he, too, had supposed that they knew it. The company would be pained to learn of the error—but no, the man made haste to slip in, there was no use asking—they were not permitted to take back a house when they had once sold it.

So they came away, and Ona went down to the yards, and at noontime saw Jurgis and told him. Jurgis took it stolidly—he had made up his mind to it by this time. It was part of fate; they would manage it somehow—and he made his usual answer, "I will work harder." It would upset their plans for a time; and it would perhaps be necessary for Ona to get work, after all. Then Ona added that Teta Elzbieta had decided that little Stanislovas would have to work too. It was not fair to let Jurgis and her support the family—the family would have to help as it could. Previously Jurgis had scouted this idea, but now knit his brows and nodded his head slowly—Yes, perhaps it would be best; they would all have to make some sacrifices now.

So Ona set out that day to hunt for work; and at night Marija came home saying that she had met a girl named Jasaitis, who had a friend that worked in one of the wrapping-rooms in Smith's, and might get a place for Ona there; only the forelady was the kind that takes presents—it was no use for anyone to ask her for a place unless at the same time they slipped a ten-dollar bill into her hand. Jurgis was not in the least surprised at this now—he merely asked what the wages of the place would be. So negotiations were opened, and after an interview Ona came home and reported that the forelady seemed to like her, and had said that, while she was not sure, she thought she might be able to put her at work sewing covers on hams—a job at which she could earn as much as eight or ten dollars a week. That was a bid, so Marija reported, after consulting her friend; and then there was an anxious conference at home. The work was done in one of the cellars, and Jurgis did not want Ona to work in such a place; but then it was easy work, and one could not have everything. So in the end Ona, with a ten-dollar bill burning a hole in her palm, had another interview with the forelady.

Meantime, Teta Elzbieta had taken Stanislovas to the priest and gotten a certificate to the effect that he was three years older than he was; and with it the little boy now sallied forth to make his fortune in the world. It chanced that Anderson had just put in a wonderful new lard-machine, and when the special policeman in front of the time-station saw Stanislovas and his document he smiled to himself and told him to go—"Czia! Czia!" pointing. And so Stanislovas went down a long stone corridor and up a flight of stairs which took him into a room lighted by electricity, with the new machines for filling lard cans at work in it. The lard was finished on the floor above, and it came in little jets, like beautiful, wriggling snow-white snakes of unpleasant odor. There were several kinds and sizes of jets, and after a certain precise quantity had come out each stopped automatically, and the wonderful machine made a turn and took the can under another jet, and so on until it was filled neatly to the brim, and pressed tightly, and smoothed off. To attend to all this and fill several hundred cans of lard per hour there were necessary two human creatures, one of whom knew how to place an empty lard can on a certain spot every few seconds, and the other of whom knew how to take a full lard can off a certain spot every few seconds and set it upon a tray.

And so, after little Stanislovas had stood gazing timidly about him for a few minutes, a man approached him and asked what he wanted, to which Stanislovas said, "Job." Then the man said, "How old?" and Stanislovas answered, "Sixtin." Once or twice every year a state inspector would come wandering through the packing plants, asking a child here and there how old he was; and so the packers were very careful to comply with the law, which cost them as much trouble as was now involved in the boss's taking the document from the little boy and glancing at it, and then sending it to the office to be filed away. Then he set some one else at a different job and showed the lad how to place a lard can every time the empty arm of the remorseless machinery came to him; and so was decided the place in the universe of little Stanislovas, and his destiny till the end of his days. He did not realize what it meant—he went home dancing with delight to tell the family of the fortune he was earning. Like all the rest of them, he was to learn by experience. Hour after hour, day after day, year after year, it was fated that he should stand upon a certain square foot of floor from seven in the morning until noon, and again from one o'clock till six, making never a motion and thinking never a thought save for the setting of lard cans. In summer the stench of the warm lard would be nauseating, and in winter the cans would all but freeze to his naked little fingers in the unheated cellar. Half the year it would be dark as night when he went in to work, and dark as night again when he came out, and so he would never know what the sun looked like on week days. And for this, at the end of the week, he would carry home three dollars to his family, being his pay at the rate of five cents per hour, and, as it happened, just about exactly his proper share of the total earnings of the million and three-quarters of children under fifteen years of age who are now engaged in earning their livings in this glorious land of freedom.

And meantime, because they were young, and hope is not to be stifled before its time, Jurgis and Ona were again calculating; for they had discovered that the wages of Stanislovas would more than pay the interest, which left them considerably better off than they had been before. It would be but fair to them to add that the little boy was delighted with his work, and at the idea of earning a lot of money; and also that the two were very much in love with each other.

ALL SUMMER long the family toiled, and in the fall they had money enough for Jurgis and Ona to be married according to home traditions of decency. In the latter part of November they hired a hall, and they invited not only all their friends, but their friends' friends, and all others who might chance to hear of it. For a week or two there was preparation; it was necessary that Ona should have a white muslin dress and Jurgis a new suit of black; and then from Saturday morning till Sunday afternoon there was baking and boiling and endless trips to everywhere to borrow knives and forks and crockery. So at last the great hour arrived, and, as we have seen, the guests came and showed them what becomes of honor and decency in the dominions of the self-made merchant.

They were over a hundred dollars in debt, and all things not yet counted. It was a bitter and cruel experience, and it left them plunged in an agony of despair. Such a time of all times for them to have it, when their hearts were made tender! Such a pitiful beginning it was for their married life; they loved each other so, and they could not have the briefest respite! It was a time when everything cried out to them that they ought to be happy; when wonder burned in their hearts, and leaped into flame at the slightest breath. They were shaken to the depths of them with the awe of love realized; and was it so very weak of them that they cried out for a little peace? They had opened their hearts, like flowers to the springtime, and the merciless winter had fallen upon them. They wondered if any love that ever had blossomed in the world before had been so crushed and trampled!

Over them, relentless and savage, there cracked the lash of want; the morning after the wedding it sought them as they slept, and drove them out before daybreak to work. Ona was scarcely able to stand with exhaustion; but if she were to lose her place they would be ruined, and she would surely lose it if she were not on time that day. They all had to go, even little Stanislovas, who was so tired that he could scarcely stand, and ill besides from over-indulgence in sausages and sarsaparilla. All that day he stood at his lard-machine, rocking unsteadily, his eyes closing in spite of him; and he all but lost his place even so, for the foreman booted him twice to waken him, and once more and he would have booted him out of the door.

It was fully a week before they were all normal again, and meantime, with whining children and cross adults, the house was not a pleasant place to live in. Marija and Jonas would have to do without their savings till Jurgis could earn the money to pay them back; and though they did not say anything, they were naturally disconcerted at this. And then there came Grajczunas, the saloon-keeper, with his bill, nearly thirty dollars more than they had expected—and he demanding that it be paid upon the instant. There was some reason for dispute within the family, for Jurgis had doubted this man from the beginning, and had wanted to have nothing to do with him. There was nothing to do now but pay him—only Jurgis recouped himself by calling him names, and they all but had a fight. In truth, it was not fair to describe him as a devourer of the poor, for he had troubles of his own. The saloons in Packingtown lie as thick as the leaves of Vallambrosa, and the competition is deadly. The goods handed out over the counter have long since reached the limit of possibility of adulteration, and so no man can get the better of another that way; and half the saloon-keepers are in debt to the big brewers, who furnish them liquor on credit, and then when they cannot pay, take over their business. Thus again were the strong devouring the weak, according to the law which prevails in the jungle.

Jurgis lost his temper very little, however, all things considered. It was because of Ona; the least glance at her was always enough to make him control himself. She was so sensitive—she was not fitted for such a life as this, the truth be told; and a hundred times a day, when he thought of her, Jurgis would clench his hands and again fling himself at the task before him. She was too good for him, he told himself, and he was afraid, because she was his. So long he had hungered to possess her, but now that the time had come he knew that he had not earned the right; that she trusted him so was all her own simple goodness and no virtue of his. But he was resolved that she should never find this out, and so was always on the watch to see that he did not betray any of his ugly self; he would take care even in little matters, such as his manners, and his habit of swearing when things went wrong. The tears came so easily into Ona's eyes, and she would look at him so appealingly—it kept Jurgis quite busy making resolutions, in addition to all the other things he had on his mind. It was true that more things were going on at this time in the mind of Jurgis than ever had in all his life before.

He had to protect her, to do battle for her against the horror he saw about them. He was all that she had to look to, and if he failed she would be lost; he would wrap his arms about her and try to hide her from the world. He had learned the ways of things about him, now—the laws of the jungle. It was a war of each against all, and the devil take the hindmost; it was a battle to death, waged without respite, and the only safety was in instant watching, ready either to fight or flee. It was best to travel in the dark, and to strike from a covert; and when you had killed you did not stop to weep over your victim—nor when you failed did you cry out for sympathy, but crawled into a hole and died—in other words, you put money in your purse. You did not give feasts to other people; you waited for them to give feasts to you. You went about with your soul full of suspicion and hatred, and if anyone talked to you about friendship or trust you were not long in finding out what he wanted. You understood that you were environed by hostile powers that were trying to get your money, and who used all the virtues to bait their traps with. The store-keepers plastered up their windows with all sorts of lies to entice you; the very fences by the wayside, the lamp-posts and telegraph-poles were pasted over with beastly lies. The great corporation which employed you lied to you, and lied to the whole country—from top to bottom it was nothing but one gigantic lie. The whole country was a lie; its freedom was a lie, a snare for pauper workingmen; its prosperity was a lie of rich employers, its justice was a lie of grafting politicians. And so no matter where you went in it, or for what purpose—to buy a house, for instance—you did not pay any attention to all the fine speeches and you were not taken in by politeness; you were polite yourself, as long as it suited you, but you understood that you were dealing with a knave, and you were ready to flash out in anger and defiance at the least occasion.

Jurgis said that he understood it; and yet it was really pitiful, for the struggle was so unfair. Some had so much the advantage! Here he was, for instance, vowing upon his knees that he would save Ona from harm, and only a week later she was suffering atrociously, and from the blow of an enemy that he could not possibly have thwarted. There came a day when the rain fell in torrents; and it being December, to be wet with it and have to sit all day long in one of the cold cellars of Smith's was no laughing matter. Ona was a working girl, and did not own waterproofs and such things, and so Jurgis took her and put her on the street car. Now, it chanced that this car line was owned by wealthy gentlemen who were trying to make money out of it; and the city having passed an ordinance requiring them to give transfers, they had fallen into a rage at this interference with the elemental right of business men to manage their own business in their own way, and were now trying to revenge themselves. First they had made a rule that transfers could be had only when the fare was paid, and later, growing still uglier, they made another—that the passenger must ask for the transfer, the conductor was not allowed to offer it. Now, Ona had been told that she was to get a transfer; but it was not her way to speak up, and so she merely waited, following the conductor about with her eyes, wondering when he would think of her. When at last the time came for her to get out she asked for the transfer, and was refused. Not knowing what to make of this, she began to argue with the conductor in a language of which he did not understand a word. After warning her several times, he pulled the bell and the car went on—at which Ona burst into tears. At the next corner she got out, of course; and as she had no more money, she had to walk the rest of the way to the yards in the pouring rain. And so all day long she sat shivering, and came home at night with her teeth chattering and pains in her head and back. For two weeks afterwards she suffered cruelly—and yet every day she had to drag herself to her work. Twice during the time she swooned dead away, but the forewoman would not let her come home, even so. Girls were all the time wanting to go home, and it made extra trouble keeping the records; so generally they are told to go and lie on the floor in the corner a while and see if they do not feel better. The forewoman was especially severe with Ona, because she believed that she was obstinate on account of having been refused a holiday the day after her wedding. Ona had an idea that her "forelady" did not like to have her girls marry—perhaps because she was old and ugly and unmarried herself.

There were many such dangers, in which the odds were all against them. Their children were not as well as they had been at home; but how could they know that there was no sewer to their house, and that the drainage of fifteen years was in a cesspool under it? How could they know that the pale blue milk that they bought around the corner was watered and doctored with formaldehyde besides? When the children were not well at home, Teta Elzbieta would gather herbs and cure them; now she was obliged to go to the drug-store and buy extracts—and how was she to know that they were all adulterated, that a pure drug is not to be bought any longer by a poor man in the United States of America? How could they find out that their tea and coffee, their sugar and flour, had all been doctored; that their canned peas had been colored with copper-salts, and their fruit jams with aniline dyes? And even if they had known it, what good would it have done them, since there was no place within miles of them where any other sort was to be had? The bitter winter was coming, and they had to save money to get more clothing and bedding; but it would not matter in the least how much they saved, they could not get anything to keep them warm. All the clothing that was to be had in the stores was made of cotton and shoddy, which is made by tearing old clothes to pieces and weaving the fiber again. If they paid higher prices they might get frills and fanciness, or be cheated; but genuine quality they could not obtain for love nor money. A young friend of Szadwilas's, recently come from abroad, had become a clerk in a store on Ashland avenue, and had taken quickly to the ways of the place; he had narrated with glee a trick he had played upon an unsuspecting countryman, thereby gaining great favor with his employer. The customer had desired to purchase an alarm clock, and the clerk had shown him two exactly similar, telling him that the price of one was a dollar and of the other a dollar seventy-five. Upon being asked what the difference was, the clerk had wound up the first half way and the second all the way, and showed the customer how the latter made twice as much noise; upon which the customer remarked that he was a sound sleeper, and had better take the more expensive clock!

There is a poet who sings that

"Deeper their heart grows and nobler their bearing
Whose youth in the fires of anguish hath died."

It is not likely that he had reference to the kind of anguish that comes with destitution, that is so endlessly bitter and cruel, and yet so sordid and petty, so ugly, so humiliating—unredeemed by the slightest touch of dignity, or even of pathos. It is a kind of anguish that poets have not commonly dealt with; its very words are not admitted into the vocabulary of poets—the details of it cannot be told in polite society at all. How, for instance, could anyone expect to excite sympathy among lovers of good literature by telling how a family found their home alive with vermin, and of all the suffering and inconvenience and humiliation they were put to, and the hard-earned money they spent in efforts to get rid of them. The cultured reader's own home is provided with a bathroom—perhaps with half a dozen; and he does not have to stand in the midst of blood and filth from seven o'clock in the morning until six, or perhaps nine, at night; and he has time to use his bathtub, and cannot understand why everyone is not as clean as he. Also, when he goes traveling he does not sleep in places where his clothing and baggage get filled with vermin; if such a deplorable accident were to happen he would probably burn them all. Our family tried to get rid of them; after long hesitation and uncertainty they paid twenty-five cents for a big package of insect powder—a powder which chanced to be ninety-five per cent gypsum, a harmless earth which had cost about two cents to prepare. Of course, it had not the least effect, except upon a few roaches which had the misfortune to drink water after eating it, and so got their inwards set in a coating of plaster of paris. The family, having no idea of this, and no more money to throw away, had nothing to do but give up and submit to one more misery for the rest of their days.

Once upon a time a great-hearted woman set forth the sufferings of the black chattel-slave, and aroused a continent to arms. She had many things in her favor which cannot be counted on by him who would paint the life of the modern slave—the slave of the factory, the sweat-shop and the mine. The lash which drives the latter cannot either be seen or heard; most people do not believe that it exists—it is the cant of the philanthropist and the political convention that it does not exist. This slave is never hunted by bloodhounds; he is not beaten to pieces by picturesque villains, nor does he die in ecstasies of religious faith. His religion is but another snare of his oppressors, and the bitterest of his misfortunes; the hounds that hunt him are disease and accident, and the villain who murders him is merely the prevailing rate of wages. And who can thrill the reader with the tale of a man-hunt in which the hunted is a lousy and ignorant foreigner, and the hunters are the germs of consumption, diphtheria and typhoid? Who can make a romance out of the story of a man whose one life adventure is the scratching of a finger by an infected butcher knife, with a pine box and a pauper's grave as the denouement? And yet it may be just as painful to die of blood-poisoning as to be beaten to death; to be tracked by bloodhounds and torn to pieces is most certainly a merciful fate compared to that which falls to thousands every year in Packingtown— to be hunted for life by bitter poverty, to be ill-clothed and badly-housed, to be weakened by starvation, cold and exposure, to be laid low by sickness or accident—and then to lie and watch, while the gaunt wolf of hunger creeps in upon you and gnaws out the heart of you, and tears up the bodies and souls of your wife and babies.

There was old Antanas, for instance; the winter came, and the place where he worked was a dark, unheated cellar, where you could see your breath all day, and where your fingers sometimes tried to freeze. So the old man's cough grew every day worse, until there came a time when it hardly ever stopped, and he had become a nuisance about the place. Then, too, a still more dreadful thing happened to him; he worked in a place where his feet were soaked in chemicals, and it was not long before they had eaten through his new boots. Then sores began to break out on his feet, and grow worse and worse; whether it was that his blood was bad, or there had been a cut, he could not say; but he asked the men about it, and learned that it was a regular thing—it was the saltpeter. Everyone felt it, sooner or later, and then it was all up with him, at least for that sort of work. The sores would never heal, but in the end his toes would drop off, if he did not quit. Yet old Antanas would not quit—he saw the suffering of his family, and he remembered what it had cost him to get a job. So he tied up his feet, and went on limping about and coughing, until at last he fell to pieces—all at once, and in a heap, like the One-Horse Shay. They carried him to a dry place and laid him on the floor, and that night two of the men helped him home. The poor old man was put to bed, and though he tried it every morning until the end, he never could get up again. He would lie there and cough and cough, day and night, wasting away to a mere skeleton. There came a time when there was so little flesh on him that the bones began to poke through—which was a horrible thing to see, or even think of. And one night he had a choking fit, and a little river of blood came out of his mouth. The family, wild with terror, sent for a doctor, and paid half a dollar to be told that there was nothing to be done. Mercifully the doctor did not say this so that the old man could hear, for he was still clinging to the faith that to-morrow or next day he would be better, and could go back to his job. The company had sent word to him that they would keep it for him—or, rather, Jurgis had bribed one of the men to come one Sunday afternoon and say they had. Diedas Antanas continued to believe it, while three more hemorrhages came and then at last one morning they found him stiff and cold. Things were not going well with them then, and though it nearly broke Teta Elzbieta's heart, they were forced to dispense with nearly all the decencies of a funeral; they had only a hearse and one hack for the women and children; and Jurgis, who was learning things fast, spent all Sunday making a bargain for these, and he made it in the presence of witnesses, so that when the man tried to charge him for all sorts of incidentals, he did not have to pay. For twenty-five years old Antanas Rudkos and his son had dwelt in the forest together, and it was hard to part in this way; perhaps it was just as well that Jurgis had to give all his attention to the task of having a funeral without being bankrupted, and so had no time to indulge in memories and grief.

Now the dreadful winter was come upon them. In the forests, all summer long, the branches of the trees do battle for light, and some of them lose and die; and then in the winter come the raging blasts, and the storms of snow and hail, and strew the ground with these weaker branches. Just so it was in Packingtown; the whole district braced itself for the struggle that was an agony, and those whose time was come died off in hordes. All the year round they had been serving as cogs in the great packing-machine; and now was the time for the renovating of the machine, and the replacing of damaged parts. There came pneumonia and grippe stalking among them, seeking for weakened constitutions; there was the annual harvest of those whom tuberculosis had been dragging down. There came cruel, cold and biting winds, and blizzards of snow, all testing relentlessly for failing muscles and impoverished blood. The packing-machines ground on remorselessly—and sooner or later came the day when the unfit one did not report for work; and then, with no time lost in waiting, and no inquiries or regrets, there was a chance for a new hand.

The new hands were here by the thousands. All day long the gates of the packing-houses were besieged by starving and penniless men; they came, literally by the thousands, every single morning, fighting with each other in mad frenzy for a chance for life. Blizzards and frightful cold made no difference to them, they were always on hand; they were on hand two hours before the sun rose, an hour before the work began. Sometimes their faces froze, sometimes their feet and their hands; sometimes they froze all together —but still they came, for they had no other place to go. One day Anderson advertised in the paper for two hundred men to cut ice; and all that day the homeless and starving of the jungle came trudging through the snow from all over its two hundred square miles. That night forty score of them crowded into the station-house of the stock-yards district—they filled the rooms, sleeping in each other's laps, toboggan fashion, and they piled on top of each other in the corridors, till the police shut the doors, and left some to freeze to death outside. On the morrow, before daybreak, there were three thousand at Anderson's, and the police reserve had to be sent for to quell the riot. Then Anderson's bosses picked out twenty of the biggest, and the papers had it that the "two hundred" was a printer's error.

Four or five miles to the eastward lay the lake, and over this the bitter winds came raging. Sometimes the thermometer would fall to ten or twenty degrees below zero at night, and in the morning the streets would be piled with snowdrifts up to the first-floor windows. The streets through which our friends had to go to their work were all unpaved and full of deep holes and gullies; in summer, when it rained hard, a man might have to wade to his waist to get to his house; and now in winter it was no joke getting through these places before light in the morning and after dark at night. They would wrap up in all they owned, but they could not wrap up against exhaustion; and many a man gave out in these battles with the snow-drifts, and lay down and fell asleep. And if it was bad for the men, one may imagine how the women and children fared. Some would ride in the cars, if the cars were running; but when you are making only five cents an hour, as was little Stanislovas, you do not like to spend that much to ride two miles. The children would come to the yards with great shawls about their ears, and so tied up that you could hardly find them—and still there would be accidents. One bitter morning in February the little boy who worked at the lard-machine with Stanislovas came about an hour late, and screaming with pain; they unwrapped him, and a man began vigorously rubbing his ears. As they were frozen stiff, it took only two or three rubs to break them short off, and then the little fellow lay down and rolled on the floor in his agony. As a result of this, little Stanislovas conceived a terror of the cold that was almost a mania. Every morning, when it came time to start for the yards, he would begin to cry and protest; nobody knew quite how to manage him, for threats did no good—it seemed to be something that he could not control, and they feared sometimes that he would go into convulsions. In the end it had to be arranged that he always went with Jurgis and came home with him again; often, when the snow was deep, the man would carry him the whole way on his shoulders. But sometimes Jurgis would be working until late at night, and then it was pitiful, for there was no place for the little fellow to wait, save in the doorways or in a corner of the killing-floor, and he would all but fall asleep there, and freeze to death.

There was no heat upon the killing-floor. The men might exactly as well have worked out of doors all winter. For that matter, there was very little heat anywhere in the building, except in the cooking-rooms and such places—and it was the men who worked in these who ran the most risk of all, because whenever they had to pass to another room they had to go through ice-cold corridors, and sometimes with nothing on above the waist except a sleeveless undershirt. In summer time the chilling-rooms were counted deadly places, for rheumatism and such things; but when it came to winter the men envied those who worked there—at least the chilling-rooms were kept at a precise temperature, and one could not freeze to death. On the killing-floor you might easily freeze, if the gang for any reason had to stop for a time. You were apt to be covered with blood, and it would freeze solid; if you leaned against a pillar you would freeze to that, and if you put your hand upon the blade of your knife, you would run a chance of leaving your skin on it. The men would tie up their feet in newspapers and old sacks, and these would be soaked in blood and frozen, and then soaked again, and so on until by night time a man would be walking on great lumps the size of the feet of an elephant. Now and then, when the bosses were not looking, you would see them plunging their feet and ankles into the steaming hot carcass of the steer, or darting across the room to the hot-water jets. The cruelest thing of all was that nearly all of them—all of those who used knives—were unable to wear gloves, and their arms would be white with frost and their hands would grow numb, and then of course there would be accidents. Also the air would be full of steam, from the hot water and the hot blood, so that you could not see five feet before you; then, with men rushing about at the speed they kept up on the killing-floor, and all with butcherknives, like razors, in their hands—well, it was to be counted as a wonder that there were not more men slaughtered than cattle.

And yet all this inconvenience they might have put up with if only it had not been for one thing—if only there had been some place where they might eat. It was not so very long ago that one of the lords of Packingtown said at a banquet that it was of no use to pay more money to the men in the yards, because it all went to the saloon-keeper. And this gentleman and his associates have provided for themselves a private dining-room, and for their managers and office-employees a great dining-hall, where they may obtain as good food as can be had in the city at cost; and for the fifty or sixty thousand men who work for them with their hands, they have not provided even so much as a bench to sit down on! When Jurgis had toiled from seven till twelve to produce wealth for this oratorical gentleman, he was welcome to eat his dinner standing upon the killing-floor, amid the stench in which he had worked; or else he might go and sit on the stairs, where it was colder yet; or he might sit outside, where it was probably below zero, and snowing; or else, finally, he might rush out, as did all his companions, to any one of the hundreds of saloons which stretched out their arms to him. To the west of the yards ran Ashland avenue, and here was an unbroken line of saloons —"Whiskey Row" they called it; to the north was Forty-seventh street, and here there were half a dozen to the block; and at the angle where these joined was "Whiskey Point," a space of fifteen or twenty acres, and containing one glue factory and about two hundred saloons, and not another store or shop of any sort whatever. One might walk among these and take his choice: "Hot pea-soup and boiled cabbage today." "Beef-stew now ready." "Sauerkraut and hot frankfurters. Walk in." "Bean soup and stewed lamb. Welcome." All of these things were printed in many languages, as were also the names of the resorts. These were infinite in their variety and appeal. There was the "Home Circle," and the "Cosy Corner." There were "Firesides," and "Hearthstones," and "Pleasure Palaces," and "Wonderlands." Nothing was too remote; there was an "Uncle Tom's Cabin," and a "Tivoli." Nothing was too fanciful; there were "Dream Castles," and "Music Lands," and "Love's Delights"— there was one place called "The Glory," and another called "The Vision." What-ever else they were called, they were sure to be called "Union Headquarters," and to hold out a welcome to working-men. There was always a warm stove, and a chair near it, and some friends to laugh and talk with. There was only one condition attached—you must drink. If you went in not intending to drink, you would be put out in no time, and if you were slow about going, like as not you would get your head split open with a beer-bottle in the bargain. But all of the men understood the convention, and drank; they believed that by it they were getting something for nothing—for they did not need to take more than one drink, and upon the strength of it they might fill themselves up with a good hot dinner. This did not always work out in practice, for there was almost sure to be a friend who would treat you, and then you would have to treat him. Then someone else would come in—and anyhow, a few drinks were good for a man who worked hard. As he went back he did not shiver so, he had more courage for his task; the deadly, brutalizing monotony of it did not afflict him so—he had ideas while he worked, and took a more cheerful view of his circumstances. On the way home, however, the shivering was apt to come on him again; and so he would have to stop once or twice to warm up against the cruel cold. As there were hot things to eat in this saloon too, he might get home late to his supper, or he might not get home at all. And then his wife might set out to look for him, and she too would feel the cold; and perhaps she would have some of the children with her—and so a whole family would drift into drinking, precisely as the current of a river drifts down stream. As if to make complete the picture, the oratorical gentleman and his associates paid their men in checks, refusing all requests to pay in coin; and where in Packingtown could a man go to have his check cashed but to a saloon, where he could pay for the favor by spending a good part of the money?

From all of these things Jurgis was saved because of Ona. He never would take but the one drink at noon-time; and so he got the reputation of being a surly fellow, and was not quite welcome at the saloons, and had to drift about from one to another. Then at night he would go straight home, helping Ona and Stanislovas, or often putting the former on a car. And when he got home perhaps he would have to trudge several blocks, and come staggering back through the snow-drifts with a bag of coal upon his shoulder. Home was not a very attractive place—at least not this winter. They had only been able to buy one stove, and this was a small one, and proved not big enough to warm even the kitchen in the bitterest weather. This made it hard for Teta Elzbieta all day, and for the children when they could not get to school. At night they would sit huddled around this stove, while they ate their supper off their laps; and then Jurgis and Jonas would smoke a pipe or two, after which they would all crawl into their beds to get warm, after putting out the fire to save the coal. Then they would have some frightful experiences, with the cruel cold. They would sleep with all their clothes on, including their overcoats, and put over them all the bedding and spare clothing they owned; the children would sleep all crowded into one bed, and yet even so they could not keep warm. The outside ones would be shivering and sobbing, crawling over the others and trying to get down into the center, and causing a fight. This old house with the leaky weather-boards was a very different thing from their cabins at home, with great thick walls plastered inside and outside with mud; and the cold which came upon them was a living thing, a demon-presence in the room. They would waken in the midnight hours, when everything was black; perhaps they would hear it yelling outside; or perhaps there would be death-like stillness, and that would be worse yet. They could feel the cold as it crept in through the cracks, reaching out for them with its icy, death-dealing fingers; and they would crouch and cower, and try to hide from it, all in vain. It would come, and it would come; a grisly thing, a spectre born in the black caverns of terror, a power primeval, cosmic, shadowing the tortures of the lost souls flung out to chaos and destruction. It was cruel, iron-hard; and hour after hour they would cringe in its grasp, alone in the silence. There would be no one to hear them if they cried out; there would be no help, no mercy. And so on until morning—when they would go out to another day of toil, a little weaker, a little nearer to the time when it would be their turn to be shaken from the tree.

8

THROUGH the earlier part of the winter our friends had plenty of work, and if they had not been just starting out housekeeping, they might have been able to lay by a little sum. As it was, however, there seemed never to be an end to the things they had to buy, and to the unforeseen contingencies. Once their water-pipes froze and burst; and when, in their ignorance they thawed them out, they had a terrible flood in their house. It happened while the men were away, and poor Teta Elzbieta rushed out into the street screaming for help, for she did not even know whether the flood could be stopped, or whether they were ruined for life. It was nearly as bad as the latter, they found in the end, for the plumber charged them seventy-five cents an hour, and seventy-five cents for another man who had stood and watched him, and included all the time the two had been going and coming; and also a charge for all sorts of material and extras. And then again, when they went to pay their January's installment on the house, the agent terrified them by asking them if they had had the insurance attended to yet. In answer to their inquiry he showed them a clause in the deed which provided that they were to keep the house insured for one thousand dollars, as soon as the present policy ran out, which would happen in a few days. Poor Teta Elzbieta, upon whom again fell the blow, demanded how much it would cost them. Seven dollars, the man said; and that night came Jurgis, grim and determined, requesting that the agent would be good enough to inform him, once for all, as to all the expenses they were liable for. The deed was signed now, he said, with sarcasm proper to the new way of life he had learned—the deed was signed, and so the agent had no longer anything to gain by keeping quiet. And Jurgis looked the fellow squarely in the eye as he said this, and so he did not waste any time in conventional protests, but read him the deed. They would have to renew the insurance every year; they would have to pay the taxes, about ten dollars a year; they would have to pay the water-tax, about six dollars a year—(Jurgis silently resolved to shut off the hydrant). This, besides the interest and the monthly installments, would be all—unless by chance the city should happen to decide to put in a sewer, or to lay sidewalk. Yes, said the agent, they would have to have these, whether they wanted them or not, if the city said so. The sewer would cost them about twenty-two dollars, and the sidewalk fifteen if it was wood, twenty-five if it was cement.

So Jurgis went home again; it was a relief to know the worst, at any rate, so that he could no more be surprised by fresh demands. He saw now how they had been plundered; but they were in for it, and there was no turning back. They could only go on and make the fight and win—for defeat was a thing that could not even be thought of.

Little by little they were paying back their debt to Jonas and Marija—though the latter, with her preposterous soft-heartedness, would spend a good part of it every week for things which she saw they needed. Marija was the capitalist of the party, for she had become an expert can-painter by this time. She was getting fourteen cents for every hundred and ten cans, and as she could paint more than two cans every minute, she was laying away a neat sum every week. Marija felt, so to speak, that she had her own hand on the throttle, and the neighborhood was vocal with her rejoicings.

Yet her friends would shake their heads and tell her to go slow; they could not prevail upon her, however, and so when the crash did come, Marija's grief was cruel to see. For her canning-factory shut down! Marija would about as soon have expected to see the sun shut down—the huge establishment had been to her a thing akin to the planets and the seasons. But now it was shut! They had not given her even a day's warning; they had not given her any explanation; they had simply posted a notice one Saturday that all hands would be paid off that afternoon, and would not resume work for at least a month. And that was all there was to it.

It was the holiday rush that was over, the girls said, in answer to Marija's inquiries; after it there was always a slack. Sometimes the factory would start up on half time after awhile, but there was no telling—it had been known to stay closed until way into the summer. The prospects were bad at present, for truckmen who worked in the store-rooms said that these were piled up to the ceilings, so that the firm could not have found room for another week's output of cans. And they had turned off three-quarters of these men, which was a still worse sign, since it meant that there were no orders to be filled. It was all a swindle, can-painting, said the girls—you were crazy with delight because you were making twelve or fourteen dollars a week, and saving half of it; but you had to spend it all keeping alive while you were out, and so your pay was really only half what you thought.

Marija came home, and because she was a person who could not rest without danger of explosion, they first had a great house-cleaning, and then she set out to search Packingtown for a job to fill up the gap. As nearly all the canning-establishments were shut down, and all the girls hunting work, it will be readily understood that Marija did not find any. Then she took to trying the stores and saloons, and when this failed she even traveled over into the far-distant regions near the lake-front, where lived the rich people in great palaces, and begged there for some sort of work that could be done by a person who did not know English. It was very hard for Marija to believe that in all this vast city there was nothing for her brawny arms to do.

The men upon the killing-floor felt also the effects of the slump which had turned Marija out; but they felt it in a different way, and a way which made Jurgis understand at last all the bitterness of the men. The big packers did not turn their hands off and close down, like the canning-factories; but they began to run for shorter and shorter hours. If they had wished to set forth the fact that all their employees together were of less importance to them than a single one of the animals they killed, they could not have managed the thing differently than they did.

They had always required the men to be on the killing-floor and ready for work at seven o'clock, although there was almost never any work to be done till the buyers out in the yards had gotten to work, and some cattle had come over the chutes. That would often be ten or eleven o'clock, which was bad enough, in all conscience; but now, in the slack season, they would perhaps not have a thing for their men to do till late in the afternoon—and still every mother's son of them had to be on the killing-floor at seven o'clock in the morning! And there they would have to loaf around, in a place where the thermometer might be twenty degrees below zero! At first one would see them running about, or skylarking with each other, trying to keep warm, but before the day was over they would become quite chilled through and exhausted, and when the cattle finally came, so near frozen that to move was an agony. And then suddenly the place would spring into activity, and the merciless "speeding-up" would begin!

There were weeks at a time when Jurgis went home after such a day as this with not more than two hours' work to his credit—which meant about thirty-five cents. There were many days when the total was less than half an hour, and others when there was none at all. Not half a dozen times in the whole long agony of that winter was there work early enough in the morning to justify their coming before daylight. The general average was about six hours a day, which meant for Jurgis about six dollars a week, and this six hours of work would be done after standing on the killing-floor till one o'clock, or perhaps even three or four o'clock in the afternoon. It would be done all in one heart-breaking rush, without allowing a single instant for rest. Like as not there would come a rush of cattle at the very end of the day, which the men would have to dispose of before they went home, often working by electric-light till nine or ten, or even twelve or one o'clock, and without a single instant for a bite of supper. Jurgis tried hard to find out the reason for all this, but the men did not understand it, except vaguely. They knew that they were at the mercy of the cattle. Perhaps the buyers would be holding off for better prices; if they could scare the shippers into thinking that they meant to buy nothing that day, they could get their own terms. For some reason the cost of fodder for cattle in the yards was much above the market price—and you were not allowed to bring your own fodder! Then, too, a number of cars were apt to arrive late in the day, now that the roads were often tied up with snow, and the packers would buy these cattle that night, to get them cheaper; and then would come into play their iron-clad rule, that all cattle must be killed the same day they were bought. There was no use kicking about this—there had been one delegation after another from the men to see about it, only to be told that it was the rule, and that there was not the slightest chance of its ever being altered. Every man who worked for them had to stay and work, over time or any other time, and it made no difference what the hour was. Sundays and holidays, as well as other days, Jurgis was liable to be called out; Christmas eve he worked till nearly one o'clock in the morning, and on Christmas day he was on the killing-floor at seven o'clock!

All this was about as near to hell as a man would care to get; and yet it was not the worst by any means. For after all the hard work they did, the chances were that they would not get any pay for a good part of it! Jurgis had once been among those who scoffed at the idea of these huge concerns cheating; and so now he could appreciate the full bitterness of the fact that it was precisely their size which enabled them to cheat with impunity. Jurgis saw now that they cheated; that they cheated constantly and systematically, that they cheated anywhere and anyhow—the tenth part of the head of a pin was not too small a thing to serve for a motive. They have made their fortune out of the discovery that the tenth part of the head of a pin is a valuable thing, if you can get a million more to add to it. One of the rules on the killing-floor was that a man who was one minute late was docked an hour; and this was economical, for he was made to work the balance of the hour—he was not allowed to "stand around." It was narrated of Charles Lamb that when rebuked for coming late to work, he replied that he went away early; and with somewhat similar ingenuity the packers had it arranged that a man was not credited with any time he might be made to work if he came ahead of time. Often when the gang was all on hand the bosses would start them up ten or fifteen minutes before the whistle, and get that much out of them for nothing. And this same custom they carried over to the end of the day—they did not pay the gang for any fraction of an hour—for "broken time." A man might work full fifty minutes, but if there was no work to fill out the hour there was no pay for him. Thus the end of every day was a sort of lottery; and sometimes there would be a struggle, all but breaking into open war, between the bosses and the men—the former trying to rush a job through, and the latter trying to stretch it out. You might tell that story to most people, and they would say it was a fairy tale; and yet it was a regular incident of Jurgis's life, the bitterness of it burning deeper into his soul every day. He blamed the bosses for it, though the truth to be told it was not always their fault; for the packers kept them frightened for their lives, each one having half a dozen trying to supplant him, and liable to succeed if he fell behind the standard. And when one was in danger of falling behind—what was easier than to catch up by making the gang work a while, "for the church?" This was a savage witticism the men had, which Jurgis had to have explained to him. They all read the newspapers, these men, and while that knew that Anderson and Smith and the rest of the packers "hogged" their money, they knew also that there were other great captains of industry who were grinding their men to pieces upon the same horrible system, and yet had a fine time posing as philanthropists and public benefactors, scattering largesses of libraries and hospitals and churches. So when the men were set to work a little early, or when they were kept half an hour over to finish up a bunch of steers, they would nod to each other and say grimly, "This is for a library," or "Now we're paying for a church."

It might be well to point out that in all this the packers were perfectly within their rights. To lie and to cheat are an essential part of that fundamental privilege of a business men to manage his own business in his own way; for if people do not like the way a man manages his business, their remedy is to leave him alone. Jurgis, for instance, now lived in a free country, and shared in its privileges; and if he did not like the way they did things at Smith's, he was perfectly at liberty to leave whenever he felt like it. He might go, let us say, to Anderson's; and when he found that Smith and Anderson, together with all the other packers in Chicago, had gotten together and agreed to treat all their hands alike, it was his privilege to take his family and pay one or two hundred dollars railroad fare and go to New York, or St. Louis, or Kansas City, or Omaha, where there were more packing-houses. And when he had discovered that these, too, were owned by Smith and by Anderson, and conducted in the same unsatisfactory manner, he was permitted to take himself out upon the broad, snow-covered prairies of this land of liberty, and lie down and die there, as a witness to the fact that he was no man's slave. That he did not do this, but stayed and worked on for Smith, and took whatever part of his pay Smith chose to give him, was probably because he was not a free-born American, but a low-down and ignorant foreigner.

The sense of justice was not altogether dead in him, however, and every day there was more hatred in his soul. One of the consequences was that he was no longer perplexed when he heard men talk of fighting for their rights. He felt like fighting now, himself, and when the Irish delegate of the butcher-helpers' union came to him a second time, Jurgis received him in a far different spirit. A wonderful idea it now seemed to him, this idea of the men—that by combining they might be able to make a stand and conquer the packers! Jurgis wondered who it was that had first thought of it; and when he was told that it was a common thing for men to do in America, he got his first inkling of the great fact that there might be some real meaning in the phrase, "a free country." The delegate explained to him how it depended upon their being able to get every man to join and stand by the organization; and then

Jurgis signified that he was willing to do his share. Before another month was by, four out of the five working members of his family had union cards—the exception being little Stanislovas, because a lard-boys' union was still a thing of the future. They all had union buttons, and wore them conspicuously and with pride; and for fully a week they were quite blissfully happy, thinking that belonging to a union meant an end of all their troubles.

But only ten days after she had joined, Marija's canning-factory closed down, and that blow quite staggered them. They could not understand why the union had not prevented it, and the very first time she attended a meeting Marija got up and made a speech about it. It was a business meeting, and was transacted in English; of the girls of the can-painters' union, probably not one-twentieth understood a word of Lithuanian. But that made no difference to Marija; she said what was in her, and all the pounding of the chairman's gavel and all the uproar and confusion in the room could not prevail—she made her speech. Quite apart from her own troubles she was boiling over with a general sense of the injustice of it, and she told what she thought of the packers, and what she thought of a world where such things were allowed to happen; and then, while the echoes of the hall rang with the shock of her terrible voice, she sat down again and fanned herself, and the meeting gathered itself together and proceeded to discuss the election of a recording secretary.

Jurgis, too, had an adventure the first time he attended a union meeting, but it was not of his own seeking. Jurgis went with the desire to get into an inconspicuous corner and see what was done—but it was precisely this attitude of silent and open-eyed attention that marked him out for a victim. Tommy Finnegan was a little Irishman, with big staring eyes and a wild aspect, a "hoister" by trade, and a harmless enough fellow, only badly cracked. Somewhere back in the far distant past Tommy Finnegan had had a strange experience, and the burden of it rested upon him. All the rest of his life he had done nothing but try to make it understood; when he talked he caught his victim by the buttonhole, and his face kept coming closer and closer—which was trying, because his teeth were so bad. Jurgis did not mind that, only he was frightened. The method of operation of the higher intelligences was Tom Finnegan's theme, and he desired to find out if Jurgis had ever considered that the representation of things in their present similarity might be altogether unintelligible upon a more elevated plane. There were assuredly wonderful mysteries about the developing of these things; and then, becoming confidential, Mr. Finnegan proceeded to tell of some experiences of his own. "If ye have iver had onything to do wid spherrits," said he and looked inquiringly at Jurgis, who kept shaking his head. "Niver mind, niver mind," continued the other, "but thair influences may be operating upon ye; it's shure as I'm tellin' ye, it's them that has the reference to the im-mejit surroundin's that has the most of influence. It was vouchsafed to me in me youthful days to be acquainted with spherrits"—and so Tommy Finnegan went on, expounding a system of philosophy, while the perspiration came out on Jurgis's forehead, so great was his agitation and embarrassment. In the end one of the men, seeing his plight, came over and rescued him; but it was a month before he was able to find some one to explain things to him, and meanwhile his fear lest the strange little Irishman should get him cornered again was enough to keep him dodging about the room a whole evening.

He never missed a meeting, however. He had picked up a few words of English by this time, and friends would help him to understand. They were often very turbulent meetings, with half a dozen men declaiming at once, in as many dialects of English; but the speakers were all desperately in earnest, and Jurgis was in earnest, too, for he understood that a fight was on, and that it was his fight. Since the time of his disillusionment, Jurgis had sworn to trust no man, except in his own family. But here suddenly he discovered that he had brothers in affliction, and allies. They had been into battle, and had lost; and wounded and bloody, crushed and trampled beneath iron hoofs—suddenly they had found a hope of deliverance, in union! And so they had united, with all the fervor of desperation. "Get together! Stay together!"—that was their cry; and they talked it, they preached it, with the ardor of religious devotees; it was their one chance for life, and the struggle became a kind of crusade. So out of all this nightmare of horror there was borne a new vision, a new hope; there was a gleam of light in the midnight sky, and men cried out that it was a dawn. Jurgis had always been a member of the church, because it was the right thing to be, but the church had never touched him, he left all that for the women. Here, however, was a new religion—one that did touch him, that took hold of every fiber of him, and with all the zeal and fury of a convert he went out as a missionary. There were many non-union men among the Lithuanians, and with these he would labor and wrestle in prayer, trying to show them the right. Sometimes they would be obstinate and refuse to see it, and, alas, Jurgis was not always patient. He forgot how he himself had been blind, a short time ago—after the fashion of all crusaders since the original ones, who set out to spread the gospel of Brotherhood by force of arms.

There was a struggle going on between the unions and the packers, a struggle that never ceased; day and night they were wrestling for the tiniest bit of advantage, and each week at the meeting there were new interviews to be reported, and wars and rumors of war in the air. The men wanted the packers to pay them in money, so that they would not have to cash checks in saloons. They wanted to prevent their taking new men on, now that they did not have half enough work for those they already had. They were trying to get them to abandon the rule of not keeping the cattle over—to set a limit to the overtime, and to the lateness of the hour at which a man was liable to work. They wanted, also, half an hour to eat supper in, when they had to work at night. And most important of all, they wanted to put a stop to the "speeding-up."

Editors of newspapers, and statesmen, and presidents of employers' associations and universities, and other pillars of things as they are, were busied to see that the public was kept informed about this. "Limitation of the output" it was called, and it was the chief of the outrages of union domination. Lazy workingmen presuming to get together and say to their employers how much work they would do for their wages! Trying to restrict the productive capacity of the factories, and bring ruin upon this great country! Trying to tie up the food industry in Chicago and raise the price of every poor man's dinner! Many other things they were trying to do, so these wise and powerful ones declared—and charity compels one to believe that not all of them really understood that what the unions were really trying to do was to put a stop to murder. For murder it was that went on there upon the killing-floor, systematic, deliberate and hideous murder—and there was no other word for it, and nothing else to be said about it. They were slaughtering men there, just as certainly as they were slaughtering cattle; they were grinding the bodies and souls of them, and turning them into dollars and cents. Jurgis talked with some who worked in the sausage-rooms, and who told him how now and then some one would lose a finger in the dangerous cutting-machines; and how when that happened they would stop the machine, but only for a minute or so; if they could not find the finger they would let it go and call it sausage. And that was grinding up men, as anyone will admit; yet it was not one bit more actually grinding them than the system of "speeding-up." A thousand devils with whips or white-hot irons could not have filled human creatures more full of terror, or goaded them to more agonized efforts than did the daily routine of the packing-houses, with spies and bosses prowling here and there, nagging and yelling at men and women and children, cursing them, kicking them, batting them over the heads, sometimes spitting into their faces—while outside the starving thousands struggled and fought for a chance to take their places, when at last they could hold out no longer, but fell in their tracks and dragged themselves home to die.

9

ONE OF the first consequences of the discovery of the union was that Jurgis became desirous of learning English. He wanted to know what was going on at the meetings, and to be able to take part in them; and so he began to look about him, and to try to pick up words. The children, who were at school, and learning fast, would teach him a few; and a friend loaned him a little book that had some in it, and Ona would read them to him. Then Jurgis became sorry that he could not read himself; and later on in the winter, when some one told him that there was a night-school that was free, he went and enrolled. After that, every evening that he got home from the yards in time he would go to the school; he would go, even if he were in time for only half an hour. They were teaching him both reading and speaking English—and they would have taught him other things, too, if only he had had a little time. He would have liked to have Ona go also; he promised himself that some day the time would come when she would not have to work herself to death, but might have some strength left to go with him.

Also the union made another great difference with him—it made him begin to pay attention to the country. It was the beginning of democracy with him. It was a little state, the union; a miniature republic; its affairs were every man's affairs, and every man had a real say about them. Every man had rights, which other men had to respect; and they did respect them, the laws were enforced. And just as soon as Jurgis had come to understand this and to get used to it, he had a standard by which to judge the larger state, the country in which he lived, in which the laws were not enforced, and in which a man, as a man, was nothing.

In other words, in the union Jurgis learned to talk politics. In the place where he had come from there had not been any politics. Lithuania constitutes five provinces of the Russian Empire, and there Jurgis had learned to think of the government as an affliction like the lightning and the hail, something that was there, and had been there and would be there forever, leaving a man nothing to do but to keep out of its way. "Duck, little brother, duck," the wise old peasants would tell one; "everything passes away." And when Jurgis had first came to America, he had supposed that it was the same. He had heard people say that America was a free country—but what did that mean to him? He found that here, precisely as in Russia, there were rich men who owned everything, so that there was no way to live save by serving them; and if one could not find any chance to serve, was not the hunger he began to feel the very same sort of hunger? Also there were policemen to see that he did not steal, and kept out of people's way; only in Russia the policemen were friendly, and would call one Brother while they pushed him along—whereas the policemen here in America were Cossacks. Out in the stockyards they were all Irishmen, and rated a Slav of any sort as lower than a yellow dog. They would curse at him and kick him; they would search him on the street, or break into his own house, if they felt like it, and if he protested, like as not they would crack his head open. And if that did not shut him up, they would drag him to the station-house and lock him in and he might stay there two or three days without any one's knowing where he was. Often they did not even enter his name on the station-house register—that was the way they laughed at the law with a poor man. It would be worse yet if he were taken to court, for they would charge him with anything that came into their heads, from drunkenness to burglary, and when he told his story to the judge, the interpreter would say that he was confessing and begging for mercy!

When Jurgis had been working about three weeks at Smith's, there had come to him one noon-time a man who was employed as a night-watchman, and who had asked him if he would not like to take out naturalization papers and become a citizen. Jurgis did not know what he meant, but the man explained the numerous advantages. In the first place it would not cost him anything, and it would get him half a day off, with his pay just the same; and then when election-time came he would be able to vote—and there were opportunities in that. Jurgis was naturally glad to accept, and so the night-watchman said a few words to the boss, and Jurgis was excused for the rest of the day. When later on he wanted a holiday to get married, he could not get it; and as for a holiday with pay just the same—what power that wrought that miracle heaven only knew! However, he went with the man, who picked up several other newly-landed immigrants, Poles, Lithuanians, and Slovaks, and took them all outside, where stood a great four-horse tally-ho coach, with fifteen or twenty men already in it. It was a fine chance to see the sights of the city, and the party had a merry time, with plenty of beer handed up from inside. So they drove downtown, and stopped before an imposing granite building, which had taken some twenty years to finish, and had cost the city uncounted millions of dollars; in it they interviewed an official, who had the papers all ready; with only the names to be filled in. Each man in turn took an oath of which he did not understand a word, and then he was presented with a handsome ornamented document with a big red seal and the shield of the United States upon it, and was told that he had become a citizen of the great republic, and the equal of the president himself.

A month or two later Jurgis had another interview with this same man, who got him a second holiday and told him where to go to register. And then finally when election-day came, the packing-houses posted a notice that men who desired to vote might remain away until nine that morning—it was supposed to be a legal holiday—and the same night-watchman took Jurgis and the rest of his flock into the back-room of a saloon, and showed each of them where and how to mark a ballot, and then gave each two dollars, and took them to the polling place, where there was a policeman on duty to see that they got through all right. Jurgis felt quite proud of this good luck, till he got home and met Jonas, who had been sharper than he. Jonas had been making inquiries for himself, and had taken the leader aside and whispered to him, offering to vote three times for four dollars, which offer had been accepted.

And now in the union Jurgis met men who explained all this mystery to him: and he learned that America differed from Russia, in that its government existed under the dead forms of a democracy. The officials who ruled it, and got all the graft, had to be elected first; and so there were two rival sets of grafters, known as political parties, and the one got the office which bought the most votes. Now and then the election was very close, and that was the time the poor man came in. In the stock-yards this was only in national and state elections, for in local elections the democratic party always carried everything. The ruler of this district was, therefore, the democratic boss, a little Irishman named Tom Cassidy. Cassidy held an important party office in the state, and bossed even the mayor of the city, it was said; it was his boast that he carried the stockyards district in his pocket. He was an enormously rich man—he had a hand in all the big graft in the neighborhood. It was Cassidy, for instance, who owned that dump which Jurgis and Ona had seen the first day of their arrival. Not only did he own the dump, but owned the brick-factory as well; and first he took out the clay and made it into bricks, and then he had the city bring garbage to fill up the hole, so that he could build flimsy houses and sell them to people for three times what they were worth. Then, too, he sold the bricks to the city, at his own price, and the city came and got them in its own wagons. And also he owned the other hole near by, where the stagnant water was; and it was he who cut the ice and sold it to the people; and what was more, if the men told truth, he had not had to pay any taxes for the water, and he had built the ice-house out of city lumber and had not had to pay anything for that. The newspapers had got hold of that story, and there had been a scandal; but Cassidy had hired somebody to confess and take all the blame and then skip the country. It was said too that he had built his brick-kiln in the same way, and that the workmen were on the city pay-roll while they did it; however, one had to press closely to get these things out of the men, for it was not their business, and Tom Cassidy was a good man to stand in with. A note signed by him was equal to a job any time at the packing-houses; and also he employed a good many men himself, and worked them only eight hours a day, and paid them the highest wages. This gave him many friends—all of whom he had gotten together into the War-whoop League, whose club house you might see just outside of the yards. It was the biggest club house, and the biggest club in all Chicago; and they had prize fights every now and then, and cockfights, and even dog-fights; all these were against the law, but the law was nothing to Cassidy. The police-men in the district all belonged to the league (which was also against the law), and instead of suppressing the fights, they sold tickets for them. The man that had taken Jurgis to be naturalized was one of these "Indians," as they were called; and on election-day there would be hundreds of them out, and all with big wads of money in their pockets, and free drinks at every saloon in the district. That was another thing, the men said—all the saloon-keepers had to be "Indians," and to put up on demand, otherwise they could not do business on Sundays, nor dare they have any gambling at all. In the same way Cassidy had all the jobs in the fire-department at his disposal, and all the rest of the city graft in that district; he was building a block of flats somewhere up on Ashland Avenue, and the man who was overseeing it for him was drawing pay as a city inspector of sewers. The city inspector of water-pipes had been dead and buried for over a year, but somebody was still drawing his pay for Cassidy. The city inspector of sidewalks was a bar-keeper at the War-whoop cafe—and maybe he could not make it uncom-fortable for any tradesman who did not stand in with Cassidy!

Even the packers were in awe of him, so the men said. It gave them pleasure to believe this, for Cassidy stood as the people's man, and boasted of it boldly when election day came. The packers had wanted a bridge at Ashland Avenue, but they had not been able to get it till they had seen Cassidy; and it was the same with "Bubbley Creek," which the city had threatened to make the packers cover over, till Cassidy had come to their aid. "Bubbley Creek" is an arm of the Chicago river, and forms the southern boundary of the yards; all the drainage of the square mile of packing-houses empties into it, so that it is really a great open sewer a hundred or two feet wide. One long arm of it is blind, and the filth stays there forever and a day. The grease and chemicals that are poured into it undergo all sorts of strange transformations, which are the cause of its name. It is constantly in motion, as if huge fish were feeding in it, or great leviathans disporting themselves in its depths; bubbles will rise to the surface and burst, and make rings two or three feet wide. Here and there the grease and filth have caked solid, and the creek looks like a bed of lava; chickens walk about on it, feeding, and many times an unwary stranger has started to stroll across, and vanished and never been seen again. The packers used to leave it that way, till every now and then the surface would catch on fire and burn furiously, and the fire-department would have to come and put it out. Once, however, an ingenious stranger came and started to gather this filth in scows, to make soap out of;

then the packers took the cue, and got out an injunction to stop him, and afterwards gathered it themselves. The banks of "Bubbley Creek" are plastered thick with hairs, and this also the packers gather, and clean.

And there were things even stranger than this, according to the gossip of the men. The packers had secret mains, it was said, and were stealing the city water by the millions of gallons every year. That meant hundreds of thousands of dollars in their pockets; and make believe that Cassidy was not coming in for a piece of that pie! Green as he was to Chicago, Jurgis could hardly believe that story; but some time afterwards the papers were full of the scandal, and the city government was forced to dig round the packing-houses and investigate. They came upon several unregistered water-mains—only the night before these had all been dug out and cut and stopped, and the plugs treated with chemicals to make it seem that they were many years old. Then, after the impudent newspapers had had time to satisfy themselves, one night the mains were again connected and buried, and once more there was a long lull, until this story too began to be whispered.

The great advantage that the packers enjoy in these things is that they are so big that people will not believe they can be dishonest; they are a national institution, and it is absurd to suppose that they would stoop to things like this. And all the time the fact is that it is exactly by stooping to things like this that they have become big! And then the foolish people keep talking about the risk—as if there were risk in doing anything at all in Chicago, unless you are poor! They talk about the loss to their reputation, and so on—as if the packers had any more need of reputation than a highwayman who knocks you out with a club! The men used to laugh at all this, understanding it to the full; they had no end of it, with visitors wandering about the place questioning them. From the room where they kill the hogs, in each of the plants, go daily a certain number of carcasses marked with red tags: "U. S. Condemned." These hogs have been found to be tuberculous, which means that the flesh had ptomaines in it. These ptomaines are deadly poisons—and not germs which cooking can kill, but poisons, which will remain and be fatal, no matter what may be done to the meat. The government requires that these carcasses be "tanked," that is, destroyed and turned into fertilizer; and it has stringent regulations as to exactly how it shall be done. The tanks are to be sealed at the bottom by a government employee, and the seals may not be removed till certain things have been done to destroy the meat. And with these laws before them, the men found it quite impossible to convince any inquirer that these tanks were ever kept open, and the condemned meat, that was thrown in at the top, taken out at the bottom and made into sausage. Yet Jurgis met man after man who had seen this done with his own eyes, and some who had helped to do it. He grew interested, and found that the knowledge of it was an every day, matter-of-fact thing among the men; and they would laugh, and tell how newspaper reporters and visiting wise men had demanded to know if they would make affidavit to it, and been answered, "Certainly, if you will go under bond to find me a job for the rest of my life!"

Yet the visitors need not have given up in despair; there were plenty of other things they might have seen with their own eyes, if they were fairly lucky in dodging the "spotters" of the companies. It was quite easy, for instance, to be an eye-witness of how the law regarding meat packed for shipment was heeded. Anyone can get this law from the Bureau of Animal Industries in Washington, and read how there must be an official inspector, with a force of assistants, wherever meat is packed and shipped; and that he shall examine each package, and then affix a numbered paper stamp, which he shall then cancel in a manner elaborately specified—so that the wavy lines of the cancellation shall run over each side of the stamp. The object, of this is, of course, that the stamp shall be canceled, after it is on the box and not before; and when the visitor has made sure of that, there are several thousands of employees in Packingtown who can tell him a dozen places to go and watch, while the foreman of the shipping-room goes over to the far-distant inspector's office and gets a big bunch of canceled stamps, and comes back and pastes one on each tightly-nailed box of meat. There were men with whom Jurgis talked at the union meetings who had been working in the shipping-room for years, and had never seen that law complied with once in all the time.

There was never any inspection of meat at all after it left the killing-floor, save by the packers themselves, and with meat intended for export. Jurgis asked why this was, and the men told him that there were some foreign countries in which the laws were enforced. For this reason all the best meat was sent abroad—it was impossible to get it in this country, not even the richest hotels and clubs could get it. The good went to France and England, and the very best to Germany, which was apparently the one country there was no deceiving. Germany had caused the packers no end of trouble—for which, with characteristic ingenuity, they had recouped themselves by putting out imitations of German meat for home markets! The great Anderson printing-plant made labels by the tens and hundreds of thousands, French, German, Italian, and what not; one of the men had some of them in his pocket and showed a whole set, for smoked and canned meats, labeled in brilliant colors; "August Bauer, Frankfort-Am-Main."

Jurgis heard of these things little by little, in the gossip of those who were obliged to perpetrate them; every time you met a person from a new department, you heard of new swindles and new crimes. There was, for instance, a Lithuanian who was a cattle-butcher for the plant where Marija had worked, which killed meat for canning only; and to hear this man describe the animals which came to his killing-floor would have been worth while for a Dante or a Zola. It seemed that they must have agencies all over the country, to hunt out old and crippled and diseased cattle to be canned. On the prairies nearby, for instance, were hundreds of farms which supplied the city with milk; and all the cows that developed lumpy jaw, or fell sick, or dried up of old age—they kept them till they had a carload, which was twenty, and then shipped them to this place to be canned. Here came also cattle which had been fed on "whiskey-malt," the refuse of the breweries, and had become what the men called "steerly"—which means covered with boils that were full of matter. It was a nasty job killing these, for when you plunged your knife into them they would burst, and splash foul-smelling stuff into your face; and when a man's sleeves were smeared with blood, and his hands steeped in it, how was he ever to wipe his face, or to clear his eyes so that he could see? It was enough to make anybody sick, to think that people had to eat such meat as this; but they must be eating it—for the canners were going on preparing it year after year! There must be a big graft in this too for the government inspectors; all they ever did was to order cut out any part of the carcass that was green and yellow, and then pass the rest. No doubt it was stuff such as this that made the "embalmed beef" that had killed several times as many United States soldiers as all the bullets of the Spaniards; only the army beef, besides, was not fresh canned, it was old stuff that had been lying for years in the cellars; and Jurgis's informant added that the old scoundrel who had been Secretary of War and gotten that graft was now an honorable senator in Washington.

Then one Sunday evening, Jurgis sat puffing his pipe by the kitchen-stove, and talking with an old fellow whom Jonas had introduced, and who worked in the canning-rooms at Anderson's, and then Jurgis learned a few things about the great and only Anderson canned-goods, which are a national institution. They were regular alchemists at Anderson's; they advertised a mushroom catsup, and the men who made it did not know what mushroom looked like. They advertised "potted chicken,"—and it was like the boarding-house soup of the comic papers, through which a chicken had walked with rubbers on. Perhaps they had a secret process for making chickens chemically—who knows? said Jurgis's friend; the things that went into the mixture were tripe, and the fat of pork, and beef suet, and hearts of beef, and finally the waste ends of veal, when they had any. They put these up in several grades, and sold them at several prices; but the contents of the cans all came out of the same hopper. And then there was "potted ham," and "devilled ham"—de-vyled, as the men called it. "De-vyled" ham was made out of the waste ends of smoked beef, that were too small to be sliced by the machines; and also tripe, dyed with chemicals so that it would not show white; and trimmings of hams and corned beef; and potatoes, skins and all;

and finally the hard cartilaginous gullets of beef, after the tongues had been cut out. All this ingenious mixture was ground up and flavored with spices to make it taste like something to the dear guileless public. Anybody who could invent a new imitation had been sure of a fortune from old Anderson, said Jurgis's informant; but it was hard to tell anything new to a man who even went out and gathered up carloads of cinder along the railroad tracks, and brought them in and powdered them, to adulterate his bone fertilizers with! Up to a year or two ago it had been the custom to kill horses in the yards—ostensibly for fertilizer; but after long agitation the newspapers had been able to make the public realize that the horses were being canned; now it was against the law to kill horses in Packingtown, and the law was really complied with—for the present at any rate. Any day, however, one might see sharp-horned and shaggy-haired creatures running with the sheep—and yet what a job you would have to get the public to believe that a good part of what it buys for lamb and mutton is really goat's flesh!

There is another interesting set of statistics that one might gather as his acquaintance broadened in Packingtown, and that is of the afflictions of the workers. When Jurgis had first inspected the packing-plants with Szadwilas, he had marveled while he listened to the tale of all the things that were made out of the carcasses of animals, and of all the lesser industries that were maintained there; now he found that each one of these lesser industries was a separate little inferno, in its way as horrible as the killing-floor, the source and fountain of them all. The workers in each of them had their own peculiar diseases; and the wandering visitor might be skeptical about all the swindles, but he could not be skeptical about these, for the worker bore the evidence of them about on his own person—generally he had only to hold out his hand.

There were the men in the pickle rooms, for instance, where old Antanas had gotten his death; scarce a one of these that had not some spot of horror on his person. Let a man so much as scrape his finger pushing a truck in the pickle-rooms, and like as not he would have a sore that would put him out of the world; all the joints in his fingers might be eaten by the acid, one by one. Of the butchers and floormen, the beef-boners and trimmers, and all those who used knives, you could scarcely find a person who had the use of his thumb; time and time again the base of it had been slashed, till it was a mere lump of flesh against which the man pressed the knife to hold it. The hands of these men would be cris-crossed with cuts, until you could no longer pretend to count them or to trace them. They would have no nails—they had worn them off pulling hides; their knuckles were swollen so that their fingers spread out like a fan. There were men who worked in the cooking-rooms, in the midst of steam and sickening odors, by artificial light; in these rooms the germs of tuberculosis might live for two years, but the supply is renewed every hour. There were the beef-luggers, who carried two hundred pound quarters into the refrigerator-cars; this was a fearful kind of work, that began at four o'clock in the morning, and that wore out the most powerful men in a few years. There were those who worked in the chilling-rooms, and whose special disease was rheumatism; the time limit that a man could work in the chilling-rooms was said to be five years. There were the wool-pluckers, whose hands went to pieces even sooner than the hands of the pickle-men; the pelts of the sheep had to be painted with acid to loosen the wool. and then the pluckers had to pull out this wool with their bare hands, till the acid had eaten their fingers off. There were those who made the tins for the canned meat; and their hands too were a maze of cuts, and any cut might cause blood-poisoning; some worked at the stamping machines, and it was very seldom that one could work long at these at the pace that was set and not give out and forget himself and have a part of his hands chopped off. There were the "hoisters," as they were called, whose task it was to press the lever which lifted the dead cattle off the floor; they ran along upon a rafter, peering down through the damp and the steam. Old man Anderson's architects had not built the killing-room for the convenience of the hoisters, and so every few feet they would have to stoop under a beam, say four feet above the one they ran on; this got them into the habit of stooping, so that in a few years they would be walking like chimpanzees. No man who worked as a hoister had ever been known to reach the age of fifty years. Worst of any, however, were the fertilizer men, and those who served in the rendering-rooms. These could not be shown to the visitor—for the odor of the fertilizer men would scare any ordinary visitor at a hundred yards, and as for the other men who worked in tank-rooms full of steam, and in which there were open vats upon a level with the floor, their peculiar trouble was that they fell into the vats; and when they were fished out there was never enough of them left to be worth exhibiting. Sometimes they would be overlooked for days, till all but the bones of them had gone out to the world as Anderson's Pure Leaf Lard!

DURING the early part of the winter the family had money enough to live and a little over to pay their debts with; but when the earnings of Jurgis fell from nine or ten dollars a week to five or six, there was no longer anything to spare. The winter went, and the spring came, and found them still living thus from hand to mouth, hanging on day by day, with literally not a month's wages between them and starvation. Marija was in despair, for there was still no word about the re-opening of the canning factory, and her savings were almost entirely gone. The family faced in terror the prospect that Marija's board money would cease, and that they would have to pay back the debt in board. Marija had been willing enough to let it wait while she had a cent left—but when she had nothing, certainly they could not turn her out into the street. So Jurgis and Ona and Teta Elzbieta would hold anxious conferences until late at night, trying to figure how they could manage this too without starving.

Such were the cruel terms upon which their life was possible—that they might never have nor expect a single instant's respite from worry, a single instant in which they were not haunted by the thoughts of money. They would no sooner escape, as by a miracle, from one difficulty, than a new one would come into view. In addition to all their physical hardships, there was thus a constant strain upon their minds, which were harried all day and nearly all night by worry and fear. This was in truth not living; it was scarcely even existing, and they felt that it was too little for the price they paid. They were willing to work all the time, and they could not do any more. When people did their best they ought to be able to keep alive.

When the springtime came they were delivered from the dreadful cold, and that was a great deal; but in addition they had counted on the money they would not have to pay for coal—and it was just at this time that Marija's board began to fail. Then, too, the warm weather brought trials of its own—each season had its trials, as they found. In the spring there were cold rains, that turned the streets into canals and bogs; the mud would be so deep that wagons would sink up to the hubs, so that half a dozen horses could not move them. Then, of course, it was impossible for anyone to get to work with dry feet; and this was bad for men that were poorly clad and shod, and still worse for women and children. Later came midsummer, with the stifling heat, and the dingy killing-floor of Anderson's became a very purgatory; once there were three men fell dead from sunstroke in a single day. All day long the rivers of hot blood poured forth, until, with the sun beating down and the air motionless, the stench was enough to knock a man down; all the old smells of a generation would be drawn out by this heat—for there was never any washing-up at Anderson's, and the walls and rafters were caked with the filth of a lifetime. The men who worked on the killing-floor would come to reek with foulness, so that you could smell one of them fifty feet away; there was simply no such thing as keeping decent, the most careful man gave it up in the end, and wallowed in uncleanness. There was not even a place where a man could wash his hands at Anderson's, and the men ate as much raw blood as food at dinner-time. When they were at work they could not even wipe off their faces—they were as helpless as newly-born babes in that respect; and it may seem like a small matter, but when the sweat began to run down their necks and tickle them, or a fly to bother them, it was a torture like being burned alive. Whether it was the slaughter-houses or the dumps that were responsible, one could not say, but with the hot weather there descended upon Packingtown a veritable Egyptian plague of flies; there could be no describing this—the houses would be black with flies. There was no escaping; you might provide all your doors and windows with screens, but their buzzing outside would be like the swarming of bees, and whenever you opened the door they would rush in as if a storm of wind were driving them.

Perhaps the summertime suggests to you thoughts of the country, visions of green fields, and mountains, and sparkling lakes. It had no such suggestion for the people in the yards. The great packing-machine ground on remorselessly, without thinking of green fields; and the men and women and children who were part of it were not supposed to think of them either. Recently one of New York's numerous millionaires took the trouble to write a magazine article about the injustice of the vacation habit, and the newspapers fell upon him mercilessly for his meanness, defending the toiler and his right to a rest. The newspapers were probably quite sincere in this—so little does the great world know about those who do its work. The newspaper editors most likely really believe that working people get vacations—that not merely the million or two of clerks and bookkeepers, but also the ten or fifteen millions of factory workers, mechanics and miners are all accustomed to rest two weeks in the year, and be paid by their generous employers while they do it!

Not only did the people of Packingtown not get any vacations, or even see the country, they never saw any green thing, not even a flower. Four or five miles to the east of them lay the blue waters of Lake Michigan; but for all the good it did them it might have been as far away as the Pacific Ocean. There were parks also, but not for poor people—they did not even know where they were. They had only Sundays, and then they were too tired to walk. They were tied to the great packing-machine, and tied to it for life; they would work on and on, night and day, as they were doing, year after year till they died, and there would never be the least relief, never an instant's freedom, no better pay, no larger opportunity, no easier work, no hope. The managers and superintendents and clerks of Packingtown were all recruited from another class, and never from the workers; they scorned the workers, the very meanest of them. A poor devil of a bookkeeper who had been working in Anderson's for twenty years at a salary of six dollars a week, and might work there for twenty more and do no better, would yet consider himself a gentleman, as far removed as the poles from the most skilled worker on the killing-floor; he would dress differently, and live in another part of the town, and come to work at a different hour of the day, and in every way make sure that he never rubbed elbows with a laboring man. Perhaps this state of affairs was due to the repulsiveness of the work; at any rate, the people who worked with their hands were a class apart, and were made to feel it. If you had had the misfortune to be born into that class, you lived and died in it, and no galley-slave was ever chained to his oar more tightly than you were chained to your place in the machine. Jurgis and his family were paying two hundred or two hundred and fifty dollars a year upon their house, and at the end of eight or ten years they would not have to pay this; and that was the one single hope they had in this world, and the one single betterment that they could expect in all their lives.

In the late spring the canning factory started up again, and so once more Marija was heard to sing. It was not for long, however; before two months more a dreadful calamity fell upon Marija. Just one year and three days after she had begun work as a can-painter she lost her job.

It is a long story. Marija insisted that it was because of her activity in the union. The packers, of course, had spies in all the unions, and in addition they made a practice of buying up a certain number of the union officials, as many as they thought they needed; so every week they received reports as to what was going on, and often they knew things before the members of the union knew them. Anyone who was considered to be dangerous by the packers would find that he was not a favorite with his boss; and Marija had been a great hand for going after the foreign people and preaching the union to them. However that might be, the known facts were that a few weeks before the factory closed Marija had been cheated out of her pay for three hundred cans. The girls worked at a long table, and behind them walked a woman with pencil and notebook, keeping count of the number they finished. This woman was, of course, only human, and sometimes made mistakes; when this happened there was no redress—if on Saturday you got less money than you had earned, you had to make the best of it. But Marija did not understand this, and made a disturbance. Marija's disturbances did not mean anything— and while she had known only Lithuanian and Polish, they had done no harm, for people only laughed at her and made her cry. But now Marija was able to call names in English, and so she got the woman who made the mistake to disliking her. Probably, as Marija claimed, she made mistakes on purpose after that; at any rate, she made them, and the third time it happened Marija went on the warpath and took the matter, first to the forelady, and when she got no satisfaction there, to the superintendent. This was an unheard of presumption, but the superintendent said he would see about it, which Marija took to mean that she was going to get her money; after waiting three days, she went to see the superintendent again. This time the man frowned, and said that he had not had time to attend to it; and when Marija, against the advice and warning of everyone, tried it once more, he ordered her back to her work in a passion. Just how things happened after that, Marija was not sure, but that afternoon the forelady told her that her services would not be any longer required. Poor Marija could not have been more dumfounded had the woman knocked her over the head; at first she could not believe what she heard—and then she grew furious and swore that she would come anyway, that her place belonged to her. In the end she sat down in the middle of the floor and wept and wailed. It was a cruel lesson; but then Marija was headstrong—she should have listened to those who had had experience. The next time she would know her place, as the forelady expressed it; and so Marija went out, and the family faced the problem of an existence again.

It was especially hard this time, for Ona was to be confined before long, and Jurgis was trying hard to save up money for this. He had heard dreadful stories as to what happened to women who had to be attended by the midwives, who grew as thick as fleas in Packingtown; and he had made up his mind that Ona must have a man-doctor. Jurgis could be very obstinate when he wanted to, and he was in this case, much to the dismay of the women, who felt that a man-doctor was an impropriety, and that the matter really belonged to them. The cheapest doctor they could find would charge them fifteen dollars, and perhaps more, when the bill came in; and here was Jurgis, declaring that he would pay it, even if he had to stop eating in the meantime!

Marija had only about twenty-five dollars left. Day after day she wandered about the yards begging a job, but this time without hope of finding it. Marija could do the work of an able-bodied man, when she was cheerful, but discouragement wore her out easily, and she would come home at night a pitiable object. She learned her lesson this time, poor creature; she learned it ten times over. All the family learned it along with her—that when you have once got a job in Packingtown, you hang on to it, come what will; you hang on even if they kick and beat you, you hang on as long as you can drag yourself there. Sometimes—so literally do the people take this lesson—they come when they are dying, and fall dead at their work.

Four weeks Marija hunted, and half of a fifth week. Of course she stopped paying her dues to the union—she lost all interest in the union, and cursed herself for a fool that she had ever been dragged into one. She had about made up her mind that she was a lost soul, when somebody told her of an opening, and she went and got a place as a "beef-trimmer." She got this because the boss saw that she had the muscles of a man, and so he discharged a man, and put Marija to do his work, paying her a little more than half what he had been paying.

When she first came to Packingtown, Marija would have scorned such work as this. She was in another canning-factory, and her work was to trim the meat of those diseased cattle that Jurgis had been told about not long before. She was shut up in one of the rooms where the people never saw the daylight; beneath her were the chilling-rooms, where the meat was frozen, and above her were the cooking-rooms; and so she stood on an ice-cold floor, while her head was often so hot that she could scarcely breathe. Trimming beef off the bones by the hundred weight, while standing up from early morning till late at night, with heavy boots on and the floor ankle-deep in blood, liable to be thrown out of work indefinitely because of a slackening in the trade, liable again to be kept overtime in rush seasons, and be worked till she trembled in every nerve and lost her grip on her slimy knife, and gave herself a poisoned wound—that was the new life that unfolded itself before Marija. But because Marija was a human horse she merely laughed and went at it—it would enable her to pay her board again, and keep the family going.

Marija's lesson came just in time, perhaps, to save Ona from a similar fate. Ona, too, was dissatisfied with her place, and had far more reason than Marija. Ona did not tell half of her story at home, because she saw it was a torment to Jurgis, and she was afraid of what he might do. For a long time Ona had seen that the forelady in her department "had a grudge" against her. At first she thought it was the old-time mistake she had made in asking for a holiday to get married. Then she concluded it must be because she did not give the forelady a present occasionally—she was the kind that took presents from the girls, Ona learned, and made all sorts of discriminations in favor of those who gave them. In the end, however, Ona discovered that it was even worse than that. The forelady was a newcomer, and it was some time before rumor made her out; finally it transpired that she was a kept woman, the former mistress of the superintendent of that department. He had put her there to keep her quiet, it seemed—and that not altogether with success, for once or twice they had been heard quarreling. She had the temper of a hyena, and soon the place she ran was a witches' cauldron. There were some of the girls who were of her own sort, who were willing to toady to her and flatter her; and these would carry tales about the rest, and so the furies were unchained in the place. Worse than this, the woman lived in a bawdy-house downtown, and some of the girls would go there with her in the slack times.

In fact, it would not be too much to say that she managed l~department at~
Smith's in conjunction with the house down-town—someti~women from~
the house would be given places alongside of decent girls,~after other~
decent girls had been turned off to make room for them. Wh~u worked~
in this woman's department the house down-town was nev~of your~
thoughts all day—there were always whiffs of it to be caught~e odor~
of the Packingtown rendering-plants at night, when the ~ifted~
suddenly. There would be stories about it going the rounds; the ~site~
you would be whispering them and winking at you. In such ~na~
would not have stayed a day but for starvation; and, as it was, sh~r~
sure that she could stay the next day. She understood now that the
that the forelady hated her was that she was a decent married g
knew that the tale-bearers and the toadies hated her for the same r
were doing their best to make her life miserable.

But there was no place a girl could go in Packingtown, if
particular about things of this sort; there was no place in it where a p
could not get along better than a decent girl. That was inevitable, as e
who is familiar with human nature would grant. Here was a populati
class and mostly foreign, hanging always on the verge of starvatic
dependent for its opportunities of life upon the whim of men every
brutal and unscrupulous as the old-time slave-drivers; under suc
cumstances immorality was exactly as inevitable, and as prevalent, as
under the system of chattel slavery. Things that were quite unspeakable
on there in the packing-houses all the time, and were taken for grante
everybody; only they did not show, as in the old slavery times, because th
was no difference in color between master and slave. One of these thi
resulted in a horrible incident, in the new department where Marija work
and only a week or two after she came. One of the women, an unmarried gi
who had been coming day after day when she ought not to have come, cre
away at last into a dark passage and gave birth to a baby boy; and no
knowing what to do with him, and in terror of losing her place, she crept up
to the floor above and dropped him into one of the carts full of beef, that was
all ready for the cooking-vats. It was by the merest chance that some one
heard the baby cry, just as the cart was in the act of being dumped. They took
this woman to the hospital—what became of her after that no one ever knew.

Perhaps it was because of this incident, which sent a shock through all the
yards, that Ona had no difficulty in getting off when her own time came. She
went home one Saturday morning, and Jurgis had the man doctor, according
to his whim, and she was safely delivered of a fine baby. It was an enormous
big boy; and Ona was such a tiny creature herself, that it seemed quite
incredible. Jurgis would stand and gaze at the stranger by the hour, unable to
believe that it had happened.

The coming this boy was a decisive event with Jurgis. It made him
irrevocably a ...ly man; it killed the last lingering impulse that he might
have had to ...t in the evenings and sit and talk with the men in the
saloons. The ...s nothing he cared for now so much as to sit and look at the
baby. This ...ry curious, for Jurgis had never been interested in babies.
But then, t... a very unusual sort of a baby, as everyone agreed. He had
the bright ...black eyes, and little black ringlets all over his head; he
was the l...age of Jurgis, they said, and Jurgis found this a fascinating
circums...was sufficiently perplexing that this tiny mite of life should
have c...e world at all, in the manner that it had; that it should have
come ...ical imitation of his father's nose, was simply uncanny.

Pe...s thought, it was intended to signify that it was his baby; that
it w...Ona's to care for all its life. Jurgis had never possessed
any...so interesting; it was, when you came to think about it,
as...elous possession. It would grow up to be a man; it would be
a...ith a personality all its own, a will of its own! These thoughts
...nting Jurgis, filling him with all sorts of strange and almost
...ents. He was wonderfully proud of little Antanas—as they
...; he was curious about all the details of him, the washing and
...d the eating, and the sleeping of him, and asked all sorts of
...ns. It took him quite a while to get over his alarm at the
...tness of the little creature's legs.

...alas, very little time to see his baby; he never felt the chains
...e than just then. When he came home at night the baby would
...it would be the merest chance if he awoke before Jurgis had
...himself. Then in the morning there was no time to look at him,
...nly chance the father had was on Sundays. This was more cruel
...ho ought to have stayed home and nursed him, the doctor said,
...ealth as well as the baby's; but Ona had to go to work, and leave
...Elzbieta to feed, upon the pale-blue poison that was called milk
...grocery. Ona's confinement lost her only a week's wages—she
...the factory the second Monday, and the best that Jurgis could
...er was to ride in the car, and let him run along behind and help her
...when she alighted. After that it would be all right, said Ona; it was
...sitting still sewing hams all day; and if she waited longer she might
...that dreadful forelady had put someone else in her place. That would
...se than ever now, Ona continued, on account of the baby. They would
...ve to work harder now on his account. It was such a responsibility—
...must not have the baby grow up to suffer as they had. That had been the
...t thing Jurgis had thought himself—he had clenched his hands and braced
...mself anew for the struggle, for the sake of that tiny mite of human
...ossibility.

And so Ona went back to Smith's and saved her place and a week's wages; and so she gave herself some one of the thousand ailments that women group under the title of "womb-trouble;" and so was never again a well person as long as she lived. It is difficult to convey in words all that this meant to Ona; it seemed such a slight offense, and the punishment was so out of all proportion that neither she nor anyone else ever connected the two. "Womb-trouble" to Ona did not mean a specialist's diagnosis, and a course of treatment, and perhaps an operation or two; it meant simply headaches and pains in the back, and depression and heartsickness, and neuralgia when she had to go to work in the rain. The great majority of the women who worked in Packingtown suffered in the same way, and from the same cause, so it was not deemed a thing to see the doctor about; instead Ona would try patent medicines, one after another, as her friends told her about them. As these all contained alcohol, or some other stimulant, she found that they all did her good, while she took them; and so she was always chasing the phantom of good health, and losing it because she was too poor to continue. All this is so familiar and common-place that one has to apologize for telling of it; though it might really be interesting to have some psychologist work out the problem why a dreadful and cruel fact that we learn about one person should immediately cease to trouble us when we are told that it is the case with millions. Perhaps it is because we feel the hopelessness of so vast a problem, and prefer to turn our limited sympathies where they can do some good; for cannot anyone in his right senses see that such troubles as Ona's must continue to be the rule so long as women whom "God in his infinite wisdom" has condemned to be manufacturing-machines will insist upon having children just as if they were ordinary human creatures?

DURING the summer the packing-houses were in full activity again, and Jurgis made more money. He did not make so much, however, as he had the previous summer, for the packers took on more hands. There were new men every week, it seemed—it was a regular system; and this number they would keep over to the next slack season, so that everyone would have less than ever, Sooner or later, by this plan, they would have all the floating labor of Chicago trained to do their work. And how very cunning a trick was that! The men were to teach new hands, who would some day come and break their strike; and meantime they were kept so poor that they could not prepare for the trial!

But let no one suppose that this superfluity of employees meant easier work for anyone! On the contrary, the speeding-up seemed to be growing more savage all the time; they were continually inventing new devices to crowd the work on—it was for all the world like the thumb-screw of the mediaeval torture chamber. They would get new pace-makers and pay them more; they would drive the men on with new machinery—it was said that in the hog-killing rooms the speed at which the hogs moved was determined by clock-work, and that it was increased a few minutes every day. In piece-work they would reduce the time, requiring the same work in a shorter time, and paying the same wages; and then, after the workers had accustomed themselves to this new speed, they would reduce the rate of payment to correspond with the reduction in time! They had done this so often in the canning establishments that the girls were fairly desperate; their wages had gone down by a full third in the past two years, and a storm of discontent was brewing that was likely to break any day. Only a month after Marija had become a beef-trimmer the canning factory that she had left posted a cut that would divide the girls' earnings almost squarely in half; and so great was the indignation at this that they marched out without even a parley, and organized in the street outside. One of the girls had read somewhere that a red flag was the proper symbol for oppressed workers, and so they mounted one, and paraded all about the yards, yelling with rage. A new union was the result of this outburst, but the impromptu strike went to pieces in three days, owing to the rush of new labor. At the end of it the girl who had carried the red flag went down-town and got a position in Marshall Field's great retail store at a salary of two dollars and a half a week.

Jurgis and Ona heard these stories with dismay, for there was no telling when their own time might come. Once or twice there had been rumors that one of the big houses was going to cut its unskilled men to fifteen cents an hour, and Jurgis knew that if this was done his turn would come soon. He had learned by this time that Packingtown was really not a number of firms at all, but one great firm, the Beef Trust. And every week the managers of it got together and compared notes, and there was one scale for all the workers in the yards, and one standard of efficiency. Jurgis was told that they also fixed the price they would pay for beef on the hoof, and the price of all dressed meat in the country; but that was something he did not understand or care about as yet.

The only one who was not afraid of a cut was Marija, who congratulated herself, somewhat naively, that there had been one in her place only a short time before she came. Marija was getting to be a skilled beef-trimmer, and was mounting to the heights again. During the summer and fall Jurgis and Ona managed to pay her back the last penny they owed her, and so she began to have a bank account. The possession of vast wealth entails cares and responsibilities, however, as poor Marija found out. She had taken the advice of a friend and invested her savings in a bank on Ashland avenue. Of course she knew nothing about it, except that it was big and imposing—what possible chance has a poor foreign working-girl to understand the banking business, as it is conducted in this land of frenzied finance? So Marija lived in continual dread lest something should happen to her bank, and would go out of her way mornings to make sure that it was still there; her principal thought was of fire, for she had deposited her money in bills, and was afraid that if they were burned up the bank would not give her any others. Jurgis made fun of her for this, for he was a man and was proud of his superior knowledge, telling her that the bank had fire-proof vaults, and all its millions of dollars hidden safely away in them.

However, one morning Marija took her usual detour and to her horror and dismay saw a crowd of people in front of the bank, filling the avenue solid for half a block. All the blood went out of her face for terror. She broke into a run, shouting to the people to ask what was the matter, but not stopping to hear what they answered till she had come to where the throng was so dense that she could no longer advance. There was a "run on the bank," they told her then, but she did not know what that was, and turned from one person to another, trying in an agony of fear to make out what they meant. Had something gone wrong with the bank? Nobody was sure, but they thought so. Couldn't she get her money? There was no telling; the people were afraid not, and they were all trying to get it. It was too early yet to tell anything—the bank would not open for nearly three hours. So, in a frenzy of despair Marija began to claw her way towards the doors of this building, through a throng of men, women and children, all as excited as herself. It was a scene of wild confusion, women shrieking and wringing their hands and fainting, and men fighting and trampling down everything in their way. In the midst of the melee Marija recollected that she did not have her bank-book, and could not get her money anyway, so she fought her way out and started on a run for home. This was fortunate for her, for a few minutes later the police-reserves arrived—and God help the people who are caught in a crowd that the police at the stock-yards are sent out to disperse.

In half an hour Marija was back, Teta Elzbieta with her, both of them breathless with running, and sick with fear. The crowd was now formed in a line, extending for several blocks, with half a hundred policemen keeping guard over it. There was nothing for them to do but to take their places at the end of it. At nine o'clock the bank opened and began to pay the waiting throng; but then, what good did that do Marija, who saw three thousand people before her—enough to take out the last penny of a dozen banks? And how in all that confusion were they going to tell her money from that of anyone else?

To make matters worse, a drizzling rain came up, and soaked them to the skin; yet all the morning they stood there, creeping slowly toward the goal— all the afternoon they stood there, heart-sick, seeing that the hour of closing was coming, and that they were going to be left out. Marija made up her mind that, come what might, she would stay there and keep her place; but as nearly all did the same, all through the long, cold night, she got very little closer to the bank for that. Toward evening Jurgis came; he had heard the story from the children, and he brought some food and dry wraps, which made it a little easier.

The next morning, before daybreak, came a bigger crowd than ever, and more policemen from down-town. Marija held on like grim death, and toward afternoon she got into the bank and got her money—all in big silver dollars—a handkerchief full. When she had once got her hands on them her fear vanished, and she wanted to put them back again; but the man at the window was savage, and said that the bank would take no more deposits from those who had taken part in the run. So Marija was forced to take her dollars home with her, watching from right to left, expecting every instant that some one would try to rob her; and when she got home she was not much better off. Until she could find another bank there was nothing to do but sew them up in her clothes, and so Marija went about for a week or more loaded down with bullion, and afraid to cross the street in front of the house, because Jurgis told her she would sink out of sight in the mud. Weighted this way she made her way to the yards, again in terror, this time to see if she had lost her place. Fortunately about twenty per cent of the working people of Packingtown had been depositors in that bank, and it was not convenient to discharge that many at once. The cause of the panic had been the attempt of a policeman to arrest a drunken man in a saloon next door, which had drawn a crowd at the hour the people were on their way to work, and so started the "run."

About this time Jurgis and Ona also began a bank-account. Besides having paid Jonas and Marija, they had almost paid for their furniture, and could have that little sum to count on. So long as each of them could bring home nine or ten dollars a week, they were able to get along finely. Also election-day came round again, and Jurgis made half a week's wages out of that, all net profit. It was a very close election that year, and the echoes of the battle reached even to Packingtown. The two rival sets of grafters hired halls and set off fireworks and made speeches, to try to get the people interested in the matter. Although Jurgis did not understand it all, he knew enough by this time to realize that it was not supposed to be right to sell your vote. However, everyone did it, and his refusal to join would not have made the slightest difference in the results. The idea of refusing would have seemed absurd, had it ever came into his head.

Now chill winds and shortening days began to warn them that the winter was coming again. The very memory of the winter was a terror; it seemed that the respite had been too short—they had not had time enough to get ready for it. Still it came, inexorably, and the hunted look began to come back into the eyes of little Stanislovas. The prospect struck fear to the heart of Jurgis also, for he knew that Ona was not fit to face the cold and the snow-drifts this year. And suppose that some day when a blizzard struck them and the cars were not running, Ona should have to give it up, and should come the next day to find that her place had been given to some one who lived nearer and could be depended on?—It was the week before Christmas that the first great storm came, and then the soul of Jurgis rose up within him like a sleeping lion. There were four days that the Ashland avenue cars were stalled, and in those days, for the first time in his life, Jurgis knew what it was to be really opposed. He had faced difficulties before, but they had been child's play; now there was a death struggle, and all the furies were unchained in him. The first morning they set out two hours before dawn, Ona wrapped all in blankets and tossed upon his shoulder like a sack of meal, and the little boy, bundled nearly out of sight, hanging by his coat-tails. There was a raging blast beating in his face, and with the thermometer below zero; the snow was never short of his knees, and in some of the drifts it was nearly up to his arm-pits. It would catch his feet and try to trip him; it would build itself into a wall before him to beat him back; and he would fling himself into it, plunging like a wounded buffalo, puffing and snorting in rage. So foot by foot he drove his way, and when at last he came to Anderson's he was staggering and almost blind, and leaned against a pillar gasping, and thanked God that the cattle came late to the killing-floor that day. In the evening the same thing had to be done again; and because Jurgis could not tell what hour of the night he would get off, he paid a saloon-keeper to let Ona sit and wait for him in a corner. Once it was eleven o'clock at night, and black as the pit, but still they got home.

That blizzard knocked many a man out, for the crowd outside begging for work was never greater, and the packers would not wait long for anyone. When it was over the soul of Jurgis was a song, for he had met the enemy and conquered, and he felt himself the master of his fate.—So it might be with some monarch of the forest, that had vanquished his foes in fair fight, and then fell into some cowardly trap in the night-time. There are so many traps in the jungle—the creature that would escape them all must never sleep.

A time of peril on the killing-floor was when a steer broke loose. In the killing of the cattle at Anderson's they had, of course, no thought save of speed. In the slaughter-houses of Europe, where there are laws, they fit over the head of the animal a leather cap having a nail in it; then, provided the knocker has only skill enough to hit the nail with a big mallet, he cannot fail to kill the animal. But they never stopped for things like that in the yards— the knockers would lean over the pens and slap away at the creatures with a pointed hammer, and if they did not kill at the first blow, they had only to try again. So now and then you might see one banging away for a full minute, with the steer plunging and bellowing in agony and terror. That was nothing—only sometimes, in the haste of speeding-up, they would dump the animal out on the floor before it was fully stunned, and it would get upon its feet and run amuck. Then there would be a yell of warning—the men would drop everything, and dash for the nearest pillar, slipping here and there on the slimy floor, and tumbling head over heels over each other. This was bad enough in the summer, when a man could see; in winter time it was enough to make your hair stand up, for the room would be so full of steam that you could not see five feet in front of you. To be sure, the steer was generally blind and frantic, and not especially bent on hurting anyone; but think of the chances of running upon a knife, while two men out of three had one in his hand! And then the floor boss would come rushing up with a rifle and begin blazing away! Jurgis had seen times when as many as eight shots had to be fired, in a room with hundreds of men in it.

It was in one of these melees that Jurgis fell into his trap. That is the very word to describe it—it was so cruel, and so utterly not to be foreseen. At first he hardly noticed it, it was such a slight accident—simply that in leaping out of the way he turned his ankle. There was a twinge of pain, but Jurgis was used to pain, and did not coddle himself. When he came to walk home, however, he realized that it was hurting him a great deal; and in the morning his ankle was swollen out nearly double its size, and he could not get his foot into his shoe. Still, even then, he did nothing more than swear a little, and wrapped his foot in old rags, and hobbled out to take the car. It chanced to be a rush day at Anderson's, and all the long morning he limped about with his aching foot; by noon-time the pain was so great that it made him faint, and after a couple of hours in the afternoon he was fairly beaten, and had to tell the boss. They sent for the company doctor, and he examined the foot and told Jurgis to go home to bed, adding that he had probably laid himself up for months by his folly. The injury was not one that Anderson and Company could be held responsible for, and so that was all there was to it, so far as the doctor was concerned.

Jurgis got home somehow, scarcely able to see for the pain, and with an awful terror in his soul. Elzbieta helped him into bed and bandaged his injured foot with cold water, and tried hard not to let him see her dismay; when the rest came home at night she met them outside and told them, and they, too, put on a cheerful face, saying it would only be for a week or two, and that they would pull him through.

When they had gotten him to sleep, however, they sat by the kitchen fire and talked it over in frightened whispers. They were in for a siege, that was plainly to be seen. Jurgis had only about sixty dollars in the bank, and the slack season was upon them. Both Jonas and Marija might soon be earning no more than enough to pay their board, and besides that there was only the wages of Ona, and the little pittance of the boy. There was the rent to pay, and still some on the furniture; there was the insurance just due, and every month there was sack after sack of coal. It was January, mid-winter, an awful time to have to face privation. Deep snows would come again; and who would carry Ona to her work now? She might lose her place—she was almost certain to lose it. And then little Stanislovas began to whimper—who would take care of him?

It was dreadful that an accident of this sort, that no man can help, and that is quite certain to happen to a workingman now and then in his life, should have meant such suffering. The bitterness of it was now the daily food and drink of Jurgis. It was of no use for them to try to deceive him—he knew as much about the situation as they did, and he knew that the family might literally starve to death. The worry of it fairly ate him up—he began to look haggard the first two or three days of it. In truth, it was almost maddening for a strong man like him, a fighter, to have to lie there helpless on his back. It was for all the world the old story of Prometheus bound; Jurgis felt like a wild animal in a trap—the more so because it was by his foot that he was held, his foot which he wrenched and twisted in his efforts to escape. The naturalists tell us of the creatures of the forest; that they never die a natural death. Day and night without rest they are hunted, and they crouch and dart from cover to cover, watching ceaselessly with eyes of terror, and in awful loneliness of soul; whenever by any chance one of them is wounded he crawls into a corner and hides, till his fate finds him out. So it was with Jurgis now; and as he lay on his bed, hour after hour, there came to him emotions that he had never known before. Before this he had met life with a welcome; it had its trials, but none that a man could not face. But now, in the night time, when he lay tossing about, there would come stalking into his chamber a grisly phantom, the sight of which made his flesh curl and his hair to bristle up. It was like seeing the world fall away from underneath his feet—plunging down into a bottomless abyss, into yawning caverns of despair. It might be true, then, after all, what others had told him about life, that the best powers of a man might not be equal to it! It might be true that, strive as he would, toil as he would, he might fail, and go down, and be destroyed! The thought of this was like an icy hand at his heart; the thought that here, in this ghastly home of all horror, he and all those who were dear to him might lie and perish of starvation and cold, and there would be no ear to hear their cry, no hand to help them! It was true, it was true—and yet did it not seem a monstrous thing that could happen, here in this huge city, with its stores of heaped-up wealth—that tens and hundreds of thousands of human creatures should be hunted and destroyed by the wild beast powers of nature, just as truly as ever they were in the days of the cave-man.

Ona was now making about forty dollars a month, and Stanislovas about thirteen. To add to this there was the board of Jonas and Marija, about forty-five dollars. Deducting from this the rent, interest and instalments on the furniture, they had left seventy dollars, and deducting the coal, they had sixty. They did without everything that human beings could do without; they went in old and ragged clothing, that left them at the mercy of the cold; when the children's shoes wore out, they tied them up with string, and they went to school, when they could go, with old rags tied about their ears, and with nothing but their pockets to keep their poor little fingers in. Half invalid as she was, Ona would do herself harm by walking in the rain and cold when she ought to have ridden; they bought literally nothing but food—and still they could not keep alive on sixty dollars a month. They might have done it if only they could have gotten pure food, and at fair prices; and if only they had known what to get—if they had not been so pitifully ignorant! But they had come to a new country, where everything was different, including the food. Here in America it was the tradition that men and women who had been working hard all day, and children who were growing, had to have plenty of meat; there was no one to tell them that the nutriment they got in meat cost them several times as much as if they had gotten it in oatmeal and beans and brown bread. Meat was cheaper (in Packingtown) than anywhere else, but then it is all the very worst of the garbage of the packing-houses, which they sell to the cheap retailers and free-lunch counters of the neighborhood, because otherwise it would have to be canned; yet it was this food the family thought they had to have—and it was amazing what quantities of it were needed every day by eleven hungry persons! Two dollars a day was simply not enough to feed them, and there was no use trying; and so each week they made an inroad upon the pitiful little bank account that Ona had begun. Because the account was in her name, it was possible for her to keep this a secret from her husband, and to keep the heart-sickness of it for her own.

It would have been better if Jurgis had been really ill; if he had not been able to think. For he had no resources such as most invalids have—he could not read to pass the time, he had nothing to read if he had known how. All he could do was to lie there and toss about from side to side. Now and then he would break into cursing, regardless of everything; and now and then his impatience would get the better of him, and he would try to get up, and poor Teta Elzbieta would have to plead with him in frenzy. Elzbieta was all alone with him the greater part of the time. She would sit and smooth his forehead by the hour and talk to him and try to make him forget. Sometimes it would be too cold for the children to go to school, and they would have to play in the kitchen, where Jurgis was, because it was the only room that was half warm. These were dreadful times, for Jurgis would get as cross as any bear; he was scarcely to be blamed, for he had enough to worry him, and it was hard when he was trying to take a nap to be kept awake by noisy and peevish children.

Teta Elzbieta's only resource in those times was the little Antanas; indeed it would be hard to say how they could have gotten along at all if it had not been for little Antanas. It was the one consolation of Jurgis's long imprisonment, that now he had time to look at his baby. Teta Elzbieta would put the clothes-basket in which the baby slept alongside of his mattress, and Jurgis would lie upon one elbow and watch him by the hour, imagining things. Then little Antanas would open his eyes—he was beginning to take notice of things now; and he would smile—how he would smile. So Jurgis would begin to forget and be happy, because he was in a world where there was a thing so beautiful as the smile of little Antanas, and because such a world could not but be of good at the heart of it. He looked more like his father every hour, Teta Elzbieta would say, and said it many times a day, because she saw that it pleased Jurgis; the poor little terror-stricken woman was planning all day and all night to soothe the prisoned giant who was entrusted to her care. Jurgis, who knew nothing about the age-long and everlasting hypocrisy of women, would take the bait and grin with delight; and then he would hold his finger in front of little Antanas's eyes, and move it this way and that, and laugh with glee to see the baby follow it. There is no pet quite so fascinating as a baby; he would look into Jurgis's face with such uncanny seriousness— and Jurgis would start and cry: "*Palauk.* Look, Muma, he knows his papa! He does, he does! *Tu mano szirdele*, the little rascal!"

12

FOR THREE weeks after his injury Jurgis never got up from bed. It was a very obstinate sprain; the swelling would not go down, and the pain still continued. At the end of that time, however, he could contain himself no longer, and began trying to walk a little every day, laboring to persuade himself that he was better. No arguments could stop him, and three or four days later he declared that he was going back to work. He limped to the cars and got to Smith's, where he found that the boss had kept his place—that is, was willing to turn out into the snow the poor devil he had hired in the meantime. Every now and then the pain would force Jurgis to stop work, but he stuck it out till nearly an hour before closing. Then he was forced to acknowledge that he could not go on without fainting; it almost broke his heart to do it, and he stood leaning against a pillar and weeping like a child. Two of the men had to help him to the car, and when he got out he had to sit down and wait in the snow till some one came along.

So they put him to bed again, and sent for the doctor, as they ought to have done in the beginning. It transpired that he had twisted a tendon out of place, and could never have gotten well without attention. Then he gripped the sides of the bed, and shut his teeth together and turned white with agony, while the doctor pulled and wrenched away at his swollen ankle. When finally the doctor left, he told him that he would have to lie quiet for two months, and that if he went to work before that time he might lame himself for life.

Three days later there came another heavy snow-storm, and Jonas and Marija and Ona and little Stanislovas all set out together, an hour before day-break, to try to get to the yards. About noon the last two came back, the boy screaming with pain. His fingers were all frosted; it seemed. They had to give up trying to get to the yards, and had nearly perished in a drift. All that they knew how to do was to hold the frozen fingers near the fire, and so little Stanislovas spent most of the day dancing about in horrible agony, till Jurgis flew into a passion of nervous rage and swore like a madman, declaring that he would kill him if he did not stop. All that day and night the family was half-crazed with fear that Ona and the boy had lost their places; and in the morning they set out earlier than ever, after the little fellow had been beaten with a stick by Jurgis. There could be no trifling in a case like this, it was a matter of life and death; little Stanislovas could not be expected to realize that he might a great deal better freeze in the snow-drift than lose his place at the lard-machine. Ona was quite certain that she would find her place gone, and was all unnerved when she finally got to Smith's, and found that the forelady herself had failed to come, and was, therefore, compelled to be lenient.

One of the consequences of this episode was that the first joints of three of the little boy's fingers were permanently disabled, and another that thereafter he always had to be beaten before he set out to work, whenever there was fresh snow on the ground. Jurgis was called upon to do the beating, and as it hurt his foot he did it with a vengeance; but it did not tend to add to the sweetness of his temper. They say that the best dog will turn cross if he be kept chained all the time, and it was the same with our friend; he had not a thing to do all day but lie and curse his fate, and the time came when he wanted to curse everything. This was never for very long, however, for when Ona began to cry Jurgis could not stay angry. The poor fellow looked like a homeless ghost, with his cheeks sunken in and his long black hair straggling into his eyes; he was too discouraged to cut it, or to think about his appearance. His muscles were wasting away, and what there was left was soft and flabby; he would feel of them and moan with anguish. He had no appetite —and they could not afford to tempt him with delicacies. It was better, he said, that he should not eat, it was a saving. About the end of March he had got hold of Ona's bank-book, and had been able to read enough to understand that there was only three dollars left to them in the world.

But perhaps the worst of the consequences of this long siege was that they lost another member of their family; Brother Jonas disappeared. One Saturday night he did not come home, and thereafter all their efforts to get trace of him were futile. It was said by the boss at Anderson's that he had gotten his week's money and left there. That might not be true, of course, for sometimes they would say that when a man had been killed; it was the easiest way out of it for all concerned—when, for instance, a man had fallen into one of the rendering tanks and had been made into pure leaf lard and peerless fertilizer, what was the use of letting the fact out, and making his family unhappy, and perhaps getting the story into the papers, and stirring up those pests who call themselves reformers? Also it might possibly be that Jonas had been robbed and murdered, a thing that happened often in the jungle. Most probable, however, was the theory that he had deserted them, and this was the one the family adopted in the end. Jonas had gone on the road, seeking happiness. He had been discontented for a long time, and it was true, also, that he had cause to be. He paid good board, and was yet obliged to live in a family where nobody had enough to eat. And Marija would keep giving them all her money, and of course he could not but feel that he was called upon to do the same. Then there were crying brats and all sorts of misery—and they were not his children, it was not his fault that anything was as it was. A man would have to be a good deal of a hero to have stood all this without grumbling, and Jonas was not in the least a hero—he was simply a weather-beaten old fellow and liked to have a good supper and sit in the corner by the fire and smoke his pipe in peace before he went to bed. Here there was not room enough for all by the fire, and through the winter the kitchen had seldom been warm enough for comfort. So, with the springtime, what was more likely than that the wild idea of escaping had come to him! Two years he had been yoked like a horse to a half-ton truck in Anderson's dark cellars, with never a rest, save on Sundays, and four holidays in the year, and with never a word of thanks—only kicks and blows and curses, such as no decent dog would have stood. And now the winter was over, and the spring winds were blowing— and with a day's walk a man might put the smoke of Packingtown behind him forever, and be where the grass was green and the flowers all the colors of the rainbow!

The men all knew about this; there were few of them who had not "hoboed it" a few times in their lives, and had not dreamed the wild dream of freedom. Out of the yards every single day there went hundreds of freight cars, and all a man had to do was to hide in one of these, or underneath on the trucks, and the next day he would be in the country. There would be streams where he could wash the stench of Packingtown out of him; there would be barns and haystacks in which he could sleep, and hen-roosts which he could rob. If the worst came, he could always earn a square meal by half an hour's work. The only drawback about it all was that the ruthless winter would be coming on again, and then he would have to make his way back to some city, one of a vast throng of hapless wretches joining the already overcrowded ranks of the unemployed. But the winter was a long way off—and if Jonas had stayed, likely as not he might lose his place by that time, or be killed in one of the elevators.

One of the first things the family thought of, that Saturday night when Jonas did not show up, was of Anderson's elevators; when they understood that he had run away, they said to themselves, "Ah, he was afraid of the elevators!" Two men had been killed there on the floor where he worked within the last two months, and Jonas had lost his nerve because of it. The law says that all elevators in factories shall have gates; but probably the law-makers did not realize what an inconvenient law this would be. There was not always gates at Anderson's; and because a man who ran an elevator was paid a little more than a man who pushed a truck, he felt that he was a little boss, and had a right to swear at a poor devil who did not make speed to suit him. He would slam over the lever of the elevator the instant the rear wheels of the truck were on, and leave it for the man to follow as best he could. The man's boots would be slippery, coming out of the pickle-rooms, and perhaps he would be out of breath and half dazed from a long run with a truck. At any rate, every now and then there was a sickening accident. The first time it happened where Jonas worked, the man was mashed right in half, and they got the body out of the way and started things up again, so that two or three minutes later, when Jonas came along, there was only the blood to show that anything had happened. But the second time he was right behind the man, who was a friend of his—and who missed his leap into the moving car, and had one of his feet cut off. It was blood-curdling even to hear Jonas tell about this thing; his eyes would pop wide open with horror. The injured man, a poor Slovak, did not faint, but instead rolled round on the floor, shrieking with agony. They sent in haste for the company doctor, and also for the company lawyer. Jonas did not understand what was going on; but he saw the latter kneel down beside the frantic wretch, and heard him ask him if he would not like to go to the hospital, if the company would pay his expenses. The man signified yes, and then the lawyer pulled out a paper and told him to sign it, giving him a pencil, and holding him while he wrote his name, with a hand that shook like a leaf. It was only afterwards that Jonas had it explained to him that what the man had really signed was a statement that he accepted ten dollars as satisfaction of all his damage claims against Anderson and Company. As for the hospital, Jonas's informant explained, that was all a damned lie—the city paid for the hospital, and took there all the men that Anderson and Company chose to slaughter. Jonas happened to know that this particular man had a wife and eight children, and he wondered if the city would take them to the hospital too.

Now the income of the family was cut down more than one-third, and the food demand was cut only one-eleventh, so they were worse off than ever. By this time also they were borrowing money from Marija, and eating up her bank-account; and so immediately it was decided that two more of the children would have to leave school.

Next to Stanislovas, who was now fifteen, there was a girl, little Kotrina; who was two years younger, and then two boys, Villimui, who was eleven, and Nikalojus, who was ten. Both of these last were bright boys, and there was no reason why their family should starve when tens of thousands of boys no older were earning their own livings and more. So one morning they were given a quarter apiece and a roll with a sausage in it, and with their minds top heavy with good advice, were sent out to make their way to the city and learn to sell newspapers. They came back late at night in tears, having walked the five or six miles, to report that a man had offered to take them to a place where they sold newspapers, and had taken their money and gone into a store to get them, and nevermore been seen. So they both received a whipping, and the next morning set out again. This time they found the newspaper place, and procured their stock; and after wandering about till nearly noontime, saying "Paper?" to everyone they saw, they had all their stock taken away and received a thrashing besides from a big newsman upon whose territory they had trespassed. Fortunately, however, they had already sold some papers, and came back with nearly as much as they started with.

After a week of mishaps such as these, the two little fellows began to learn the ways of the jungle—the names of the different papers that are sold there, and how many of each to get and where to get them, and what sort of people to offer them to, and where to go and where to stay away from. After this leaving home at four o'clock in the morning, and running about the streets, first with morning papers and then with evening, they might come home late at night with twenty or thirty cents apiece—possibly as much as forty cents —in their pockets. From this they had to deduct their car-fare, since the distance was so great; but after awhile they made friends, and learned still more, and then they would save their car-fare. They would get on a car when the conductor was not looking, and hide in the crowd. Three times out of four he would not ask for their fares, either not seeing them, or thinking they had already paid; and if he did ask, they would hunt through their pockets, and then begin to cry, and either have their fares paid by some kind old lady, or else try the trick again on a new car. All this was fair play in the jungle; they felt it dimly and instinctively, but had they known the facts they might have justified it by arguments—saying that the street-car companies were as much entitled to just dealing as the crews of so many pirate-ships. Not a franchise or a right that they had not stolen, with the help of scoundrelly politicians; and whose fault was it that at the hours when workingmen were going to their work and back, the cars were so crowded that the conductor could not collect all the fares? Not only would the people inside be jammed like rats in a trap, but the platforms would be packed, and men would be hanging to the the steps and windows, and even riding upon the roof, in the bitterest winter weather.

Now the family finances were about as they had been before Jonas left. This meant that they still had to live on Marija, and so about the same time Teta Elzbieta accepted with joy an opportunity that came to her. It had always been intended that Teta Elzbieta should have the care of the house; but then it had also been intended that the children should go to school, and learn to read English, instead of picking up all the vices of the "Levee;" it had been intended that Ona should stay at home and take care of her child, instead of dragging herself to Smith's to sew hams. All these fine intentions had been abandoned one by one, and now they abandoned the last. The son of Grandmother Majauszkis belonged to a club with a man who worked as a coachman over in Hyde Park, the swell district near the lake-front; and there a woman was wanted to do the dirty work of the kitchen, and would get her board and fifteen dollars a month. That would about make things even, and so little Kotrina also left school and came home while her mother went away. It was humiliating to Teta Elzbieta, who had once considered herself a lady, to have to serve as a kitchen-wench; but she took it as a penance, to try to retrieve the disgrace of the brother's desertion. Elzbieta took this much to heart, for to her it meant one more victory of America over Lithuania.

Little Kotrina was like most children of the poor, prematurely made old; she had to take care of her little brother and sister, both of them cripples, and also of the baby, and of Jurgis. She had to cook all the meals, and wash the dishes and clean house, and then have supper ready when the workers came home in the evening. She was only thirteen, and small for her age, but she did all this without a murmur, and did it beautifully. She and Jurgis would get on famously, for Kotrina had learned things in school and could borrow games and picture books from her former teacher.

Now that the winter was by, and there was no more danger of snow, and no more coal to buy, and another room warm enough to put the children into when they cried, and enough money to get along from week to week with, Jurgis was less terrible than he had been. A man can get used to anything in the course of time, and Jurgis had gotten used to lying about the house. Ona saw this and was very careful not to destroy his peace of mind, by letting him know how very much pain she was suffering. It was now the time of the spring rains, and Ona had often to ride to her work, in spite of the expense; she was getting paler every day, and sometimes, in spite of her good resolutions, it pained her that Jurgis did not notice it. She wondered if he cared for her as much as ever, if all this misery was not wearing out his love. She had to be away from him all the time, and bear her own troubles while he was bearing his; and then, when she came home, she was so worn out; and whenever they talked they had only their worries to talk of—truly it is hard, in such a life, to keep any sentiment alive. The woe of this would flame up in Ona sometimes—at night she would suddenly clasp her big husband in her arms and break into passionate weeping, demanding to know if he really loved her. Poor Jurgis, who had in truth grown more matter-of-fact, under the endless pressure of penury, would not know what to make of these things, and could only try to recollect when he had last been cross; and so Ona would have to forgive him and sob herself to sleep.

The latter part of April Jurgis went to see the doctor, and was given a bandage to lace about his ankle, and told that he might go back to work. It needed more than the permission of the doctor, however, for when he showed up on the killing-floor of Smith's he was told by the foreman that it had not been possible to keep his job for him. Jurgis knew what this meant, simply that the foreman had found some one else to do the work as well, and did not want to bother to make a change. He stood in the doorway, looking mournfully on, seeing his friends and companions at work, and feeling like an outcast. Then he went out and took his place with the mob of the un-employed.

This time, however, Jurgis did not have the same fine confidence, nor the same reason for it. He was no longer the finest-looking man in the throng, and the bosses no longer made for him; he was thin and haggard, and his clothes were seedy, and he looked miserable. And there were hundreds who looked and felt just like him, and who had been wandering about Packingtown for months begging for work. This was a critical time in Jurgis's life, and if he had been a weaker man he would have gone the way the rest did. Those out-of-work wretches would stand about the packing-houses every morning till the police drove them away, and then they would scatter among the saloons. Very few of them had the nerve to face the rebuffs that they would encounter by trying to get into the buildings to interview the bosses; if they did not get a chance in the morning, there would be nothing to do but hang about the saloons the rest of the day and night. Jurgis was saved from all this—partly, to be sure, because it was pleasant weather, and there was no need to be indoors—but mainly because he carried with him always the pitiful little face of Ona. He must get work, he told himself, fighting the battle with despair every hour of the day. He must get work. He must have a place again and some money saved up before the next winter came.

But there was no work for him. He sought out all the members of his union—Jurgis had stuck to the union through all this—and begged them to speak a word for him. He went to every one he knew, asking for a chance, there or anywhere. He wandered all day through the buildings, asking everyone; and in a week or two, when he had been all over the yards, and into every room to which he had access, and learned that there was not a job anywhere—he persuaded himself that there might have been a change in the places he had first visited, and began the round all over, till finally the watchmen and the "spotters" of the companies came to know him by sight, and to order him out with threats. Then there was nothing more for him to do but go with the crowd in the morning, and keep in the front row and look eager, and when he failed, go back home, and play with little Kotrina and the baby.

The peculiar bitterness of all this was that Jurgis saw so plainly the meaning of it. In the beginning he had been fresh and strong, and he had gotten a job the first day; but now he was second-hand, so to speak, and they did not want him. He was a damaged article, to put it exactly. And yet it was in their service that he had been damaged! They had got the best out of him, there was the truth—they had worn him out, with their speeding up and their damned carelessness, and now they had thrown him away! And Jurgis would make the acquaintance of some of these unemployed men; he would stroll away with them, and perhaps sit in a saloon and talk a while with them; and he found that they had all had the same experience. The packers had gotten the best out of them all. There were some, of course, who had wandered in from other places, who had been ground up in other mills; there were others, who were out from their own fault—some, for instance, who had not been able to stand the awful grind without drink. The vast majority, however, were simply the worn-out parts of the great merciless packing-machine; they had toiled there, and kept up with the pace, some of them for ten or twenty years, until finally the time had come when they could not keep up with it any more. Some had been frankly told that they were too old, that a spryer man was needed; others had given occasion, by some act of carelessness or incompetence; with most, however, the occasion had been the same as with Jurgis. They had been overworked and underfed so long, and finally some disease laid them on their backs; or they had cut themselves, and had blood-poisoning, or met with some other accident. When a man came back after that he would get his place back only by the courtesy of the boss. The only exception to this was when the accident was one for which the firm was liable; in that case they would send a slippery lawyer to see him, first to try to get him to sign away his claims, but if he was too smart for that, to promise him that he would always be provided with work. This promise they would keep strictly and to the letter—for two years. Two years was the "statute of limitations," and after that a man could not sue.

What happened to a man after any of these things all depended upon the circumstances. If a man were of the highly-skilled workers, he would probably have enough saved up to tide him over. The best-paid men, the "splitters," made fifty cents an hour, which would be five or six dollars a day in the rush seasons, and one or two in the dullest. A man could live and save on that; but then there were only half a dozen splitters in each place, and one of them that Jurgis knew had a family of twenty-two children, all hoping to grow up to be splitters, like their father. For an unskilled man, who made ten dollars a week in the rush seasons and five in the dull, it all depended upon his age and the number he had dependent upon him. An unmarried man could save, if he did not drink, and if he was absolutely selfish—that is, if he paid no heed to the demands of his old parents, or of his little brothers and sisters, or of any other relatives he might have, as well as of the members of his union, and his chums, and the people who might be starving to death next door. For a man with a family, there were periods when a brief accident would not be apt to wreck him, and others when almost certainly it would. The ups and downs of it might have been shown on a chart. The first year both he and his wife would be at work, and saving; but then the babies would begin to come, one at a time, or possibly two or three at a time—and then the man's chances would go steadily downward, and stay down till the children began to reach an age where they could sell papers or pass for sixteen at the yards. Then the line of his fate would rise again, until the man had a number of grown children, when it would be highest of all. Finally, however, his children would begin to marry and incur responsibilities of their own, and then the line would sink again, to the lowest point of all, and never to rise. The most striking single fact about Packingtown is the large number of the children, and the next most striking fact is the small number of the old people. This is in accordance with two well-known laws of nature, the first that those creatures whose order is the lowest and whose existence is the most precarious, cast out into the world the largest number of offspring; and the other—which has been mentioned before—that the creatures of the jungle never die a natural death. The age at which they began to die an unnatural death in Packingtown could have been ascertained by taking a census of the unemployed who thronged the yards. The number that was there now, in a time of the fullest "prosperity," was appalling; and yet they represented but a very small part of those who were thrown out into the packers' scrap-heap every year. Of those who fell sick, or met with accident, a good many never came back to ask for work; and of those who did, the vast majority had given up in despair, and either were living upon others, or dying of starvation and exposure, and the diseases to which these made them liable. Or else they had wandered off to beg for work in some other place; or had gone down into the heart of the city and became prostitutes and beggars and criminals; or had gone out into the country and became tramps and vagrants—all of them certain to perish in the end, of the same cold, the same hunger, and the same diseases, as if they had stayed at home. For the place which is here called The Jungle is not Packingtown, nor is it Chicago, nor is it Illinois, nor is it the United States—it is Civilization.

DURING this time that Jurgis was looking for work occurred the death of little Kristoforas, one of the children of Teta Elzbieta. Both Kristoforas and hia brother, Juozapas, were cripples, the latter having lost one leg by having it run over, and Kristoforas having congenital dislocation of the hip, which made it impossible for him ever to walk. He was the last of Teta Elzbieta's children, and perhaps he had been intended by nature to let her know that she had had enough. At any rate he was wretchedly sick and undersized; he had the rickets, and, though he was over three years old, he was no bigger than an ordinary child of one. All day long he would crawl around the floor in a filthy little dress, whining and fretting; because the floor was full of draughts he was always catching cold, and snuffling because his nose ran. This made trouble in the family. For his mother, with unnatural perversity, loved him best of all her children, and made a perpetual fuss over him; she would let him do anything undisturbed, and would burst into tears when his fretting drove Jurgis wild.

And now he died. Perhaps it was the smoked sausage he had eaten that morning—which may have been made out of some of the tuberculosis pork that is taken out at the bottom of the tank. At any rate, an hour after eating it the child had begun to cry with pain and in another hour he was rolling about on the floor in convulsions. Little Kotrina, who was all alone with him, ran out screaming for help, and after a while a doctor came, but not until little Kristoforas had howled his last howl. No one was really sorry about this except poor Elzbieta, who was inconsolable. Jurgis announced that so far as he was concerned the child would have to be buried by the city, since they had no money for a funeral; and at this the poor woman almost went out of her senses, wringing her hands and screaming with grief and despair. Her child to be buried in a pauper's grave! And her own step-daughter to stand by and hear it said without protesting! It was enough to make Ona's father rise up out of his grave to rebuke her! If it had come to this, they might as well give up at once, and be buried all of them together! . . . In the end Marija said that she would help with ten dollars; and Jurgis being still obdurate, Elzbieta went in tears and begged a month's wages in advance where she worked, and so little Kristoforas had a mass and a hearse with white plumes on it, and a tiny plot in a graveyard with a wooden cross to mark the place. The poor mother was not the same for months after that—on Sunday afternoons, when she could get away from the place where she worked, she would come over, and the mere sight of the floor where little Kristoforas had crawled about would set her weeping. He had never had a fair chance, poor little fellow, she would say. He had been handicapped from his birth. He really had the best heart—if only she had heard about it, so that she might have had the great doctor to cure him of his lameness! . . . Some time ago, Elzbieta was told, a Chicago billionaire, whose occupation shall be unspecified here, but whose name was Ogden Armour, had paid a sum equal to the lifetime's earnings of several men such as Jurgis, to bring a great European surgeon over to cure his little daughter of a dislocation of the hip, the same disease from which little Kristoforas suffered. And because this surgeon had to have bodies to demonstrate upon, he announced that he would treat the children of the poor, a piece of magnanimity over which the papers became quite maudlin. Elzbieta, alas, did not read the papers, and no one had told her; but perhaps it was as well, for just then they would not have had the carfare to spare to go every day to wait upon the surgeon, nor for that matter anybody with the time to take the child; besides, there were the ten times as many poor children applying as the surgeon could treat, and so nearly all had to go back home and stay crippled, belonging as they did to that greater portion of the population of the civilized world for which medical and surgical science does not exist. It is sufficiently obvious that it is hopeless to doctor people whose conditions of life breed diseases ten times as fast as science can cure them; and that the Almighty cannot have intended the science of healing to apply to human beings who have unventilated and filthy homes to live in, and dangerous and exhausting work to do, and insufficient food and clothing—who in other words are not human beings at all, but simply parts of a machine for pro-ducing wealth.

All this time that he was seeking for work, there was a dark shadow hanging over Jurgis; as if a savage beast were lurking somewhere in the pathway of his life, and he knew it, and yet could not help approaching. There are all stages of being out of work, and he faced in dread the prospect of reaching the lowest. There is a place in Packingtown that waits for the lowest man—the fertilizer plant!

The men would talk about it in awe-stricken whispers. Not more than one in ten had ever really tried it; the other nine had contented themselves with hearsay evidence and a peep through the door. There were some things worse than even starving to death. They would ask Jurgis if he had worked there yet, and if he meant to; and Jurgis would debate the matter with himself. As poor as they were, and making all the sacrifices that they were, would he dare to refuse any sort of work that was offered to him, be it as horrible as ever it could? Would he dare to go home and eat bread that had been earned by Ona, weak and complaining as she was, knowing that he bad been given a chance, and had not had the nerve to take it? And yet he might argue that way with himself all day, and one glimpse into the fertilizer works would send him away again shuddering. He went there every day, like a prisoner to an execution; he was a man, and he would do his duty; he went and made application —but surely he was not also required to hope for success! He knew perfectly well, however, that his chance of getting employment there was greater than of getting it in all the rest of the yards together.

The fertilizer works of Anderson's lay to the south of the rest of the plant. Few visitors ever saw them, and the few who did would come out looking like Dante, of whom the peasants would say that he had been into hell. To this part of the yards came all the "tankage," and the waste products of all sorts. Here they dried out the bones, and in suffocating cellars where the daylight never came you might see men and women and children bending over whirling machines and sawing them into all sorts of shapes, breathing their lungs full of the fine dust, and doomed to die, every one of them, within a certain definite time. Here they made the blood into albumen, and made other foul-smelling things into things still more foul-smelling. In the corridors and caverns where it was done you might lose yourself as in the great caves of Kentucky. In the dust and the steam, the electric lights would shine like far-off twinkling stars—red and blue, green and purple stars, according to the color of the mist and the brew from which it came. For the odors in these ghastly charnel-houses there may be words in Lithuanian, but there are none in English. The person entering would have to summon his courage as for a cold-water plunge. He would go on like a man swimming under water; he would put his handkerchief over his face, and begin to cough and choke; and then if he were still obstinate, he would find his head beginning to ring, and the veins in his forehead to throb, until finally he would be assailed by an overpowering blast of ammonia fumes, and would turn and run for his life, and come out half dazed.

On top of this were the suffocating rooms where they dried the "tankage," as it was called, the mass of brown stringy stuff that was left after the waste portions of the carcasses have had the lard and tallow dried out of them. This dried tankage they would then grind to a fine powder, and after they had adulterated it with railroad cinders and an innocuous brown rock which they brought in and ground up by the hundreds of car loads for that purpose, the substance was ready to be put into bags and sent out to the world as any one of a hundred different brands of standard bone-phosphate. And then the farmer in Maine or California or Texas would buy this, at say twenty-five dollars a ton, and plant it with his corn; and for several days after the operation the fields would have a strong odor, and the farmer and his wagon, and the very horses that had hauled it, would all have it too. The next planting-time, let the farmer ponder the matter and imagine what this odor would be if the fertilizer were pure, instead of being a flavoring, and if instead of a ton or so spread out on several acres under the open sky, there were hundreds and thousands of tons of it in one building, heaped here and there in hay-stack piles, covering the floor several inches deep, and filling the air with a choking dust that became a blinding sandstorm when the wind stirred.

It was to this building that Jurgis came daily, as if dragged by an unseen hand. The month of May was an exceptionally cool one, and his secret prayers were granted—he was not offered a job. But early in the June there came a record-breaking hot spell, and after that there was "no longer any excuse for a man's being idle" (to use the common phrase) in Packingtown. There were men wanted—in the fertilizer-mill!

The boss of the grinding-room had come to know Jurgis by this time, and had marked him for a likely man; and so when he came to the door about two o'clock this breathless hot day, he felt a sudden spasm of pain shooting through him—the man beckoned to him! In ten minutes more Jurgis had pulled off his coat and overshirt, and set his teeth together and gone to work. Here was one more difficulty for him to meet and conquer!

His labor took him about one minute to learn. Before him was one of the vents of the mill in which the fertilizer was being ground; it came out in a great brown river, with a spray of the finest dust flung forth in clouds. Jurgis was given a shovel, and along with half a dozen others it was his task to shovel this fertilizer into cars. That others were at work, he knew by the sound, and by the fact that he sometimes collided with them; otherwise they might as well not have been there, for in the blinding clouds of dust a man could not see six feet in front of his face. When he had filled one cart he had to grope around him until another came, and if there was none on hand he continued to grope until one arrived. In five minutes he was, of course, a mass of fertilizer from head to feet; they gave him a sponge to tie over his mouth, so that he could breathe, but the sponge did not prevent his lips and eyelids from caking up with it, and his ears from filling solid. He looked like a brown ghost at twilight—from hair to shoes he became the color of the building, and of everything in it, and for that matter a hundred yards outside it. The building had to be left open, and when a wind blew, Anderson and Company lost a great deal of fertilizer; doubtless, however, they had figured it out, and found that they would lose more in extra wages than they would have saved in fertilizer, had they closed it up tight. As it was, it was hard to retain—not common laborers, for these were always to be had in droves—but bosses and trusty men to take charge; in the month of November, 1900, there was one week when one hundred and twenty-six men were employed and only six were able to continue.

It was possible for Jurgis to conquer his revulsion from the odor of the fertilizer, but he could not prevent his body from rebelling. Working in his shirt-sleeves and with the thermometer at over a hundred, the phosphates soaked in through every pore of his skin, and in five minutes he had a headache, and in fifteen was almost dazed. The blood was pounding in his brain like an engine's throbbing; there was a frightful pain in the top of his skull, and he could hardly control his hands. Still, with the memory of his four months' siege behind him, he fought on, in a frenzy of determination; and half an hour later he began to vomit—he vomited until it seemed as if his insides must be torn to shreds. A man could get used to the fertilizer-mill, the boss had said, if he would only make up his mind to it; but Jurgis now began to see that it was a question of making up his stomach.

At the end of that day of horror, he could scarcely stand. He had to catch himself now and then, and lean against a building and get his bearings. Most of the men, when they came out, made straight for a saloon—they seemed to place fertilizer and rattle-snake poison in one class. But Jurgis was too ill to think of drinking—he could only make his way to the street and stagger onto a car. He had a sense of humor, and later on, when he became an old hand, he used to think it fun to get on a street car and see what happened. Now, however, he was too ill to see it—how the people in the car began to gasp and sputter, to put their handkerchiefs to their noses, and transfix him with furious glances. Jurgis only knew that a man in front of him immediately got up and gave him a seat; and that half a minute later the two people on each side of him got up; and that in a full minute the crowded car was nearly empty—those passengers who could not get room on the platform having gotten out to walk.

Of course, Jurgis had made his home a miniature fertilizer-mill a minute after entering. The stuff was half an inch deep in his skin—his whole system was full of it, and it would have taken a week, not merely of scrubbing, but of vigorous exercise, to get it out of him. As it was, he could be compared with nothing known to men, save that newest discovery of the savants, a substance which emits energy in large quantities and for unlimited time, without being itself in the least diminished in power. Jurgis smelt so that he made all the food at the table taste, and set the whole family to vomiting; for himself, it was three days before he could keep anything upon his stomach—he might wash his hands and use a knife and fork, but were not his mouth and throat filled with the poison?

And still Jurgis stuck it out! In spite of splitting headaches he would stagger down to the plant and take his stand once more, and begin to shovel in the blinding clouds of dust. And so at the end of the week he was a fertilizer-man for life—he was able to eat again, and though his head never stopped aching, it ceased to be so bad that he could not work. Every man who worked in the fertilizer plant was dying slowly of deadly diseases; but so long as the process was slow enough, it did not trouble them much—the men outside were dying more rapidly still.

So there passed another summer. It was a summer of prosperity all over the country, and the country ate generously of packing-house products, and there was plenty of work for all the family, in spite of the packers' efforts to keep a superfluity of labor. They were again able to pay their debts, and to begin to save a little sum. They could have become quite well off, by their standards, had they worked just so all the time. But there were one or two sacrifices they considered too heavy to be made for long—it was too bad that their home should go all to wreck, while Teta Elzbieta remained a kitchen-woman; and also it was too bad that the two boys should have to sell papers at their age. It was quite useless to caution them and plead with them; quite without knowing it they were taking on the tone of their new environment, and anyone could see that they were growing rougher and less obedient. They were learning to swear in voluble English; they were learning to pick up cigar stumps and smoke them, to pass hours of their time gambling with pennies and dice and cigarette-cards; they were learning the location of all the houses of prostitution on the "Levee," and the names of the "madames" who kept them, and the days when they gave their gorgeous banquets, which the police-captains and the big politicians all attended. If a visiting "country customer" were to ask them they could show him which was "Hinkydink's" famous saloon, and could even point out to him by name the different gamblers and thugs and "hold-up men" who made the place their head-quarters. Among other things the boys were getting out of the habit of coming home at night. What was the use, they would ask, of wasting time and energy and a possible car-fare riding out to the stock-yards every night, when the weather was pleasant, and they could crawl under a truck or into an empty doorway and sleep exactly as well? So long as they brought home a half dollar for each day, what mattered it when they brought it? But Jurgis declared that from this to ceasing to come at all would not be a very long step, and so as soon as he was at work again it was decided that Teta Elzbieta should give up her place and come home, and that Vilimui and Nikalojus and little Kotrina should all return to school in the fall.

And so in September the family was again just making out upon the earnings of Jurgis and Ona, and the board of Marija—when suddenly, without so much as half an hour's warning, Ona lost her place at Smith's.

There was no complicated story to this. It was all quite simple and obvious. Ona had now been working in the ham-wrapping room for two years, and every day during that time she had been half expecting what now happened, when the forelady came and told her that her services were no longer needed. Ona stood still, quite white about the lips; she caught at her breath two or three times, and then managed to gasp out an inquiry as to what she had done. She had done nothing in particular, the forelady answered coldly; she was no longer needed. She would be paid for the time she had worked. And so Ona got her things together and went out and sat down on the steps and wept to break her heart.

The next day Ona was told by Jadwiga Marciukus that the forelady had put in her place one of the girls from the house down on the "Levee." That had happened so often that Ona was not surprised at all; though she felt the cruel injustice of it, there was nothing that she could do. There was no one higher up that she could complain to; the superintendent was this woman's paramour and accomplice, and in all the time that she had been there the will of these two people had been Ona's law. For her to have inquired for or sought any higher authority would have been an unpardonable piece of impertinence. In Packingtown the discipline is the same as in an army—every official has full sway in his own department, and is responsible only to the official next in rank, and responsible, of course, for results. The ham-wrapping department of Smith's was competing with all the other ham-wrapping departments in the yards; and every week the reports of all would be submitted, and the managers would compare them. Anyone who is guileless enough may believe that what these hard-headed business men discussed was which had kept the highest moral standard among its workers, and had been kindest to the old and trusted hands—and not which of them had wrapped the most hams!

So the family faced one siege more. It was commonly much easier for a woman to get a place in the yards than for a man—with the introduction of new machinery and the perfecting of the processes, it was an every-day matter for men to be turned off and women and children put in their places. But then Ona was not an ordinary woman; she could not hope to succeed like Marija, for instance, who would do the work of the average man and a little more. So there was great anxiety—and corresponding surprise and delight when one of the girls that had worked with Ona came and told her of a chance that she might get in the sausage department. It was all the more strange because the girl who told Ona was one who had been most chummy with the forelady, and a frequent visitor to the house downtown, and, therefore, the last person in the world that Ona would have looked to for a favor. At first she thought it must be a cruel jest; and this became almost a certainty when she went to the sausage-rooms and saw the boss, a coarse-looking, red-faced Irishman whom she had frequently seen with her "forelady." But the man, after looking her over and asking her a few questions, told her that he would give her a chance, and added that if she did her work she could earn more than she had in the place she had left.

So Ona became the servant of a sausage-machine. The change would have been a cruel one, even had she made several times as much money; for while she was wrapping hams she had been able to sit down, and now she had to be upon her feet from seven in the morning till noon, and again from one till six.

For the first few days it seemed to her that she could not stand it—she suffered almost as much as Jurgis had from the fertilizer, and would come out at sundown with her head fairly reeling. Besides this, she was now working in one of the dark holes, by electric light; the dampness, too, was deadly—there was always a thin layer of water on the floor and a sickening odor of moist flesh in the room. The people who worked here followed the ancient custom of nature, whereby the ptarmigan is the color of dead leaves in the fall and of snow in the winter, and the chameleon, who is black when he lies upon a stump, turns green when he moves to a leaf. The men and women who work in this department were precisely the color of the "fresh country sausage" they made.

The sausage-room was an interesting place to visit for two or three minutes, and provided that you did not look at the people; the sausage-machines were perhaps the most wonderful things in the entire plant. Presumably sausages were once chopped and stuffed by hand, and if so it would be interesting to know how many workers had been displaced by these machines. On one side of the room were the hoppers, into which men shoveled loads of meat, and wheelbarrows full of spices; in these great bowls were whirling knives that made two thousand revolutions a minute, and when the meat was ground fine and well mixed with water it was was forced to the stuffing-machines on the other side of the room. These machines were tended by women; there was a sort of spout, like the nozzle of a hose, and one of the women would take a long string of gut and put the end over the nozzle and then work the whole thing on, as one works the fingers of a tight glove. This string of casing would be twenty or thirty feet long, but the woman would have it all on in a jiffy; and when she had several on she would press a lever and a stream of sausage meat would be shot out, taking the casing with it as it came. Thus one might stand and see appear, miraculously born from the machine, a wriggling snake of sausage of incredible length. In front was a big pan which caught these creatures, and two more women, who seized them as fast as they appeared and twisted them into links. This was for the uninitiated the most perplexing work of all; for all that the woman had to give was a single turn of the wrist, and in some way she contrived to give it so that instead of an endless chain of sausage, one after another, there grew under her hands a bunch of strings, all dangling from a single center. It was quite like the feat of a prestidigitator—for the woman worked so fast that the eye could literally not follow her, and there was only a mist of motion and tangle after tangle of sausages appearing. In the midst of the mist, however, the visitor would suddenly notice the tense set face, with the two wrinkles graven in the forehead, and the ghastly pallor of the cheeks, and then he would suddenly recollect that it was time he was going on. The woman did not go on; she stayed right there—hour after hour, day after day, week after week, year after year, twisting sausage links and racing with death. It was piece-work, and she was apt to have a family to keep alive; and stern and ruthless economic laws had arranged it that she could only do this by working just as she did, with all her soul upon her work, and with never an instant for thought, nor a glance at the well-dressed ladies and gentlemen who came to stare at her, as at some wild beast in a menagerie.

WITH ONE member trimming beef in a cannery and another working in a sausage factory, our family had now a first-hand knowledge of the great majority of Packingtown swindles. For it was the custom, as they found, whenever meat was so spoiled that it could not be used for anything else, either to can it, or else to chop it up into sausage. With what had been told them by Jonas, who had worked in the pickle-rooms, they could now study the whole of the spoiled meat industry on the inside, and read a new and grim meaning into that old Packingtown jest—that they use everything of the pig except the squeal.

Jonas had told them how the meat that was taken out of pickle would often be found sour, and how they would rub it up with soda to take away the smell, and sell it to be eaten on free-lunch counters. In the pickling of hams they had an ingenious apparatus, by which they saved time and increased the capacity of the plant—a machine consisting of a hollow needle attached to a pump; by plunging this needle into the meat and working with his foot, a man cold fill a ham with pickle in a few seconds. And yet, in spite of this, there would be hams found spoiled, some of them with an odor so bad that a man could hardly bear to be in the room with them. To pump into these the frugal packers had a second and much stronger pickle which destroyed the odor—a process known to the workers as "giving them thirty per cent." Also, after the hams had been smoked, there would be found some that had gone to the bad. Formerly these had been sold as "Number Three Grade," but later on some ingenious person had hit upon a new device, and now they would extract the bone, about which the bad part generally lay, and insert in the hole a white-hot iron. After this invention there was no longer Number One, Two and Three Garde—there was only Number One Grade.

It was only when the whole ham was spoiled that it came into the department of Ona. Cut up by the two-thousand-revolutions-a-minute flyers, and mixed with half a ton of other meat, no odor that was ever in a ham could make any difference; and if people all over the world ate the sausage and died of ptomaine poisoning, the packers would not even have to know it. There was never the least attention paid to what was cut up for sausage; there would come all the way back from Europe old sausage that had been rejected and that was moldy and white—it would be dosed with borax and glycerine, and dumped into the hoppers, and made over again for home consumption. There would be meat that had tumbled out on the floor, in the dirt and saw-dust, where the workers had tramped and spit uncounted billions of consumption germs. There would be meat stored in great piles in rooms; and the water from leaky roofs would drip over it, and thousands of rats would race about on it. It was too dark in these storage places to see well, but a man could run his hand over these piles of meat and sweep off handfuls of the dried dung of rats. These rats were nuisances, and the packers would put poisoned bread out for them; they would die, and then rats, bread and meat would go into the hoppers together. This is no fairy-story, and no joke; the meat would be shoveled into carts, and the man who did the shoveling would not trouble to lift out a rat even when he saw one—there were things that went into the sausage in comparison with which a poisoned rat was a tidbit. There was no place for the men to wash their hands before they ate their dinner, and so they made a practice of washing them in the water that was to be ladled into the sausage. There were the butt-ends of smoked meat, and the scraps of corned beef, and all the odds and ends of the waste of the plants, that would be dumped into old barrels in the cellar and left there. Under the system of rigid economy which the packers enforced there were some jobs that it only paid to do once in a long time, and among these was the cleaning out of the waste-barrels. Every spring they did it; and in the barrels would be dirt, and rust, and old nails, and stale water—and filth that cannot be named. The meat would be moldy and white, stinking and full of maggots; and still, cartload after cartload, it would be taken up and dumped into the hoppers with fresh meat, and sent out to the dear public's breakfast. Some of it they would make into "smoked" sausage—but as the smoking took time, and was therefore expensive, they would preserve it with borax, and color it with gelatine to make it brown. All of their sausage came out of the same bowl, but when they came to pack it they would stamp some of it "special," and for this they would charge two cents more a pound.

Such were the new surroundings in which Ona was placed, and such was the work she was compelled to do. It was stupefying, brutalizing work; it left her no time to think, no strength for anything. She was part of the machine she tended, and every faculty that was not needed for the machine was doomed to be crushed out of existence. There was only one mercy about the cruel grind—that it gave her the gift of insensibility. Little by little she sank into a torpor—she fell silent—Ona, who had once gone about all day singing like a bird. She had nothing to sing about now, nothing to think about. She had barely strength to drag herself home at night; she would meet Jurgis at the corner, and often they would not say a word all the way. At home they would eat what they had to eat, and then, because there was only their misery to talk of, they would crawl into bed and fall into a stupor and never stir until it was time to get up again, and dress by candle light, and go back to the machine. They were so numbed that they did not even suffer much from hunger, now; only the children continued to fret when the food ran short.

Yet their souls were not dead, they were only sleeping; now and then they would waken, and these were cruel times. The gates of memory would roll open—old joys would stretch out their arms to them, old hopes and dreams would call to them, and they would stir beneath the burden that lay upon them and feel its forever unmeasurable weight. They could not even cry out beneath it; but anguish would seize them more dreadful than the agony of death. It was a thing scarcely to be spoken—a thing never spoken by the world, that will not know its own defeat.

They were beaten; they had lost the game; they were swept aside. It was not less tragic because it was so sordid, because that it had to do with wages, and grocery bills, and rents. They had dreamed of freedom; of a chance to look about them and learn something; to be decent and clean, to see their child grow up to be strong. And now it was all gone—it would never be. They had played the game and they had lost. Six years more of toil they had before them before they could expect the least respite, the cessation of the payments upon the house; and how cruelly certain it was that they could never stand six years of such a life as they were living! They were lost, they were going down! And there was no deliverance for them, no hope; for all the help it gave them the vast city in which they lived might have been an ocean waste, a wilderness, a desert, a tomb. So often this mood would come to Ona, in the night time, when something wakened her; she would lie, afraid of the beating of her own heart, fronting the blood-red eyes of the old primeval terror of life.

Once Ona cried aloud, and woke Jurgis, who was tired and cross. After that she learned to weep silently—their moods so seldom came together now! It was as if their hopes were buried in separate graves.

Jurgis, being a man, had troubles of his own. There was another specter following him. He had never spoken of it, nor would he allow anyone else to speak of it—he had never acknowledged. its existence to himself. Yet the battle with it took all the manhood that he had—and once or twice, alas, a little more. Jurgis had discovered drink. He was working in the steaming pit of hell; day after day, week after week, until now there was not an organ of his body that did its work without pain, until the sound of ocean breakers echoed in his head day and night, and the building swayed and danced before him as he went down the street. And from all the unending horror of this there was a respite, a deliverance—he could drink! He could forget the pain, he could slip off the burden; he would see clearly again, he would be master of his brain, of his thoughts, of his will. His dead self would stir in him, and he would find himself laughing, and cracking jokes with his companions—he would be a man again, and master of his life.

It was not an easy thing for Jurgis to take more than two or three drinks. With the first drink he could eat a meal, and he could persuade himself that

that was economy; with the second he could eat another meal—but there would come a time when he could eat no more, and then to pay for a drink was an unthinkable extravagance, a defiance of the age-long instincts of his hunger-haunted class. One day, however, he took the plunge, and drank up all that he had in his pockets, and went home half "canned," as the men called it. He was happier than he had been in a year; and yet, because he knew that the happiness would not last, he was savage, too—with those who would wreck it, and with the world, and with his life; and then again, beneath this, he was sick with the shame of himself. Afterwards, when he saw the despair of his family, and reckoned up the money he had spent, the tears came into his eyes, and he began the long battle with the specter.

It would not have been so bad but for the fact that it was a battle that had no end, that never could have one. Jurgis did not realize that very clearly; he was not given much time for reflection; he lived wholly in the present. He simply knew that he was always fighting. Steeped in misery and despair as he was, it was to be put upon the rack merely to walk down the street. There was surely a saloon on the corner—perhaps on all four corners, and some in the middle of the block as well; and each one stretched out a hand to him— each one had a personality of its own, allurements unlike any others. Going and coming—before sunrise and after dark—there was warmth and a glow of light, and the steam of hot food, and perhaps music or a friendly face, and a word of good cheer. Jurgis developed a fondness for having Ona on his arm whenever he went out on the street, and he would hold her tightly and walk fast. It was pitiful to have Ona know of this—it drove him wild to think of it; the thing was not fair, for Ona had never tasted drink, and so could not understand. Sometimes, in desperate hours, he would find himself wishing that she might learn what it was, so that he need not be ashamed in her presence. They might drink together, and escape from the horror—escape for a while, come what would.

There came a time when nearly all the conscious life of Jurigs consisted of a struggle with the craving for drink. He would have ugly moods, when he hated Ona and the whole family because it so stood in his way. He was a fool to have married; he had tied himself down, and made himself a slave. It was all because he was a married man that he was compelled to stay in the yards; if it had not been for that he might have gone off like Jonas, and to hell with the packers. There were few single men in the fertilizer-mill—and those few were working only for a chance to escape. Meantime, too, they had some-thing to think about while they worked—they had the memory of the last time they had been drunk, and the hope of the time when they would be drunk again. As for Jurgis, he was expected to bring home every penny; he could not even go with the men at noontime—he had to sit down and eat his dinner on a pile of fertilizer dust.

This was not always his mood, of course—he still loved his family. But just now was a time of trial. Poor little Antanas, for instance—who had never failed to win him with a smile—little Antanas was not smiling just now, being a mass of fiery red pimples. He had had all the diseases that babies are heir to in quick succession, scarlet fever, mumps and whooping-cough, all in the first year, and now he was down with the measles. There was no one to attend him but Teta Elzbieta; there was no doctor to help him, because they were too poor, and children did not die of the measles—at least, not often. Now and then Elzbieta would find time to sob over his woes; but for the greater part of the time he had to be barricaded upon the bed. The floor was full of draughts, and if he caught cold he would die. At night he was tied down lest he should kick the covers off him, while the family lay in their stupor of exhaustion. He would lie and scream for hours, almost in convulsions; and then, when he was worn out, he would lie whimpering and wailing in his torment. He was burning up with fever, and his eyes were running sores; in the day time he was a thing uncanny and impish to behold, in his plaster of pimples and sweat—a great purple lump of misery.

All this was not really as cruel as it sounds, for, sick as he was, little Antanas was the least unfortunate member of that family. He was quite able to bear his sufferings—it was as if he had all these complaints to show what a prodigy of health he was. He was the child of his parents' youth and joy; he grew up like the conjurer's rose-bush, and all the world was his oyster. In general he toddled around the kitchen all day with a lean and hungry look— the portion of the family's allowance that fell to him was not enough, and he was restrainable in his demand for more. Antanas was but little over a year old, and already no one but his father could manage him.

It seemed as if he had taken all of his mother's strength—had left nothing for those that might come after him. Ona was with child again now, and it was a dreadful thing to contemplate; even Jurgis, dumb and despairing as he was, could not but understand that yet other agonies were on the way, and shudder at the thought of them. Ona was visibly going to pieces. In the first place, she was developing a cough, like the one that had killed old Diedas Antanas. She had had a trace of it ever since that fatal morning when the greedy streetcar corporation had turned her out into the rain; but now it was beginning to grow serious, and to wake her up at night. Even worse than that was the fearful nervousness from which she suffered; it had begun almost the first day she had entered the sausage-rooms, and it had grown worse every day since. She would have frightful headaches and fits of aimless weeping; sometimes she would come home at night shuddering and moaning, and would fling herself down upon the bed and burst into tears. Several times she was quite beside herself and hysterical; and then Jurgis would go half mad with fright. Elzbieta would explain to him that it could not be helped, that a woman was subject to such things when she was pregnant; but he was hardly to be persuaded, would beg and plead to know what had happened. She had never been like this before, he would argue—it was monstrous and unthinkable. It was the life she had to live, the accursed work she had to do, that was killing her by inches. She was not fitted for it—no woman was fitted for it, no woman ought to be allowed to do such work; if the world could not keep them alive any other way it ought to kill them at once and be done with it. They ought not to marry, to have children; no workingman ought to marry— if he had known what a woman was like, he would have had his eyes torn out first. So Jurgis would carry on, becoming half hysterical himself, which was an unbearable thing to see in a big man; Ona would pull herself together and fling herself into his arms, begging him to stop, to be still, that she would be better, it would be all right. So she would lie and sob out her grief upon his shoulder, while he gazed at her, as helpless as a wounded animal, the target of unseen enemies.

The beginning of these things was in September; each time Ona would promise him with terror in her voice that it would, not happen again—but in vain. Each crisis would leave Jurgis more and more perplexed and frightened, more disposed to distrust Elzbieta'a consolations, and to believe that there was some terrible thing about all this that he was not allowed to know. Once or twice in these outbreaks he caught Ona's eye, and it seemed to him like the eye of a hunted animal; there were broken phrases of anguish and despair now and then amid her frantic weeping. It was only because he was so numb and beaten that Jurgis did not worry himself more about this; he never thought of it, except when he was dragged to it—he lived like a dumb beast of burden, knowing only the moment in which he was.

15

THE WINTER was coming on again, more menacing and cruel than ever. It was November, and the holiday rush had begun—it was necessary for the machines to grind till late at night, to provide the millions of extra sausages that would be eaten at holiday breakfasts; and Ona, as part of the machine, began working fifteen or sixteen hours a day. There was no choice about this—whatever work there was to be done she had to do, if she wished to keep her place, besides that, it added another pittance to her income, so she staggered on with the awful load. She would start to work every morning at seven, and eat her dinner at noon, and then work until ten or eleven at night without another mouthful of food. Jurgis wanted to wait for her, to help her home at night, but she would not think of this, the fertilizer-mill was not running overtime, and there was no place for him to wait save in a saloon. She would stagger out into the darkness, and make her way to the corner, where there was a chance of finding Marija, who was also working overtime. If Marija had gone, she would get into a car, and begin a painful struggle to keep awake; once or twice, in fear of failure, she asked the conductor to call out her street, and was insulted for her trouble. When she got home, she was always too tired either to eat or to undress; she would crawl into bed with her shoes on and lie like a log. If she should fail, they would certainly be lost; if she held out they might have enough coal for the winter.

A day or two before Thanksgiving day there came a snow-storm. It began in the afternoon, and by evening two inches had fallen. Jurgis tried to wait for his wife, but went into a saloon to get warm, and took two drinks, and came out and ran home to escape from the demon; there he lay down to wait for her and instantly fell asleep. When he opened his eyes again he was in the midst of a nightmare, and found Elzbieta shaking him and crying with fright. At first he could not realize what she was saying—Ona had not come home. What time was it, he asked. It was morning—time to be up. Ona had not been home that night! And it was bitter cold, and a foot of snow on the ground.

Jurgis sat up with a start. Marija was crying with fright and the children were wailing in sympathy—little Stanislovas in addition, because the terror of the snow was upon him. Jurgis had nothing to put on but his shoes and his coat, and in half a minute he was out of the door. Then, however, he realized that there was no need of haste, that he had no idea where to go. It was still dark as midnight. And the thick snowflakes were sifting down—everything was so silent that he could hear the rustle of them as they fell. In the few seconds that he stood there hesitating, he was covered white.

He set off at a run for the yards, stopping by the way to inquire in the saloons that were open. Ona might have been overcome on the way; or else she might have met with an accident in the machines. When he got to the place where she worked he inquired of one of the watchmen—there had not been any accident, so far as the man had heard. At the time-office, which he found already open, the clerk told him that Ona's check had been turned in the night before, showing that she had left her work.

After that there was nothing for him to do but to wait, pacing back and forth in the snow, meantime, to keep from freezing. Already the yards were full of activity—cattle were being unloaded from the cars in the distance, and across the way the "beef-luggers" were toiling in the darkness, carrying two hundred pound quarters of bullocks into the refrigerator cars. Before the first streaks of daylight came the crowding throngs of workingmen, shivering, and swinging their dinner pails as they hurried by, Jurgis took up his stand by the time-office window, where alone there was light enough for him to see; the snow fell so thick that it was only by peering closely that he could make sure that Ona did not pass him.

Seven o'clock came, the hour when the great packing-machine began to move. Jurgis ought to have been at his place in the fertilizer-mill; but instead he was waiting, in an agony of fear, for Ona. It was fifteen minutes after the hour when he saw a form emerge from the snow-mist, and sprang towards it with a cry. It was she, running swiftly; as she saw him, she staggered forward, and half fell into his outstretched arms.

"What has been the matter?" he cried anxiously. "Where have you been?"

It was several seconds before she could get breath to answer him. "I couldn't get home," she exclaimed. "The snow—the cars had stopped."

"But where were you then?" he demanded.

"I had to go home with a friend," she panted—"with Jadwiga."

Jurgis drew a deep breath; but then he noticed that she was sobbing and trembling—as if in one of those nervous crises that he dreaded so. "But what's the matter?" he cried. "What has happened?"

"Oh, Jurgis, I was so frightened!" she said, clinging to him wildly. "I have been so worried!"

They were near the time-station window, and people were staring at them. Jurgis led her away. "How do you mean?" he asked, in perplexity.

"I was afraid—I was just afraid!" sobbed Ona. "I knew you wouldn't know where I was, and I didn't know what you might do. I tried to get home, but I was so tired. Oh, Jurgis, Jurgis!"

He was so glad to get her back that he could not think clearly about anything else; it did not seem strange to him that she should be so very much upset; all her fright and incoherent protestations did not matter since he had her back. He let her cry away her fears; and then, because it was nearly eight o'clock, and they would lose another hour if they delayed, he left her at the packing-house door, with her ghastly white face and her haunted eyes of terror.

There was another brief interval. Christmas was almost come; and because the snow still held, and the searching cold, morning after morning Jurgis half carried his wife to her post, staggering with her through the darkness. Until at last, one night, came the end.

It lacked but three days of the holidays. About midnight Marija came home, exclaiming in alarm when she found that Ona had not come. Marija had agreed to meet her; and after waiting, had gone to the room where she worked, only to find that the sausage hands had quit work an hour before, and left. There was no snow that night, nor was it especially cold; and still Ona had not come! Something more serious must be wrong this time.

They aroused Jurgis, and he sat up and listened crossly to the story. She must have gone home again with Jadwiga, he said; Jadwiga lived only two blocks from the yards, and perhaps she had been tired. Nothing could have happened to her—and even if there had there was nothing could be done about it until morning. Jurgis turned over in his bed, and was snoring again before the two had closed the door.

In the morning, however, he was up and out nearly an hour before the usual time. Jadwiga Marciukus lived on the other side of the yards, beyond Halstead street, with her mother and sisters in a single basement room—for Mikolas had recently lost one hand from blood-poisoning, and their marriage had been put off forever. The door of the room was in the rear, reached by a narrow court, and Jurgis saw a light in the window and heard something frying as he passed; he knocked, half expecting that Ona would answer.

Instead there was one of Jadwiga's little sisters, who gazed at him through a crack in the door. "Where's Ona?" he demanded; and the child looked at him in perplexity. "Ona?" she said.

"Yes," said Jurgis, "isn't she here?"

"No," said the child, and Jurgis gave a start. A moment later came Jadwiga, peering over the child's head. When she saw who it was, she slid around out of sight, for she was not quite dressed. Jurgis must excuse her, she began, her mother was very ill—"

"Ona isn't here?" Jurgis demanded, too alarmed to wait for her to finish.

"Why, no," said Jadwiga. "What made you think she would be here? Had she said she was coming?"

"No," he answered. "But she hasn't come home—and I thought she would be here the same as before."

"As before?" echoed Jadwiga, in perplexity.

"The time she spent the night here," said Jurgis.

"There must be some mistake," she answered quickly. "Ona has never spent the night here."

He was only half able to realize her words. "Why—why," he exclaimed. "Two weeks ago, Jadwiga! She told me so—the night it snowed, and she could not get home."

"There must be some mistake," declared the girl, again; "she didn't come here."

He steadied himself by the door sill; and Jadwiga in her anxiety—for she was fond of Ona—opened the door wide, holding her jacket across her throat. "Are you sure you didn't misunderstand her?" she cried. "She must have meant somewhere else. She—"

"She said here," insisted Jurgis. "She told me all about you, and how you were, and what you said. Are you sure? You haven't forgotten? You weren't away?"

"No, no!" she exclaimed—and then came a peevish voice—"Jadwiga, you are giving the baby a cold. Shut the door!" Jurgis stood for half a minute more, stammering his perplexity through an eighth of an inch of crack; and then, as there was really nothing more to be said, he excused himself and went away.

He walked on half dazed, without knowing where he went. Ona had deceived him! She had lied to him! And what could it mean—where had she been? Where was she now? He could hardly grasp the thing—much less try to solve it; but a hundred wild surmises came to him, and a sense of impending calamity rushed over him.

Because there was nothing else to do, he went back to the time-office to watch again. He waited until nearly an hour after seven, and then went to the room where Ona worked to make inquiries of Ona's "boss." The "boss," who was named Connor, he found had not yet come; all the lines of cars that came from downtown were stalled—there had been an accident in the power-house, and no cars had been running since last night. Meantime, however, the sausage-machines were grinding on with someone else in charge of them. The man who answered Jurgis was shovelling meat into a hopper, and as he talked he looked to see if he were being watched. Then another came up, wheeling a truck; he knew Jurgis for Ona's husband, and was curious about the mystery.

Maybe the cars had something to do with it he suggested—maybe she had gone downtown. No, said Jurgis, she never went downtown. "Perhaps not," said the man. Jurgis thought he saw him exchange a swift glance with the other as he spoke, and he demanded quickly: "What do you know about it?"

But the man had seen that the boss was watching him; he started on again pushing his truck. "I don't know anything about it," he said over his shoulder. "How should I know where your wife goes?"

Then Jurgis went out again, and paced up and down before the building.

All the morning he stayed there, with no thought of his work. About noon he went to the police-station to make inquiries, and then came back again for another anxious vigil. Finally, towards the middle of the afternoon, he set out for home again.

He was walking out Ashland avenue. The street cars had began running again, and several passed him, packed to the steps with people. The sight of them set Jurgis to thinking again of the man's sarcastic remark; and half involuntarily he found himself watching the cars—with the result that he gave a sudden startled exclamation, and stopped short in his tracks.

Then he broke into a run. For a whole block he tore after the car, only a little ways behind. Then gave up, and let it go. That rusty black hat with the drooping red flower, it might not be Ona's, but there was very little likelihood of it. He would know for certain very soon, for she would get out two blocks ahead.

She got out; and as soon as she was out of sight on the side street Jurgis broke into a run. Suspicion was rife in him now, and he was not ashamed to shadow her; he saw her turn the corner near their home, and then he ran again, and saw her as she went up the porch-steps of the house. After that he turned back, and for five minutes paced up and down, his hands clenched tightly and his lips set, his mind in a turmoil. Then he went home and entered.

As he opened the door, Teta Elzbieta was coming out of one of the bed-rooms. She was on tip-toe, and had a finger on her lips. Jurgis waited until she was close to him.

"Don't make any noise," she whispered, hurriedly.

"What's the matter?" he asked.

"Ona is asleep," she panted. "She's been very ill. I'm afraid her mind's been wandering, Jurgis. She was lost on the street all night, and I've only just succeeded in getting her quiet."

"When did she come in?" he asked. "Soon after you left this morning," said Elzbieta. "And has she been out since?" "No, of course not. She's so weak, Jurgis, she—"

And he set his teeth hard together. "You are lying to me," he said.

Elzbieta started, and turned pale. "Why!" she gasped. "What do you mean?

But Jurgis did not answer. He pushed her aside, and strode to the bed-room door and opened it.

Ona was sitting on the bed. She turned a startled look upon him as he entered. He closed the door in Elzbieta's face, and went towards his wife. "Where have you been?" he demanded.

She had her hands clasped tightly in her lap, and he saw that her face was as white as paper, and drawn with pain. She gasped once or twice as she tried to answer him, and then began, speaking low, and swiftly, "Jurgis, I—I think I have been out of my mind. I started to come last night, and I could not find the way. I walked—I walked all night, I think, and—and I only got home—this morning."

"You needed a rest," he said in a hard tone. "Why did you go out again?"

He was looking her fairly in the face, and he could read the sudden fear and wild uncertainty that leaped into her eyes. "I—I had to go to—to the store," she gasped, almost in a whisper, "I had to go—"

"You are lying to me." said Jurgis.

Then he clenched his hands and took a step towards her. "Why do you lie to me?" he cried fiercely. "What are you doing that you have to lie to me?"

"Jurgis!" she exclaimed, starting up in fright, "Oh, Jurgis, how can you?"

"You have lied to me, I say!" he cried. "You told me you had been to Jadwiga's house that other night, and you hadn't. You had been where you were last night—somewhere's downtown, for I saw you get off the car. Where were you?"

It was as if he had struck a knife into her. She seemed to go all to pieces. For half a second she stood, reeling and swaying, staring at him with horror in her eyes; then, with a cry of anguish, she tottered forward, stretching out her arms to him.

But he stepped aside, deliberately, and let her fall. She caught herself at the side of the bed, and then sunk down, burying her face in her hands and bursting into frantic weeping.

There came one of those hysterical crises that had so often dismayed him. Ona sobbed and wept, her fear and anguish building themselves up into long climaxes. Furious gusts of emotion would come sweeping over her, shaking her as the tempest shakes the trees upon the hills; all her frame would quiver and throb with them—it was as if some dreadful thing rose up within her and took possession of her, torturing her, tearing her. This thing had been wont to set Jurgis quite beside himself with fear; but now he stood with his lips set tightly, and his hands clenched—she might weep till she killed herself, but she should not move him this time—not an inch, not an inch. Yet the sounds she made set his blood to running cold, and his lips to quivering in spite of himself, and he was glad of the diversion when Teta Elzbieta, pale with fright, opened the door and rushed in.

He turned upon her with an oath. "Go out!" he cried, "Go out!" And then, as she stood hesitating, about to speak, he seized her by the arm, and half flung her from the room, slamming the door and barring it with a table. Then he turned again and faced Ona, crying—"Now, answer me!"

But she did not hear him—she was still in the grip of the fiend. Jurgis could see her outstretched hands, shaking and twitching, roaming here and there over the bed at will, like living things; he could see convulsive shudderings start in her body, and run through her limbs. She was sobbing and choking—it was as if there were too many sounds for one throat, they came chasing each other, like waves upon the sea. Then her voice would begin to rise into screams, louder and louder, until it broke in wild, horrible peals of laughter. Jurgis bore it until he could bear it no longer, and then he sprang at her, seizing her by the shoulders and shaking her, shouting into her ear: "Stop it, I say! Stop it!"

She looked up at him, out of her agony; then she fell forward at his feet. She caught them in her hands in spite of his efforts to step aside, and with her face upon the floor lay writhing. It made a choking in Jurgis's throat to hear her, and he cried again more savagely than before: "Stop it, I say!"

This time she heeded him, and caught her breath and lay silent, save for the gasping sobs that wrenched all her frame. For a long minute she lay there, perfectly motionless, until a cold fear seized her husband, thinking that she was dying. Suddenly, however, he heard her voice, faintly: "Jurgis! Jurgis!"

"What is it?" he said.

He had to bend down to her, she was so weak. She was pleading with him, in broken phrases, painfully uttered; "Have faith in me! Believe me!"

"Believe what?" he cried. "Believe that I—that I know best—that I love you! And do not ask me—what you did. Oh, Jurgis, please, please! It is for the best—it is—"

He started to speak again, but she rushed on, frantically, heading him off. "If you will only do it! If you will only—only believe me! It wasn't my fault—I couldn't help it—it will be all right—it is nothing—it is no harm. Oh, Jurgis—please, please!"

She had hold of him, and was trying to raise herself to look at him; he could feel the palsied shaking of her hands, and the heaving of the bosom she pressed against him. She managed to catch one of his hands and gripped it convulsively, drawing it to her face, and bathing it in her tears. "Oh, believe me, believe me!" she wailed again; and he shouted in fury: "I will not!"

But still she clung to him, wailing aloud in her despair: "Oh, Jurgis, think what you are doing! It will ruin us—it will ruin us! Oh, no, you must not do it! No, don't, don't do it. You must not do it! It will drive me mad—it will kill me—no, no, Jurgis, I am crazy—it is nothing. You do not really need to know. We can be happy—we can love each other, just the same. Oh, please, please, believe me!"

Her words fairly drove him wild. He tore his hands loose, and flung her off. "Answer me," he cried, "God damn it, I say—answer me!"

She sunk down upon the floor, beginning to cry again. It was like listening to the moan of a damned soul, and Jurgis could not stand it. He smote his fist upon the table by his side, and shouted again at her, "Answer me!"

She began to scream aloud, her voice like the voice of some wild beast:

"Ah! Ah! I can't! I can't do it!"

"Why can't you do it?" he shouted. "I don't know how!"

He sprang and caught her by the arm, lifting her up, and glaring into her face. "Tell me where you were last night!" he panted. "Quick, out with it!"

Then she began to whisper, one word at a time: "I—was in—a house—downtown—"

"What house? What do you mean?" She tried to hide her eyes away, but he held her. "Miss Henderson's house," she gasped.

He did not understand at first, "Miss Henderson's house," he echoed. Miss Henderson was the "forelady" of the ham-wrapping room, Ona's former place. And then suddenly, as in an explosion, the horrible truth burst over him, and he reeled and staggered back with a scream. He caught himself against the wall, and put his hand to his forehead, staring about him, and whispering, "Jesus! Jesus!"

Then suddenly he leaped at her, as she lay grovelling at his feet. He seized her by the throat. "Tell me!" he gasped, hoarsely, "Quick! Who took you to that place?"

She tried to get away, making him furious; he thought it was fear, or the pain of his clutch—he did not understand that it was the agony of her shame. Still she answered him, "My boss."

He tightened his grip in his frenzy, and only when he saw her eyes closing did he realize that he was choking her. Then he relaxed his fingers, and crouched, waiting, until she opened her lids again. His breath beat hot into her face.

"Tell me," he whispered, at last, "tell me about it."

She lay perfectly motionless, and he had to hold his breath to catch her words: "I did not want—to do it," she said; "I tried—I tried not to do it. I only did it—to save us. It was our only chance."

Again, for a space, there was no sound but his panting. Ona's eyes closed, and when she spoke again she did not open them. "He told me—he would discharge me. He told me he would—we would all of us lose our places. We could never get anything to do—here—again. He—he meant it—he would have ruined us."

Jurgis's arms were shaking so that he could scarcely hold himself up, and lurched forward now and then as he listened. "When—when did this begin?" he gasped.

"At the very first," she said. She spoke as if in a trance. "It was all—it was their plot—Miss Henderson's plot. She hated me. And he—he wanted me. She discharged me, so that he could give me a place. Then he began to—to make love to me. He offered me money. He begged me—he said he loved me. Then he threatened me. He knew all about us, he knew we would starve. He knew your boss—he knew Marija's. He would hound us to death, he said—then he said if I would—if I—we would all of us be sure of work—always. Then one day he caught hold of me—he would not let go—he—he—"

"Where was this?" "In the hall-way—at night—after everyone had gone. I could not help it—I thought of you—of the baby—of mother and the children. I was afraid of him—afraid to cry out."

A moment ago her face had been ashen grey, now it was scarlet. She was beginning to breathe hard again. Jurgis made not a sound.

"That was a month ago. Then he wanted me to come—to that house. He wanted me to stay there. He said all of us—that we would not have to work. He made me come there—in the evenings. I told you—you thought I was at the factory. Then—one night it snowed, and I couldn't get back. And then—last night—the cars were stopped. It was such a little thing—to ruin us all. I tried to walk, but I couldn't. I didn't want you to know. It would have—it would have been all right. We could have gone on—just the same—you need never have known about it. He was getting tired of me—he would have let me alone soon. I am going to have a baby—I am getting ugly. He told me that—twice, he told me, last night. He kicked me—last night —too. And now you will kill him—you—you will kill him—and we shall die."

All this she had said without a quiver; she lay still as death—not an eyelid moving. And Jurgis, too, said not a word. He lifted himself by the bed, and stood up. He did not stop for another glance at her, but went to the door and opened it. He did not see Elzbieta, crouching terrified in the corner; he went out, hatless, leaving the street door open behind him. The instant his feet were on the sidewalk he broke into a run.

He ran like one possessed, blindly, furiously, looking neither to the right nor left. He was on Ashland Avenue before exhaustion compelled him to slow down, and then, noticing a car, he made a dart for it, and drew himself aboard. His eyes were wild and his hair flying, and he was breathing hoarsely, like a wounded bull; but the people on the car did not notice this particularly—perhaps it seemed natural to them that a man who smelt as Jurgis smelt should exhibit an aspect to correspond. They began to give way before him, as usual. The conductor took his nickel gingerly, with the tips of his fingers, and then left him with the platform to himself. Jurgis did not even notice it—his thoughts were far away. Within his soul it was like a roaring furnace; he stood waiting, waiting, crouching as if for a spring.

He had some of his breath back when the car came to the entrance of the yards, and so he leaped off and started again, racing at full speed. People turned and stared at him, but he saw no one—there was the factory, and he bounded through the doorway, and up the stairs, three at a time. He knew the room where Ona worked—he had been there once, at night, out of curiosity.

He knew Connor—he looked for him as he sprang into the room.

The machines were racing at full speed, and men and women were toiling busily. He shot one swift glance about the room—the man was not in it. But then suddenly he heard a voice in the corridor and started for it with a bound. In an instant more he fronted the boss.

He was a big, red-faced Irishman, coarse-featured, and smelling of liquor. He saw Jurgis as he crossed the threshold, and turned white. He hesitated one second, as if meaning to run; and in the next his assailant was upon him. He put up his hands to protect his face, but Jurgis, lunging with all the power of his arm and body, struck him fairly between the eyes and knocked him backwards. The next moment he was on top of him, burying his fingers in his throat.

To Jurgis this man's whole presence reeked of the crime he had committed; the touch of his body was madness to him—it set every nerve of him a-tremble, it aroused all the demon in his soul. It had worked its will upon Ona, this great beast—and now he had it, he had it! It was his turn now! Things swam blood before him, and he screamed aloud in his fury, lifting his victim and smashing his head upon the floor.

The room, of course, was in an uproar; women fainting and shrieking, and men rushing in. Jurgis was so bent upon his task that he knew nothing of this, and scarcely realized that people were trying to interfere with him; it was only when half a dozen men had seized him by the legs and shoulders and were pulling at him, that he understood that he was losing his prey. In a flash he had bent down and sunk his teeth into the man's cheek; and when they tore him away he was dripping with blood, and little ribbons of skin were hanging in his mouth.

They got him down upon the floor, clinging to him by his arms and legs, and still they could hardly hold him. He fought like a tiger, writhing and twisting, half flinging them off, and starting toward his unconscious enemy. But yet others rushed in, until there was a little mountain of twisted limbs and bodies, heaving and tossing, and working its way about the room. In the end, by their sheer weight they choked the breath out of him, and then they carried him to the company police station, where he lay still until they had summoned a patrol-wagon to take him away.

WHEN JURGIS got up again he went quietly enough. He was exhausted and half dazed, and besides he saw the blue uniforms of the policemen. He drove in a patrol-wagon with half a dozen of them watching him; keeping as far away as possible, however, on account of the fertilizer. Then he stood before the sergeant's desk and gave his name and address, and saw a charge of assault and battery entered against him. On his way to his cell a burly policeman cursed him because he started down the wrong corridor, and then added a kick when he was not quick enough; nevertheless Jurgis did not even lift his eyes—he had lived two years and a half in Packingtown and he knew what the police were. It was as much as a man's very life was worth to anger them, here in their inmost lair; like as not a dozen would pile on to him at once, and pound his face into a pulp. It would be nothing unusual if he got his skull cracked in the melee—in which case they would report that he had been drunk and had fallen down, and there would be no one to know the difference, or to care.

So a barred door clanged upon Jurgis and he sat down on a bench and buried his face in his hands. He was alone; and he had the afternoon and all of the night to himself.

At first he was like a wild beast that has glutted itself; he was in a dull stupor of satisfaction. He had done up the scoundrel pretty well—not as well as he would have if they had given him a minute more, but still pretty well; the ends of his fingers were still tingling from their contact with the fellow's throat. But then, little by little, as his strength came back and his senses cleared, he began to see beyond his momentary gratification; that he had nearly killed the boss would not help Ona—not the horrors that she had borne, nor the memory that would haunt her all her days. It would not help to feed her and her child; she would certainly lose her place, while he—what was to happen to him, God only knew.

Half the night he paced the floor, wrestling with this nightmare; and when he was exhausted he lay down, trying to sleep, but finding instead, for the first time in his life, that his brain was too much for him. In the cell next to him was a drunken wife-beater, and in the one beyond a yelling maniac. At midnight they opened the station-house to the homeless wanderers who were crowded about the door, shivering in the winter blast; they thronged into the corridor outside of the cells. Some of them stretched themselves out on the bare stone floor and fell to snoring; others sat up, laughing and talking, cursing and quarreling. The air was fetid with their breath, yet in spite of this some of them smelt Jurgis and called down the torrents of hell upon him. He lay in a far corner of his cell, upon the ground, counting the throbbings of the blood in his forehead.

They had brought him his supper, which was "duffers and dope"—being hunks of dry bread on a tin plate, and coffee, called "dope" because it was drugged to keep the prisoners quiet. Jurgis had not known this, or he would have swallowed the stuff in desperation; as it was, every nerve of him was a-quiver with shame and rage. Toward morning the place fell silent and then he got up and began to pace his cell; within the soul of him there rose up a fiend, red-eyed and cruel, and tore out the strings of his heart.

It was not for himself that he suffered—what did a man who had worked in Anderson's fertilizer-mill care about anything that the world might do to him! What was any tyranny of prison compared with the tyranny of the past, of the thing that had happened and could not be recalled, of the memory that could never be effaced! The horror of it drove him mad; he stretched out his arms to heaven, crying out for deliverance from it—and there was no deliverance, there was no power in heaven that could undo the past. It was a ghost that would not down; it followed him, it seized upon him and beat him to the ground. Ah, if only he could have known of it—but he would have known of it if he had not been a fool! He smote his hands upon his forehead, cursing himself because he had ever allowed her to work where she had, because he had not stood between her and a fate which every one knew to be so common. Every one laughed at it; but he—he should have taken her away, even if it were to lie down and die of starvation in the gutters of Chicago's streets! And now—oh, it could not be true; it was too monstrous, too horrible!

It was a thing that could not be faced; a new shuddering seized him every time he tried to think of it. No, there was no bearing the load of it, there was no living under it. There would be none for her—he knew that he might pardon her, might plead with her on his knees, but she would never look him in the face again, she would never be his wife again. The shame of it would kill her—there could be no other deliverance, and it was best that she should die.

This was simple and clear, and yet, with cruel inconsistency, whenever he escaped from this nightmare, it was to suffer and cry out at the vision of Ona starving. They had put him in jail, and left his family to perish! And he saw it all happening; the long series of inevitabilities filed and refiled before him in gloomy procession. They would keep him here a long time, years maybe. And Ona would surely not go to work again, broken and crushed as she was; Marija, too, might lose her place—if that hell-fiend Connor chose to set to work to ruin them they would all be turned out. And even if he did not, they could not live—even if the boys left school again and Elzbieta went out to service, they could surely not pay all the bills without him and Ona. They had only a few dollars now—they had just paid the rent of the house a week ago, and that after it was two weeks over-due. So it would be due again in a week! They would have no money to pay it then—and they would lose the house, after all their long, heart-breaking struggle. Three times now the agent had warned him that he would not tolerate another delay. Perhaps it was very base of Jurgis to be thinking about the house, when he had the other unspeakable thing to fill his mind; yet, how much he had suffered for this house, how much they had all of them suffered! It was their one hope of respite, as long as they lived; they had put all their money into it—and they were working people, poor people, whose money was their strength, the very substance of them, body and soul, the thing by which they lived and for lack of which they died.

And they would lose it all; they would be turned out into the streets, and have to hide in some icy garret, and live or die as best they could! Jurgis had all the night—and all of many more nights—to think about this, and he saw the thing in its details; he lived it all, as if he were there. They would sell their furniture, and then run into debt at the stores, and then be refused credit; they would borrow a little from the Szadwilases, whose delicatessen store was tottering on the brink of ruin; the neighbors would come and help them a little—poor, sick Jadwiga would bring a few spare pennies, as she always did when people were starving, and Tamoszius Kuszlejka would bring them the proceeds of a night's fiddling. So they would struggle to hang on until he got out of jail—or would they know that he was in jail, would they be able to find out anything about him! Would they be allowed to see him—or was it to be part of his punishment to be kept in ignorance about their fate?

His mind would hang upon the worst possibilities; he saw Ona ill and tortured, Marija out of her place, little Stanislovas unable to get to work for the snow, the whole family turned out on the street. God Almighty! would they actually let them lie down in the street and die? Would there be no help even then—would they wander about in the snow till they froze? Jurgis had never seen any dead bodies in the streets, but he had seen people evicted and disappear, no one knew where; and though the city had a relief-bureau, though there was a charity organization society in the stock-yards district, in all his life there he had never heard of them. They did not advertise their activities, having ten times as many calls as they could attend to without that.

So on until morning. Then he had another ride in the patrol wagon, along with the drunken wife-beater and the maniac, several "plain drunks" and "saloon fighters," a burglar and two men who had been arrested for stealing meat from the packing-houses. Along with them he was driven into a large, white-walled room, stale-smelling and crowded. In front, upon a raised platform behind a rail, sat a stout, florid-faced Irishman, with a nose broken out in purple blotches.

Our friend realized, vaguely, that he was about to be tried. He wondered what for—whether or not his victim might be dead, and if so, what they would do with him. Boil him alive, perhaps, or tear him to pieces—nothing would have surprised Jurgis, who knew little of the laws. Yet he had picked up gossip enough to have it occur to him that the loud-voiced man upon the bench might be the notorious Justice Callahan, about whom the people of Packingtown spoke with bated breath.

"Pat" Callahan—"Growler" Pat, as he had been known before he ascended the bench—had begun life as a butcher boy and a bruiser of local reputation; he had gone into politics almost as soon as he had learned to talk, and had held two offices at once before he was old enough to vote. If Cassidy was the thumb, Pat Callahan was the first finger of the unseen hand whereby the packers held down the people of the district. No politician in Chicago ranked higher in their confidence; he had been at it a long time—had been the business agent in the city council of old man Anderson, the self-made merchant, way back in the early days, when the whole city of Chicago had been up at auction. "Growler" Pat had given up holding city offices very early in his career—caring only for party power, and giving the rest of his time to superintending his dives and brothels. Of late years, however, since his children were growing up, he had begun to hunger for respectability, and had had himself made a magistrate; a position for which he was admirably fitted, because of his strong conservatism.

Jurgis sat gazing about the room for an hour or two; he was in hopes that some one of the family would come, but in this he was disappointed. Finally he was led before the bar, and a lawyer for the company appeared against him. Connor was under the doctor's care, the lawyer explained briefly, and if his honor would hold the prisoner for a week—"Three hundred dollars," said His Honor, promptly.

Jurgis was staring from the judge to the lawyer in perplexity. "Have you anyone to go on your bond?" demanded the judge, and then a clerk who stood at Jurgis's elbow explained to him what this meant. The latter shook his head, and before he realized what had happened the policeman was leading him away again. They took him to a room where other prisoners were waiting, and here he stayed until court adjourned, when he had another long and bitterly cold ride in a patrol wagon to the county jail, which is on the north side of the city, and nine or ten miles from the stock-yards.

Here they searched Jurgis, leaving him only his money, which consisted of fifteen cents. Then they led him to a room and told him to strip for a bath; after which he had to walk down a long gallery, past the grated cell-doors of the inmates of the jail. This was a great event to the latter—the daily review of the new arrivals—all stark naked—and many and diverting were the comments. Jurgis was required to stay in the bath longer than anyone, in the vain hope of getting out of him a few of his phosphates and acids. The prisoners roomed two in a cell, but that day there was one left over and he was the one. The cells were in tiers, opening upon galleries. His cell was about five feet by seven in size, with a stone floor and a heavy wooden bench built into it. There was no window—the only light came from windows near the roof at one end of the court outside. There were two bunks, one above the other, each with a straw mattress and a pair of gray blankets—the latter stiff as boards with filth, and alive with fleas, bed-bugs and lice. When Jurgis lifted up the mattress he discovered beneath it a layer of skurrying roaches almost as badly frightened as himself.

Here they brought him more "duffers and dope," with the addition of a bowl of soup. Many of the prisoners had their meals brought in from a restaurant, but Jurgis had no money for that. Some had books to read and cards to play, with candles to see by night, but Jurgis was all alone in darkness and silence. He could not sleep again; there was the same maddening procession of thoughts that lashed him like whips upon his naked back. When night fell he was pacing up and down his cell like a wild beast that breaks its teeth upon the bars of a cage. Now and then in his frenzy he would fling himself against the walls of the place, beating his hands upon them. They cut him and bruised him—they were cold and merciless as the men who had built them.

In the distance there was a church-tower bell that tolled the hours one by one. When it came to midnight Jurgis was lying upon the floor with his head in his arms, listening. Instead of falling silent at the end, the bell broke into a sudden clangor. Jurgis raised his head; what could that mean—a fire? God! suppose there were to be a fire in this jail? But then he made out a melody in the ringing; there were chimes. And they seemed to waken the city—all around, far and near, there were bells, ringing wild music; for fully a minute Jurgis lay lost in wonder, before, all at once, the meaning of it broke over him—that this was Christmas eve!

Christmas eve—he had forgotten it entirely! There was a breaking of floodgates, a whirl of new memories and new griefs rushing into his mind. In far Lithuania they had celebrated Christmas; and it came to him as if it had been yesterday—himself a little child, with his lost brother and his dead father in the cabin in the deep black forest, where the snow fell all day and all night and buried them from the world. It was too far off for Santa Claus in Lithuania, but it was not too far for peace and good will to men, for the wonder-bearing vision of the Christ-child. And even in Packingtown they had not forgotten it—some gleam of it had never failed to break their darkness even in the jungle. Last Christmas eve and all Christmas day Jurgis had toiled on the killing-floor, and Ona at wrapping hams, and still they had found strength enough to take the children for a walk upon the avenue, to see the store-windows all decorated with Christmas-trees and ablaze with electric lights. In one window there would be live geese, in another marvels in sugar —pink and white canes big enough for ogres and cakes with cherubs upon them; in a third there would be rows of fat yellow turkeys, decorated with rosettes, and rabbits and squirrels hanging; in a fourth would be a fairy-land of toys—lovely dolls with pink dresses; and woolly sheep and drums and soldier-hats. Nor did they have to go without their share of all this, either—the last time they had had a big basket with them and all their Christmas marketing to do—a roast of pork and a cabbage, and some rye-bread, and a pair of mittens for Ona, and a rubber doll that squeaked, and a little green cornucopia full of candy, to be hung from the gas jet and gazed at by half a dozen pairs of longing eyes.

Even half a year of the sausage machines and the fertilizer-mill had not been able to kill the thought of Christmas in them; there was a choking in Jurgis's throat as he recalled that the very night Ona had not come home Teta Elzbieta had taken him aside and shown him an old valentine that she had picked up in a paper store for three cents—dingy and shop-worn, but with bright colors, and figures of angels and doves. She had wiped all the specks off this, and was going to set it on the mantle, where the children could see it. Great sobs shook Jurgis at this memory—for now they would spend their Christmas in misery and despair, with their mother ill, and their father in prison, and their home in desolation. Ah, it was too cruel! Why at least had they not left him alone—why, after they had shut him in jail, must they be ringing Christmas chimes in his ears!

But no, their bells were not ringing for him—their Christmas was not meant for him. They were simply not counting him at all. He was of no consequence—he was flung aside, like a bit of trash, the carcass of some dead animal. He had got into their way—and they had put him out of it, without ever a thought of the consequences. It was horrible, horrible! His wife might be dying, his baby might be starving, his whole family might be perishing in the cold—and all the while they were ringing their Christmas chimes. And the bitter mockery of it—all this was punishment for him! They put him in a place where the snow could not beat in, where the cold could not eat through his bones; they brought him food and drink—why, in the name of heaven, if they must punish him, did they not put his family in jail and leave him outside? Why punish him by leaving three weak women and six helpless children to starve and freeze?

That was their law, that was their justice! Jurgis stood upright, trembling with passion, his hands clenched and his arms upraised, his whole soul ablaze with hatred and defiance. Ten thousand curses upon them and their law! Their justice, it was a lie, it was a lie, a hideous, brutal lie—a thing too black and hateful for any world but a world of nightmares. It was a sham and a loathsome mockery—there was no justice, there was no right, anywhere in it—it was only force, it was tyranny, the will and the power, reckless and unrestrained! They had ground him beneath their heel, they had devoured all his substance; they had murdered his old father, they had broken and wrecked his wife; they had crushed and cowed his whole family; and now they were through with him, they had no further use for him—and because he had interfered with them, had gotten in their way, this was what they had done with him! They had put him behind bars, as if he had been a wild beast, a thing without sense or reason, without rights, without affections, without feelings. Nay, they would not even have treated a beast as they had treated him! Would any man in his senses have trapped a wild thing in its lair and left its young to die?

These midnight hours were fateful ones to Jurgis; in them was the beginning of his rebellion, of his outlawry and his unbelief. He had no wit to trace back the social crime to its far sources—he could not say that it was the thing men call "the system" that was crushing him to the earth—that it was the packers, his masters, who had brought up the law of the land and had dealt out their brutal will to him from the seat of justice. He only knew that he was wronged, and that the world had wronged him, that the law, society, with all its powers, had declared itself his foe. And every hour his soul grew blacker, every hour he dreamed new dreams of vengeance, of defiance, of raging, frenzied hate.

> The vilest deeds, like poison weeds,
> Bloom well in prison air;
> It is only what is good in Man
> That wastes and withers there:
> Pale Anguish keeps the heavy gate,
> And the Warder Is Despair.

So wrote a poet, to whom the world had dealt its justice[1]—

> I know not whether Laws be right,
> Or whether Laws be wrong;
> All that we know who lie in gaol
> Is that the wall is strong.
> And they do well to hide their Hell,
> For in it things are done
> That Son of God nor son of Man
> Ever should look upon!

---

1. Oscar Wilde. These stanzas are from "The Ballade of Reading Gaol."

17

AT SEVEN o'clock the next morning Jurgis was let out to get water to wash his cell—a duty which he performed faithfully, but which most of the prisoners were accustomed to shirk, until their cells became so filthy that the guards interposed. Then he had more "duffers and dope," and afterward was allowed three hours for exercise, in a long cement-walled court roofed with glass. Here were all the inmates of the jail crowded together. At one side of the court was a place for visitors, cut off by two heavy wire screens, a foot apart, so that nothing could be passed in to the prisoners; here Jurgis watched anxiously, but there came no one to see him.

Soon after he went back to his cell a keeper opened the door to let in another prisoner. He was a dapper young fellow, with a light brown mustache and blue eyes, and a graceful figure. He nodded to Jurgis, and then, as the keeper closed the door upon him, began gazing critically about him.

"Well, pal," he said, as his glance encountered Jurgis again. "Good morning."

"Good morning," said Jurgis.

"A rum go for Christmas, eh?" added the other. Jurgis nodded.

The new-comer went to the bunks and inspected the blankets; he lifted up the mattress, and then dropped it with an explanation. "My God!" he said, "that's the worst yet."

He glanced at Jurgis again. "Looks as if it hadn't been slept in last night. Couldn't stand it, eh?"

"I didn't want to sleep last night," said Jurgis.

"When did you come in?"

"Yesterday."

The other had another look round, and then wrinkled up his nose. "There's the devil of a stink in here," he said suddenly. "What is it?"

"It's me," said Jurgis.

"You?"

"Yes, me."

"Didn't they make you wash."

"Yes, but this don't wash."

"What is it?"

"Fertilizer."

"Fertilizer! The deuce! What are you?"

"I work in the stock-yards—at least I did until the other day. It's in my clothes."

"That's a new one on me," said the new-comer. "I thought I'd been up against 'em all. What are you in for?"

"I hit my boss."

"Oh—that's it. What did he do?"

"He—he treated me mean."

"I see. You're what is called an honest workingman!"

"What are you?" Jurgis asked.

"I?" the other laughed. "They say I'm a cracksman," he said.

"What's that?" asked Jurgis.

"Safes, and such things," answered the other.

"Oh," said Jurgis wonderingly, and stared at the speaker in awe. "You mean you break into them—you—you—"

"Yes," laughed the other, "that's what they say."

He did not look to be over twenty-two or three, though, as Jurgis found afterwards, he was thirty. He spoke like a man of education, like what the world calls a "gentleman."

"Is that what you're here for?" Jurgis inquired.

"No," was the answer. "I'm here for 'disorderly conduct.' They were mad because they couldn't get any evidence."

"What's your name?" the young fellow continued after a pause. "My name's Duane—Jack Duane. I've more than a dozen, but that's my company one." He seated himself on the floor, with his back to the wall and his legs crossed, and went on talking easily; he soon put Jurgis on a friendly footing—he was evidently a man of the world, used to getting on, and not too proud to hold conversation with a mere laboring man. He drew Jurgis out, and heard all about his life—all but the one unmentionable thing; and then he told stories about his own life. He was a great one for stories, not always of the choicest. Being sent to jail had apparently not disturbed his cheerfulness; he had "done time" twice before, it seemed, and he took it all with a frolic welcome. What with women and wine and the excitement of his vocation, a man could afford to rest now and then.

Naturally, the aspect of prison life was changed for Jurgis by the arrival of a cell-mate. He could not turn his face to the wall and sulk, he had to speak when he was spoken to; nor could he help being interested in the conversation of Duane—the first educated man with whom he had ever talked. How could he help listening with wonder while the other told of midnight ventures and perilous escapes, of feastings and orgies, of fortunes squandered in a night? The young fellow had an amused contempt for Jurgis, as a sort of working-mule; he too had felt the world's injustice, but instead of bearing it patiently he had struck back, and struck hard. He was striking all the time—there was war between him and society. He was a genial free-booter, living off the enemy, without fear or shame; he was not always victorious, but then defeat did not mean annihilation, and need not break his spirit.

Withal he was a good-hearted fellow—too much so, it appeared. His story came out, not on the first day, nor the second, but in the long hours that dragged by, in which they had nothing to do but talk, and nothing to talk of but themselves. Jack Duane was from the East; he was a college-bred man —had been studying electrical engineering. Then his father had met with misfortune in business and killed himself; and there had been his mother, and a younger brother and sister. The sister was beautiful; Jurgis could not be sure, as it was dark when they were talking, but he fancied that there were tears in the other's eyes as he told about her. He had not laid eyes upon her for six years—he would have had an arm torn out rather than have her know what had become of him.

Their hopes had all been in an invention of Duane's; Jurgis could not understand it clearly; but it had to do with telegraphing, and it was a very important thing—there were fortunes in it, millions upon millions of dollars —yes, really. The trouble had been that they were poor, and this device had to be patented so carefully. Duane had taken all he owned to pay lawyers; and then at last he had taken his model to a great company, which, understanding his position, had offered him for his rights about a thousandth part of what they were worth. He had refused the offer; and a few weeks later he had found that they were beginning to infringe upon his patent. Then he had tried to stop them, and got tangled up in law-suits and technicalities—it would have taken a fortune and half a lifetime to get justice done, and meantime they went on using his patent, and he had not a cent and was ruined. Then somebody had given him a tip on a horse race, and he had tried to retrieve his fortune with another person's money, and then run away, and all the rest had come from that. Jurgis asked him what had led him to safe-breaking—to Jurgis a wild and appalling occupation to think about; a man he had met, his cell-mate had replied—one thing leads to another. Didn't he ever wonder about his family, Jurgis asked. Sometimes, the other answered, but not often —he didn't allow it. Thinking about it would make it no better. This wasn't a world in which a man had any business with a family; sooner or later Jurgis would find that out also, and give up the fight and shift for himself.

Jurgis was so transparently what he pretended to be that his cell-mate was as open with him as a child; it was pleasant to tell him adventures, he was so full of wonder and admiration, he was so new to the ways of the country. Duane did not even bother to keep back names and places—he told all his triumphs and his failures, his loves and his griefs. Also he introduced Jurgis to many of the other prisoners, nearly half of whom he knew by name. The crowd had already given Jurgis a name—they called him "the stinker." This was cruel, but they meant no harm by it, and he took it with a good-natured grin.

Our friend had caught now and then a whiff from the sewers over which he lived, the cess-pools and fens of the jungle; but this was the first time that he had ever been splashed by its filth. This jail was a Noah's ark of the city's crime—there were murderers, "hold up men" and burglars, embezzlers, counterfeiters and forgers, bigamists, "shoplifters," confidence men, petty thieves and pickpockets, gamblers and procurers, brawlers, beggars, tramps and drunkards; they were black and white, old and young, Americans and natives of every nation under the sun. There were hardened criminals and innocent men too poor to give bail; old men and boys literally not yet in their teens. They were the drainage of the great festering ulcer of society; they were hideous to look upon, sickening to talk to. All life had turned to rottenness and stench in them—love was a beastly filthiness, joy was a snare and God was an imprecation. They strolled here and there about the court-yard, and Jurgis listened to them; he was ignorant and they were wise—they had been everywhere and tried everything, they could tell the whole hateful story of it, set forth the inner soul of a city in which justice and honor, women's bodies and men's souls were for sale in the market-place, and human beings writhed and fought and fell upon each other like wolves in a pit; in which lusts were raging fires, and men were fuel, and humanity was festering and stewing and wallowing in its own corruption. Into this wild beast tangle these men had been born without their consent, they had taken part in it because they could not help it; that they were in jail was no disgrace to them, for the game had never been fair, the dice were loaded. They were swindlers and thieves of pennies and dimes, and they had been trapped and put out of the way by the swindlers and thieves of millions of dollars.

To most of this Jurgis tried not to listen. They frightened him with their savage mockery; and all the while his heart was far away, where his loved ones were calling. Now and then in the midst of it his thought would take flight, and then the tears would come into his eyes—and he would be called back by the jeering laughter of his companions.

He spent a week in this company, and during all that time he had no word from his home. He paid one of his fifteen cents for a postal card and his companion wrote a note to the family telling them where he was and when he would be tried. There came no answer to it, however, and at last, the day before New Year's, Jurgis bade good-bye to Jack Duane. The latter gave him his address, or, rather, the address of his mistress, and made Jurgis promise to look him up. "Maybe I could help you out of a hole some day," he said, and added that he was sorry to have him go. Jurgis rode in the patrol wagon back to Justice Callahan's court for trial.

One of the first things he made out as he entered the room was Teta Elzbieta and little Kotrina, looking pale and frightened, seated far in the rear. His heart began to pound, but he did not dare to try to signal to them, and neither did Elzbieta. He took his seat in the prisoner's pen and sat gazing at them in helpless agony. He saw that Ona was not with them, and was full of forebodings as to what that might mean. He spent half an hour brooding over this—and then suddenly he straightened up and the blood rushed to his face. A man had come in—Jurgis could not see his features for the bandages that swathed him, but he knew the burly figure. It was Connor! A trembling seized him, and his limbs bent as if for a spring. Then suddenly he felt a hand on his collar, and heard a voice behind him—"Sit down, you son of a —!"

He subsided, but he never took his eyes off his enemy. The fellow was still alive, which was a disappointment, in one way; and yet it was pleasant to see him, all in penitential plasters. He and the company lawyer who was with him came and took seats within the judge's railing; and a minute later the clerk called Jurgis's name, and the policeman jerked him to his feet and led him before the bar, gripping him tightly by the arm, lest he should spring upon the boss.

Jurgis listened while the man entered the witness chair, took the oath, and told his story. The wife of the prisoner had been employed in his department, and he had discharged her for inefficiency. Half an hour later he had been violently attacked, knocked down and almost choked to death. He had brought witnesses—

"They will probably not be necessary," observed the judge, and he turned to Jurgis. "You admit attacking the plaintiff?" he asked.

"Him?" inquired Jurgis, pointing at the boss.

"Yes," said the judge.

"I hit him, sir," said Jurgis.

"Say 'Your Honor,'" said the officer, pinching his arm hard.

"Your Honor," said Jurgis, obediently.

"You tried to choke him?"

"Yes, sir, Your Honor."

"Ever arrested before?"

"No, sir, Your Honor."

"What have you to say for yourself?"

Jurgis hesitated. What had he to say? In two years and a half he had learned to speak English for practical purposes, but these had never included the statement that someone had intimidated and seduced his wife. He tried once or twice, stammering and balking, to the annoyance of the judge, who was gasping from the odor of fertilizer. Finally the prisoner made it understood that his vocabulary was inadequate, and there stepped up a dapper young man with waxed mustaches, bidding him speak in any language he knew.

Jurgis began; supposing that he would be given time, he explained how the boss had procured Ona's discharge from another place, and how, after giving her employment, he had taken advantage of his position to make advances to her. When the interpreter had translated this the judge, whose calendar was crowded, and whose automobile was ordered for a certain hour, interrupted with the remark: "Oh, I see. Well, if he made love to your wife, why didn't she complain to the superintendent or leave the place?"

Jurgis hesitated, somewhat taken aback; he began to explain that they were very poor—that work was hard to get—

"I see," said Justice Callahan; "so instead you thought you would knock this gentleman down." He turned to the plaintiff, inquiring, "Is there any truth in this story, Mr. Connor?"

"Not a particle, Your Honor," said the boss. "It is very unpleasant—they tell some such tale every time you have to discharge a woman—"

"Yes, I know," said the judge, "I hear it often enough. The fellow seems to have handled you pretty roughly. Thirty days and costs. Next case."

Jurgis had been listening in perplexity. It was only when the policeman who had him by the arm turned and started to the door that he realized that sentence had been passed. He gazed around him wildly. "Thirty days!" he panted—and then he whirled upon the judge. "What will my family do?" he cried frantically. "I have a wife and baby, sir, and they have no money—my God, they will starve to death!"

"You would have done well to think about them before you committed the assault," said the judge, drily, as he turned to look at the next prisoner.

Jurgis would have spoken again, but the policeman had seized him by the collar and was twisting it, and a second policeman was making for him with evidently hostile intentions. So he let them lead him away. Far down the room he saw Elzbieta and Kotrina, risen from their seats, staring in fright; he made one effort to go to them, and then, brought back by another twist at his throat, he bowed his head, and gave up the struggle. They thrust him into a cell-room, where other prisoners were waiting; and as soon as court had adjourned they led him down with them into the "Black Maria," and drove him away.

This time Jurgis was bound for the "Bridewell," a petty jail where Cook county prisoners serve their time. It was even filthier and more crowded than the county jail; all the smaller fry out of the latter had been sifted into it—the petty thieves and swindlers, the brawlers and vagrants. For his cell-mate Jurgis had an Italian fruit-seller who had refused to pay his graft to the policeman and been arrested for carrying a large pocket-knife; as he did not understand a word of English, our friend was glad when he left. He gave place to a Norwegian sailor, who had lost half an ear in a drunken brawl, and who proved to be quarrelsome, cursing Jurgis because he moved in his bunk and caused the roaches to drop upon the lower one. It would have been quite intolerable, staying in a cell with this wild beast, but for the fact that all day long the prisoners were put at work breaking stone.

Ten days of his thirty Jurgis spent thus, without hearing a word from his family; then one day a keeper came and informed him that there was a visitor to see him. Jurgis turned white, and so weak at the knees that he could hardly leave his cell.

The man led him down the corridor and a flight of steps to the visitors' room, which was barred like a cell. Through the grating Jurgis could see some one sitting in a chair; and as he came into the room the person started up and he saw that it was little Stanislovas. At the sight of some one from home the big fellow nearly went to pieces—he had to steady himself by a chair, and he put his other hand to his forehead, as if to clear away a mist. "Well?" he said, weakly.

Little Stanislovas, also trembling, and all but too frightened to speak. "They—sent me to tell you—" he said, with a gulp.

"Well?" Jurgis repeated.

He followed the boy's glance to where the keeper was standing watching them. "Never mind that," Jurgis cried, wildly. "How are they?"

"Ona is very sick," Stanislovas said; "and we are almost starving. We can't get along; we thought you might be able to help us."

Jurgis gripped the chair tighter; there were beads of perspiration on his forehead, and his hand shook. "I—can't—help you," he said.

"Ona lies in her room all day," the boy went on, breathlessly. "She won't eat anything, and she cries all the time. She won't tell what is the matter and she won't go to work at all. Then a long time ago the man came for the rent. He was very cross. He came again last week. He said he would turn us out of the house. And then Marija—"

A sob choked Stanislovas, and he stopped. "What's the matter with Marija?" cried Jurgis.

"She's cut her hand!" said the boy. "She's cut it bad this time, worse than before. She can't work, and it's all turning green, and the company doctor says she may—she may have to have it cut off. And Marija cries all the time—her money is nearly all gone, too, and we can't pay the rent, and the interest on the house; and we have no coal, and nothing more to eat, and the man at the store, he says—"

The little fellow stopped again, beginning to whimper. "Go on!" the other panted in frenzy—"Go on!"

"I—I will," sobbed Stanislovas. "It's so—so cold all the time. And last Sunday it snowed again—a deep, deep snow—and I couldn't—couldn't get to work all alone—"

"God!" Jurgis half shouted, and he took a step towards the child. There was an old hatred between them because of the snow—ever since that dreadful morning when the boy had had his fingers frozen and Jurgis had had to beat him to send him to work. Now he clenched his hands, looking as if he would try to break through the grating. "You little villain," he cried, "you didn't try!"

"I did—I did!" wailed Stanislovas, shrinking from him in terror. "I tried all day—two days. I couldn't walk at all, it was so deep. And I had nothing to eat, and oh, it was so cold; I tried and then the third day Ona went with me—"

"Ona!"

"Yes. She tried to go to work, too. She had to. We were all starving. But she had lost her place—"

Jurgis reeled and gave a gasp. *"She went back to that place?"* he screamed.

"She tried to," said Stanislovas, gazing at him in perplexity. "Why not, Jurgis?"

The man breathed hard, three or four times. "Go—on," he panted, finally.

"I went with her," said Stanislovas, "but the boss wouldn't take her back. He cursed her. He was still bandaged up—why did you hit him, Jurgis?" (There was some fascinating mystery about this the little fellow knew; but he could get no satisfaction.)

Jurgis could not speak; he could only stare, his eyes starting out. "She has been trying to get other work," the boy went on, "but she's so weak she can't keep up. And my boss would not take me back, either—Ona says he knows Connor, and that's the reason; they've all got a grudge against us now. So I've got to go down-town and sell papers, with the rest of the boys and Kotrina—"

"Kotrina!"

Yes, she's been selling papers, too. She does best, because she's a girl. Only the cold is so bad—it's terrible coming home at night, Jurgis. Sometimes they can't come home at all—I'm going to try to find them tonight and sleep where they do, it's so late, and it's such a long ways home. I've had to walk, and I didn't know where it was—I don't know how to get back, either. Only Teta Elzbieta said I must come, because you would want to know, and maybe somebody would help your family, when they had put you in jail so you couldn't work. And I walked all day to get here—and I only had a piece of bread for breakfast, Jurgis. Teta Elzbieta, she tried to get some work where she was before, but they didn't need her; and so she goes and begs at houses with a basket, and people give her food. Only she didn't get much yesterday; it was too cold for her fingers, and today she was crying—"

So little Stanislovas went on, sobbing as he talked; and Jurgis stood, gripping the table tightly, saying not a word, but feeling that his head would burst; it was like having weights piled upon him, one after another, crushing the life out of him. He struggled and fought within himself—as if in some terrible nightmare, in which a man suffers an agony, and cannot lift his hand, nor cry out, but feels that he is going mad, that his brain is bursting—

Just when it seemed to him that another turn of the screw would kill him, little Stanislovas stopped. "You can not help us?" he said, weakly.

Jurgis shook his head.

"They won't give you anything here?"

He shook it again.

"When are you coming out?"

"Three weeks yet," Jurgis answered. And the boy gazed around him uncertainly. "Then I might as well go," he said.

Jurgis nodded. Then, suddenly recollecting, he put his hand into his pocket and drew it out, shaking. "Here," he said, holding out the fourteen cents. "Take this to them."

And Stanislovas took it, and after a little more hesitation, started for the door. "Goodbye, Jurgis," he said, and the other noticed that he walked unsteadily as he passed out of sight.

For a minute or so Jurgis stood clinging to the chair, reeling and swaying; then the keeper touched him on the arm, and he turned and went back to breaking stone.

JURGIS did not get out of the Bridewell quite as soon as he had expected. To his sentence there were added "court costs" of $1.50—he was supposed to pay for the trouble of putting him in jail, and not having the money was obliged to work it off by three days more of toil. Nobody had taken the trouble to tell him this—only after counting the days and looking forward to the end in an agony of impatience, when the hour came that he expected to be free he found himself still set at the stone-heap, and laughed at when he ventured to protest. Then he concluded he must have counted wrong; but as another day passed, he gave up all hope—and was sunk in the depths of despair when one morning after breakfast a keeper came to him with the word that his time was up at last. So he doffed his prison garb and put on his old fertilizer clothing, and heard the door of the prison clang behind him.

He stood upon the steps, bewildered; he could hardly believe that it was true—that the sky was above him again and the open street before him—that he was a free man. But then the cold began to strike through his clothes, and he started quickly away.

There had been a heavy snow, and now a thaw had set in; a fine, sleety rain was falling, driven by a wind that pierced Jurgis to the bone. He had not stopped for his overcoat when he set out to "do up" his boss, and so his rides in the patrol-wagons had been cruel experiences; his clothing was old and worn thin, and it never had been very warm. Now as he trudged on the rain soon wet him through; there were six inches of watery slush on the side-walks, so that his feet would soon have been soaked, even had there been no holes in his shoes.

Jurgis had had enough to eat in the jail, and the work had been the least trying of any that he had done since he came to Chicago; but even so, he had not grown strong—the fear and grief that had preyed upon his mind had worn him thin. Now he shivered and shrunk from the rain, hiding his hands in his pockets and hunching his shoulders together. The Bridewell grounds were on the outskirts of the city and the country around them was unsettled and wild—on one side was the big drainage canal, and on the other a maze of railroad tracks, and so the wind had full sweep. After walking a ways Jurgis met a little ragmuffin, whom he hailed: "Hey, sonny!"

The boy cocked one eye at him—he knew that Jurgis was a "jail bird" by his shaven head. "Wot yer want?" he queried.

"How do you go to the stock-yards?" Jurgis demanded.

"I don't go," replied the boy.

Jurgis hesitated a moment, nonplussed. Then he said: "I mean which is the way?"

"Why don't you say so, then?" was the response, and he pointed to the northwest, across the tracks. "That way."

"How far is it?" Jurgis asked.

"I dunno," said the other—"mebby twenty miles or so."

"Twenty miles!" Jurgis echoed, and his face fell. He had to walk every foot of it, for they had turned him out of jail without a penny in his pockets.

Yet, when he once got started, and his blood had warmed with walking, he forgot everything in the fever of his thoughts. All the dreadful imaginations that had haunted him in his cell now rushed into his mind at once. The agony was almost over—he was going to find out; and he clenched his hands in his pockets as he strode, following his flying desire, almost at a run. Ona—the baby—the family—the house—he would know the truth about them all! And he was coming to the rescue—he was free again! His hands were his own, and he could help them, he could do battle for them against the world.

For an hour or so he walked thus, and then he began to look about him. He seemed to be leaving the city altogether—the street was turning into a country road, leading out to the westward; there were snow-covered fields on either side of him. Soon he met a farmer driving a two-horse wagon loaded with straw, and he stopped him.

"Is this the way to the stock-yards?" he asked.

The farmer scratched his head. "I dunno jest where they be," he said. "But they're in the city somewhere, and you're going dead away from it now."

Jurgis looked dazed. "I was told this was the way," he said.

"Who told you?"

"A boy."

"Well, mebbe he was playing a joke on ye. The best thing ye kin do is to go back, and when ye git into town ask a policeman. I'd take ye in, only I've come a long ways an' I'm loaded heavy. Git up!"

So Jurgis turned and followed, and toward the end of the morning he began to see Chicago again. Past endless blocks of two-story shanties he walked, along wooden sidewalks and unpaved pathways treacherous with deep slush-holes. Every few blocks there would be a railroad crossing, on a level with the sidewalk, a death-trap for the unwary; long freight trains would be passing, the cars clanking and crashing together, and Jurgis would pace about waiting, burning up with a fever of impatience. Occasionally the cars would stop for some minutes, and wagons and street-cars would crowd together waiting, the drivers swearing at each other, or hiding beneath umbrellas out of the rain; at such times Jurgis would dodge under the gates and run across the tracks and between the cars, taking his life into his hands.

He crossed a long bridge over a river, frozen solid and covered with slush. Not even on the river bank was the snow white—the rain which fell was a diluted solution of smoke, and Jurgis's hands and face were streaked with black. Then he came into the business part of the city, where the streets were sewers of inky blackness, with horses slipping and plunging, and women and children flying across in panic-stricken droves. These streets were huge canyons formed by towering black buildings, echoing with the clang of car-gongs and the shouts of drivers; the people who swarmed in them were as busy as ants—all hurrying breathlessly, never stopping to look at anything nor at each other. The solitary trampish-looking foreigner, with water-soaked clothing, and haggard face and anxious eyes, was as much alone as he hurried past them, as much unheeded and as lost, as if he had been a thousand miles deep in a wilderness.

A policeman gave him his direction and told him that he had five miles to go. He came again to the slum districts, to avenues of saloons and cheap stores, with long, dingy red factory buildings, and coal-yards and railroad tracks; and then Jurgis lifted up his head and began to sniff the air like a startled animal—scenting the far-off odor of home. It was late afternoon then, and he was hungry, but the dinner invitations hung out of the saloons were not for him.

So he came at last to the stock-yards, to the black volcanoes of smoke and the lowing cattle, and the stench. Then, seeing a crowded car, his impatience got the better of him and he jumped aboard, hiding behind another man, unnoticed by the conductor. In ten minutes more he had reached his street, and home.

He was half running as he came around the corner. There was the house, at any rate—and then suddenly he stopped and stared. What was the matter with the house?

Jurgis looked twice, bewildered; then he glanced at the house next door, and at the one beyond—then at the saloon on the corner. Yes, it was the right place, quite certainly—he had not made any mistake. But the house—the house was a different color.

He came a couple of steps nearer. Yes; it had been gray, and now it was yellow! The trimmings around the windows had been red, and now they were green! It was all newly painted! How strange it made it seem!

Jurgis went closer yet, but keeping on the other side of the street. A sudden and horrible spasm of fear had come over him. His knees were shaking beneath him, and his mind was in a whirl. New paint on the house! And new weather-boards, where the old had begun to rot off, and the agent had got after them! New shingles over the hole in the roof, too, the hole that had for six months been the bane of his soul—he having no money to have it fixed, and no time to fix it himself, and the rain leaking in, and overflowing the pots and pans he put to catch it, and flooding the attic and loosening the plaster. And now it was fixed! And the broken window-pane replaced! And curtains in the windows! New, white curtains, stiff and shiny!

Then suddenly the front door opened. Jurgis stood, his chest heaving as he struggled to catch his breath. A boy had come out, a stranger to him; a big, fat, rosy-cheeked youngster, such as had never been seen in his home before.

Jurgis started at the boy, fascinated. He came down the steps whistling, kicking off the snow. He stopped at the foot and picked up some, and then leaned against the railing, making a snow-ball. A moment later he looked around and saw Jurgis, and their eyes met; it was a hostile glance, the boy evidently thinking that the other had suspicions of the snow-ball. When Jurgis started slowly across the street toward him he gave a quick glance about, meditating retreat, but then he concluded to stand his ground.

Jurgis took hold of the railing of the steps, for he was a little unsteady. "What—what are you doing here?" he managed to gasp.

"Go on!" said the boy.

"You—" Jurgis tried again, "what do you want here?"

"Me?" answered the boy, angrily. "I live here."

"You live here!" Jurgis panted. He turned white, and clung more tightly to the railing. "You live here! Then where's my family?"

The boy looked surprised. "Your family?" he echoed.

And Jurgis started towards him. "I—I live here!" he cried.

"Come off!" said the boy; then suddenly the door upstairs opened, and he called: "Hey, ma! Here's a fellow says he lives here."

A stout Irish woman came to the top of the steps. "What's that?" she demanded.

Jurgis turned toward her. "Where is my family!" he cried, wildly. "I left them here! This is my home! What are you doing in my home?"

The woman stared at him in frightened wonder; she must have thought she was dealing with a maniac—Jurgis looked like one. "Your home!" she echoed.

"My home!" he half shrieked. "I lived here, I tell you!"

"You must be mistaken," she answered him. "No one ever lived here. This is a new house. They told us so. They—"

"What have they done with my family?" shouted Jurgis, frantically.

A light had begun to break upon the woman; perhaps she had had doubts of what "they" had told her. "I don't know where your family is," she said; "I bought the house only three days ago, and there was nobody here, and they told me it was all new. Do you really mean you had ever rented it?"

"Rented it!" panted Jurgis. "I bought it! I paid for it! I own it! And they— my God, can't you tell me where my people went?"

She made him understand at last that she knew nothing. Jurgis's brain was so in a whirl that he could not grasp the situation. It was as if his family had been wiped out of existence; as if they were proving to be dream people, who never had existed at all. He was quite lost—but then suddenly he thought of Grandmother Majauszkis, who lived on the next block. She would know! He turned and started at a run.

Grandmother Majauszkis came to the door herself. She cried out when she saw Jurgis, wild-eyed and shaking. Yes, yes, she could tell him. The family had moved; they had not been able to pay the rent and they had been turned out into the snow, and the house had been repainted and sold again the next week. No, she had not heard how they were, but she could tell him that they had gone back to Panei Aniele Juknos, with whom they had stayed when they first came to the yards. Wouldn't Jurgis come in and rest? It was certainly too bad—if only he had not got into jail—

And so Jurgis turned and staggered away. He did not go very far—around the corner he gave out completely, and sat down on the steps of a saloon, and hid his face in his hands, and shook all over with dry, racking sobs.

Their home! Their home! They had lost it! Grief, despair, rage, over-whelmed him—what was any imagination of the thing to this heart-breaking, crushing reality of it—to the sight of strange people living in his house, hanging their curtains in his windows, staring at him with hostile eyes! It was monstrous, it was unthinkable—they could not do it—it could not be true! Only think what he had suffered for that house—what miseries they had all suffered for it—the price they had paid for it!

The whole long agony came back to him. Their sacrifices in the beginning, their three hundred dollars that they had scraped together, all they owned in the world, all that stood between them and starvation! And then their toil, month by month, to get together the twelve dollars, and the interest as well, and now and then the taxes, and the other charges, and the repairs, and what not! Why, they had put their very souls into their payments on that house, they had paid for it with their sweat and tears—yes, more, with their very life-blood. Diedas Antanas had died of the struggle to earn that money—he would have been alive and strong today if he had not had to work in Anderson's dark cellars to earn his share. And Ona, too, had given her health and strength to pay for it—she was wrecked and ruined because of it; and so was he, who had been a big, strong man three years ago, and now sat here shivering, broken, cowed, weeping like a hysterical child. Ah! they had cast their all into the fight; and they had lost, they had lost! All that they had paid was gone—every cent of it. And their house was gone—they were back where they had started from, flung out into the cold to starve and freeze!

Jurgis could see all the truth now—could see himself, through the whole long course of events, the victim of ravenous vultures, that had torn into his vitals and devoured him; of fiends that had racked and tortured him, mocking him meantime, jeering in his face. Ah, God, the horror of it, the monstrous, hideous, demoniacal wickedness of it! He and his family, helpless women and children, struggling to live, ignorant and defenseless and forlorn as they were—and the enemies that had been lurking for them, crouching upon their trail and thirsting for their blood! That first lying circular, that smooth-tongued, slippery agent! That trap of the extra payments, the interest and all the other charges that they had not the means to pay, and would never have attempted to pay! And then all the tricks of the packers, their masters, the tyrants who ruled them; the shut-downs and the scarcity of work, the irregular hours and the cruel speeding-up, the lowering of wages, the raising of prices! The mercilessness of nature about them, of heat and cold, rain and snow; the mercilessness of the city, of the country in which they lived—of its laws and customs that they did not understand! All of these things had worked together for the company that had marked them for its prey and was waiting for its chance. And now, with this last hideous injustice, its chance had come, and the company had turned them out bag and baggage, and taken their house and sold it again! And they could do nothing, they were tied hand and foot; the law was against them—the whole machinery of society was at their oppressors' command! If Jurgis so much as raised a hand against them, back he would go into that wild-beast pen from which he had just escaped!

To get up and go away was to give up, to acknowledge defeat, to leave the strange family in possession; and Jurgis might have sat shivering in the rain for hours before he could do that, had it not been for the thought of his family. It might be that he had worse things yet to learn—and so he got to his feet and started away, walking on, wearily, half-dazed.

To Panei Aniele's house, in back of the yards, was a good two miles; the distance had never seemed longer to Jurgis, and when he saw the familiar dingy gray shanty his heart was beating fast. He ran up the steps and began to hammer upon the door.

The old woman herself came to open it. She had shrunk all up with her rheumatism since Jurgis had seen her last, and her yellow parchment face stared up at him from a little above the level of the door-knob. She gave a start when she saw him. "Is Ona here?" he cried, breathlessly.

"Yes," was the answer, "she's here."

"How—" Jurgis began, and then stopped short, clutching convulsively at the side of the door. From somewhere within the house had come a sudden cry, a wild, horrible scream of anguish. And the voice was Ona's.

For a moment Jurgis stood half-paralyzed with fright; then he bounded past the old woman, and into the room.

It was Panei Aniele's kitchen, and huddled around the stove were half a dozen women, pale and frightened. One of them started to her feet as Jurgis entered; she was haggard and frightfully thin, with one arm tied up in bandages—he hardly realized that it was Marija. He looked first for Ona; then, not seeing her, he stared at the women, expecting them to speak. But they sat dumb, gazing back at him, panic-stricken; and a second later came another piercing scream.

It was from the rear of the house, and upstairs. Jurgis bounded to a door of the room and flung it open; there was a ladder leading through a trap door to the garret, and he was at the foot of it, when suddenly he heard a voice behind him, and saw Marija at his heels. She seized him by the sleeve with her good hand, panting wildly, "No, no, Jurgis! Stop!"

"What do you mean?" he gasped.

"You mustn't go up," she cried. Jurgis was half-crazed with bewilderment and fright. "What's the matter?" he shouted. "What is it?"

Marija clung to him tightly; he could hear Ona sobbing and moaning above, and he fought to get away and climb up, without waiting for her reply. "No, no," she rushed on. "Jurgis! You mustn't go up! It's—it's the child!"

"The child?" he echoed in perplexity. "Antanas?"

Marija answered him, in a whisper: "The new one!"

And then Jurgis went limp and caught himself on the ladder. He stared at her as if she were a ghost. "The new one!" he gasped. "But it isn't time," he added, wildly.

Marija nodded. "I know," she said; "but it's come."

And then again came Ona's scream, smiting him like a blow in the face, making him wince and turn white. Her voice died away into a wail—then he heard her sobbing again: "My God—let me die, let me die!" And Marija flung her arms about him, crying: "Come out! Come away!"

She dragged him back into the kitchen, half carrying him, for he had gone all to pieces. It was as if the pillars of his soul had fallen in—he was blasted with horror. In the room he sunk into a chair, trembling like a leaf, Marija still holding him, and the women staring at him in dumb, helpless fright.

And then again Ona cried out; he could hear it nearly as plainly here, and he staggered to his feet. "How long has this been going on?" he panted.

"Not very long," Marija answered, and then, at a signal from Panei Aniele, she rushed on: "You go away, Jurgis—you can't help—go away and come back later. It's all right—it's—"

"Who's with her?" Jurgis demanded; and then, seeing Marija hesitating, he cried again: "Who's with her?"

"She's—she's all right," she answered. "Elzbieta's with her."

"But the doctor!" he panted. "Someone who knows!"

He seized Marija by the arm; she trembled, and her voice sank beneath a whisper as she replied: "We—we have no money." Then, frightened at the look on his face, she exclaimed: "It's all right, Jurgis! You don't understand —go away—go away! Ah, if you only had waited!"

Above her protests Jurgis heard Ona again; he was almost out of his mind. It was all new to him, raw and horrible—it had fallen upon him like a lightning stroke. When little Antanas was born he had been at work, and had known nothing about it until it was over; and now he was not to be controlled. The frightened women were at their wit's end; one after another they tried to reason with him, to make him understand that this was the lot of woman. In the end they half drove him out into the rain, where he began to pace up and down, bareheaded and frantic. Because he could hear Ona from the street, he would first go away to escape the sounds, and then come back because he could not help it. At the end of a quarter of an hour he rushed up the steps again, and for fear that he would break in the door they had to open it and let him in.

There was no arguing with him. They could not tell him that all was going well—how could they know? he cried—why, she was dying, she was being torn to pieces. Listen to her—listen! Why, it was monstrous—it could not be allowed—there must be some help for it! Had they tried to get a doctor? They might pay him afterwards—they could promise—

"We couldn't promise, Jurgis," protested Marija. "We had no money—we have scarcely been able to keep alive."

"But I can work," Jurgis exclaimed; "I can earn money!"

"Yes," she answered—"but we thought you were in jail. How could we know when you would return? They will not work for nothing."

Marija went on to tell how she had tried to find a midwife, and how they had demanded ten, fifteen, even twenty-five dollars, and that in cash. "And I had only a quarter," she said. "I have spent every cent of my money—all that I had in the bank; and I owe the doctor who has been coming to see me, and he has stopped because he thinks I don't mean to pay him. And we owe Panei Aniele for two weeks' rent, and she is nearly starving, and is afraid of being turned out. We have been borrowing and begging to keep alive, and there is nothing more we can do—"

"And the children?" cried Jurgis.

"The children have not been home for three days, the weather has been so bad. They could not know what is happening—it came suddenly, two months before we expected it."

Jurgis was standing by the table, and he caught himself with his hands; his head sunk and his arms shook—it looked as if he were going to collapse. Then suddenly Panei Aniele got up and came hobbling towards him, fumbling in her skirt pocket. She drew out a dirty rag, in one corner of which she had something tied.

"Here, Jurgis!" she said, "I have some money. Palauk! See!"

She unwrapped it and counted it out—thirty-four cents. "You go, now," she said, "and try and get somebody yourself. And maybe the rest can help

—give him some money, you; he will pay you back some day, and it will do him good to have something to think about, even if he doesn't succeed. When he comes back maybe it will be over."

And so the other women turned out the contents of their pocketbooks; most of them had only pennies and nickels, but they gave him all. Mrs. Oiszewski, who lived next door, and had a husband who was a skilled cattle-butcher, but a drinking man, gave nearly half a dollar, enough to raise the whole sum to a dollar and a quarter. Then Jurgis thrust it into his pocket, still holding it tightly in his fist, and started away at a run.

"MADAME HAUPT, Hebamme," ran a sign, swinging from a second-story window over a saloon on the avenue; at a side door was another sign, with a hand pointing up a dingy flight of steps. Jurgis went up them, three at a time.

Madame Haupt was frying pork and onions, and had her door half open to let out the smoke. When he tried to knock upon it it swung open the rest of the way, and he had a glimpse of her, with a black bottle turned up to her lips. Then he knocked louder, and she started and put it away. She was a Dutch woman, enormously fat—when she walked she rolled like a small boat on the ocean, and the dishes in the cupboard jostled each other. She wore a filthy blue wrapper, and her teeth were black. "Vot is it?" she said, when she saw Jurgis.

He had run like mad all the way and was so out of breath he could hardly speak. His hair was flying and his eyes wild—he looked like a man that had risen from the tomb. "My wife!" he panted. "Come quickly!"

Madame Haupt set the frying pan to one side and wiped her hands on her wrapper. "You vant me to come for a case?" she inquired.

"Yes," gasped Jurgis.

"I haf yust come back from a case," she said, "I haf had no time to eat my dinner. Still—if it is so bad—" "Yes—it is!" cried he. "Vell, den, perhaps—vot you pay?"

"I—I—how much do you want?" Jurgis stammered.

"Twenty-five dollars." His face fell. "I can't pay that," he said.

The woman was watching him narrowly. "How much do you pay?" she demanded.

"Must I pay now—right away?"

"Yes; all my customers do."

"I—I haven't much money," Jurgis began, in an agony of dread. "I've been in—in trouble—and my money is gone. But I'll pay you—every cent—just as soon as I can. I can work—"

"Vot is your work."

"I have no place now. I must get one. But I—" "How much haf you got now?"

He could hardly bring himself to reply. When he said "A dollar and a quarter," the woman laughed in his face.

"I vould not put on my hat for a dollar und a quarter," she said.

"It's all I've got," he pleaded, his voice breaking. "I must get some one—my wife will die. I can't help it—I—"

Madame Haupt had put back her pork and onions on the stove. She turned to him and answered, out of the steam and noise: "Git me ten dollars cash, und so you can pay me de rest next mont'."

"I can't do it—I haven't got it!" Jurgis protested. "I tell you I have only a dollar and a quarter."

The woman turned to her work. "I don't believe you," she said. "Dot is all to try to sheat me. Vot is de reason a big man like you has got only a dollar und a quarter?"

"I've just been in jail," Jurgis cried—he was ready to get down upon his knees to the woman—"and I had no money, and my family has almost starved."

"Vere is your friends, dot ought to help you?"

"They are all poor," he answered. "They gave me this. I have done everything I can—"

"Haven't you got notting you can sell?"

"I have nothing, I tell you—I have nothing," he cried frantically.

"Can't you borrow it, den? Don't your store people trust you?" Then, as he shook his head, she went on, "Listen to me—if you get me you will be glad of it. I vill save your wife und baby for you, und it vill not seem like mooch to you in de end. If you lose dem now how you tink you feel den? Und here is a lady dot knows her business—I could send you to people in dis block, und dey vould tell you—"

Madame Haupt was pointing her cooking-fork at Jurgis persuasively; but her words were more then he could bear. He flung up his hands with a gesture of despair and turned and started away. "It's no use," he exclaimed—but suddenly he heard the woman's voice behind him again:

"I vill make it five dollars for you."

She followed behind him, arguing with him. "You vill be foolish not to take such an offer," she said. "You von't find nobody to go out on a rainy day like dis for less. Vy, I haf never took a case in my life so sheap as dot. I couldn't pay mine room rent—"

Jurgis interrupted her with an oath of rage: "If I haven't got it," he shouted "how can I pay it? Damn it, I would pay you if I could, but I tell you I haven't got it. I haven't got! Do you hear me—I haven't got it!"

He turned and started away again. He was half way down the stairs before Madame Haupt could shout to him: "Vait! I vill go mit you! Come back!"

He went back into the room again. "It is not goot to tink of anybody suffering," she said, in a melancholy voice. "I might as vell go mit you for notting as vot you offer me, but I will try to help you. How far is it?"

"Three or four blocks from here."

"Tree or four! Und so I shall get soaked! Gott in Himmell, it ought to be worth more! Vun dollar und a quarter, und a day like dis! But you understand now—you vill pay me de rest of twenty-five dollars soon?"

"As soon as I can."

"Some time dis mont'?"

"Yes, within a month," said poor Jurgis. "Anything! Hurry up!"

"Vere is de dollar und a quarter?" persisted Madame Haupt, relentlessly.

Jurgis put the money on the table and the woman counted it and stowed it away. Then she wiped her greasy hands again and proceeded to get ready, complaining all the time; she was so fat that it was painful for her to move, and she grunted and gasped at every step. She took off her wrapper without even taking the trouble to turn her back to Jurgis, and put on her corsets and dress. Then there was a black bonnet which had to be adjusted carefully, and an umbrella which was mislaid, and a bag full of necessaries which had to be collected from here and there—poor Jurgis being nearly crazy with anxiety in the meantime. When they were on the street he kept about four paces ahead of her, turning now and then, as if he could hurry her on by the force of his desire. But Madame Haupt could only go so far at a step, and it took all her attention to get the needed breath for that.

They came at last to the house, and to the group of frightened women in the kitchen. It was not over yet, Jurgis learned—he heard Ona crying still; and meantime Madame Haupt removed her bonnet and laid it on the mantel-piece, and got out of her bag first an old dress, and then a saucer of goose-grease, which she proceeded to rub upon her hands. The more cases this goose-grease is used in, the better luck it brings to the midwife, and so she keeps it upon her kitchen mantel-piece, or stored away in a cupboard with her dirty clothes, for months, and sometimes even for years.

Then they escorted her to the ladder, and Jurgis heard her give an exclamation of dismay. "Gott in Himmell, vot for haf you brought me to a place like dis? I could not climb up dot ladder. I could not git troo a trap door! I vill not try it—vy, I might kill myself already. Vot sort of a place is dot for a woman to bear a child in—up in a garret mit only a ladder to it? You ought to be ashamed of yourselves!" Jurgis stood in the doorway and listened to her scolding, half drowning out the horrible moans and screams of Ona.

At last Panei Aniele succeeded in pacifying her, and she essayed the ascent; then, however, she had to be stopped while the old woman cautioned her about the floor of the garret. They had no real floor—they had laid old boards in one part to make a place for the family to live; it was all right and safe there, but the other part of the garret had only the joists of the floor, and the lath and plaster of the ceiling below, and if one stepped on this there would be a catastrophe. As it was half dark up above, perhaps one of the others had best go up first with a candle. Then there were more outcries and threatening, until at last Jurgis had a vision ot a pair of elephantine legs disappearing through the trap-door, and felt the house shake as Madame

Haupt started to walk. Then suddenly Panei Aniele came to him and took him by the arm.

"Now," she said, "you go away. Do as I tell you—you have done all you can, and you are only in the way. Go away and stay away."

"But where shall I go?" Jurgis asked, helplessly.

"I don't know where," she answered. "Go on the street, if there is no other place—only go! And stay all night!"

In the end she and Marija pushed him out of the door and shut it behind him. It was just about sundown, and it was turning cold—the rain had changed to snow, and the slush was freezing. Jurgis shivered in his thin clothing, and put his hands into his pockets and started away. He had not eaten since morning, and he felt weak and ill; with a sudden throb of hope he recollected he was only a few blocks from the saloon where he had been wont to eat his dinner. They might have mercy on him there, or he might meet a friend. He set out for the place as fast as he could walk.

"Hello, Jack," said the saloon-keeper, when he entered—they call all foreigners and unskilled men "Jack" in Packingtown. "Where've you been?"

Jurgis went straight to the bar. "I've been in jail," he said, "and I've just got out. I walked home all the way, and I've not a cent, and had nothing to eat since this morning. And I've lost my home, and my wife's ill, and I'm done up."

The saloon-keeper gazed at him, with his haggard white face and his blue trembling lips. Then he pushed a big bottle toward him. "Fill her up!" he said.

Jurgis could hardly hold the bottle, his hands shook so.

"Don't be afraid," said the saloon-keeper; "fill her up!"

So Jurgis drank a huge glass of whiskey, and then turned to the lunch-counter, in obedience to the other's suggestion. He ate all he dared, stuffing it in as fast as he could; and then, after trying to speak his gratitude, he went and sat down by the big red stove in the middle of the room.

It was too good to last, however—like all things in this hard world. His soaked clothing began to steam, and the horrible stench of fertilizer to fill the room. In an hour or so the packing-houses would be closing and the men coming in from their work; and they would not come into a place that smelt of Jurgis. Also it was Saturday night, and in a couple of hours would come a violin and a cornet, and in the rear part of the saloon the families of the neighborhood would dance and feast upon Wienerwurst and lager, until two or three o'clock in the morning. The saloon-keeper coughed once or twice, and then remarked: "Say, Jack, I'm afraid you'll have to quit."

He was used to the sight of human wrecks, this saloon-keeper; he "fired" dozens of them every night, just as haggard and cold and forlorn as this one. But they were all men who had given up and been counted out, while Jurgis was still in the fight, and had reminders of decency about him. As he got up meekly, the other reflected that he had always been a steady man, and might soon be a good customer again. "You've been up against it, I see," he said. "Come this way."

In the rear of the saloon were the cellar stairs. There was a door above and another below, both safely padlocked, making the stairs an admirable place to stow away a customer who might still chance to have money, or a political light whom it was not advisable to kick out of doors.

So Jurgis spent the night. The whiskey had only half warmed him, and he could not sleep, exhausted as he was; he would nod forward, and then start up, shivering with the cold, and begin to remember again. Hour after hour passed, until he could only persuade himself that it was not morning by the sounds of music and laughter and singing that were to be heard from the room. When at last these ceased, he expected that he would be turned out into the street; as this did not happen, he fell to wondering whether the man had forgotten him.

In the end, when the silence and suspense was no longer to be borne, he got up and hammered on the door, and the proprietor came, yawning and rubbing his eyes. He was keeping open all night, and dozing between customers.

"I want to go home," Jurgis said. "I'm worried about my wife—I can't wait any longer."

"Why the hell didn't you say so before?" said the man. "I thought you didn't have any home to go to."

Jurgis went outside. It was four o'clock in the morning, and as black as night. There were three or four inches of snow on the ground, and the flakes were falling thick and fast. He turned towards Panei Aniele's and started at a run.

There was a light burning in the kitchen window and the blinds were drawn. The door was unlocked and Jurgis rushed in.

Panei Aniele, Marija, and the rest of the women were huddled about the stove, exactly as before; with them were several new comers, Jurgis noticed—also he noticed that the house was silent.

"Well?" he said.

No one answered him; they sat staring at him with their pale faces. He cried again: "Well?"

And then, by the light of the smoky lamp, he saw Marija, who sat nearest him, shaking her head slowly. "Not yet," she said.

And Jurgis gave a cry of dismay. "Not yet?"

Again Marija's head shook. The poor fellow stood dumbfounded. "I don't hear her," he said suddenly.

"She's been quiet a long time," replied the other.

There was another pause—broken suddenly by a voice from the attic:

"Hello, there!"

Several of the women ran into the next room, while Marija sprang towards Jurgis. "Wait here!" she cried, and the two stood, pale and trembling, listening. In a few moments it became clear that Madame Haupt was engaged in descending the ladder, scolding and exhorting again, while the ladder creaked in protest. In a moment or two she reached the ground, angry and breathless, and they heard her coming into the room. Jurgis gave one glance at her, and then turned white and reeled. She had her jacket off, like one of the workers on the killing floor. Her hands and arms were smeared with blood, and blood was splashed upon her clothing and her face.

She stood breathing hard, and gazing around her; no one made a sound.

"I haf done my best," she began suddenly. "I can do notting more—dere is no use to try."

Again there was silence. "It ain't my fault," she said. "You had ought to haf had a doctor, und not vaited so long—it vas too late already ven I come." Once more there was deathlike stillness. Marija was clutching Jurgis with all the power of her one well arm.

Then suddenly Madame Haupt turned to Panei Aniele. "You haf not got someting to drink, hey?" she queried. "Some brandy?"

Aniele shook her head.

"Herr Gott!" exclaimed Madame Haupt. "Such people! Perhaps you vill give me someting to eat den—I have had notting since yesterday morning, und I have vorked myself near to death here. If I could have known it vas like dis, I vould never haf come for such money as you gif me."

At this moment she chanced to look round, and saw Jurgis. She shook her finger at him. "You understand me," she said, "you pays me dot money yust de same! It is not my fault you send for me so late I can't help your vife. It is not my fault if her baby comes mit one arm first, so dot I can't save it. I haf tried all night, und in dot place vere it is not fit for dogs to be born, und mit notting to eat only vot I brings in mine own pockets."

Here Madame Haupt paused for a moment to get her breath; and Marija, seeing the beads of sweat on Jurgis's forehead, and feeling the quivering of his frame, broke out in a low voice: "How is Ona?"

"How is she?" echoed Madame Haupt. "How do you tink she can be ven you leave her to kill herself so? I told dem dot ven dey send for de priest. She is young, und she might haf got over it, und been vell und strong, if she had been treated right. She fight hard, dot girl—she is not yet quite dead."

And Jurgis gave a frantic scream. "Dead!"

"She vill die, of course," said the other, angrily. "Der baby is dead now."

The garret was lighted by a candle stuck upon a board; it had almost burned itself out, and was spluttering and smoking, as Jurgis rushed up the ladder. He could make out dimly in one corner a pallet of rags and old blankets, spread upon the floor; at the foot of it was a crucifix, and near it a priest muttering a prayer. In a far corner crouched Elzbieta, moaning and wailing. Upon the pallet lay Ona.

She was covered with a blanket, but he could see her shoulders and one arm lying bare; she was so shrunken he would scarcely have known her—she was all but a skeleton, and as white as a piece of chalk. Her eye-lids were closed, and she lay still as death. He staggered towards her and fell upon his knees with a cry of anguish: "Ona! Ona!"

She did not stir. He caught her hand in his, and began to clasp it frantically, calling: "Look at me! Answer me! It is Jurgis come back—don't you hear me?"

There was the faintest quivering of her eye-lids, and he called again in frenzy: "Ona! Ona!"

Then suddenly her eyes opened—one instant—and then closed. One instant she looked at him—there was a flash of recognition between them, he saw her afar off, as through a dim vista, standing forlorn. He stretched out his arms to her, he called her in wild despair; a fearful yearning surged up in him, hunger for her that was agony, desire that was a new being born within him, tearing his heart-strings, torturing him. But it was all in vain—she faded from him, she slipped back and was gone. And a wail of despair burst from him, great sobs shook all his frame, and hot tears ran down his cheeks and fell upon her. He clutched her hands, he shook her, he caught her in his arms and pressed her to him; but she lay cold and still—she was gone—she was gone! The word rang through him like the sound of a bell, echoing in the far depths of him, making forgotten chords to vibrate, old shadowy fears to stir—fears of the dark, fears of the void, fears of annihilation. She was dead! she was dead! He would never see her again, never hear her again! An icy horror of loneliness seized him; he saw himself standing apart, and watching all the world fade away from him—a world of shadows, of fickle dreams. He was like a little child, in his fright and grief; he called and called, and got no answer, and his cries of anguish echoed through the house, making the women down stairs draw nearer to each other in fear. He was inconsolable, beside himself—the priest came and laid his hand upon his shoulder and whispered to him, but he heard not a sound. He was gone away himself, stumbling through the shadows and groping after the soul that had fled.

So she lay. The gray dawn came up and crept into the attic. The priest left, the women left, and he was alone with the still, white figure—quieter now, but moaning and shuddering, wrestling with the grisly fiend. Now and then he would raise himself and stare at the white mask before him, then hide his eyes, because he could not bear it. Dead! Dead! And she was only a girl, she was barely eighteen! Her life had hardly begun—and here she lay murdered —mangled, tortured to death!

It was morning when he rose up and came down into the kitchen—haggard and ashen gray, reeling and dazed. More of the neighbors had come in, and they stared at him in silence as he sunk down upon a chair by the table, and buried his face in his arms.

A few minutes later the front door opened; a blast of cold and snow rushed in, and behind it little Kotrina, breathless from running and blue with the cold. "I'm home again!" she exclaimed. "I could hardly—"

And then, seeing Jurgis, she stopped with an exclamation. Looking from one to another she saw that something had happened, and she asked, in a lower voice: "What's the matter?"

Before any one could reply, Jurgis started up; he went toward her, walking unsteadily. "Where have you been?" he demanded.

"Selling papers with the boys," she said. "The snow—"

"Have you any money?" he demanded. "Yes."

"How much?" "Nearly three dollars, Jurgis."

"Give it to me." Kotrina, frightened by his manner, glanced at the others. "Give it to me!" he commanded again, and she put her hand into her pocket and pulled out a lump of coins tied in a bit of rag. Jurgis took it without a word, and went out of the door and down the street.

Three doors away was a saloon. "Whiskey," he said, as he entered, and as the man pushed him some, he tore at the rag with his teeth and pulled out half a dollar. "How much is the bottle?" he said. "I want to get drunk."

20

BUT A big man cannot stay drunk very long on three dollars. That was Sunday morning, and Monday night Jurgis came home, sober and sick, realizing that he had spent every cent the family owned, and had not bought a single instant's forgetfulness with it.

Ona was not yet buried; but the police had been notified, and on the morrow they would put the body in a pine coffin and take it to the potter's field. Elzbieta was out begging now; a few pennies from each of the neighbors, to get enough to pay for a mass for her; and the children were upstairs starving to death, while he, good-for-nothing rascal, had been spending their money on drink. So spoke Panei Aniele, scornfully, and when he started towards the fire she added the information that her kitchen was no longer for him to fill with his phosphate stinks. She had crowded all her boarders into one room on Ona's account, but now he could go up in the garret where he belonged—and not there much longer, either, if he did not pay her some rent.

Jurgis went without a word, and stepping over half a dozen sleeping boarders in the next room, ascended the ladder. It was dark up above; they could not afford any light; also it was nearly as cold as out-doors. In a corner, as far away from the corpse as possible, sat Marija, holding little Antanas in her one good arm and trying to soothe him to sleep. In another corner crouched poor little Juozapas, wailing because he had had nothing to eat all day. Marija said not a word to Jurgis; he crept in like a whipped cur, and went and sat down by the body.

Perhaps he ought to have meditated upon the hunger of the children, and upon his own baseness; but he thought only of Ona, he gave himself up again to the luxury of grief. He shed no tears, being ashamed to make a sound; he sat motionless and shuddering with his anguish. He had never dreamed how much he loved Ona, until now that she was gone; until now that he sat here, knowing that on the morrow they would take her away, and that he would never lay eyes upon her again—never all the days of his life. His old love, which had been starved to death, beaten to death, awoke in him again; the floodgates of memory were lifted—he saw all their life together, saw her as he had seen her in Lithuania, the first day at the fair, beautiful as the flowers, singing like a bird. He saw her as he had married her, with all her tenderness, with her heart of wonder; the very words she had spoken seemed to ring now in his ears, the tears she had shed to be wet upon his cheek. The long, cruel battle with misery and hunger had hardened and embittered him, but it had not changed her—she had been the same hungry soul to the end, stretching out her arms to him, pleading with him, begging him for love and tenderness. And she had suffered—so cruelly she had suffered, such agonies, such infamies—ah, God, the memory of them was not to be borne. What a monster of wickedness, of heartlessness, he had been! Every angry word that he had ever spoken came back to him and cut him like a knife; every selfish act that he had done—with what torments he paid for them now! And such devotion and awe as welled up in his soul—now that it could never be spoken, now that it was too late—too late! His bosom was choking with it, bursting with it; he crouched here in the darkness beside her, stretching out his arms to her—and she was gone forever—she was dead! He could have screamed aloud with the horror and despair of it; a sweat of agony beaded his forehead, yet he dared not make a sound—he scarcely dared to breathe, because of his shame and loathing of himself.

Late at night came Elzbieta, having gotten the money for a mass, and paid for it in advance, lest she should be tempted too sorely at home. She brought also a bit of stale rye-bread that someone had given her, and with that they quieted the children and got them to sleep. Then she came over to Jurgis and sat down beside him.

She said not a word of reproach—she and Marija had chosen that course before; she would only plead with him, here by the corpse of his dead wife. Already Elzbieta had choked down her tears, grief being crowded out of her soul by fear. She had to bury one of her children—but then she had done it three times before, and each time risen up and gone back to take up the battle for the rest. Elzbieta was one of the primitive creatures; like the angle-worm, which goes on living though cut in half; like a hen, which, deprived of her chickens one by one, will mother the last that is left her. She did this because it was her nature—she asked no questions about the justice of it, nor the worthwhileness of life in which destruction and death ran riot.

And this old common-sense view she labored to impress upon Jurgis, pleading with him with tears in her eyes. Ona was dead, but the others were left, and they must be saved. She did not ask for her own children. She and Marija could care for them somehow, but there was Antanas, his own son. Ona had given Antanas to him—the little follow was the only remembrance of her that he had; he must treasure it and protect it—he must show himself a man. He knew what Ona would have had him do, what she would ask of him at this moment, if she could speak to him. It was a terrible thing that she should have died as she had; but the life had been too hard for her, and she had to go. It was terrible that they were not able to bury her, that he could not even have a day to mourn her—but so it was. Their fate was pressing; they had not a cent, and the children would perish—some money must be had. Could he not be a man for Ona's sake, and pull himself together? In a little while they would be out of danger—now that they had given up the house they could live more cheaply, and with all the children working they could get along, if only he would not go to pieces. So Elzbieta went on, with feverish intensity. It was a struggle for life with her; she was not afraid that Jurgis would go on drinking, for he had no money for that, but she was wild with dread at the thought that he might desert them, might take to the road, as Jonas had done.

But with Ona's dead body beneath his eyes, Jurgis could not well think of treason to his child. Yes, he said, he would try, for the sake of Antanas. He would give the little fellow his chance—would get to work at once, yes, tomorrow, without even waiting for Ona to be buried. They might trust him, he would keep his word, come what might.

And so he was out before daylight the next morning, headache, heartache and all. He went straight back to Anderson's fertilizer-mill, to see if he could get back his job. But the boss shook his head when he saw him—no, his place had been filled long ago, and there was no room for him.

"Do you think there will be?" Jurgis asked, "I may have to wait."

"No," said the other, "it will not be worth your while to wait—there will be nothing for you here."

Jurgis stood gazing at him in perplexity. "What is the matter?" he asked. Didn't I do my work?"

The other met his look with one of cold indifference, and answered: "There will be nothing for you here, I said."

Jurgis had his suspicions as to the dreadful meaning of that incident, and he went away with a sinking at the heart. He went and took his stand with the mob of hungry wretches who were standing about in the snow before the time-station. Here he stayed, breakfastless, for two hours, until the throng was driven away by the clubs of the police. There was no work for him that day.

Jurgis had made a good many acquaintances in his long services at the yards—there were saloon-keepers who would trust him for a drink and a sandwich, and members of his old union who would lend him a dime at a pinch. It was not a question of life and death for him therefore; he might hunt all day, and come again on the morrow, and try hanging on thus for weeks, like hundreds and thousands of others. Meantime Teta Elzbieta would go and beg, over in the Hyde Park district, and the children would bring home enough to pacify Panei Aniele, and keep them all alive.

It was at the end of a week of this sort of waiting, roaming about in the bitter winds or loafing in saloons, that Jurgis stumbled on a chance in one of the cellars of Morton's big packing plant. He saw a foreman passing the open doorway, and hailed him for a job.

"Push a truck?" inquired the man, and Jurgis answered "Yes, sir!" before the words were well out of his mouth.

"What's your name?" demanded the other.

"Jurgis Rudkos."

"Worked in the yards before?"

"Yes."

"Where abouts?"

"Two places—Smith's killing-floor, and Andersons fertilizer-mill."

"Why did you leave there?"

"The first time I had an accident, and the last time I was sent up for a month."

"I see. Well, I'll give you a trial. Come early tomorrow and ask for Mr. Thomas."

So Jurgis rushed home with the wild tidings that he had a job—that the terrible siege was over. The remnants of the family had quite a celebration that night; and in the morning Jurgis was at the place half an hour before the time of opening. The foreman came in shortly afterwards, and when he saw Jurgis he frowned.

"Oh," he said, "I promised you a job, didn't I?"

"Yes, sir," said Jurgis.

"Well, I'm sorry, but I made a mistake. I can't use you."

Jurgis stared, dumbfounded. "What's the matter?" he gasped.

"Nothing," said the man, "only I can't use you."

There was the same cold, hostile stare that he had had from the boss of the fertilizer-mill. He knew that there was no use in saying a word, and he turned and went away.

Out in the saloons the men could tell him all about the meaning of it; they gazed at him with pitying eyes—poor devil, he was black-listed! What had he done? they asked—knocked down his boss? Good heavens, then he might have known! Why, he stood as much chance of getting a job in Packingtown as of being chosen mayor of Chicago. Why had he wasted his time hunting? They had him on a secret list in every office, big and little, in the place. They had his name by this time in St. Louis and New York, in Omaha and Boston, in Kansas City and St. Joseph. He was condemned and sentenced, without trial and without appeal; he could never work for the packers again—he could not even clean cattle-pens or drive a truck in any place where they controlled. He might try it, if he chose, as hundreds had tried it, and found out for themselves. He would never be told anything about it; he would never get any more satisfaction than he had gotten just now; but he would always find when the time came that he was not needed. It would not do for him to give any other name, either—they had company "spotters" for just that purpose, and he wouldn't keep a job in Packingtown three days. It was worth a fortune to the packers to keep their black-list effective, as a warning to the men, and a means of keeping down union agitation and political discontent.

Jurgis went home, carrying these new tidings to the family council. It was a most cruel thing; here in this district was his home, such as it was, the place he was used to and the friends he knew—and now every possibility of employment in it was closed to him. There was nothing in Packingtown but packing-houses; and so it was the same thing as evicting him from his home.

He and the two women spent all day and half the night discussing it. It would be convenient, downtown, to the children's place of work; but then Marija was on the road to recovery, and had hopes of getting a job in the yards, and also Elzbieta had heard something about a chance to scrub floors in Anderson's offices. In the end it was decided that Jurgis should go downtown to strike out for himself, and they would decide after he got a job. As there was no one from whom he could borrow there, and he dared not beg for fear of being arrested, it was arranged that every day he should meet one of the children and be given fifteen cents of their earnings, upon which he could keep going. Then all day he was to pace the streets with hundreds and thousands of other homeless wretches, inquiring at stores, warehouses and factories for a chance; and at night he was to crawl into some door-way, or underneath a truck, and hide there until midnight, when he might get into one of the station-houses, and spread a newspaper upon the floor, and lie down in the midst of a throng of "bums" and beggars, reeking with alcohol and tobacco, and filthy with vermin and disease.

So for two weeks more Jurgis fought with the demon of despair. Once he got a chance to load a truck for half a day, and again he carried an old woman's valise and was given a quarter. This let him into a lodging-house on several nights when he might otherwise have frozen to death; and it also gave him a chance now and then to buy a newspaper in the morning and hunt up jobs while his rivals were watching and waiting for a paper to be thrown away. This, however, was really not the advantage it seemed, for the newspaper advertisements were a cause of much loss of precious time and of many weary journeys. Nine-tenths of these were "fakes," put in by the endless variety of establishments which preyed upon the helpless ignorance of the unemployed. If Jurgis lost only his time, it was because he had nothing else to lose; whenever a smooth-tongued agent would tell him of the wonderful positions he had on hand, he could only shake his head sorrowfully and say that he had not the necessary dollar to deposit; when it was explained to him what "big money" he and all his family could make by coloring photographs he could only promise to come in again when he had two dollars to invest in the outfit.

In the end Jurgis got a chance through an accidental meeting with an old-time acquaintance of his union days. He met this man on his way to work, in the giant factories of the Harvester Trust; and his friend told him to come along and he would speak a good word for him to his boss, whom he knew well. So Jurgis trudged four or five miles, and passed through a waiting throng of unemployed at the gate under the escort of his friend. His knees nearly gave way beneath him when the foreman, after looking him over and questioning him, told him that he could find an opening for him.

How much this accident meant to Jurgis he realized only by stages; for he found that the harvester-works were the sort of place to which our philanthropists and reformers point with pride. It had some thought for its employes; its work-shops were big and roomy, it provided a restaurant where the workmen could buy good food at cost, it had even a reading-room, and decent places where its girl-hands could rest; also the work was free from many of the elements of filth and repulsiveness that prevailed at the stock-yards. Day after day Jurgis discovered these things—things never expected nor dreamed of by him—until this new place came to seem a kind of a heaven to him.

It was an enormous establishment, covering a hundred and sixty acres of ground, employing five thousand people, and turning out over three hundred thousand machines every year—a good part of all the harvesting and mowing machines used in the country. Jurgis saw very little of it, of course—it was all specialized work, the same as at the stock-yards; each one of the hundreds of parts of a mowing-machine was made separately, and sometimes handled by hundreds of men. Where Jurgis worked there was a machine which cut and stamped a certain piece of steel about two square inches in size; the pieces came tumbling out upon a, tray, and all that human hands had to do was to pile them in regular rows, and change the trays at intervals. This was done by a single boy, who stood with eyes and thought centered upon it, and fingers flying so fast that the sounds of the bits of steel striking upon each other was like the music of an express train as one hears it in a sleeping-car at night. This was "piece-work," of course; and besides it was made certain that the boy did not idle by setting the machine to match the highest possible speed of human hands. Thirty thousand of these pieces he handled every day—nine or ten millions every year—how many in a lifetime it rested with the gods to say. Nearby him men sat bending over whirling grindstones, putting the finishing touches to the steel knives of the reaper; picking them out of a basket with the right hand, pressing first one side and then the other against the stone, and finally dropping them with the left hand into another basket. One of these men told Jurgis that he had sharpened three thousand pieces of steel a day for thirteen years. In the next room were wonderful machines that ate up long steel rods by slow stages, cutting them off, seizing the pieces, stamping heads upon them, grinding them and polishing them, threading them and finally dropping them into a basket, all ready to bolt the harvesters together. From yet another machine came tens of thousands of steel burrs to fit upon these bolts. In other places all these various parts were dipped into troughs of paint and hung up to dry, and then slid along on trolleys to a room where men streaked them with red and yellow, so that they might look cheerful in the harvest-fields.

Jurgis's friend worked upstairs in the casting-rooms, and his task was to make the moulds of a certain part. He shovelled black sand into an iron receptacle and pounded it tight and set it aside to harden; then it would be taken out and molten iron poured into it. This man, too, was paid by the mould—or rather for perfect castings, nearly half his work going for naught. You might see him, along with dozens of others, toiling like one possessed by a whole community of demons; his arms working like the driving rods of an engine, his long, black hair flying wild, his eyes starting out, the sweat rolling in rivers down his face. When he had shovelled the mould full of sand, and reached for the pounder to pound it with, it was after the manner of a canoeist running rapids and seizing a pole at sight of a submerged rock. All day long this man would toil thus, his whole being centered upon the purpose of making twenty-three instead of twenty-two and a half cents an hour; and then his product would be reckoned up by the census-taker, and jubilant captains of industry would boast of it in their banquet-halls, telling how our workers are nearly twice as efficient as those of any other country. If we are the greatest nation the sun ever shown upon, it would seem to be mainly because we have been able to goad our wage-earners to this pitch of frenzy; though there are a few other things that are great among us, including our drink-bill, which is a billion and a quarter of dollars a year, and doubling itself every decade.

There was a machine which stamped out the iron plates, and then another which, with a mighty thud, mashed them to the shape of the sitting-down portion of the American farmer. Then they were piled upon a truck, and it was Jurgis's task to wheel them to the room where the machines were "assembled." This was child's play for him, and he got a dollar and seventy five a day for it; on Saturday he paid Panei Aniele the seventy-five cents a week he owed her for the use of her garret, and also redeemed his overcoat, which Elzbieta had put in pawn when he was in jail.

This last was a great blessing. A man cannot go about in mid-winter in Chicago with no overcoat and not pay for it, and Jurgis had to walk or ride five or six miles back and forth to his work. It so happened that half of this was in one direction and half in another, necessitating a change of cars; the law required that transfers be given at all intersecting points, but the railway corporation had gotten round this by arranging a pretence at separate owner-ship. So whenever he wished to ride, he had to pay ten cents each way, or over ten per cent of his income, to this pirate power, which had gotten its franchises long ago by buying up the city council, in the face of popular clamor amounting almost to a rebellion. Tired as he felt at night, and dark and bitter cold as it was in the morning, Jurgis generally chose to walk; at the hours other workmen were traveling, the street-car monopoly saw fit to put on so few cars that there would be men hanging to every foot of the backs of them and often crouching upon the snow-covered roof. Of course, the doors could never be closed, and so the cars were as cold as out-doors; Jurgis, like many others, found it better to spend his fare for a drink and a free lunch, to give him strength to walk.

These, however, were all slight matters to a man who had escaped from Anderson's fertilizer-mill. Jurgis began to pick up heart again and to make plans. He had lost his house, but then the awful load of the rent and interest was off his shoulders, and when Marija was well again they could start over and save. In the shop where he worked was a man, a Lithuanian like himself, whom the others spoke of in admiring whispers, because of the mighty feats he was performing. All day he sat at a machine turning bolts; and then in the evening he went to the public-school to study English and learn to read. In addition, because he had a family of eight children to support and his earnings were not enough, on Saturdays and Sundays he served as a watchman; he was required to press two buttons at opposite ends of the building every five minutes, and as the walk only took him two minutes, he had three minutes to study between each trip. Jurgis felt jealous of this fellow; for that was the sort of thing he himself had dreamed of, two or three years ago. He might do it even yet, if he had a fair chance—he might attract attention and become a skilled man, or a boss, as some had done in this place. Suppose that Marija could get a job in the big mill where they made binder-twine—then they would move into this neighborhood, and he would really have a chance. With a hope like that, there was some use in living; to find a place where you were treated like a human being—by God! he would show them how he could appreciate it. He laughed to himself as he thought how he would hang on to this job!

And then one afternoon, the ninth of his work in the place, when he went to get his overcoat he saw a group of men crowded before a placard on the door, and when he went over and asked what it was, they told him that beginning with the morrow the National Harvester Works would be closed until further notice!

21

THAT WAS the way they did it! There was not half an hour's warning—the works were closed! It had happened that way before, said the men, and it would happen that way forever. They had made all the harvesting-machines that the world needed, and now they had to wait till some wore out! It was nobody's fault—that was the way of it; and five thousand men and women were turned out in the dead of winter, to live upon their savings if they had any, and otherwise to die. So many tens of thousands already in the city, homeless and begging for work, and now five thousand more added to them!

Jurgis walked home with his pittance of pay in his pocket, heart-broken, overwhelmed. One more bandage had been torn from his eyes, one more pitfall of the jungle was revealed to him! Of what help was kindness and decency on the part of employers—when they could not keep a job for him, when there were more harvesting-machines made than the world was able to buy! What a hellish mockery it was, anyway, that a man should slave to make harvesting-machines for the country, only to be turned out to starve for doing his duty too well!

It took him two days to get over this heart-sickening disappointment. He did not drink anything, because Elzbieta got his money for safekeeping and knew him too well to be in the least frightened by his angry demands. He stayed up in the garret, however, and sulked—what was the use of a man's hunting a job when it was taken from him before he had time to learn the work? But then their money was going again, and little Antanas was hungry, and crying with the bitter cold of the garret. Also Madame Haupt, the midwife, was after him for some money. And so he went out once more.

For another ten days he roamed the streets and alleys of the huge city, sick and hungry, begging for any work. He tried in stores and warehouses, in restaurants and hotels, along the docks and in the railroad yards, in warehouses and mills and factories where they made products that went to every corner of the world. There were often one or two chances—but there were always a hundred men for every chance, and his turn would not come. At night he crept into sheds and cellars and doorways—until there came a spell of belated winter weather, with a raging gale and the thermometer five degrees below zero at sundown and falling all night. Then Jurgis fought like a wild beast to get into the big Harrison street police-station and slept down in a corridor, crowded with two other men upon a single step.

He had to fight often in these days—to fight for a place near the factory gates, and now and again with gangs on the street. He found, for instance, that the business of carrying satchels for railroad-passengers was a preempted one—whenever he essayed it, eight or ten men and boys would fall upon him and force him to run for his life. They always had the policeman "squared," and so there was no use in expecting protection.

That Jurgis did not starve to death was due solely to the pittance the children brought him. And even this was never certain. For one thing, the cold was almost more than the children could bear; and then they, too, were in perpetual peril from rivals who plundered and beat them. The law was against them, too—little Vilimui, who was really eleven, but did not look to be eight, was stopped on the streets by a severe old lady in spectacles, who told him that he was too young to be working, and that if he did not stop selling papers she would send a truant-officer after him. Also one night a strange man caught little Kotrina by the arm and tried to persuade her into a dark cellar-way, an experience which filled her with such terror that she was hardly to be kept at work.

At last on a Sunday, as there was no use looking for work, Jurgis went home by stealing rides on the cars. He found that they had been waiting for him for three days—there was a chance of a job for him.

It was quite a story. Little Juozapas, who was near crazy with hunger these days, had gone out on the street to beg for himself. Juozapas had only one leg, having been run over by a wagon when a little child, but he had got himself a broomstick, which he put under his arm for a crutch. He had fallen in with some other children and found the way to Tom Cassidy's dump, which lay three or four blocks away. To this place there came every day many hundreds of wagonloads of garbage and trash, from the lake-front where the rich people lived; and in the heaps the children raked for food—there were hunks of bread, and potato peelings, and apple-cores, and meat-bones, all of it half-frozen and quite unspoiled. Little Juozapas gorged him-self, and came home with a newspaper full, which he was feeding to Antanas when his mother came in. Elzbieta was horrified, for she did not believe that the food out of the dumps was fit to eat. The next day, however, when no harm came of it and Juozapas began to cry with hunger, she gave in and said that he might go again. And that afternoon he came home with a story of how, while he had been digging away with a stick, a lady upon the street had called him. A real fine lady, the little boy explained, a beautiful lady; and she wanted to know all about him, and whether he got the garbage for chickens, and why he walked with a broomstick, and why Ona had died, and how Jurgis had come to go to jail, and what was the matter with Marija, and everything. In the end she had asked where he lived, and said that she was coming to see him, and bring him a new crutch to walk with. She had on a hat with a bird on it, Juozapas added, and a long fur snake around her neck.

She really came, the very next morning, and climbed the ladder to the garret, and stood and stared about her, turning pale at the sight of the blood-stains on the floor where Ona had died. She was a "settlement-worker," she explained to Elzbieta—she lived around on Ashland avenue. Elzbieta knew the place, over a feed-store; somebody had wanted her to go there, but she had not cared to, for she thought that it must have something to do with religion, and the priest did not like her to have anything to do with strange religions. They were rich people who came to live there to find out about the poor people; but what good they expected it would do them to know, one could not imagine. So spoke Elzbieta, naively, and the young lady laughed and was rather at a loss for an answer—she stood there and gazed about her, and thought of a cynical remark that had been made to her, that she was standing upon the brink of the pit of hell and throwing in snowballs to lower the temperature.

Elzbieta was glad to have somebody to listen, and she told all their woes—what had happened to Ona, and the jail, and the loss of their home, and Marija's accident, and how Ona had died, and how Jurgis could get no work. As she listened the pretty young lady's eyes filled with tears, and in the midst of it she burst into weeping and hid her face on Elzbieta's shoulder, quite regardless of the fact that the woman had on a dirty old wrapper and that the garret was full of fleas. Poor Elzbieta was ashamed of herself for having told so woeful a tale, and the other had to beg and plead with her to get her to go on. The end of it was that the young lady sent them a basket of things to eat, and left a letter that Jurgis was to take to a gentleman who was superintendent in one of the mills of the great steel-works in South Chicago. "He will get Jurgis something to do," the young lady had said, and added, smiling through her tears—"if he doesn't he will never marry me."

The steel-works were fifteen miles away, and as usual it was so contrived that one had to pay two fares to get there. Far and wide the sky was flaring with the red glare that leaped from rows of towering chimneys—for it was pitch dark when Jurgis arrived. The vast works, a city in themselves, were surrounded by a stockade; and already a full hundred men were waiting at the gate where new hands were taken on. Soon after daybreak whistles began to blow, and then suddenly thousands of men appeared, streaming from saloons and boarding-houses across the way, leaping from trolley-cars that passed—it seemed as if they rose out of the ground, in the dim gray light. A river of them poured in through the gate—and then gradually ebbed away again, until there were only a few late ones running, and the watchman pacing up and down, and the hungry strangers stamping and shivering.

Jurgis presented his precious letter. The gatekeeper was surly, and put him through a catechism, but he insisted that he knew nothing, and as he had taken the precaution to seal his letter, there was nothing for the gatekeeper to do but send it to the person to whom it was addressed. A messenger came back to say that Jurgis should wait, and so he came inside the gate, perhaps not sorry enough that there were others less fortunate watching him with greedy eyes.

The great mills were getting under way—one could hear a vast stirring, a rolling and rumbling and hammering. Little by little the scene grew plain— towering black buildings here and there, long rows of shops and sheds, little railways branching everywhere, bare gray cinders under foot and oceans of billowing black smoke above. On one side of the grounds ran a railroad with a dozen tracks, and on the other side lay the lake, where steamers came to load.

Jurgis had time enough to stare and speculate, for it was two hours before he was summoned. He went into the office-building, where a company time-keeper interviewed him. The superintendent was busy, he said, but he (the timekeeper) would try to find Jurgis a job. He had never worked in a steelmill before? But he was ready for anything? Well, then, they would go and see.

So they began a tour, among sights that made Jurgis stare amazed. He wondered if ever he could get used to working in a place like this, where the air shook with deafening thunder, and whistles shrieked warnings on all sides of him at once; where miniature steam-engines came rushing upon him, and sizzling, quivering, white-hot masses of metal sped past him, and explosions of fire and flaming sparks dazzled him and scorched his face. The men in these mills were all black with soot, and hollow-eyed and gaunt; they worked with feverish intensity, rushing here and there, and never lifting their eyes from their tasks. Jurgis clung to his guide like a scared child to its nurse, and while the latter hailed one foreman after another to ask if they could use another unskilled man, he stared about him and marveled.

He was taken to the Bessemer furnace, where they made billets of steel—a dome-like building the size of a big theater. Jurgis stood where the balcony of the theater would have been, and opposite, by the stage, he saw three giant cauldrons, big enough for all the devils of hell to brew their broth in, full of something white and blinding, bubbling and splashing, roaring as if volcanoes were blowing through it—one had to shout to be heard in the place. Liquid fire would leap from these cauldrons and scatter like bombs below—and men were working there, seeming careless, so that Jurgis caught his breath with fright. Then a whistle would toot, and across the curtain of the theater would come a little engine with a carload of something to be dumped into one of the receptacles; and then another whistle would toot, down by the stage, and another train would back up—and suddenly, without an instant's warning, one of the giant kettles began to tilt and topple, flinging out a jet of hissing, roaring flame. Jurgis shrank back appalled, for he thought it was an accident; there fell a pillar of white flame, dazzling as the sun, swishing like a huge tree falling in the forest. A torrent of sparks swept all the way across the building, overwhelming everything, hiding it from sight; and then Jurgis looked through the fingers of his hands, and saw pouring out of the cauldron a cascade of living, leaping fire, white with a whiteness not of earth, scorching the eyeballs. Incandescent rainbows shone above it; blue, red and golden lights played about it; but the stream itself was white, ineffable. Out of regions of wonder it streamed, the very river of life; and the soul leaped up at the sight of it, fled back upon it, swift and resistless, back into far-off lands where beauty and terror dwell. Then the great cauldron tilted back again, empty, and Jurgis saw, to his relief, that no one was hurt, and turned and followed his guide out into the sunlight.

They went through the blast-furnaces, through, rolling-mills where bars of steel were tossed about and chopped like bits of cheese. All around and above giant machine-arms were flying, giant wheels were turning, giant hammers crashing; traveling cranes creaked and groaned overhead, reaching down iron hands and seizing iron prey—it was like standing in the center of the earth, where the machinery of time was revolving.

Bye and bye they came to the place where steel rails were made; and Jurgis heard a toot behind him, and jumped out of the way of a car with a white-hot ingot upon it the size of a man's body. There was a sudden crash and the car came to a halt, and the ingot toppled out upon a moving platform, where steel fingers and arms seized hold of it, punching it and prodding it into place, and hurrying it into the grip of huge rollers. Then it came out upon the other side, and there were more crashings and clatterings, and over it was flopped, like a pancake on a gridiron, and seized again and rushed back at you through another squeezer. So amid deafening uproar it clattered to and fro, growing thinner and flatter and longer. The ingot seemed almost a living thing; it did not want to run this mad course, but it was in the grip of fate; it was tumbled on, screeching and clanking and shivering in protest. Bye and bye it was long and thin, a great red snake escaped from purgatory; and then, as it slid through the rollers, you would have sworn that it was alive—it writhed and squirmed, and wriggles and shudders passed out through its tail, all but flinging it off by their violence. There was no rest for it until it was cold and black—and then it needed only to be cut and straightened to be ready for a railroad. It was at the end of this rail's progress that Jurgis got his chance. They had to be moved by men with crowbars, and the boss here could use another man—so he took off his coat and set to work on the spot.

It took him two hours to get to this place, and a dollar and twenty cents a week; as this was out of the question, he wrapped his bedding in a bundle and took it with him, and one of his fellow-workingmen introduced him to a Polish lodging-house, where be might have the privilege of sleeping upon the floor for ten cents a night. He got his meals at free-lunch counters, and every Saturday night he went home—bedding and all—and took the greater part of his money to the family. Elzbieta was sorry for this arrangement, for she feared that it would get him into the habit of living without them, and once a week was not very often for him to see his baby—but there was no other way of arranging it. There was no chance for a woman at the steel-works, and Marija was now ready to work again, and lured on from day to day by the hope of finding it at the yards.

In a week Jurgis got over his sense of helplessness and bewilderment in the rail-mill. He learned to find his way about and to take all the miracles and terrors for granted, to work without hearing the rumbling and crashing. From blind fear he went to the other extreme; he became reckless and indifferent, like all the rest of the men, who took but little thought of themselves in the ardor of their work. It was wonderful, when one came to think of it, that these men should have taken an interest in the work they did; they had no share in it—they were paid by the hour, and paid no more for being interested. Also they knew that if they were hurt they would be flung aside and forgotten—and still they would hurry to their task by dangerous short-cuts, would use methods that were quicker and more effective in spite of the fact that they were also risky. His fourth day at his work Jurgis saw a man stumble while running in front of a car, and have his foot mashed off; and before he had been there three weeks he was witness of a yet more dreadful accident. There was a row of brick-furnaces, shining white through every crack with the molten steel inside. Some of these were bulging dangerously, yet men worked before them, wearing blue glasses when they opened and shut the doors. One morning, as Jurgis was passing, a furnace blew out, spraying two men with a shower of liquid fire. As they lay screaming and rolling upon the ground in agony, Jurgis rushed to help them, and as a result he lost a good part of the skin from the inside of one of his hands. The company doctor bandaged it up, but he got no other thanks from anyone, and was laid up for eight working days without any pay.

Most fortunately, at this juncture, Elzbieta got the long-awaited chance to go at five o'clock in the morning and help scrub the office-floors of one of the packers. Jurgis came home and covered himself with blankets to keep warm, and divided his time between sleeping and playing with little Antanas. Juozapas was away raking in the dump a good part of the time, and Elzbieta and Marija were hunting for more work.

Antanas was now over a year and a half old, and was a perfect talking-machine. He learned so fast that every week when Jurgis came home it seemed to him as if he had a new child. He would sit down and listen and stare at him, and give vent to delighted exclamations—"*Palauk! Mumal! Tu mano szirdele!*" The little fellow was now really the one delight that Jurgis had in the world—his one hope, his one victory. Thank God, Antanas was a boy! And he was as tough as a pine-knot, and with the appetite of a wolf. Nothing had hurt him, and nothing could hurt him: he had come through all the suffering and deprivation unscathed—only shriller-voiced and more determined in his grip upon life. He was a terrible child to manage, was Antanas, but his father did not mind that—he would watch him and smile to himself with satisfaction. The more of a fighter he was the better—he would need to fight before he got through.

Jurgis had got the habit of buying the Sunday paper, whenever he had the money; a most wonderful paper could be had for only five cents, a whole armful, with all the news of the world set forth in big headlines, that Jurgis could spell out slowly, with the children to help him at the big words. There was battle and murder and sudden death—it was marvelous how they ever heard about so many entertaining and thrilling happenings; they must be all true, for surely no man could have made such things up, and, besides, there were pictures of them all, as real as life. One of these papers was as good as a circus, and nearly as good as a spree—certainly a most wonderful treat for a workingman who was tired out and stupefied, and had never had any education—whose work was one dull, sordid grind, day after day, and year after year, with never a sight of a green field, nor an hour's entertainment, nor anything but liquor to stimulate his imagination. Among other things, these papers had pages full of comical pictures, and these were the main joy in life to little Antanas. He treasured them up, and would drag them out and make his father tell him about them; there were all sorts of animals among them, and Antanas could tell the name of all of them, lying upon the floor for hours and pointing them out with his chubby little fingers. Whenever the story was plain enough for Jurgis to make out, Antanas would have it repeated to him, and then he would remember it, prattling funny little sentences and mixing it up with other stories in an irresistible fashion. Also his quaint pronunciation of words was such a delight—and the phrases he would pick up and remember, the most outlandish and impossible things! The first time that the little rascal burst out with "God-damn" his father nearly rolled off the chair with glee; but in the end he was sorry for this, for Antanas was soon "God-damning" everything and everybody.

Jurgis had two visitors during his illness—one the young lady from the settlement, and the other Miss Wheeler. The Wheelers were a family that had rented a room in Panei Aniele's basement a month or two before. No one in the neighborhood knew them, for they kept to themselves; it was not clear why they were there, for they were people of a far different class from the Packingtown workers. There was a mother, who was a helpless invalid, and a daughter, and a son of about twenty-five. Once a week the daughter went down-town for a bundle of sewing, except for that never going out at all. As for the son, he worked in the factory of one of the "independent" packers, but as no one else in the vicinity worked there, the neighbors knew no more about him, except that he played the violin half the night—and played it in a way that none of them had ever heard or dreamed of, wild, wonderful music that made them tremble to their finger-tips, and sent them away wondering and awestricken. They noticed that it was always mournful, heart-breaking music that he played—never by any chance had anyone heard so much as half a dozen notes of happy music coming from that little basement room with the curtains drawn.

That the mystery was ever solved for the neighborhood was due to this accident to Jurgis. Miss Wheeler heard of it somehow, and she asked Elzbieta if she might come up and see him. She came in the evening, when they were all home; and she sat in the dark and talked with them. She had heard that Jurgis had injured his hand, she said, and she could sympathize with them, because of the dreadful misfortune her brother Harry had met with. He was a musician, as they knew, and he worked at a stamping machine, and had had two fingers of his left hand taken off by it. That made it impossible for him really to play anything upon his violin for the rest of his life; and of course it had made him very unhappy. The young lady spoke in a low, sweet voice that was like a violin itself; it was the first time that Jurgis had ever spoken to a woman of her class in his life, and he was speechless with confusion when she went on to say that she had heard of the sorrow he had met with, and that if it would give him pleasure during his helplessness, she would be glad to have him come down and visit them, and meet her mother, and talk with her while she was doing her sewing. Elzbieta had to kick Jurgis in the dark to make him answer, and then apologize for him because he was such a clumsy bear.

Jurgis returned the call, of course; he felt like a fish out of water, but he soon found himself at home watching Miss Wheeler's fingers fly, and listening to her gentle voice. She was a little fairy of a woman, pale and thin, and in the daylight he could see that her eyes were red from the strain of the sewing. She never ceased for an instant, except when she ran to attend to her mother, a white-haired old lady, who would lie upon her back on the sofa, as silent as a corpse, for an hour at a time.

The daughter was interested in this big, strange, foreign man, who had suffered so much and was so silent. She drew him out and got him to telling her about his life, and the way things were in Lithuania. She never said anything about her own life, but Jurgis could see that they were nearly as poor as he was. Yet everything they had was different from what one saw in Packingtown. The women had their bed hung round with a curtain, and with a screen the brother had made a tiny room to himself. Also they had pictures, and little knick-knacks that told of another life. It was long afterwards that Jurgis heard the story of the Wheelers. Their father had been a business-man in a town in Connecticut, and had been ruined and had blown out his brains. Then the son, who was studying music, and was called a man of genius, had set out to support them by playing in a theater; and hearing of a chance in Chicago he had brought them there, and after being ill, and going from one place to another, he had come to be a cashier in a tailor-shop, earning six dollars a week. Then he had made up his mind to work with his hands; and had been first in a printing office, and then a motorman on a street-car; finally, unable to stand the exposure and killing hours of this trade, he had drifted into the stock-yards, and learned to tend a tin-stamping machine.

Before he had been two weeks at the work he had had blood-poisoning, and in a month, more he had lost his fingers. This had not prevented his working, but it had broken his heart; he was dying inch by inch, and half the night he would sit and sob out his anguish through such fitful snatches of music as he could still manage to achieve.

When he was able to use his hands Jurgis took his bedding again and went back to his task of shifting rails. It was now April, and the snow had given place to cold rains, and the unpaved street in front of Panei Aniele's house was turned into a canal. Jurgis would have to wade through it to get home, and if it was late he might easily get stuck to his waist in the mire. But he did not mind this much—it was a promise that summer was coming. Marija had now gotten a place as beef-trimmer in one of the smaller packing-plants; and he told himself that he had learned his lesson now, and would meet with no more accidents—so that at last there was prospect of an end to their long agony. They were within sight of the promised land, and those of them who were left were to be happy! So once more Jurgis began to make plans and to dream dreams. They could save money again, and when another winter came they would have a comfortable place; and the children would be off the streets and in school again—so they might all set to work to nurse back into life their habits of decency and kindness.

And then one Saturday night Jurgis jumped off the car and started home with the sun shining low under the edge of a bank of clouds that had been pouring floods of water into the mud-soaked street. There was a rainbow in the sky and another in his breast—for he had thirty-six hours' rest before him, and a chance to see his family. Then suddenly he noticed that there was a crowd before the door of the house, and he started in alarm. He ran up the steps and pushed his way in, and saw that Panei Aniele's kitchen was crowded with excited women. It reminded Jurgis so vividly of the time when he had come home from jail and found Ona dying that his heart almost stood still.

"What's the matter?" he cried.

A dead silence had fallen in the room, and he saw that every one was staring at him. "What's the matter?" he exclaimed again.

And then, up in the garret, he heard sounds of wailing, in Marija's voice, he started for the ladder—and Panei Aniele seized him by the arm. "No, no!" she exclaimed. "Don't go up there!"

"What is it?" he yelled.

And the old woman answered him weakly: "It's Antanas. He's dead. He was drowned in the street!"

JURGIS took the news In a peculiar way. He turned deadly pale but he caught himself, and for half a minute stood in the middle of the room, clutching his hands tightly and setting his teeth. Then he pushed Panei Aniele aside and strode into the next room and climbed the ladder.

In the corner was a blanket, with a form half showing beneath it; and beside it lay Elzbieta, whether crying or in a faint, Jurgis could not tell. Marija was pacing the room, screaming and wringing her hands. He clenched his hands tighter yet, and his voice was hard as he spoke.

"How did it happen?" he asked.

Marija scarcely heard him in her agony. He repeated the question, louder yet and more harshly. "He fell off the sidewalk!" she wailed. The sidewalk in front of the house was a platform made of half-rotten boards, about three feet above the level of the sunken street.

"How did he come to be there?" he demanded.

"He went—he went out to play," Marija sobbed, her voice choking her. "We couldn't make him stay in. He must have got caught in the mud!"

"Are you sure that he is dead?" he demanded.

"Ai! ai!" she wailed, "yes, we had the doctor."

Then Jurgis stood a few seconds, wavering. He did not shed a tear. He took one glance more at the blanket with the little form beneath it, and then turned suddenly to the ladder and climbed down again. A silence fell once more in the room as he entered. He went straight to the door, passed out, and started down the street.

When his wife had died, Jurgis made for the nearest saloon, but he did not do that now, though he had his week's wages in his pocket. He walked and walked, seeing nothing, splashing through mud and water. Later on he sat down upon a step and hid his face in his hands, and for half an hour or so he did not move. Now and then he would whisper to himself: "Dead! Dead!"

Finally he got up and walked on again. It was about sunset, and he went on and on until it was dark, when he was stopped by a railroad crossing. The gates were down, and a long train of freight-cars was thundering by. He stood and watched it; and all at once a wild impulse seized him, a thought that had been lurking within him, unspoken, unrecognized, leaped into sudden life. He started down the track, and when he was past the gate-keeper's shanty he sprang forward and swung himself onto one of the cars.

Bye and bye the train stopped again, and Jurgis sprang down and ran under the car, and hid himself upon the truck. Here he sat, and when the train started again, he fought a battle with his soul. He gripped his hands and set his teeth together—he had not wept, and he would not—not a tear! It was past and over, and he was done with it—he would fling it off his shoulders, be free of it, the whole business, that night. It should go like a black, hateful nightmare, and in the morning he would be a new man. And every time that a thought of it assailed him—a tender memory, a trace of a tear—he rose up, cursing with rage, and pounded it down.

He was fighting for his life; he gnashed his teeth together in his desperation. He had been a fool, a fool! He had wasted his life, he had wrecked himself, with his accursed weakness; and now he was done with it—he would tear it out of him, root and branch! There should be no more tears, and no more tenderness; he had had enough of them—they had sold him into slavery! Now he was going to be free, to tear off his shackles, to rise up and fight. He was glad that the end had come—it had to come some time, and it was just as well now. This was no world for women and children, and the sooner they got out of it the better for them. Whatever Antanas might suffer where he was, he could suffer no more than he would have had he stayed upon earth. And meantime his father had thought the last thought about him that he meant to; he was going to think of himself, he was going to fight for himself, against the world that had baffled him and tortured him!

So he went on, tearing up all the flowers from the garden of his soul, and setting his heel upon them. The train thundered deafeningly, and a storm of dust blew in his face; but though the train stopped now and then through the night, he clung where he was—he would cling there until he was driven off, for every mile that he got from Packingtown meant another load from his mind.

Whenever the cars stopped a warm breeze blew upon him, a breeze laden with the perfume of fresh fields, of honey-suckle and clover. He snuffed it, and it made his heart beat wildly—he was out in the country again. He was going to live in the country! When the dawn came he was peering out with hungry eyes, getting glimpses of meadows and woods and rivers. At last he could stand it no longer, and when the train stopped again he crawled out. Upon the top of the car was a brakeman, who shook his fist and swore; Jurgis waved his hand derisively, and started across the country.

Only think that he had been a countryman all his life; and for three long years he had never seen a country sight nor heard a country sound! Excepting for that one walk when he left jail, when he was too much worried to notice anything, and for a few times that he had rested in the city parks, in the winter time when he was out of work, he had literally never seen a tree! And now he felt like a bird lifted up and borne away upon the gale; he stopped and stared at each new sight of wonder—at a herd of cows, and a meadow full of daisies, hedgerows set thick with June roses, and little birds singing in the trees. He was only a poor, dirty tramp, and he did not know any poetry; but he understood all these things, and that they were glad to see him, and not ashamed of him.

Then he came to a farm-house, and after getting himself a stick for protection, he approached it. The farmer was greasing a wagon in front of the barn, and Jurgis went to him. "I would like to get some breakfast, please," he said.

"Do you want to work?" said the farmer.

"No," said Jurgis, "I don't."

"Then you can't get anything here," snapped the other.

"I meant to pay for it," said Jurgis.

"Oh," said the farmer, and then added sarcastically: "We don't serve breakfast after seven a.m."

"I am very hungry," said Jurgis, gravely; "I would like to buy some food."

"Ask the woman," said the farmer, nodding over his shoulder. The "woman" was more tractable, and for a dime Jurgis secured two thick sandwiches and a piece of pie and two apples. He walked off eating the pie, as the least convenient thing to carry. In a few minutes he came to a stream, and he climbed a fence and walked down the bank, along a woodland path. Bye and bye he found a comfortable spot, and there he devoured his meal, slaking his thirst at the stream. Then he lay for hours, just gazing, and drinking in joy; until at last he felt sleepy, and lay down in the shade of a bush.

When he awoke the sun was shining hot in his face. He sat up and stretched his arms, and then gazed at the water sliding by. There was a deep pool, sheltered and silent, below him, and a sudden wonderful idea rushed upon him. He might have a bath! The water was free, and he might get into it—all the way into it! It would be the first time that he had been all the way into the water since he left Lithuania!

When Jurgis had first came to the stock-yards he had been as clean as any workingman could well be—on Saturday nights he had never failed to scrub out his kitchen sink and plug it up and take a bath. But later on, what with sickness and cold and hunger and discouragement, and the filthiness of his work, and the vermin in his home, Jurgis had given up washing in winter, and in summer only as much of him as would go into a basin. He had had a shower-bath in jail, but nothing since—and now he would have a swim.

The water was warm, and he splashed about like a very boy in his glee. Afterwards he sat down in the water near the bank, and proceeded to scrub himself—soberly and methodically, scouring every inch of him with sand. While he was doing it he would do it thoroughly, and see how it felt to be clean. He even scrubbed his head with sand, and combed what the men called "crumbs" out of his long black hair, holding his head under water as long as he could, to see if he could not kill them all. Then, seeing that the sun was still hot, he took his clothes from the bank and proceeded to wash them piece by piece; as the dirt and grease went floating off downstream he grunted with satisfaction and soused the clothes again, venturing even to dream that he might get rid of the fertilizer.

He hung them all up, and while they were drying he lay down in the sun and had another long sleep. They were hot and stiff as boards on top and a little damp on the under-side, when he awakened; but being hungry, he put them on and set out again. He had no knife, but with some labor he broke himself a good stout club, and armed with this he marched down the road again.

Before long he came to a big farmhouse, and turned up the lane that led to it. It was just supper-time; and the farmer was washing his hands at the kitchen-door. "Please, sir," said Jurgis, "can I have something to eat? I can pay." To which the farmer responded promptly: "We don't feed tramps here. Get out!"

Jurgis went without a word; but as he passed round the barn he came to a freshly plowed and harrowed field, in which the farmer had set out some young peach-trees; and as he walked he jerked up a row of them by the roots, more than a hundred trees in all, before he reached the end of the field. That was his answer and it showed his mood; from now on he was fighting, and the man who hit him would get all that he gave, every time.

Beyond the orchard Jurgis struck through a patch of woods, and then a field of winter-grain, and came at last to another road. Before long he saw another farm-house, and as it was beginning to cloud over a little, he asked here for shelter as well as food. Seeing the farmer eyeing him dubiously, he added: "I'll be glad to sleep in the barn."

"Well, I dunno," said the other. "Do you smoke?"

"Sometimes," said Jurgis, "but I'll do it out of doors." When the man had assented, he inquired, "How much will it cost me? I haven't very much money."

"I reckon about twenty cents for supper," replied the farmer; "I won't charge ye for the barn."

So Jurgis went in, and sat down at the table with the farmer's wife and half a dozen children. It was a bountiful meal—there were baked beans and mashed potatoes and asparagus chopped and stewed, and a dish of strawberries, and great, thick slices of bread, and a pitcher of milk. Jurgis had not had such a feast since his wedding day, and he made a mighty effort to put in his twenty cents' worth.

They were all of them too hungry to talk; but afterwards they sat upon the steps and smoked, and the farmer questioned his guest. When Jurgis had explained that he was a workingman from Chicago and that he did not know just whither he was bound, the other said: "Why don't you stay here and work for me?"

"I'm not looking for work just now," Jurgis answered.

"I'll pay ye good," said the other, eyeing his big form—"a dollar a day and board ye. Help's terrible scarce round here."

"Is that winter as well as summer?" Jurgis demanded, quickly.

"N—no," said the farmer, "I couldn't keep ye after October—I ain't got a big enough place for that." "I see," said the other, "that's what I thought. When you get through working your horses this fall will you turn them out in the snow to shift for themselves?" (Jurgis was beginning to think for himself nowadays.)

"It ain't quite the same as that," the farmer answered, seeing the point. "A horse ain't a man. There ought to be work a strong fellow like you can find to do, in the cities, or some place, in the winter time."

"Yes," said Jurgis, "that's what they all think; and so they crowd into the cities, and when they have to beg or steal to live, then people ask 'em why they don't go into the country, where help is so terrible scarce."

The farmer meditated over that awhile. "There's some here-abouts," he said finally, "that keep help all winter, and don't get it any too easy. The men say it's too lonesome—they like to get where there's a crowd."

"Well," said Jurgis, "I like company once in a while myself. It's hard to work all the time with nothing to work for. I don't suppose any of your farmers would keep a man with a wife and family, would they?"

"No, hardly," was the reply.

"Would they give him a house where he could keep them on his wages?"

"They ain't generally got but their own house," was the reply.

"Yes," said Jurgis, "they want to marry themselves, but they expect the men who work for them to be made different. I had a family myself, but they're all dead—and so now I can get a job again! But I ain't looking for jobs just now."

"How about when your money's gone?" inquired the farmer, "you'll have to then, won't you?"

"Wait till she's gone," said Jurgis, "and then I'll see."

He had a long sleep in the barn and afterwards a big breakfast of coffee and bread and oatmeal and stewed cherries, for which the man charged him only fifteen cents, perhaps having been influenced by his arguments. Then Jurgis bade farewell, and went his way. Such was the beginning of his life as a tramp. It was seldom he got as fair treatment as from this last farmer, and so as time went on he learned to shun the houses, and to prefer sleeping in the fields. When it rained he would find a deserted building, if he could, and if not, he would wait until after dark and then, with his stick ready, begin a stealthy approach upon a barn. Generally he could get in before the dog got scent of him, and then he would hide in the hay and be safe until morning; if not, and the dog attacked him, he would rise up and make a retreat in battle order. Our friend was not the mighty man he had once been, but his arms were still good, and there were few farm dogs he needed to hit more than once.

Before long there came raspberries, and then blackberries, to help him save his money; and there were apples in the orchards and potatoes in the ground—he learned to note the places, and fill his pockets after dark. Twice he even managed to capture a chicken, and had a feast, once in a deserted barn, and the other time in a lonely spot alongside of a stream. When all of these things failed him he used his money, carefully, but without worry—for he saw that he could earn more whenever he chose. Half an hour's chopping wood in his lively fashion was enough to bring him a meal, and when the farmer had seen him working he would sometimes try to bribe him to stay.

But Jurgis was not staying. He was a free man now, a buccaneer. The old *Wanderlust* had got into his blood, the joy of the unbound life, the joy of seeking, of hoping without limit. There were mishaps and discomforts—but at least there was always something new; and only think what it meant to a man who for years had been penned up in one place, seeing nothing but one dreary prospect of shanties and factories—to be suddenly set loose beneath the open sky, to behold new landscapes, new places and new people every hour! To a man whose whole life had consisted of doing one certain thing all day, until he was so exhausted that he could only lie down and sleep until the next day—and to be now his own master, working as he pleased and when he pleased, and facing a new adventure every hour!

Then, too, his health came back to him, all his lost youthful vigor, his joy and power, that he had mourned and forgotten! It came with a sudden rush, bewildering him, startling him; it was as if his dead child had come back to him, laughing and calling! What with plenty to eat, and fresh air, and exercise that was taken as it pleased him, he would waken from his sleep and start off not knowing what to do with his energy, stretching his arms, laughing, singing old songs of home that came back to him. Now and then, of course, he could not help but think of little Antanas, whom he should never see again, whose little voice he should never hear; and then he would have to battle with himself. Sometimes at night he would waken dreaming of Ona, and stretch out his arms to her, and wet the ground with his tears. But in the morning he would get up and shake himself, and stride away again to battle with the world.

He never asked where he was nor where he was going; the country was big enough, he knew, and there was no danger of his coming to the end of it. And of course he could always have company for the asking—everywhere he went there were men living just as he lived, and whom he was welcome to join. He was a stranger at the business, but they were not clannish, and they taught him all their tricks—what towns and villages it was best to keep away from, and how to read the secret signs upon the fences, and when to beg and when to steal, and just how to do both. They laughed at his ideas of paying for anything with money or with work—for they got all they wanted without either. Now and then Jurgis camped out with a gang of them in some woodland haunt, and foraged with them in the neighborhood at night. And then among them some one would take a "shine" to him, and they would go off together and travel for a week, exchanging reminiscences.

Of these professional tramps a great many had, of course, been shiftless and vicious all their lives. But the vast majority of them had been workingmen, had fought the long fight as Jurgis had, and found that it was a losing fight, and given up. Later on he encountered yet another sort of men, those from whose ranks the tramps were recruited, men who were homeless and wandering, but still seeking work—finding it in the harvest-fields. Of these there was an army, the huge surplus-labor army of society, called into being, under the stern system of nature, to do the casual work of the world, the tasks which were transient and irregular, and yet which had to be done. They did not know that they were such, of course; they only knew that they sought the job, and that the job was fleeting. In the early summer they would be in Texas, and as the crops were ready they would follow north with the season, ending with the fall in Manitoba. Then they would seek out the big lumber-camps, where there was winter work; or failing in this, would drift to the cities and live upon what they had managed to save, with the help of such transient work as was there, the loading and unloading of steamships and drays, the digging of ditches and the shoveling of snow. If there were more of them on hand than chanced to be needed, the weaker ones died off of cold and hunger, again according to the stern system of nature.

It was in the latter part of July, when Jurgis was in Missouri, that he came upon the harvest-work. Here were crops that men had worked for three or four months to prepare, and of which they would lose nearly all unless they could find others to help them for a week or two. So all over the land there was a cry for labor—agencies were set up and all the cities were drained of men, even college boys were brought by the car load, and hordes of frantic farmers would hold up trains and carry off wagon loads of men by main force. Not that they did not pay them well—any man could get two dollars a day and his board, and the best men could get two dollars and a half or three. The harvest fever was in the very air, and no man with any spirit in him could be in that region and not catch it. Jurgis joined a gang and worked from dawn till dark, eighteen hours a day, for two weeks without a break. Then he had a sum of money that would have been a fortune to him in the old days of misery—but what could he do with it now? To be sure he might have put it in a bank, and if he were so fortunate as to find a bank whose officers were not involved in the frenzied finances of Wall street, he could get it back again when he wanted it. But Jurgis was now a homeless man, wandering over a continent; and what did he know about banking and drafts and letters of credit? If he carried the money about with him, he would surely be robbed in the end; and so what was there for him to do but enjoy it while he could? On a Saturday night he drifted into a town with his fellows; and because it was raining, and there was no other place provided for him, he went to a saloon. And there were some who treated him and whom he had to treat, and there was laughter and singing and good cheer; and then out of the rear part of the saloon a girl's face, red-cheeked and merry, smiled at Jurgis, and his heart thumped suddenly in his throat. He nodded to her, and she came and sat by him, and they had more drink, and then he went upstairs into a room with her, and the wild beast rose up within him and screamed, as it has screamed in the jungle from the dawn of time. And then, because of his memories and his shame, he was glad when others joined them, men and women; and they had more drink, and spent the night in wild rioting and debauchery.

In the van of the surplus-labor army there followed another, an army of women; they also struggling for life under the stern system of nature. Because there were rich men who sought pleasure, there has been ease and plenty for them so long as they were young and beautiful; and when they were crowded out by others younger and more beautiful, they went out to follow upon the trail of the workingmen. Sometimes they came of themselves, and the saloon-keepers shared with them! or sometimes they were handled by agencies, the same as the labor army. They were in the towns in harvest-time, near the lumber-camps in the winter, in the cities when the men came there; if an army were encamped, or a railroad or canal being made, or a great exposition getting ready, the crowd of women were on hand, living in shanties or saloons or tenement-rooms, sometimes eight or ten of them together, according to the stern system of nature.

In the morning Jurgis had not a cent, and he went out upon the road again. He was sick and disgusted, but after the new plan of his life he crushed his feelings down. He had made a fool of himself, but that was his life; he could not help it now—all he could do was to see that it did not happen again. So he tramped on until exercise and fresh air banished his headache, and his strength and joy returned. This happened to him every time, for Jurgis was still a creature of impulse, and his pleasures had not yet become business. It would be a long time before he could be like the majority of these men of the road, who roamed until the hunger for drink and for women mastered them, and then went to work with a purpose in mind, and stopped when they had the price of a spree.

On the contrary, try as he would, Jurgis could not help being made miserable by his conscience. It was the ghost that would not down. It would come upon him in the most unexpected places—sometimes it fairly drove him to drink.

One night he was caught by a thunder-storm, and he sought shelter in a little house just outside of a town. It was a workingman's home, and the owner was a Slav like himself, a new emigrant from White Russia; he bade Jurgis welcome in his home language, and told him to come to the kitchen-fire and dry himself. He had no bed for him, but there was straw in the garret, and he could make out. The man's wife was cooking the supper, and their children were playing about on the floor. Jurgis sat and exchanged thoughts with him about the old country, and the places there they had been and the work they had done. Then they ate, and afterwards sat and smoked and talked more, about America, and how they found it; in the middle of a sentence, however, Jurgis stopped, seeing that the woman had brought a big basin of water and was proceeding to undress her youngest baby. The rest had crawled into the closet where they slept, but the baby was to have a bath, the workingman explained. The nights had begun to be chilly, and his mother, ignorant as to the climate in America, had sewed him up for the winter; then it had turned warm again, and some kind of a rash had broken out on the child. The doctor had said she must bathe him every night, and she, foolish woman, believed him.

Jurgis scarcely heard the explanation; he was watching the baby. He was about a year old, and a sturdy little fellow, with soft, fat legs, and a round ball of a stomach, and eyes as black as coals. His pimples did not seem to bother him much, and he was wild with glee over the bath, kicking and squirming and chuckling with delight, pulling at his mother's face, and then at his own little toes. When she put him in the basin he sat in the midst of it and grinned, splashing the water over himself and squealing like a little pig. He spoke in Russian, of which Jurgis knew some; he spoke it with the quaintest of baby accents—and every word of it brought back to Jurgis some word of his own dead little one, and stabbed him like a knife. He sat perfectly motionless, silent, but gripping his hands tightly, while a storm gathered in his bosom and a flood heaped itself up behind his eyes. And in the end he could bear it no more, but buried his face in his hands and burst into tears, to the alarm and amazement of his hosts. Between the shame of this and his woe, Jurgis could not stand it, and got up and rushed out into the rain.

He went on and on down the road, finally coming to a black woods, where he hid and wept as if his heart would break. Ah, what agony was that, what despair, when the tomb of memory was rent open and the ghosts of his old life came forth to scourge him! What woe, to see, what he had been and now could never be—to see Ona, and his child, and his own dead self, stretching out their arms to him, calling to him across a bottomless abyss—and to know that they were gone from him forever, and he writhing and suffocating in the mire of his own vileness!

EARLY IN the fall Jurgis set out for Chicago again. All the joy went out of tramping as soon as a man could not keep warm in the hay; and, like many thousands of others, he deluded himself with the hope that by coming early he could avoid the rush. He brought fifteen dollars with him, hidden away in one of his shoes, a sum which had been saved from the saloon-keepers, not so much by his conscience, as by the deadly terror which filled him at the thought of being out of work in the city in the winter-time.

He travelled upon the railroad with several other men, hiding in freight-cars at night, and liable to be thrown off at any time regardless of the speed of the train. When he reached the city he left the rest, for he had money and they did not, and he meant to save himself in this fight. He would bring to it all the skill that practice had brought him, and he would stand, whoever fell. On fair nights he would sleep in the park or on a truck or an empty barrel or box, and when it was rainy or cold he would stow himself upon a shelf in a ten-cent lodging-house or pay three cents for the privileges of a "squatter" in a tenement hallway. He would eat at free lunches, five cents a meal, and never a cent more—so he might keep alive for two months and more, and in that time he would surely find a job. He would have to bid farewell to his summer cleanliness, of course, for he would come out of the first night's lodging with his clothes alive with vermin. There was no place in the city where he could wash even his face, unless he went down to the lake front—and there it would soon be all ice.

First he went to the steel-mill and the harvester-works, and found that his places there had been filled long ago. He was careful to keep away from the stock-yards—he was a single man now, he told himself, and he meant to stay one, to have his wages for his own when he got a job. He began the long, weary round of factories and warehouses, tramping all day, from one end of the city to the other, finding everywhere from ten to a hundred men ahead of him. He watched the newspapers, too—but no longer was he to be taken in by smooth-spoken agents. He had been told of all those tricks while "on the road."

In the end it was through a newspaper that he got a job, after nearly a month of seeking. It was a call for a hundred laborers, and though he thought it was a "fake," he went because the place was near by. He found a line of men a block long, but as a wagon chanced to come out of an alley and break the line, he saw his chance and sprang to seize a place. Men threatened him and tried to throw him out, but he cursed and made a disturbance to attract a policeman, upon which they subsided, knowing that if the latter interfered it would be to "fire" them all.

An hour or two later he entered a room and confronted a big Irishman behind a desk.

"Ever worked in Chicago before?" the man inquired; and whether it was a good angel that put it into Jurgis's mind, or an intuition of his sharpened wits, he was moved to answer, "No, sir."

"Where do you come from?"

"Kansas City, sir."

"Any references?"

"No, sir. I'm just an unskilled man. I've got good arms."

"I want men for hard work—it's all underground, digging tunnels for telephones. Maybe it won't suit you."

"I'm willing, sir—anything for me. What's the pay?"

"Fifteen cents an hour."

"I'm willing, sir."

"All right; go back there and give your name."

So within half an hour he was at work, far underneath the streets of the city. The tunnel was a peculiar one for telephone-wires—it was about eight feet high, and with a level floor nearly as wide. It had innumerable branches—a perfect spider-web beneath the city; Jurgis walked over half a mile with his gang to the place where they were to work. Stranger yet, the tunnel was lighted by electricity, and upon it was laid a double-tracked, narrow-gauge railroad!

But Jurgis was not there to ask questions, and he did not give the matter a thought. It was nearly a year afterwards that he finally learned the meaning of this whole affair. The City Council had passed a quiet and innocent little bill allowing a company to construct telephone-conduits under the city streets; and upon the strength of this, a great corporation had proceeded to tunnel all Chicago with a system of railway freight-subways. In the city there was a combination of employers, representing hundreds of millions of capital, and formed for the purpose of crushing the labor-unions. The chief union which troubled it was the teamsters and when these freight tunnels were completed, connecting all the big factories and stores with the railroad depots, they would have the teamsters' union by the throat. Now and then there were rumors and murmurs in the Board of Aldermen, and once there was a committee to investigate—but each time another small fortune was paid over, and the rumors died away; until at last the city woke up with a start to find the work completed. There was a tremendous scandal, of course; it was found that the city records had been falsified, and other crimes committed, and some of Chicago's big capitalists got into jail—figuratively speaking. The aldermen declared that they had had no idea of it all, in spite of the fact that the main entrance to the work had been in the rear of the saloon of one of them.

It was in a newly-opened cut that Jurgis worked, and so he knew that he had an all-winter job. He was so rejoiced that he treated himself to a spree that night, and with the balance of his money he hired himself a place in a tenement-room, where he slept upon a big home-made straw mattress along with four other workingmen. This was one dollar a week, and for four more he got his food in a boarding house near his work. This would leave him four dollars extra each week, an unthinkable sum for him. At the outset he had to pay for his digging-tools, and also to buy a pair of heavy boots, since his shoes were falling to pieces, and a flannel shirt, since the one he had worn all summer was in shreds. He spent a week meditating whether or not he should also buy an overcoat. There was one belonging to a Hebrew collar-button peddler who had died in the room next to him, and which the landlady was holding for her rent; in the end, however, Jurgis decided to do without it, as he was to be underground by day and in bed at night.

This was an unfortunate decision, however, for it drove him more quickly than ever into the saloons. From now on Jurgis worked from seven o'clock until half-past five, with half an hour for dinner; which meant that except while running across the street to the meal he never saw the sunlight on week-days. In the evenings there was no place for him to go except a bar-room; no place where there was light and warmth, where he could hear a little music, or sit with a companion and talk. Our friend had now no home to go to, no children to laugh and play with, no wife to greet him, to plead with him and save him from himself; he had no affection now in his life, only the pitiful mockery of it in the *camaraderie* of vice. On Sundays the churches were open—but where was there a church in which an ill-smelling working-man with vermin crawling upon his neck, could sit without seeing people edge away and look annoyed? He had, of course, his corner in a close, though unheated, room, with a window opening upon a blank wall two feet away; and also he had the bare streets, with the winter gales sweeping through them; beside this he had only the saloons—and, of course, he had to drink to stay in them; if he drank now and then he was free to make himself at home, to gamble with dice or a pack of greasy cards, to play at a dingy pool-table for money, or to look at a beer-stained pink "sporting paper," with pictures of murderers and half-naked women. It was for such pleasures as these that he spent his money; and such was his life during the six weeks and a half that he toiled for the merchants of Chicago, to enable them to break the grip of their teamsters' union.

In a work carried out by criminal conspirators, it may be imagined how much thought was given to the welfare of the laborers. On an average, the tunneling cost a life a day, and several manglings; it was seldom, however—

scattered in widely branching tunnels as they were—that more than a dozen or two men heard of any one accident. The work was all done by the new boring-machinery, with as little blasting as possible; but there would be falling rocks, and crushed supports, and premature explosions—and in addition all the dangers of railroading. So it was that one night, as Jurgis was on his way out with his gang, an engine and a loaded car dashed round one of the innumerable right-angle branches upon him; he was in front, and leaped too late, and the engine struck him upon the shoulder, hurling him against the concrete wall and knocking him senseless.

When he opened his eyes again it was to the clanging of the bell of an ambulance. He was lying in it, covered by a blanket, and it was threading its way slowly through the holiday-shopping crowds. They took him to the County Hospital, where a young surgeon set his arm; then he was washed and laid upon a bed in a ward with a score or two more of maimed and mangled men.

Jurgis spent his Christmas in this hospital, and it was the pleasantest Christmas he had had in America. Every year there were scandals and investigations in the institution, the newspapers charging that doctors were allowed to try fantastic experiments upon the patients; but Jurgis knew nothing of this. His only complaint was that they used to feed him upon tinned meat, which no man who had ever worked in Packingtown would feed to his dog. Jurgis had often wondered just who ate the canned corned-beef and "roast beef," the "veal loaf" and potted ham of the stockyards; now he began to understand—it was what you might call "graft-meat," put up to be sold to corrupt army and navy officers, public officials and contractors, and eaten by soldiers and sailors, prisoners and inmates of institutions, "shanty-men" and gangs of railroad laborers.

Jurgis was ready to leave the hospital at the end of two weeks. This did not mean that his arm was strong and that he was able to go back to work, but simply that he could get along without further attention, and that his place was needed for some one worse off than he. That he was utterly helpless, and had no means of keeping himself alive in the meantime, was something which did not concern the hospital authorities, nor anyone else in the city.

As it chanced, he had been hurt on a Monday, and had just paid for his last week's board and his room rent, and spent nearly all the balance of his Saturday's pay. He had less than seventy-five cents in his pockets, and a dollar and a half due him for the day's work he had done before he was hurt. He might, possibly have sued the company, and got some damages for his injuries, but he did not know this, and it was not the company's business to tell him. He went and got his pay, and his tools, which he left in a pawn-shop for fifty cents. Then he went to his land-lady, who had rented his place and had no other for him; and then to his boarding-house keeper, who looked him over and questioned him. As he must certainly be helpless for a couple of months, and had boarded there only six weeks, she decided very quickly that it would not be worth the risk to board him on trust.

So Jurgis went out into the streets, in a most dreadful plight. It was bitterly cold, and a heavy snow was falling, beating into his face. He had no overcoat, and no place to go, and two dollars and sixty-five cents in his pocket, with the certainty that he could not earn another cent for months. The snow meant no chance to him now; he must walk along and see others shovelling, vigorous and active—and he with his left arm bound to his side! He could not hope to tide himself over by odd jobs of loading trucks; he could not sell newspapers—he could not even carry satchels, because he was now at the mercy of any rival. Words could not paint the terror that came over him as he realized this. He was now a wounded animal in the jungle. He was forced to compete with his enemies upon unequal terms. There would be no consideration for him because of his weakness—it was no one's business to help him in such distress, to make the fight the least bit easier for him. Even if he took to begging, he would be at a disadvantage—for reasons which he was to discover in good time.

In the beginning he could not think of anything except getting out of the awful cold. He went into one of the saloons he had been wont to frequent, and bought a drink, and then stood by the fire shivering and waiting to be ordered out. According to an unwritten law, the buying a drink included the privilege of loafing for just so long; then one had to buy another drink, or move on. That Jurgis was an old customer entitled him to a somewhat longer stop; but then he had been away two weeks, and was evidently "on the bum." He might plead and tell his "hard-luck story," but that would not help him much; a saloon-keeper who was to be moved by such means would soon have his place jammed to the doors with "hoboes" on a day like this.

So Jurgis went out into another place and paid another nickel. He was so hungry this time that he could not resist the hot beef-stew, an indulgence which cut short his stay by a considerable time. When he was again told to move on, he made his way to a "tough" place in the "levee" district, where now and then he had gone with a certain rat-eyed Bohemian workingman of his acquaintance, seeking a woman. It was Jurgis's vain hope that at this place the proprietor would let him remain as a "sitter." In low-class saloons, in the dead of winter, saloon-keepers would often allow one or two forlorn-looking bums who came in covered with snow or soaked with rain, to sit by the fire and look miserable to attract custom. A workingman would come in, feeling cheerful after his day's work was over, and it would trouble him to have to take his glass with such a sight under his nose; and so he would call out: "Hello, Bud, what's the matter? You look as if you'd been up against it!" And then the other would begin to pour out some tale of misery, and the man would say, "Come have a glass, and maybe that'll brace you up." And so they would drink together, and if the tramp was sufficiently wretched-looking, or good enough at the "gab," they might have two; and if they were to discover that they were from the same country, or had lived in the same city, or worked at the same trade, they might sit down at a table and spend an hour or two in talk—and before they got through the saloon-keeper would have taken in a dollar. All of this may seem diabolical, but the saloon-keeper was in nowise to blame for it. He had either to do it or be driven out of business, just as now-a-days every manufacturer has to adulterate and misrepresent his product. If he does not, some one else will; and the saloon-keeper, unless he is also an alderman, is apt to be in debt to the big brewers, and on the verge of being sold out.

The market for "sitters" was glutted that day, however, and there was no place for Jurgis. In all, he had to spend six nickels in keeping a shelter over him that frightful day, and then it was just dark, and the station-houses would not open until midnight! At the last place, however, there was a bartender who knew him and liked him, and let him doze at one of the tables until the boss came back; and also, as he was going out, the man gave him a tip—on the next block there was a religious revival of some sort, with preaching and singing, and hundreds of hoboes would go there for the shelter and warmth.

Jurgis went straightway, and saw a sign hung out, saying that the door would open at seven-thirty; then he walked, or half ran, a block, and hid awhile in a doorway and then ran again, and so on until the hour. At the end he was all but frozen, and fought his way in with the rest of the throng (at the risk of having his arm broken again) and got close to the big stove.

By eight o'clock the place was so crowded that the speakers ought to have been flattered, the aisles were packed half way up, and at the door men were packed tight enough to walk upon. There were three elderly gentlemen in black upon the platform, and a young lady who played the piano in front. First they sang a hymn, and then one of the three, a tall, smooth-shaven man, very thin, and wearing black spectacles, began an address. Jurgis heard smatterings of it, for the reason that terror kept him awake—he knew that he snored abominably, and to have been put out just then would have been like a sentence of death to him.

The evangelist was preaching "sin and redemption," the infinite grace of God and His pardon for human frailty. He was very much in earnest, and he meant well, but Jurgis, as he listened, found his soul filled with contempt for him—he would have liked to stand up and hoot at him, to get up there and punch him. What did he know about sin and suffering—with his smooth, black coat and his neatly-starched collar, his body warm, and his belly full, and money in his pocket—and lecturing men who were struggling for their lives, men at the death-grapple with the demon powers of hunger and cold!

He had managed to get the good things of life, somehow—but why at least could he not go off and enjoy them, without coming to taunt the poor with their misfortune?—This, of course, was very disrespectful, even impious; but it was how Jurgis felt, and it was how the vast majority of the men felt, while they listened, held prisoners by the cold. These men were out of touch with the life they discussed; they were unfitted to solve its problems; nay, they themselves were part of the problem—they were part of the order established, that was crushing men down and beating them! They were of the triumphant and insolent possessors—they had a hall, and a fire, and food and clothing and money, and so they might preach to hungry men, and the hungry men must be humble and listen! They were trying to save their souls—and who but a fool could fail to see that all that was the matter with their souls was that they had not been able to get a decent existence for their bodies? They were preaching about vice—and why did a workingman have to live with low women, save that he could not afford to marry a decent girl? They were preaching about drunkenness—and what made workingmen drink but repulsive homes, exposure and hunger, over-work and uncertain employment—the fact, in a word, that his life was a hell, and that a man who has to live in hell had better be drunk than sober.

At eleven the meeting closed, and the desolate audience filed out into the snow, muttering curses upon the few traitors who had got repentance and gone upon the platform, and would get some food and coddling for their self-abasement. It was yet an hour before the station-house would open, and Jurgis had no overcoat—and was weak from a long illness. During that hour he nearly perished. He was obliged to run hard to keep his blood moving at all—and then he came back to the station-house and found a crowd blocking the street before the door! This was in the month of January, 1904, when the country was on the verge of "hard times," and the newspapers were reporting the shutting down of factories every day—it was estimated that a million and a half of men were thrown out of work before the spring. So all the hiding-places of the jungle were crowded, and before that station-house door men fought and tore each other like savage beasts. When at last the place was jammed and they shut the doors, half the crowd was still outside, and Jurgis, with his helpless arm, was among them. There was no choice then but to go to a lodging-house and spend another dime. It really broke his heart to do this, at half-past twelve o'clock, after he had wasted the night at the meeting and on the street. He would be turned out of the lodging-house promptly at seven—they had the shelves which served as bunks so contrived that they could be dropped, and any man who was slow about obeying orders could be tumbled to the floor.

This was one day, and the cold spell lasted for fourteen of them. At the end of six days every cent of Jurgis's money was gone; and then he went out on the streets to beg for his life.

He would begin as soon as the business of the city was moving. He would sally forth from a saloon, and after making sure there was no policeman in sight, would approach every likely-looking person who passed him, telling his woeful story and pleading for a nickel or a dime. Then, when he got one, he would dart around the corner and return to his base to get warm; and his victim, seeing him do this, would go away vowing that he would never give a cent to a beggar again, since they went straight to a saloon every time. The victim never paused to ask where else Jurgis could have gone under the circumstances—where he, the victim, would have gone. At the saloon Jurgis could not only get more food and better food than he could buy in any restaurant for the same money, but a drink in the bargain to warm him up. Also he could find a comfortable seat by a fire, and could chat with a companion until he was as warm as toast. At the saloon, too, he felt at home—it was the place where he was supposed to be, where everything was understood, without questions or apologies. Part of the saloon-keeper's business was to offer a home and refreshment to beggars in exchange for the proceeds of their foragings; and was there anyone else in the whole city who would do this—would the victim have done it himself?

Poor Jurgis might have been expected to make a successful beggar. He was just out of the hospital, and desperately sick-looking, and with a helpless arm; also he had no overcoat, and shivered pitifully. But, alas, his case was like that of the honest merchant—he found that the genuine and unadulterated article was driven to the wall by the artistic counterfeit. Jurgis, as a beggar, was simply a blundering amateur in competition with organized and scientific professionalism. He was just out of the hospital—but the story was worn threadbare, and how could he prove it? He had his arm in a sling—and it was a device a regular beggar's little boy would have scorned. He was pale and shivering—but they were made up with cosmetics, and had studied the art of chattering their teeth. As to his being without an overcoat, among them you would meet men you could swear had on nothing but a ragged linen duster and a pair of cotton trousers—so cleverly had they concealed the several suits of all-wool underwear beneath. Many of these professional mendicants had comfortable homes, and families, and thousands of dollars in the bank; some of them had retired upon their earnings, and gone into the business of fitting out and doctoring others, or working children at the trade. There were some who had both their arms bound tightly to their sides, and padded stumps in their sleeves, and a sick child hired to carry a cup for them. There were some who had no legs, and pushed themselves upon a wheeled platform—some who had been blessed with blindness, and were led by pretty little dogs. Some less fortunate had mutilated themselves or burned themselves, or had brought horrible sores upon themselves with chemicals; you might suddenly encounter upon the street a man holding out to you a finger rotting and discolored with gangrene—or one with livid scarlet wounds half escaped from their filthy bandages. These desperate ones were the dregs of the city's cesspools, wretches who hid at night in the rain-soaked cellars of old ramshackle tenements, in "stale-beer dives" and opium-joints, with abandoned women in the last stages of the harlot's progress—women who had been kept by Chinamen and turned away at last to die. Every day the police net would drag hundreds of them off the streets, and in the Detention Hospital you might see them, herded together in a miniature inferno, with hideous, beastly faces, bloated and leprous with disease, laughing, shouting, screaming, in all stages of drunkenness, barking like dogs, gibbering like apes, raving and tearing themselves in the last stages of delirium.

IT WAS really a fact that every circumstance that might have been expected to help Jurgis was in reality a hindrance to him, in competition with the professional mendicants. It was a hindrance that he was actually suffering from weakness and cold, while they were strong and hardy. It was a hindrance that he told the truth, while they had a hundred different tales, adapting them by shrewd intuition to the character of every victim. They had their haunts to retire to, and confederates to help them, and also they had "squared" the police; Jurgis, on the other hand, had to be always upon the move—if they observed him working they would tip the patrolman, and he would get a clubbing.

In the face of handicaps such as these, he was obliged to make the price of a lodging, and of a drink every hour or two, under penalty of freezing to death. Day after day he roamed about in the arctic cold, his soul filled full of bitterness and despair. He saw the world of the jungle then more plainly than ever he had seen it before: a world in which nothing counted but brutal might; an order devised by those who had it for the subjugation of those who had not. He was one of the latter; and all outdoors, all life, was to him one colossal prison, which he paced like a pent-up tiger, trying one bar after another, and finding them all beyond his power. He had lost in the fierce battle of greed, and so he was doomed to be exterminated; and all society was busied to see that he did not escape the sentence. Everywhere that he turned were prison-bars, and hostile eyes followed him; the well-fed, sleek policeman, from whose glances he shrank, and who seemed to grip their clubs more tightly when they saw him; the saloon-keepers, who never ceased to watch him while he was in their places, who were jealous of every moment he lingered after he had paid his money; the hurrying throngs upon the streets, who were deaf to his entreaties, oblivious of his very existence—and savage and contemptuous when he forced himself upon them. They had their own affairs, and there was no place for him among them. There was no place for him anywhere—every place he turned his gaze, this fact was forced upon him. Everything was built to express it to him; the residences, with their heavy walls and bolted doors, and basement-windows barred with iron; the great ware-houses filled with the products of the whole world, and guarded by iron shutters and heavy gates; the banks with their unthinkable billions of wealth, all buried in safes and vaults of steel.

And it was not enough that these heaped-up treasures were there, and he with no share in them—but their owners must flaunt them in his face! Jurgis had known all along that there was wealth in Chicago; but while he was working or seeking work in the factories and mills, and living in slum tenements, he had no occasion to see it. Now, however, he was free to roam the shopping district, gazing through miles upon miles of plate-glass windows, that blazed by night with electric lights, and were crowded with all the dazzling, blasphemous, soul-terrifying splendor of the city. He was perishing of cold; and here were literally blocks upon blocks of clothing—whole windows full of shoes, others full of gloves, others of robes of every kind of rich and gorgeous fur, others blazing with diamonds and rubies, and ornaments of silver and pearl and gold. He was half-dead from long-continued and habitual under-feeding; and here were tempting viands gathered from all the corners of the world, clubs and hotels and banquet-halls ablaze with light and glowing with flowers and palms, in which he might have glimpses of the rich rejoicing in their power—sleek and immaculate men, beautiful women in luxurious raiment. These were the victors of the struggle, they were the rulers, the masters of life. The factories and the mills and the stores were theirs; it was for them that he had labored, by them that he had been dispossessed—if was they who were crushing him down! It was they who made the laws, and enforced them—it was by them that the world was run. Before this Jurgis's bitterness had all been impersonal; it was the way of things that he had hated, it was life, that was so cruel and so hard. But now he saw people for whom life was not hard, and his hatred became personal and direct—he hated the rich. He would wander out along the great boulevards and driveways, where they had built their palaces, where they lived in their haughty magnificence, flaunting their greatness to the world. He saw them glide past him in their automobiles and their sleighs; he saw their children, parading on exhibition with their nurses; he saw their wives, in bejeweled and disdainful splendor, emerging from jewelry-shops and florists; he saw their coroneted equipages, with lackeys robed in bearskins, their faces charged to the point of bursting with insolence and contempt. Shivering, starving, agonized, he wandered about among sights such as these, one helpless arm tied fast, and the other outstretched for a pittance of money or a bit of bread, and a rage that was almost madness heaping itself up within him, a longing to hurl himself upon it, to smash it and crush it, to fling a bomb into the midst of it all, and blow it into eternity.

Then one day there befell him the one adventure of his life. It was late at night, and he had failed to get the price of a lodging. Snow was falling, and he had been out so long that he was covered with it, and was chilled to the bone. He was working among the theater crowds, flitting here and there, taking large chances with the police, in his desperation half hoping to be arrested. When he saw a blue-coat start toward him, however, his heart failed him, and he dashed down a side street and fled a couple of blocks. When he stopped again he saw a man coming towards him, and placed himself in his path.

"Please, sir" he began, in the usual formula, "will you give me the price of a lodging? I've had a broken arm, and I can't work, and I've not a cent in my pocket. I'm an honest workingman, sir, and I never begged before. It's not my fault, sir—"

Jurgis usually went on until he was interrupted, but this man did not interrupt, and so at last he came to a breathless stop. The other had halted, and Jurgis suddenly noticed that he stood a little unsteadily. "Whuzzat you say?" he queried, suddenly, in a thick voice.

Jurgis began again, speaking more slowly and distinctly; before he was half through the other put out his hand and rested it upon his shoulder. "Poor ole chappie!" he said. "Been up—hic—up—against it, hey?"

Then he lurched toward Jurgis, and the hand upon his shoulder became an arm about his neck. "Up against it myself, ole sport," he said. "She's a hard ole world."

They were close to a lamp-post, and Jurgis got a glimpse of his face. He was a young fellow—not much over eighteen, with a handsome, boyish face. He wore a silk hat and a rich, soft overcoat with a fur collar; and he smiled at Jurgis with benignant sympathy. "I'm hard up, too, my goo' fren'," he said. "I've got cruel parents, or I'd set you up. Whuz-zamatter whizyer?"

"I've been in the hospital."

"Hospital!" exclaimed the young fellow, still smiling sweetly, "thass too bad! Same's my Aunt Polly—hic—my Aunt Polly's in the hospital, too—ole auntie's been havin' twins! Whuzzamatter whiz you!"

"I've got a broken arm—" Jurgis began.

"So?" said the other, sympathetically. "That ain't so bad—you get over that. I wish somebody'd break my arm, ole chappie—damfidont! Then they's treat me better—hic—hole me up, ole sport! Whuzzit you wamme do?"

"I'm hungry, sir," said Jurgis.

"Hungry? Why don't you hassome supper?"

"I've got no money, sir." "No money! Ho, ho—less be chums, ole boy— Jess like me! No money, either ole chappie—almost busted! Why don't you go home, then, same's me?"

"I haven't any home," said Jurgis.

"No home? Stranger in the city, hey? Goo' God, thass bad! Better come home wiz me—yes, by Harry, thass the trick, you'll come home an' hassome supper—hic—wiz me! Awful lonesome—nobody home! Guv'ner gone abroad—Bubby on's honeymoon—Polly havin' twins every damn soul gone away! Nuff—hic—nuff to drive a feller to drink, I say! Only ole Ham standin' by' passin' plates—damfican eat like that, no, sir! The club for me every time, my boy, I say. But then they won't lemme sleep there—guv'ner's orders, by Harry—home every night, sir! Ever hear anythin' like that? 'Every mornin' do?' I asked him. 'No, sir, every night, or no allowance at all, sir.' Thass my guv'ner—hic—hard as nails, by Harry! Tole ole Ham to watch me, too—servants spyin' on me—whuzyer think of that, my fren'? A nice, quiet—hic—good-hearted young feller like me, an' his daddy can't go to Europe—hup!—an' leave him in peace! Ain't that a shame, sir? An' I gotter go home every evenin' an' miss all the fun, by Harry! Thass whuzzamatter now—thass why I'm here! Hadda come away an' leave Kitty—hic—left her cryin', too—whujja think of that, ole sport? 'Lemme go, Kittens,' says I—'come early an' often—I go where duty—hic—calls me. Farewell, farewell, my own true love—farewell, farewe-hell, my-own-true-love!'"

This last was a song, and the young gentleman's voice rose mournful and wailing, while he swung upon Jurgis's neck. The latter was glancing about nervously, lest some one should approach. They were still alone, however.

"But I came all right, all right," continued the youngster, aggressively. "I can—hic—I can have my own way when I want it, by Harry—Freddie Jones is a hard man to handle when he gets goin'! 'No, sir,' says I, 'by thunder, and I don't need anybody goin' home with me, either—whujja take me for, hey? Think I'm drunk, dontcha, hey?—I know you! But I'm no more drunk than you are, Kittens,' says I to her. And then she answered, 'Thass true, Freddie dear' (she's a smart one, is Kitty), 'but I'm stayin' in the flat, an' you're goin' out into the cold, cold night!' 'Put it in a pome, lovely Kitty,' said I. 'No jokin', Freddie, my boy,' said she. 'Lemme call a cab now, like a good dear'—but I can call my own cabs, dontcha fool yourself—I know what I'm a-doin', you bet! Say, my fren', whatcha say—willya come home an' see me, an' hassome supper? Come long, like a good fellow—don't be haughty—'I like you, ma honey, 'deed I do!' You're up against it, same as me, an' you can unnerstan' a feller; your heart's in the right place, by Harry—come long, ole chappie, an' we'll light up the house, an' have some fizz, an' we'll raise hell, we will—whoop-la! 'Slong's I'm inside the house I can do as I please—the guvner's own very orders, b' God! Hip! hip!"

They had started down the street, arm in arm, the young fellow pushing Jurgis along, half dazed. Jurgis was trying to think what to do—he knew he could not pass any crowded place with his new acquaintance without attracting attention and being stopped. It was only because of the falling snow that people who passed here did not notice anything wrong.

Suddenly, therefore, Jurgis stopped. "Is it very far?" he inquired.

"Not very," said the other. "Tired, are you, though? Well, we'll ride—whatcha say? Good! Call a cab!"

And then, gripping Jurgis tight with one hand, the young fellow began searching his pockets with the other. "You call, ole sport, an' I'll pay," he suggested. "How's that, hey?"

And he pulled out from somewhere a big roll of bills. It was more money than Jurgis had ever seen in his life before, and he stared at it with startled eyes.

"Looks like a lot, hey?" said Master Freddie, fumbling with it. "Fool you, though, ole chappie—they're all little ones! I'll be busted in one week more, sure thing—word of honor. An' not a cent more till the first—hic—guvners orders—hic—not a *cent,* by Harry! Nuff to set a feller crazy, it is. I sent him a cable this af'noon—thass one reason more why I'm goin' home. 'Hangin' on the verge of starvation,' I said—'for the honor of the family—hic—sen' me some bread. Hunger will compel me to join you.—Freddie.' Thass what I wired him, by Harry, an' I mean it—I'll run away from school, b' God, if he don't sen' me some."

After this fashion the young gentleman continued to prattle on—and meantime Jurgis was trembling with excitement. He might grab that wad of bills and be out of sight in the darkness before the other could collect his wits. Should he do it? What better had he to hope for, if he waited longer? But Jurgis had never committed a crime in his life, and now he hesitated half a second too long. "Freddie" got one bill loose and then stuffed the rest back into his trousers pocket.

"Here, ole man," he said, "you take it." He held it out fluttering; they were in front of a saloon—and by the light of the window Jurgis saw that it was a hundred-dollar bill!

"You take it," the other repeated. "Pay the cabbie an' keep the change— I've got—hic—no head for business! Guv'ner says so hisself, an' the guv'ner knows—the guv'ner's got a head for business, you bet! 'All right, guv'ner,' I told him, 'you run the show, an' I'll take the tickets!' An' so he set Aunt Polly to watch me—hic—an' now Polly's off in the hospital havin' twins, an' me out raisin' the devil! Hello, there! Hey! Call him!"

A cab was driving by; and Jurgis sprang and called, and it swung round to the curb. Master Freddie clambered in with some difficulty, and Jurgis had started to follow, when the driver shouted: "Hi, there! Get out—you!"

Jurgis hesitated, and was half obeying; but his companion broke out: "Whuzzat? Whuzzamatter wiz you, hey?"

And the cabbie subsided, and Jurgis climbed in. Then Freddie gave a number on the Lake Shore drive, and the carriage started away. The youngster leaned back and snuggled up to Jurgis, murmuring contentedly; in half a minute he was sound asleep. Jurgis sat shivering, speculating as to whether he might not still be able to get hold of the roll of bills. He was afraid to try to go through his companion's pockets, however; and besides, the cabbie might be on the watch. He had the hundred safe, and he would have to be content with that.

At the end of half an hour or so the cab stopped. They were out on the water-front, and from the east a freezing gale was blowing off the ice-bound lake. "Here we are," called the cabbie, and Jurgis awakened his companion. Master Freddie sat up with a start. "Hello!" he said. "Where are we? Whuzzis? Who are you, hey? Oh, yes, sure nuff! Mos' forgot you—hic—ole chappie! Home, are we? Lessee! B-r-r—it's cold! Yes—come 'long— we're home—be it ever so—hic—humble!"

Before them there loomed an enormous granite pile, set far back from the street, and occupying a whole block. By the light of the driveway-lamps Jurgis could see that it had towers and huge gables, like a mediaeval castle. He thought that the young fellow must have made a mistake—it was inconceivable that any person could have a home like a hotel or the city hall. But he followed in silence, and they went up the long flight of steps, arm in arm.

"There's a button here, ole sport," said Master Freddie. "Hole my arm while I find her! Steady, now—Oh, yes, here she is—saved!"

A bell rang, and in a few seconds the door was opened. A man in blue livery stood holding it, and gazing before him, silent as a statue.

They stood for a moment blinking in the light. Then Jurgis felt his companion pulling, and he stepped in, and the blue automaton closed the door. Jurgis's heart was beating wildly; it was a bold thing for him to do—into what strange, unearthly place he was venturing he had no idea. Aladdin entering his cave could not have been more excited.

The place where he stood was dimly lighted; but he could see a vast hall, with pillars fading into the darkness above, and a great staircase opening at the far end of it. The floor was of tesselated marble, smooth as glass, and from the walls strange shapes loomed out, woven into huge portiers in rich, harmonious colors, or gloaming from paintings, wonderful and mysterious-looking in the half-light, purple and red and golden, like sunset glimmers in a shadowy forest.

The man in livery had moved silently towards them; Master Freddie took off his hat and handed it to him, and then, letting go of Jurgis's arm, tried to get out of his overcoat. After two or three attempts he accomplished this with the lackey's help; and meantime a second man had approached, a tall and portly personage, solemn as an executioner. He bore straight down upon Jurgis, who shrunk away nervously; he seized him by the arm without a word, and started towards the door with him. Then suddenly came Master Freddie's voice: "Hamilton! My fren' will remain wiz me."

The man paused and half released Jurgis. "Come 'long, ole chappie," said the other, and Jurgis started towards him.

"Master Frederick!" exclaimed the man.

"See that the cabbie—hic—is paid," was the other's response; and he linked his arm in Jurgis's. Jurgis was about to say, "I have the money for him," but he restrained himself. The stout man in uniform signaled to the other, who went out to the cab, while he followed Jurgis and his young master.

They went down the great hall, and then turned. Before them were two huge doors.

"Hamilton," said Master Freddie.

"Well, sir?" said the other.

"Whazzamatter wizze dinin'-room doors?"

"Nothing is the matter, sir."

"Then why doncha openum?" The man rolled them back! another vista lost itself in the darkness. "Lights," commanded Master Freddie; and the butler pressed a button, and a flood of brilliant incandescence streamed from above, half-blinding Jurgis. He stared; and little by little he made out the great apartment, with a domed ceiling from which the light poured, and walls that were one enormous painting—nymphs and dryads dancing in a flower-strewn glade, Diana with her hounds and horses, dashing headlong through a mountain streamlet, a group of maidens bathing in a forest-pool—all life-size, and so real that Jurgis thought it was some work of enchantment, that he was in a dream-palace. Then his eye passed to the long table in the center of the hall, a table black as ebony, and gleaming with wrought silver and gold. In the center of it was a huge carven bowl, with the glistening gleam of ferns and the red and purple of rare orchids, glowing from a light hidden somewhere in their midst.

"This's the dinin'-room," observed Master Freddie. "How you like it, hey, ole sport?"

He always insisted on having an answer to his remarks, leaning over Jurgis and smiling into his face. Jurgis liked it.

"Rummy ole place to feed in all 'lone, though," was Freddie's comment—"rummy's hell! Whazya think, hey?" Then another idea occurred to him and he went on, without waiting: "Maybe you never saw anything—hic—like this 'fore? Hey, old chappie?"

"No," said Jurgis.

"Come from country, maybe—hey?"

"Yes," said Jurgis.

"Aha! I thosso! Lossa folks from country never saw such a place. Guv'ner brings 'em—free show—hic—regular circus! Go home tell folks about it. Ole man Jones's place—Jones the packer—beef-trust man. Made it all out of hogs, too, damn ole scoundrel. Now we see where our pennies go—rebates, an' private car-lines—hic—by Harry! Bully place, though—worth seein'! Ever hear of Jones the packer, hey, old chappie?"

Jurgis had started involuntarily; the other, whose active eyes missed nothing, demanded: "Whuzzamatter, hey? Heard of him?"

And Jurgis managed to stammer out: "I have worked for him in the yards."

"What!" cried Master Freddie, with a yell. "You! In the yards? Ho, ho! Why, say, thass good! Shake hands on it, ole man—by Harry! Guv'ner ought to be here—glad to see you. Great fren's with the men, guv'ner—labor an' capital, community 'f interests, an' all that—hic! Funny things happen in this world, don't they, ole man? Hamilton, lemme interduce you—fren' the family—ole fren' the guv'ner's—works in the yards. Come to spend the night wiz me, Hamilton—have a hot time. My fren', Mr.—whuzya name, ole chappie? Tell us your name."

"Rudkos—Jurgis Rudkos."

"My fren', Mr. Rudnose, Hamilton—shake han's."

The stately butler bowed his head, but made not a sound; and suddenly Master Freddie pointed an eager finger at him. "I know whazzam after wiz you, Hamilton—lay you a dollar I know! You think—hic—you think I'm drunk! Hey, now?"

And the butler again bowed his head. "Yes, sir," he said, at which Master Freddie hung tightly upon Jurgis's neck and went into a fit of laughter. "Hamilton, you damn ole scoundrel!" he roared, "I'll 'scharge you for impudence, you see 'f I don't! Ho, ho, ho! I'm drunk! Ho, ho!"

The two waited until his fit had spent itself, to see what new whim would seize him. "Whatcha wanta do?" he queried suddenly. "Wanta see the place, ole chappie? Want me play the guv'ner —show you 'roun'? State parlors— Looee Cans—Looee Sez—chairs cost three thousand apiece. Tea-room— Maryanntnet—picture of shepherds dancing—Ruysdael—twenty-three thousan'! Ball-room—balcony pillars—hic—imported—special ship— sixty-eight thousan'! Ceilin' painted in Rome—whazzat feller's name, Hamilton—Mattatoni? Macaroni? Then the conservatory—flowers an' music —hic! Country folks got lost in it once! Then this place—silver bowl— Benvenuto Cellini—rummy ole Dago! An' the organ—thirty thousan' dollars, sir—starter up, Hamilton, let Mr. Rednose hear it. No—never mind— clean forgot—says he's hungry, Hamilton—less have some supper. Only— hic—don't less have it here—come up to my place, ole sport—nice an' cosy. This way—steady, now, don't slip on the floor. Hamilton, we'll have a cole spread, an' some fizz—don't leave out the fizz, by Harry. We'll have some of the eighteen-thirty Madeira. Hear me, sir?"

"Yes, sir," said the butler, "but Master Frederick, your father left orders—"

And Master Frederick drew himself up to a stately height. "My father's orders were left to me—hic—an' not to you," he said. Then, clasping Jurgis tightly by the neck, he staggered out of the room; on the way another idea occurred to him, and he asked: "Any—hic—cable message for me, Hamilton?"

"No, sir," said the butler.

"Guv'ner must be travelin'. An' how's the twins, Hamilton?"

"They are doing well, sir."

"Good!" said Master Freddie; and he added fervently: "God bless 'em, the little lambs!"

They went up the great staircase one step at a time; at the top of it there gleamed at them out of the shadows the figure of a nymph crouching by a fountain, a figure ravishingly beautiful, the flesh warm and glowing with the hues of life. Above was a huge court, with domed roof, the various apartments opening into it. The butler had passed below but a few minutes to give orders, and then followed them; now he pressed a button, and the hall blazed with light. He opened a door before them, and then pressed another button, as they staggered into the apartment.

It was fitted up as a study. In the center was a mahogany table, covered with books, and smokers' implements; the walls were decorated with college trophies and colors, flags, posters, photographs and knick-knacks—tennis-rackets, canoe-paddles, golf-clubs, and polo-sticks. An enormous moose-head, with horns six feet across, faced a buffalo-head on the opposite wall, while bear and tiger skins covered the polished floor. There were lounging chairs and sofas, window-seats covered with soft cushions of fantastic designs; there was one corner fitted in Persian fashion, with a huge canopy and a jeweled lamp beneath. Beyond, a door opened upon a bed-room, and beyond that was a swimming pool of the purest marble, that had cost about forty thousand dollars.

Master Freddie stood for a moment or two, gazing about him; then out of the next room a dog emerged, a monstrous bull-dog, the most hideous object that Jurgis had ever laid eyes upon. He yawned, opening a mouth like a dragon's; and he came towards the young man, wagging his tail. "Hello, Dewey!" cried his master. "Been having a snooze, ole boy? Well, well—hello, there, whuzza matter?" (The dog was snarling at Jurgis.) "Why, Dewey—this my fren' Mr. Rednose—ole fren' the gun'ner's! Mr. Rednose, Admiral Dewey; shake han's—hic. Ain't he a daisy, though—blue ribbon at the New York show—twenty-three thousan' dollars at a clip! How's that, hey?"

The speaker sank into one of the big arm-chairs, and Admiral Dewey crouched beneath it; he did not snarl again, but he never took his eyes off Jurgis—he was perfectly sober, was the Admiral.

A moment or two, and then the young fellow's restless eye was caught by a leather dress-suit case, with name-plate and trimmings of gold. "Hello," he said, "it's come, has it?"

He jumped up and ran to it. "Ain't that a peacherina?" he cried. "Look a-here—hic—ole chappie—ever see anything like that? Chris'mas presen' from the guv'ner—thass why I'm so good! Come near—it won't bite you—jes look at that!" It contained a shaving and toilet set, with half a hundred implements for purposes unimaginable. Each of them was carved with individual designs; and all of them were of solid gold.

The butler had closed the door, and he stood by it, watching Jurgis every second. Now there came footsteps outside, and, as he opened the door, a man in livery entered, carrying a folding-table, and behind him came two men with covered trays. They stood like statues while the first spread the table and set out the contents of the trays upon it. There were cold pates, and thin slices of meat, tiny bread and butter sandwiches with the crust cut off, a bowl of sliced peaches and cream (in January), little fancy cakes, pink and green and yellow and white, and half a dozen ice-cold bottles of wine.

"Thass the stuff for you!" cried Master Freddie, exultantly, as he spied them. "Come 'long, ole chappie, move up."

And he seated himself at the table; the waiter pulled a cork, and he took the bottle and poured three glasses of its contents in succession down his throat. Then he gave a long-drawn sigh, and cried again to Jurgis to seat himself.

The butler held the chair at the opposite side of the table, and Jurgis thought it was to keep him out of it; but finally he understood that it was the other's intention to put it under him, and so he sat down, cautiously and mistrustingly. Master Freddie perceived that the attendants embarrassed him, and he remarked, with a nod to them, "You may go."

They went, all save the butler.

"You may go too, Hamilton," he said.

"Master Frederick—" the man began.

"Go!" cried the youngster, angrily. "Damn you, don't you hear me?"

The man went out and closed the door; Jurgis, who was as sharp as he, observed that he took the key out of the lock, in order that he might peer through the keyhole.

Master Frederick turned to the table again. "Now," he said, "go for it."

Jurgis gazed at him doubtingly. "Eat!" cried the other. "Pile in, ole chappie!"

"Don't you want anything?" Jurgis asked.

"Ain't hungry," was the reply—"only thirsty. Kitty and me had some candy—you go on."

So Jurgis began, without further parley. He ate as with two shovels, his fork in one hand and his knife in the other; when he once got started his wolf-hunger got the better of him, and he did not stop for breath until he had cleared every plate. "Gee whiz!" said the other, who had been watching him in wonder.

Then he held Jurgis the bottle. "Lessee you drink now," he said; and Jurgis took the bottle and turned it up to his mouth, and a wonderful, unearthly liquid ecstasy poured down his throat, tickling every nerve of him, thrilling him with joy. He drank the very last drop of it, and then he gave vent to a long-drawn "Ah!"

"Good stuff, hey?" said Freddie, sympathetically; he had leaned back in the big chair, putting his arm behind his head and gazing at Jurgis. And Jurgis gazed back at him. He was clad in spotless evening-dress, was Freddie, and looked very handsome—he was a beautiful boy, with light golden hair and the head of an Antinous. He smiled at Jurgis confidingly, and then started talking again, with his blissful insouciance. This time he talked for ten minutes at a stretch, and in the course of his speech he told Jurgis all of his family history. His big brother Charlie was in love with the guileless maiden who played the part of "Little Bright-Eyes" in "The Kaliph of Kamskatka." He had been on the verge of marrying her once, only "the guv'ner" had sworn to disinherit him, and had presented him with a sum that would stagger the imagination, and that had staggered the virtue of "Little Bright-Eyes." Now Charlie had got leave from college, and had gone away in his auto-mobile on the next best thing to a honeymoon. "The guv'ner" had made threats to disinherit another of his children also, sister Gwendolen, who had married an Italian marquis with a string of titles and a dueling record. They lived in his chateau, or rather had, until he had taken to firing the breakfast-dishes at her; then she had cabled for help, and the old gentleman had gone over to find out what were his grace's terms. So they had left Freddie all alone, and he with less than two thousand dollars in his pocket. Freddie was up in arms and meant serious business, as they would find in the end—if there was no other way in bringing them to terms he would have his "Kittens" wire that she was about to marry him, and see what happened then.

So the cheerful youngster rattled on, until he was tired out. He smiled his sweetest smile at Jurgis, and then he closed his eyes, sleepily. Then he opened them again, and smiled once more, and then he closed them and forgot to open them.

For several minutes Jurgis sat perfectly motionless, watching him, and reveling in the strange sensations of the champagne. Once he stirred, and the dog growled; after that he sat almost holding his breath—until after a while the door of the room opened softly, and the butler came in.

He walked toward Jurgis upon tip-toe, scowling at him; Jurgis rose up, and retreated, scowling back. So until he was against the wall, and then the butler came close, and pointed toward the door. "Get out of here!" he whispered.

Jurgis hesitated, giving a glance at Freddie, who was snoring softly. By making a noise he might awaken him.

"If you do, you son of a" hissed the butler, "I'll mash in your face for you before you get out of here!"

And Jurgis wavered but an instant more. He saw "Admiral Dewey" coming up behind the man and growling softly, to back up his threats. Then he surrendered and started towards the door.

They went out without a sound, and down the great echoing stair-case, and through the dark hall. At the front door he paused, and the butler strode close to him.

"Hold up your hands!" he snarled. Jurgis took a step back, clenching his one well fist. "Hold up your hands," the man ordered again.

"What for?" Jurgis cried, and then understanding that the fellow proposed to search him, answered, "I'll see you in hell first."

"Do you want to go to jail?" demanded the butler, menacingly. "I'll have the police onto you so quick—"

"Have 'em, then!" roared Jurgis, with fierce passion. "But you won't put your hands on me till you do! I haven't touched anything in your damned house, and I'll not have you touch me!"

So the butler, who was terrified lest his young master should waken, stepped suddenly to the door, and opened it. "Go on out of here!" he said; and then as Jurgis passed through the opening, he gave him a ferocious kick that sent him down the great stone steps at a run, and landed him sprawling in the snow at the bottom.

JURGIS got up, wild with rage; but the door was shut and the great castle was dark and impregnable. Then the icy teeth of the blast bit into him and he turned and went away at a run.

When he stopped again it was because he was coming to frequented streets and did not wish to attract attention. His heart was thumping fast with triumph. He had come out ahead on that deal! He put his hand into his trousers pocket every now and then to make sure that the precious hundred-dollar bill was still there.

Yet he was in a plight—a curious and even dreadful plight, when he came to realize it. He had not a single cent but that one bill! And he had to find some shelter that night—he had to change it! How could it be done?

Jurgis spent half an hour walking and debating the problem. There was no one he could go to for help—he had to manage it all alone. To get it changed in a lodging-house would be to take his life in his hands—he would almost certainly be robbed, and perhaps murdered, before morning. He might go to some hotel or railroad-depot and ask to have it changed; but what would they think, seeing a "bum" like him with a hundred dollars? He would probably be arrested if he tried it; and what story could he tell? On the morrow Freddie Jones would discover his loss, and there would be a hunt for him, and he would lose his money. The only other plan he could think of was to try in a saloon. He might pay them to change it if it could not be done otherwise.

He began peering into places as he walked; he passed several as being too crowded, and finally, chancing upon one where the bartender was all alone, he gripped his hands in sudden resolution and went in.

"Can you change me a hundred-dollar bill?" he demanded.

The bartender was a big, husky fellow, with the jaw of a prize fighter, and a three weeks' stubble of hair upon it. He stared at Jurgis. "What's that youse say?" he demanded.

"I said could you change me a hundred-dollar bill?"

"Where'd youse get it?" he inquired, incredulously.

"Never mind," said Jurgis; "I've got it, and I want it changed. I'll pay you if you'll do it."

The other stared at him hard. "Lemme see it," he said.

"Will you change it?" Jurgis demanded, gripping it tightly in his pocket.

"How the hell can I know if it's good or not?" retorted the bartender. "Whatcher take me for, hey?"

Then Jurgis slowly and warily approached him; he took out the bill, and fumbled it for a moment, while the man stared at him with hostile eyes across the counter. Then finally he handed it over.

The other took it and began to examine it; he smoothed it between his fingers, and he held it up to the light; he turned it over, and upside down, and edgeways. It was new and rather stiff, and that made him dubious. Jurgis was watching him like a cat all the time.

"Humph!" he said, finally, and gazed at the stranger, sizing him up—a ragged, ill-smelling tramp; with no overcoat and one arm in a sling—and a hundred-dollar bill! "Want to buy anything?" he demanded.

"Yes," said Jurgis, "I'll take a glass of beer."

"All right," said the other, "I'll change it." And he put the bill in his pocket, and poured Jurgis out a glass of beer and set it on the counter. Then he turned to the cash-register and punched up five cents, and began to pull money out of the drawer. Finally he faced Jurgis, counting out—two dimes, a quarter, and fifty cents. "There's your change," he said.

For a second Jurgis waited, expecting to see him turn again. "My ninety-nine dollars," he said.

"What ninety-nine dollars?" demanded the bartender.

"My change!" he cried—"the rest of my hundred!"

"Go on," said the bartender, "you're nutty!"

And Jurgis stared at him with wild eyes. For an instant horror reigned in him—black, paralyzing, awful horror clutching him at the heart; and then came rage, in surging, blinding floods—he screamed aloud, and seized the glass and buried it at the scoundrel's head. The other ducked, and it missed him by half an inch; then he rose again, and faced Jurgis, who was vaulting over the bar with his one well arm, and dealt him a smashing blow in the face, hurling him backward upon the floor. Then, as Jurgis scrambled to his feet again and started round the counter after him, he shouted at the top of his voice, "Help! help!"

Jurgis seized a bottle off the counter as he ran; and as the bartender made a wild leap he hurled the bottle at him with all his force. It just grazed his head, and shivered into a thousand pieces against the post of the door. Then Jurgis started back, rushing at the man again in the middle of the room. This time, in his blind frenzy, he came without a bottle, and that was all the bartender wanted—he rushed at him, meeting him half way and flooring him with a sledge-hammer drive between the eyes. An instant later the screen-doors flew open, and two men rushed in—just as Jurgis was getting to his feet again, foaming at the mouth with rage, and trying to tear his broken arm out of its bandages.

"Look out!" shouted the bartender—"he's got a knife!" Then, seeing that the two were disposed to join in the fray, he made another rush at Jurgis, and knocked aside his feeble defense and sent him tumbling again; and the three flung themselves upon him, rolling and kicking about the place.

A second later a policeman dashed in, and the bartender yelled once more—"Look out for his knife!" Jurgis had fought himself half to his knees, when the policeman made a leap for him, and cracked him across the face with his club. Though the blow staggered him, the wild beast frenzy still blazed in him, and he got to his feet, lunging into the air. Then again the club descended, full upon his head, and he dropped like a log to the floor. The policeman crouched over him, clutching his stick, waiting for him to try to rise again; and meantime the barkeeper got up, and put his hand to his head. "Christ!" he said, "I thought I was done. for that time. Did he cut me?"

"Don't see anything, Jake," said the policeman. "What's the matter with him?"

"Just crazy drunk," said the other. "A lame duck, too—but he most got me under the bar. Youse had better call the wagon, Billy."

"No," said the officer. "He's got no more fight in him, I guess—and he's only got a block to go." He twisted his hand in Jurgis's collar and jerked at him. "Git up here, you!" he commanded.

But Jurgis did not move, and the bartender went behind the bar, and after stowing the hundred-dollar bill away in a safe hiding place, came and poured a glass of water over Jurgis. Then, as the latter began to moan feebly, the policeman got him to his feet and dragged him out of the place. The station-house was just around the corner, and so in a few minutes Jurgis was in a cell.

He spent half the night lying unconscious, and the balance moaning in torment, with a blinding headache and a racking thirst. Now and then he cried aloud for a drink of water, but there was no one to hear him; there were others in that same station-house with split heads and a fever; there were hundreds of them in the great city, and tens of thousands of them in the great land, and there was no one to hear any of them.

In the morning he was given a cup of water and a piece of bread, and then hustled into a patrol-wagon and driven to the nearest police-court. He sat in the pen with a score of others, until his turn came.

The bartender—who proved to be a well-known bruiser—was called to the stand. He took the oath and told his story. The prisoner had come into his saloon after midnight, fighting drunk, and had ordered a glass of beer and tendered a dollar bill in payment. He had been given ninety-five cents change, and had demanded ninety-nine dollars more, and before the plaintiff could even answer, had hurled the glass at him and then attacked him with a bottle of bitters, and nearly wrecked the place.

Then the prisoner was sworn—a forlorn object, haggard and unshorn, with an arm done up in a filthy bandage, a cheek and head cut and bloody, and one eye purplish black and entirely closed. "What have you to say for yourself?" queried the magistrate.

"Your Honor," said Jurgis, "I went into his place and asked the man if he could change me a hundred-dollar bill. And he said he would if I bought a drink. I gave him the bill and then he wouldn't give me the change."

The magistrate was staring at him in amazement. "You gave him a hundred-dollar bill!" he exclaimed.

"Yes, Your Honor," said Jurgis.

"Where did you get it?"

"A man gave it to me, Your Honor."

"A man? What man, and what for?"

"A young man I met upon the street, Your Honor. I had been begging."

There was a titter in the court-room; the officer who was holding Jurgis put up his hand to hide a smile, and the magistrate smiled without trying to hide it. "It's true, Your Honor!" cried Jurgis, passionately.

"You had been drinking as well as begging last night, had you not?" inquired the magistrate.

"No, Your Honor—" protested Jurgis. "I—"

"You had not had anything to drink?"

"Why yes, Your Honor, I had—"

"What did you have?"

"I had a bottle of something—I don't know what it was—something that burned—"

There was again a laugh round the court-room, stopping suddenly as the magistrate looked up and frowned. "Have you ever been arrested before?" he asked abruptly.

The question took Jurgis aback. "I—I—" he stammered.

"Tell me the truth, now!" commanded the other, sternly.

"Yes, Your Honor."

"How often?"

"Only once, Your Honor."

"What for?"

"For knocking down my boss. Your Honor. I was working in the stock-yards, and he—"

"I see," said His Honor; "I guess that will do. You ought to stop drinking if you can't control yourself. Ten days and costs. Next case."

Jurgis gave vent to a cry of rage, cut off suddenly by the policeman, who seized him by the collar. He was jerked out of the way, into a room with the convicted prisoners, where he sat and wept like a child in his impotent rage. It seemed monstrous to him that policemen and judges should esteem his word as nothing in comparison with the bartender's; poor Jurgis could not know that the owner of the saloon paid five dollars each week to the policeman alone for Sunday privileges and general favors—nor that the pugilist bar-tender was one of the most trusted henchmen of the "Democratic" leader of the district, having helped only a few months before to hustle out a record-breaking vote as a testimonial to the magistrate, who had been made the target of odious kid-gloved reformers.

Jurgis was driven out to the Bridewell for the second time. In his tumbling around he had hurt his arm again, and so could not work, but had to be attended to by the physician. Also his head and his eye had to be tied up—and so he was a pretty-looking object when, the second day after his arrival, he went out into the exercise-court and encountered—Jack Duane!

The young fellow was so glad to see Jurgis that he almost hugged him. "By God if it isn't 'the Stinker!'" he cried. "And what is it—have you been through a sausage-machine?"

"No," said Jurgis, "but I've been in a railroad wreck and a fight." And then, while some of the other prisoners gathered round, he told his wild story; most of them were incredulous, but Duane knew that Jurgis could never have made up such a yarn as that.

"Hard luck, old man," he said, when they were alone; "but maybe it's taught you a lesson."

"I've learned some things since I saw you last," said Jurgis mournfully. Then he explained how he had spent the last summer, "hoboing it," as the phrase was. "And you?" he asked, finally. "Have you been here ever since?"

"Lord, no!" said the other. "I only came in the day before yesterday. It's the second time they've sent me up on a trumped-up charge—they're trying to drive me out of Chicago. I guess I'll have to quit, too—I've had hard luck and can't pay them what they want. Why don't you quit along with me, Jurgis?"

"I've no place to go," said Jurgis, sadly.

"Neither have I," replied the other, laughing lightly. "But we'll wait till we get out and see."

In the Bridewell Jurgis met few who had been there the last time, but he met scores of others, old and young, of exactly the same sort. It was like breakers upon a beach; there was new water, but the wave looked just the same. He strolled about and talked with them, and the biggest of them told tales of their prowess, while those who were weaker or younger and inexperienced gathered round and listened in admiring silence. The last time Jurgis had thought of little but his family; but now he was free to listen to these men, and to realize that he was now one of them—that their point of view was his point of view, and that the way they kept themselves alive in the world was the way he meant to do it in future.

And so, when he was turned out of prison again, without a penny in his pocket, he went straight to Jack Duane. Duane had left an address, and offered him an asylum; and he went, full of humility and gratitude. For Duane was a gentleman, and a man with a profession—and it was marvelous that he should be willing to throw his lot with a humble workingman, one who had even been a beggar and a tramp. Jurgis could not see what help he could be to him; he did not understand that a man like himself—who could be trusted to stand by anyone who was kind to him—was as rare among criminals as among any other class of men.

The rendezvous was a garret-room in the Ghetto district, the home of a pretty little French girl, Duane's mistress, who sewed all day, and eked out her living by prostitution. He had left an address, she told Jurgis—he was afraid to stay there now, on account of the police; he was threatening to go away and leave her forever, and her eyes were red with weeping. She had been arrested for street-walking, she said, and was afraid she would have to go into a brothel, the police tax upon independent prostitution was so high.

The new address was a cellar dive. The proprietor had never heard of Duane, but after he had put Jurgis through a catechism he showed him a back-stairs which led to a "fence" in the rear of a pawn-broker's shop, and to a number of assignation-rooms, in one of which Duane was hiding.

He was going to leave the city that very night, he told Jurgis—the police were after him again. But he was without a cent and had first to get his carfare. The other suggested that he try a freight-train, but Duane did not travel that way, least of all in midwinter. He was going to get the money, all right, and Jurgis should help him and share with him. Duane explained his plan; and as it was the other's first lesson, and was likely to be his last, Duane spent the day in laying bare to him the criminal world of the city, and in showing him how he might earn himself a living in it. That winter he would have a hard time, on account of his arm and of an unwonted fit of activity of the police; but so long as he was unknown to them he would be safe if he were careful. Here at "Papa" Hanson's (so they called the old man who kept the dive) he might rest at ease, for "Papa" Hanson was "square"—would stand by him so long as he paid, and give him an hour's notice if there were to be a police-raid. Also Rosensteg, the pawn-broker, would buy anything he had for a third of its value, and guarantee to keep it hidden for a year.

There was an oil-stove in the little cupboard of a room, and they had some supper; and then about eleven o'clock at night they sallied forth together, by a rear entrance to the place, Duane armed with a slung-shot. They came to a residence district, and he sprang up a lamp-post and blew out the light, and then the two dodged into the shelter of an area-step and hid in silence.

Pretty soon a man came by, a workingman—and they let him go. Then after a long interval came the heavy tread of a policeman, and they held their breath till he was gone. Though half frozen, they waited a full quarter of an hour after that—and then at last came footsteps, walking briskly. Duane nudged Jurgis, and the instant the man had passed they rose up. Duane stole out, as silently as a shadow, and second later Jurgis heard a thud and a stifled cry. He was only a couple of feet behind, and he leaped to stop the man's mouth, while Duane held him fast by the arms, as they had agreed. But the man was limp, and showed a tendency to fall, and so Jurgis had only to hold him by the collar while the other, with swift fingers, went through his pockets—ripping open, first his overcoat, and then his coat, and then his vest, searching inside and outside, and transferring the contents into his own pockets. At last, after feeling of the man's finger and in his neck-tie, Duane whispered, "That's all!" and they dragged him to the area and dropped him in. Then Jurgis went one way and his friend the other, walking briskly.

The latter arrived first, and Jurgis found him examining the "swag." There was a gold watch, for one thing, with a chain and locket; there was a silver pencil, and a match-box, and a handful of small change, and finally a card-case. This last Duane opened feverishly—there were letters and checks, and two theater-tickets, and finally, in the back part, a wad of bills. He counted them—there was a twenty, five tens, four fives and three ones. Duane drew a long breath. "That lets me out!" he said.

After further examination they burned the card-case and its contents, all but the bills, and likewise the picture of a little girl in the locket. Then Duane took the watch and trinkets down-stairs, and came back with sixteen dollars. "The old scoundrel said the case was filled," he said. "It's a lie, but he knows I want to get away."

They divided up the spoils, and Jurgis got as his share fifty-five dollars and some change. He protested that it was too much, but the other had agreed to divide even. That was a good haul, he said, better than the average. It would be enough to take him to New York, so he would wait until the next evening—he was afraid to start in the daytime, and he was perfectly safe here.

When they got up in the morning Jurgis was sent out to buy a paper; one of the pleasures of committing a crime was the reading about it afterwards. "I had a pal that always did it," Duane remarked, laughing—"until one day he read that he had left three thousand dollars in a lower inside pocket of his party's vest."

Nothing like that happened this time, but the newspaper reading led to a terrible misfortune, none the less. There was a half-column account of the robbery—it was evident that a gang was operating in the neighborhood, said the paper, for it was the third within a week, and the police were apparently powerless. The victim was an insurance agent, and he had lost a hundred and ten dollars that did not belong to him. He had chanced to have his name marked on his shirt, otherwise he could not have been identified yet. His assailant had hit him too hard, and he was suffering from concussion of the brain; and also he had been half-frozen when found, and would lose three fingers of his right hand. The enterprising newspaper-reporter had taken all this information to his family, and told how they had received it.

Since it was Jurgis's first experience, these details naturally caused him some worriment; but the other laughed coolly—it was the way of the game, and there was no helping it. Before long Jurgis would think no more of it than they did in the yards of knocking out a bullock. "It's a case of us or the other fellow, and I say the other fellow every time," he observed.

"Still," said Jurgis, reflectively, he never did us any harm."

"He was doing it to somebody as hard as he could, you can be sure of that," said Duane.

To which Jurgis made no response for a moment or two. Then he chanced to say: "Three fingers gone! He will be worse off than poor Harry Wheeler." And at that remark, made casually and carelessly, he was amazed to see his companion turn deadly pale, and start as if he had been struck in the face.

"What's the matter?" Jurgis cried.

"Harry Wheeler!" gasped Duane.

"Yes," said Jurgis, "what about him?"

And Duane could hardly speak, for his agitation. "I—I had a friend—" he panted. "What—how—"

"It was a fellow I met in the stockyards," said Jurgis. "They had a room in the house where I lived. They—" "Who were they?" cried Duane. "His mother and sister. They came from a place in Connecticut—"

And Duane reached over towards him, his hand shaking like an aspen leaf. "It's—it's the same people!" he whispered, breathlessly. "What—what was the matter with his hand?"

"He worked in a tin-can factory at the yards," said Jurgis, "and he'd had two fingers of his left hand cut off. And he could not play his violin any more—that was why it was so terrible—"

And the other went all in a heap—he buried his face in his arms, and burst into tears. Jurgis started up in fright. "What—what is it?" he cried wildly. "Who are they?"

The other sobbed: "Oh, my God, why did you tell me? Why did you have to say it just now—why couldn't you let me go away in peace? Oh, it's too horrible!"

"Who are they?" Jurgis shouted again.

And the other replied: "It's my brother! It's my mother and sister, that I went away and left. My brother Harry!"

"Your brother!" Jurgis gasped, in horror.

"Yes," said the man. "My real name is Wheeler! Oh, why did you have to tell me!"

"I didn't know—" Jurgis began, stammering.

"Tell me about them!" the other broke in. "How did they live—when was this?"

"It was after I left you last," Jurgis answered, and told all he knew—how Mrs. Wheeler was helpless, and how the sister sewed, and how pale she was, and how the brother sat half the night, trying to play the violin with two fingers. His companion was almost beside himself with grief as he listened.

"And working in the stock-yards!" he panted, suddenly. "To be sacrificed to the packers! Good God, they will murder us all before they finish!"

Jurgis did not understand this remark; and later on, as the other repeated it, he asked what he meant. "Didn't they tell you," cried Duane, "that it was the packers that ruined my father?"

"No," Jurgis answered; "they told me nothing."

And then Duane—for his companion still called him that—explained to him how his father had been the president of a bank in his town; and how the principal industry there had been a slaughter-house, upon which the bank had a mortgage, and some of its notes besides. Then one day there came to the company a man, offering, in the name of one of the big packers, to buy the plant for about a quarter of what it had cost, and saying that if the company would not sell it would be ruined by competition. The company refused to sell, and to get money to fight the trust it borrowed still more from the bank, and without telling of the threat; and meantime the trust began to bid up the price of cattle in the neighborhood, and opened a big wholesale business in a town near by, and sold all its slaughter-house products at less than cost. Also, when the company tried to ship its products to Boston and New York, the railroad-rates went up all of a sudden; and the refrigerator-cars which it had to use, and which all belonged to the trust, were never to be had on time, and the charges became so preposterous that the company had to give up and abandon its property. So the bank was ruined also, and Duane's father killed himself. "And that was the Beef Trust!" the man cried, wildly—"and now my brother comes out here, and it maims him for life, and all but kills him!"

He sat staring in front of him, twisting his fingers together nervously. "I can't go away from here now," he exclaimed suddenly. "I've got to pay the police and stay—I've got to help them somehow! How could I leave them in a plight like that—and it was six months ago you saw them, and God only knows what may have happened since then!"

"Jurgis," Duane burst out, after a moment's pause—"will you go out there for me and see if you can find them? I don't dare to show myself, but you can go. I know you didn't want to meet your people—"

"I'll go for you," said Jurgis, quickly.

"What do you want me to do?"

"Find them," said Duane. "Find out how they are—take them some money for me!"

"Shall I tell them it's from you?" "No, not yet. If you did I should have to try to find some work, for they wouldn't take a cent if they knew—"

"But they won't take it from me," objected Jurgis. "I shouldn't dare to offer it to them."

"Go and see," said Duane, abruptly. "Hurry up!"

JURGIS rode out to the stock-yards and hurried down the familiar street. Panei Aniele's house was newly painted, and he knew what that meant without asking. He went up the steps and knocked, and a German woman came to the door. All the people who had lived there before were gone, she said, and she knew nothing at all about them. Jurgis went to the flat of Mrs. Oiszewski, the cattle-butcher's wife. Yes, Oiszewski could tell him—poor Aniele had been three months behind with her rent, and they had dumped her furniture out into the street about a month ago, and she had wandered off, and they had found her frozen stiff in an area-way the next morning. The newspapers had printed all about it, and there had been a tremendous stir; some people had come, and had taken Aniele's three children to some sort of an institution. The fuss had been all the greater because it was found that the tenement, which was unsafe and disease-ridden, was the property of the great Standard Oil university, which had its buildings over near the lake, and was one of the most conscienceless exploiters of the poor in all Chicago. As for the Wheelers, they had moved away before that; Mrs. Oiszewski had no idea where—they had never talked about their affairs with anyone.

Then Jurgis asked about his own people, feeling that he had to, but hoping that he would not find out anything. The woman could only tell him that Elzbieta and the children had gone away, Marija's canning-factory having shut down. Perhaps the Szadwilases would be able to tell him, she added.

But Jurgis did not go to the Szadwilases. He went instead to the factory where Harry Wheeler had worked. The place was very busy, running over-time, and so the foreman was little disposed to talk. Wheeler had left some time ago, because he had been too sick to work. What had become of him he had no idea, and he did not think any one else had. He pointed out a couple of men Jurgis might ask, but they, too, shook their heads. And so Jurgis went back to his friend.

All the joy was gone out of Jack Duane's face, and he looked old and haggard. When he heard the news, he said: "I can't leave now, Jurgis; I've got to stay and hunt for them."

He had already explained to Jurgis that a man of their trade might pay the police, and be let alone so long as he was not caught red-handed. It did not pay to do it, except for a few "big" men, because one had to work all the time to satisfy their demands. Therefore, it would be better for Jurgis to stay in hiding and never be seen in public with his pal.

But Jurgis soon got very tired of staying in hiding. It was no fun to eat and drink alone—and paying for it more than he would have to pay elsewhere, with company and good cheer. In a couple of weeks he was feeling strong and beginning to use his arm, and then he could not stand it any longer. Duane, who had done a job of some sort by himself, and made a truce with the powers, brought over Marie, his little French girl, to share with him—but even that did not avail for long, and in the end the other took him out and gave him his introduction to the saloons and "sporting-houses" where the big crooks and "hold-up men" hung out.

And so Jurgis got a glimpse of the high-class criminal world of Chicago. A city nominally ruled by the people, but in reality administered by a business aristocracy, a huge army of graft was necessary for the purpose of effecting the transfer of power. Twice a year, in the spring and fall elections, millions of dollars were furnished by the business men and expended by this army; meetings were held and clever speakers were hired, bands played and rockets sizzled, tons of documents and reservoirs of drinks were distributed, and tens of thousands of votes were bought for cash. And this army of graft had, of course, to be maintained the year round. The leaders and organizers were maintained by the business men directly—aldermen and legislators by means of bribes, party officials out of the campaign funds, lobbyists and corporation lawyers in the form of salaries, contractors by means of jobs, labor union leaders by subsidies, and newspaper proprietors and editors by advertisements. The rank and file, however, were either foisted upon the city, or else lived off the populace directly. There was the police department, and the fire and water departments, and the whole balance of the civil list, from the meanest office-boy to the head of a city department; and for the horde who could find no room in these, there was the world of vice and crime, there was license to seduce, to swindle and plunder and prey. The wives and the preachers of the business men had made it against the law to drink on Sunday; and this had delivered the saloon-keepers into the hands of the police, and made an alliance between them necessary. The wives and the preachers had said that there should be no prostitution; and so they had brought the hand-maidens and concubines of the business men into the combination. It was the same with the gambling-house keeper and the pool-room man, and the same with any other man or woman who had a means of getting "graft," and was willing to pay over a share of it; the green-goods man and the highwayman, the pickpocket and the sneak-thief, and the receiver of stolen goods, the seller of adulterated milk, of stale fruit and diseased meat, the proprietor of unsanitary tenements, the fake doctor and the usurer, the beggar and the "push-cart man," the prize fighter and the professional slugger, the race track "tout," the procurer, the white-slave agent, and the expert seducer of young girls. All of these agencies of corruption were banded together, and leagued in blood brotherhood with the politician and the police; more often than not they were one and the same person—the police-captain would own the brothel he pretended to raid, and the politician would open his headquarters in his saloon. "Hinky Dink," or "Bath-house John," or others of that ilk, were proprietors of the most notorious dives in Chicago, and also the "grey wolves" of the city council, who gave away the streets of the city to the business men; and those who patronized their places were the gamblers and prize fighters who set the law at defiance, and the burglars and hold-up men who kept the whole city in terror. On election day all these powers of vice and crime were one power; they could tell within one per cent what the vote of their district would be and they could change it at an hour's notice.

A month ago Jurgis had all but perished of starvation upon the streets; and now suddenly, as by the gift of a magic key, he had entered into a world where money and all the good things of life came freely. He was introduced by his friend to an Irishman named "Buck" Halloran, who was a political "worker" and on the inside of things. This man talked with Jurgis for a while, and then told him that he had a little plan by which a man who looked like a workingman might make some easy money; but it was a private affair, and had to be kept quiet. Jurgis expressed himself as agreeable, and the other took him that afternoon (it was Saturday) to a place where city laborers were being paid off. The pay-master sat in a little booth, with a pile of envelopes before him, and two police-men standing by. Jurgis went, according to directions, and gave the name of "Michael O'Flaherty," and received an envelope, which he took around the corner and delivered to Halloran, who was waiting for him in a saloon. Then he went again, and gave the name of "Johann Schmidt," and a third time and gave the name of "Serge Ostrinski." Halloran had quite a list of imaginary workingmen, and Jurgis got an envelope for each one. For this work he received five dollars, and was told that he might have it every week, so long as he kept quiet. As Jurgis was excellent at keeping quiet, he soon won the trust of "Buck" Halloran, and was introduced to others as a man who could be depended upon.

This acquaintance was useful to him in another way, also; before long Jurgis made his discovery of the meaning of "pull," and just why his boss, Connor, and also the pugilist bar-tender, had been able to send him to jail. One night there was given a ball, the "benefit" of "One-eyed Larry," a lame man who played the violin in one of the big "high-class" houses of prostitution on Clark street, and was a wag and a popular character on the "Levee." This ball was held in a big dance-hall, and was one of the occasions when the city's powers of debauchery gave themselves up to madness. Jurgis attended and got half insane with drink, and began quarreling over a girl; his arm was pretty strong by then, and he set to work to clean out the place, and ended in a cell in the police-station. The police-station being crowded to the doors, and stinking with "bums," Jurgis did not relish staying there to sleep off his liquor, and sent for Halloran, who called up the district leader and had Jurgis bailed out by telephone at four o'clock in the morning. When he was arraigned that same morning, the district leader had already seen the clerk of the court and explained that Jurgis Rudkos was a decent fellow, who had been indiscreet and so Jurgis was fined ten dollars and the fine was "suspended"—which meant that he did not have to pay it, and never would have to pay it, unless somebody chose to bring it up against him in the future.

Among the people Jurgis lived with now money was valued according to an entirely different standard from that of the people of Packingtown; yet, strange as it may seem, he did a great deal less drinking than he had as a workingman. He had not the same provocations of exhaustion and hopelessness; he had now something to work for, to struggle for. He soon found that if he kept his wits about him, he would come upon new opportunities; and being naturally an active man, he not only kept sober himself, but helped to steady his friend, who was a good deal fonder of both wine and women than he.

One thing led to another. In the saloon where Jurgis met "Buck" Halloran he was sitting late one night with Duane when a "country customer" (a buyer for an out of town merchant) came in, a little more than half "canned." There was no one else in the place but the bar-tender, and as the man went out again Jurgis and Duane followed him; he went round the corner and in a dark place made by a combination of the elevated railroad and an un-rented building, Jurgis leapt forward and shoved a revolver under his nose while Duane with his hat pulled over his eyes, went through the man's pockets with lightning fingers. They got his watch and his "wad," and were round the corner again and into the saloon before he could shout more than once. The bar-tender, to whom they had tipped the wink, had the cellar-door open for them, and they vanished, making their way to a secret entrance to a brothel next door. From the roof of this there was access to three similar places beyond; by means of these passages the customers of any one place could be gotten out of the way, in case a falling out with the police chanced to lead to a raid, and also it was necessary to have a way of getting a girl out of reach in case of an emergency. Thousands of them came to Chicago answering advertisements for "servants" and "factory hands," and found themselves trapped by fake employment-agencies, and locked up in a bawdy-house. It was generally enough to take all their clothes away from them; but sometimes they would have to be "doped" and kept prisoners for weeks; and meantime their parents might be telegraphing the police, and even coming on to see why nothing was done. Occasionally there was no way of satisfying them but to let them search the place to which the girl had been traced.

For his help in this little job, the bartender received twenty out of the hundred and thirty odd dollars that the pair secured; and naturally this put them on friendly terms with him, and a few days later he introduced them to a little "sheeny" named Goldberger, one of the "runners" of the "sporting-house" where they had been hidden while the police were seeking the assailants of the stranded "country customer." After a few drinks Goldberger began, with some hesitation, to narrate how he had had a quarrel over his best girl with a professional "card-sharp," who had hit him in the jaw. The fellow was a stranger in Chicago, and if he was found some night with his head cracked there would be no one to care very much. Jurgis, who by this time would cheerfully have cracked the heads of all the gamblers in Chicago, inquired what would be coming to him; at which the Jew became still more confidential, and said that he had some tips on the New Orleans races, which he got direct from the police-captain of the district, whom he had got out of a bad scrape, and who "stood in" with a big syndicate of horse-owners. Duane took all this in at once, but Jurgis had to have the whole race-track situation explained to him before he realized the importance of such an opportunity.

There was the gigantic Racing Trust. It owned the assemblies and the legislatures in every city and state in which it did business—or else it owned the police and the politicians, and disobeyed the laws, instead of making them. It even owned some of the big newspapers, and made public opinion—there was no power in the land that could oppose it, unless, perhaps, it were the Pool-room Trust. It built magnificent racing-parks all over the country, and by means of enormous purses it lured the people to come, and then it organized a gigantic shell-game whereby it plundered them of hundreds of millions of dollars every year. Horse-racing had once been a sport, but nowadays it was a business; a horse could be "doped" and doctored, under-trained or over-trained; it could be made to fall at any moment—or its gait could be broken by lashing it with the whip, which all the spectators would take to be a desperate effort to keep it in the lead. There were scores of such tricks; and sometimes it was the owners who played them and made fortunes, sometimes it was the jockeys and trainers, sometimes it was outsiders, who bribed them—but most of the time it was chiefs of the trust. Now, for instance, they were having winter-racing in New Orleans, and a syndicate was laying out each day's programme in advance, and its agents in all the Northern cities were "milking" the pool-rooms. The word came by long-distance telephone in a cipher code, just a little while before each race; and any man who could get the secret had as good as a fortune. If Jurgis did not believe it, he could try it, said the little Jew—let them meet at a certain house on the morrow and make a test. Jurgis was willing, and so was Duane, and so they went to one of the high-class pool-rooms where brokers and merchants gambled (with society women in a private room), and they put up ten dollars each upon a horse called "Black Beldame," a six to one shot, and won. For a secret like that they would have done a good many pluggings—but the next day Goldberger informed them that the offending gambler had got wind of what was coming to him, and had skipped the town.

There were ups and down at the business; but there was always a living, inside of a jail, if not out of it. Early in April the city elections were due, and that meant prosperity for all the powers of graft. Jurgis, hanging round in dives and gambling-houses and brothels, met with the heelers of both parties, and from their conversation he came to understand all the ins and out of the game, and to hear of a number of ways in which he could make himself useful about election time. "Buck" Halloran was a "Democrat," and so Jurgis became a Democrat also; but it was not a bitter one—the Republicans were good fellows, too, and were to have a pile of money in this next campaign. At the last election the Republicans had paid four dollars a vote to the Democrats' three, and "Buck" Halloran sat one night playing cards with Jurgis and another man, who told how Halloran had been charged with the job of voting a "bunch" of thirty-seven newly-landed Italians, and how he, the narrator, had met the Republican worker who was after the very same gang, and how the three had effected a bargain whereby the Italians were to vote half and half, for a glass of beer apiece, while the balance of the fund went to the conspirators!

Not long after this Jurgis, wearying of the risks and vicissitudes of miscellaneous crime, was moved to give up the career for that of a politician. Just at this time there was a tremendous uproar being raised by the reformers concerning the alliance between the criminals and the police; they had been publishing facts, and had succeeded in stirring the big business men to action. For the criminal graft was one in which the business men had no part—it was what is called a "side-line," carried by the police. "Wide-open" gambling and debauchery made the city pleasing to "trade" but burglaries and hold-ups did not. One night it chanced that while Jack Duane was drilling a safe in a clothing-store he was caught red-handed by the night-watchman, and turned over to a policeman, who chanced to know him well, and who took the responsibility of letting him make his escape. Such a howl from the newspapers followed this that Duane was slated for a sacrifice, and barely got out of town in time.

And just about now it happened that Jurgis was introduced to a man named Harper, whom he recognized as the foreman at Smith's who had been instrumental in making him an American citizen, the first year of his arrival at the yards. The other was interested in the coincidence, but did not remember Jurgis—he had handled too many "green ones" in his time, he said. He sat in a dance-hall with Jurgis and Halloran until one or two in the morning, exchanging experiences. He had a long story to tell of his quarrel with the superintendent of his department, and how he was now a plain workingman, and a good union man as well. It was not until some months afterwards that Jurgis understood that the quarrel with the superintendent had been prearranged, and that Harper was in reality drawing a salary of twenty dollars a week from the packers for an inside report of his union's secret proceedings. The yards were seething with agitation just then, said the man (speaking as a unionist). The people of Packingtown had borne about all that they would bear, and it looked as if a strike might begin any week.

After this talk the man made inquiries concerning Jurgis, and a couple of days later he came to him with an interesting proposition. He was not absolutely certain, he said, but he thought that he could get him a regular salary if he would come to Packingtown and do as he was told, and keep his mouth shut. Harper—"Bush" Harper, he was called—was a right-hand man of Tom Cassidy, the Democratic boss of the stock-yards; and in the coming election there was a peculiar situation. There had come to Cassidy a proposition to nominate a certain rich brewer who lived upon a swell boulevard that skirted the district, and who coveted the big badge and the "honorable" of an alderman. The brewer was a Jew, but he had no brains, and was harmless, and would put up a rare campaign-fund. Cassidy had accepted the offer, and then gone to the Republicans with a proposition. He was not sure that he could manage the "Sheeny" and he did not mean to take any chances with his district; let the Republicans nominate a certain obscure but amiable friend of Cassidy's, who was now setting ten-pins in the cellar of an Ashland avenue saloon, and he, Cassidy, would elect him with the "Sheeny's" money and the Republicans might have the glory, which was more then they would get otherwise. To this the Republicans had assented at once; but the hell of it was—so Harper explained—that the Republicans were all of them fools—a man had to be a fool to be a Republican in the stock-yards, where Cassidy was king. And they didn't know how to work, and of course it would not do for the Democratic workers, the noble redskins of the War Whoop League, to support the Republican openly. The difficulty would not have been so great except for another fact—there had been a curious development in stock-yards politics in the last year or two, a new party having leaped into being. They were the Socialists; and it was a devil of a mess, said "Bush" Harper. The one image which the word "Socialist" brought to Jurgis was of poor little Tamoszius Kuslejka, who had called himself one, and would go out with a couple of other men and a soap-box, and shout himself hoarse on a street corner Saturday nights. Tamoszius had tried to explain to Jurgis what it was all about, but Jurgis, who was not of an imaginative turn, had never quite got it straight; at present he was content with his companion's explanation that the Socialists were the enemies of American institutions—could be neither scared nor bought, and would not combine or make any sort of a "dicker." Whenever such a thing was so much as hinted to them they would reply with an insolent letter, and then print the letter and circulate it amongst the workingmen! Tom Cassidy was very much worried over the opportunity which his last deal gave to them—the stock-yards Democrats were furious at the idea of a rich capitalist for their candidate, and while they were changing they might possibly conclude that a Socialist firebrand was preferable to a Republican bum. And so right here was a chance for Jurgis to make himself a place in the world, explained "Bush" Harper; he had been a union man, and he was known in the yards as a workingman; he must have hundreds of acquaintances, and as he had never talked politics with them he might come out as a Republican now without exciting the least suspicion. There were barrels of money for the use of those who could deliver the goods; and Jurgis might count upon Tom Cassidy, who had never yet gone back on a friend. Just what could he do? Jurgis asked in some perplexity, and the other explained in detail. To begin with, he would have to go to the yards and work, and he mightn't relish that; but he would have what he earned, as well as the rest that came to him. He would get active in the union again, and perhaps try to get an office, as he, Harper, had; he would tell all his friends the good points of Doyle, the Republican nominee, and the bad ones of the "Sheeny;" and then Cassidy would furnish a meeting-place, and he would start the "Young Men's Republican Association," or something of that sort, and have the rich brewer's best beer by the hogshead, and fire-works and speeches, just like the War Whoop League. Surely Jurgis must know hundreds of men who would like that sort of fun; and there would be the regular Republican leaders and workers to help him out, and they would deliver a big enough majority on election-day.

When he had heard all this explanation to the end, Jurgis demanded: "But how can I get a job in Packingtown? I'm blacklisted."

At which "Bush" Harper laughed. "I will attend to that all right," he said.

And the other replied: "It's a go, then; I'm your man."

So Jurgis went out to the stock-yards again, and was introduced to the great Tom Cassidy, political lord of the district, and boss of Chicago's mayor. It was Cassidy who owned the brick-yards, and the dump, and the ice-pond—from which last year had come the typhoid germs that had killed little Sebastijonas, though Jurgis did not know it. It was Cassidy who was to blame for the unpaved street in which Jurgis's child had been drowned; it was Cassidy who had put in office the magistrate who had first sent Jurgis to jail; it was Cassidy who was principal stockholder in the company which had sold him the ramshackle tenement, and then robbed him of it. But Jurgis knew none of these things—any more than he knew that Cassidy was but a tool and puppet of the packers. To him Cassidy was simply a power, the "biggest" man he had ever met.

He was a little dried-up Irishman, whose hands shook—he had made himself the head politician of Chicago, and a millionaire as well, but he had wrecked his health in the process. He had a brief talk with his visitor, watching him with his rat-like eyes, and making up his mind about him; and then he gave him a note to Mr. Harmon, one of the head managers of Anderson's:

"The bearer, Jurgis Rudkos, is a particular friend of mine, and I would like you to find him a good place, for important reasons. He was once indiscreet, but you will perhaps be so good as to overlook that."

Mr. Harmon looked up inquiringly when he read this. "What does he mean by 'indiscreet?'" he asked.

"I was blacklisted, sir," said Jurgis.

At which the other frowned. "Blacklisted?" he said. "How do you mean?"

And Jurgis turned red with embarrassment. He had forgotten that a blacklist did not exist. "I—that is—I had difficulty in getting a place," he stammered.

"What was the matter?"

"I got into a quarrel with a foreman—not my own boss, sir—and struck him."

"I see," said the other, and meditated for a few moments. "What do you wish to do?" he asked.

"Anything, sir," said Jurgis—"only I had a broken arm this winter, and so I have to be careful."

"How would it suit you to be a night-watchman?"

"That wouldn't do, sir. I have to be among the men at night."

"I see—politics. Well, would it suit you to trim hogs?"

"Yes, sir," said Jurgis.

And Mr. Harmon called a time-keeper and said: "Take this man to Pat Murphy and tell him to find room for him somehow."

And so Jurgis marched into the hog-killing room, a place where, in the days gone by, he had come cringing, begging, week after week for a chance to keep his family from starving. Now, at last, he had got into touch with things, and was the master; and he walked jauntily and smiled to himself, seeing the frown that came to the boss' face as the time-keeper said: "Mr. Harmon says to put this man on." It would over-crowd his department and spoil the record he was trying to make—but he said not a word except "All right."

And so Jurgis became a working-man once more; and straightway he sought out his old friends and joined the union and began to "root" for "Scotty" Doyle. Doyle had done him a good turn once, he explained, and was really a bully chap; Doyle was a workingman himself, and would represent the workingman—why did they want to vote for a millionaire "Sheeny," and what the hell had Tom Cassidy ever done for them that they should back his candidates all the time? And meantime Cassidy had given Jurgis a note to the Republican leader of the ward, and he had gone there and met the crowd he was to work with. Already they had hired a big hall with some of the brewer's money, and every night Jurgis brought in a dozen new members to the "Doyle Republican Association." Pretty soon they had a grand opening night; and there was a brass band, which marched through the streets, and fire-works and bombs and red lights in front of the hall; and there was an enormous crowd, with two over-flow meetings—so that the pale and trembling candidate had to recite three times over the little speech which one of Cassidy's henchmen had written, and which he had been a month learning by heart. Best of all, the famous and eloquent Senator Spareshanks, perpetual presidential candidate, came all the way from Indiana and rode out in an automobile to discuss the sacred privileges of American citizenship, and protection and prosperity for the American workingmen. His inspiring address was quoted to the extent of half a column, in all the morning newspapers, which also said that it could be stated upon excellent authority that the unexpected popularity developed by Doyle, the Republican candidate for Alderman, was giving great anxiety to Mr. Cassidy, the chairman of the Democratic county committee.

The chairman was still more worried when the monster torch-light procession came off, with the members of the Doyle Republican Association all in red capes and hats, and free beer for every voter in the ward—the best beer ever given away in a political campaign, as the whole electorate testified. During this parade, and at innumerable cart-tail meetings as well, Jurgis labored tirelessly. He did not make any speeches—there were lawyers and other experts for that; but he helped to manage things, distributing notices, and posting placards, and bringing out the crowds, and when the show was on he attended to the fireworks and the beer. Thus in the course of the campaign he handled many hundreds of dollars of the Hebrew brewer's money, administering it with naive and touching fidelity. Towards the end, however, he learned that he was regarded with rage by the rest of the "boys," because he compelled them either to make a poorer showing than he, or to do without their share of the pie. After that Jurgis did his best to please them, and to make up for the time he had lost before he discovered the extra bung-holes of the campaign barrel.

He pleased Tom Cassidy, also; on election morning he was out at four o'clock, "getting out the vote;" he had a two-horse carriage to ride in, and he went from house to house for his friends, and escorted them in triumph to the polls. He voted half a dozen times himself, and voted some of his friends as often; he brought bunch after bunch of the newest foreigners—Lithuanians, Poles, Bohemians, Slovaks—and when he had put them through the mill he turned them over to another man to take to the next polling-place. When Jurgis first set out, the captain of the precinct gave him a hundred dollars, and three times in the course of the day he came for another hundred, and not more than twenty-five out of each one got stuck in his pocket. The balance all went for actual votes, and on a day of Democratic landslides they elected "Scotty" Doyle, the ex-ten-pin setter, by nearly a thousand plurality—and beginning at five o'clock in the afternoon, and ending at three the next morning, Jurgis treated himself to a most unholy and horrible "jag." Nearly every one else in Packingtown did the same, however, for there was universal exultation over this triumph of popular government, this crushing defeat of a purse-proud plutocrat by the power of the common people.

AFTER THE election Jurgis stayed on in Packingtown and kept his job. The agitation to break up the police protection of criminals was continuing, and it seemed to him best to "lay low" for the present. He had nearly three hundred dollars in bank, and might have considered himself entitled to a vacation; but he had an easy job, and force of habit kept him at it. Besides, Tom Cassidy, whom he consulted, advised him that something might "turn up" before long.

Jurgis got himself a place in a boarding-house with some congenial friends. Having ascertained that Elzbieta and her family had gone downtown, he gave no further thought to them; nor did he seek out his old acquaintances —he went with a new set, now, young unmarried fellows who were "sporty." Jurgis had long ago cast off his fertilizer clothing, and since going into politics he had donned a linen collar and a greasy red neck-tie. He had some reason for thinking of his dress, for he was making about eleven dollars a week, and two-thirds of it he might spend upon his pleasures without ever touching his savings.

Some times he would go downtown with a party of friends to the cheap theatres, and the music halls and other haunts with which they were familiar. Many of the saloons in Packingtown had pool-tables, and some of them bowling-alleys, by means of which he could spend his evenings in petty gambling. Also, there were cards and dice. One time Jurgis got into a game on a Saturday night and won prodigiously, and because he was a man of spirit he stayed in with the rest and the game continued until late Sunday afternoon and by that time he was "out" over twenty dollars. On Saturday nights, also, a number of balls were generally given in Packingtown; each man would bring his "girl" with him, paying half a dollar for a ticket, and several dollars additional for drinks in the course of the festivities, which continued until three or four o'clock in the morning, unless broken up by fighting. During all this time the same man and woman would dance together, half stupefied with sensuality and drink, and the things that were done when they went out may be better imagined, than described.

Before long Jurgis discovered what Cassidy had meant by something "turning up." In May the agreement between the packers and the unions expired, and a new agreement had to be signed. Negotiations were going on, and the yards were full of talk of a strike. The old scale had dealt with the wages of the skilled men only; and of the members of the National Meat Workers' Union about two-thirds were unskilled men. In Chicago these latter were receiving, for the most part, eighteen and a half cents and hour, and the unions wished to make this the general wage for the next year. It was not nearly so large a wage as it seemed; in the course of the negotiations the union officers examined time-checks to the amount of ten thousand dollars, and they found that the highest wages paid had been fourteen dollars a week, the lowest two dollars and five cents, and the average of the whole, six dollars and sixty-five cents. That meant that each man had been given about six hours' work a day—a little more than Jurgis would have expected from his own experience. And six dollars and sixty-five cents was hardly too much for a man to keep a family on. Considering the fact that the price of dressed meat had for some reason increased nearly fifty per cent in the last five years, while the price of "beef on the hoof" had decreased correspondingly, it would have seemed that the packers ought to be able to pay it; but the packers were unwilling to pay it—they rejected the union demand, and to show what their purpose was, a week or two after the agreement expired they put down the wages of about a thousand men to sixteen and a half cents, and it was said by everybody in the yards that old man Morton had banged his fist on his desk, and said that, by God, he would put them to fifteen before he got through. There were a million and a half of men in the country looking for work, a hundred thousand of them right in Chicago; there were two thousand before the gates of his place every morning, and if he put an advertisement in the papers he could bring the whole hundred thousand in a day, and every man Jack of them ready and glad to work for fifteen cents. And now were they to let the union stewards march into their places and bind them to a contract that would lose them several thousand dollars a day for a year. Not much!

The point of view of the men Jurgis heard gone over and over by the speakers at his union meetings. Some of these men had worked in Packing-town for thirty years; they had helped to build up the business, they said, and they had a right to some consideration, and to a living out of it. And since by this time it was perfectly clear that the packers did not mean to give it to them, it was time they set about taking it. They had been suffering and sacrificing for four years to build up their unions, in the face of hatred and persecution; and now it was time to put them to use, if they ever meant to. Their enemies were laboring without rest to destroy them; keeping the workers on starvation wages by employing twice too many men, and weeding out the old hands, and taking on new ones to teach them the business. A union under such conditions was like a pail with a hole in it—the quicker you drank off your beer the better for you. So they would strike if they could not hold their wage up otherwise; the skilled men would stand by the unskilled, making common cause with them.

All this was in June; and before long the question was submitted to a referendum vote of the unions, and the decision was for a strike. It was the same in all the packing-house cities—and suddenly the newspapers and public woke up to face the gruesome spectacle of a meat famine. Immediately, of course, there was an uproar, and everyone fell to talking of "the paramount rights of the public." Year after year the people of Packingtown toiled and the public gave never a thought to them, to their rights or their wrongs; only now, when they were driven mad by their sufferings, did the public discover their existence—and then it was only to rail at them and denounce them for their turbulence and presumption.

All sorts of pleas for a reconsideration were made; but the packers were obdurate. And all the while they were reducing wages, and heading off shipments of cattle, and rushing in wagon-loads of mattresses and cots. So the men boiled over, and one night telegrams went out from the union head-quarters to all the big packing-house cities—to St. Paul, South Omaha, Sioux City, St. Joseph, Kansas City, East St. Louis and New York—and the next day at noon between fifty and sixty thousand men drew off their working clothes and cleaned their tools, and marched out of the factories. The great "Beef Strike" was on.

Jurgis went to his dinner, and afterwards he walked over to see Tom Cassidy, who lived in a fine house upon a street which had been decently paved and lighted especially for his especial benefit. Cassidy had gone into semi-retirement and looked nervous and worried. "What do you want?" he demanded abruptly when he saw Jurgis.

"I came to see if maybe you could get me a place during the strike," the other replied.

And Cassidy knit his brows and eyed him narrowly. In that morning's papers Jurgis had read a fierce denunciation of the packers by Cassidy, who had declared that if they did not treat their people decently the city authorities would end the matter by tearing down their plants. Now, therefore, Jurgis was not a little taken aback when the other demanded suddenly: "See here, Rudkos, why don't you stick by your job?"

Jurgis started. "Work as a scab?" he cried.

"Why not?" demanded Cassidy. "What's that to you?"

"But—but—" stammered Jurgis. He had somehow taken it for granted that he should go out with his union.

"The packers need good men, and need them bad," continued the other, "and they'll treat a man right that stands by them. Why don't you take your chance and fix yourself?"

"But," said Jurgis, "how could I ever be of any use to you—in politics?"

"You couldn't be it anyhow," said Cassidy, abruptly.

"Why not?" asked Jurgis. "Hell, man!" cried the other. "Don't you know you're a Republican? And do you think I'm always going to elect Republicans? My brewer has found out already how we served him, and there is the deuce to pay."

Jurgis looked dumbfounded. He had never thought of that aspect of it before. "I could be a Democrat," he said.

"Yes," reflected the other, "but not right away—a man can't change his politics every day. And besides, I don't need you—there'd be nothing for you to do. And it's a long time to election day, anyhow; and what are you going to do meantime?"

"I thought I could count on you," began Jurgis.

"Yes," responded Cassidy, "so you could—I never yet went back on a friend. But is it fair to leave the job I got you and come to me for another? I have had a hundred fellows after me today, and what can I do? I have put seventeen men on the city pay-roll to clean streets this one week, and do you think I can keep that up forever? It wouldn't do for me to tell other men what I tell you, but you've been on the inside, and you ought to have sense enough to see for yourself. What have you to gain by a strike?"

"I hadn't thought," said Jurgis.

"Exactly," said Cassidy, "but you'd better. Take my word for it, the strike will be over in a few days and the men will be beaten; and meantime what you get out of it will belong to you. Do you see?"

And Jurgis saw. He went back to the yards, and into the work-room. The men had left a long line of hogs in various stages of preparation, and the foreman was directing the feeble efforts of a score or two of clerks and stenographers and office-boys to finish up the job and get them into the chilling-rooms. Jurgis went straight up to him and announced: "I have come back to work, Mr. Murphy."

The boss's face lighted up. "Good man!" he cried. "Come ahead!"

"Just a moment," said Jurgis, checking his enthusiasm. "I think I ought to get a little more wages."

"Yes," replied the other, "of course. What do you want?"

Jurgis had debated on the way. His nerve almost failed him now, but he clenched his hands. "I think I ought to have three dollars a day," he said.

"All right," said the other promptly; and before the day was out our friend discovered that the clerks and stenographers and office-boys were getting five dollars a day, and then he could have kicked himself.

So Jurgis became one of President Eliot's "American heroes," a man whose virtues merited comparison with those of the martyrs of Lexington and Valley Forge. The resemblance was not complete, of course—for Jurgis was generously paid and comfortably clad, and was provided with a spring-cot and a mattress, and three substantial meals a day; also he was perfectly at ease, and safe from all peril of life and limb, save only in the case that a desire for beer should lead him to venture outside of the stock-yards gates. And even in the exercise of this privilege he was not left unprotected; a good

246 ◆ CHAPTER 27

part of the inadequate police force of Chicago was suddenly diverted from its work of hunting criminals, and rushed out to serve him; and also the union leaders had hired horses and buggies, which they could not well afford, and were driving about to make certain that their orders of "no violence" were being obeyed. They had even paid to have the neighborhood placarded with posters in five languages, warning the men "to molest no person or property, and abide strictly by the laws of this country. *Your organization will not assist you if you get into unlawful trouble.*"

But if the police and strikers were both determined that there should be no violence, there was another party interested, which was minded to the contrary—and that was the press. The newspapers of Chicago were of two kinds—those which were dependent upon the pennies of the masses, and whose income varied according to the number of hair-raising sensations they could concoct; and those which lived upon the millions of dollars worth of advertising subsidies distributed by the packers, and by the employers' associations of the city, whose purpose was the destruction of the unions. When to these facts it is added that the editors of the papers did not themselves go to the scene of the strike, but sent young men to get the news, and paid them according to the quantity of space they could fill, it may be believed that the people of the city, and of the entire country, were certain of adequate accounts of stock-yards violence. On the first day of his life as a strike-breaker Jurgis quit work early, and in a spirit of bravado he challenged three men of his acquaintance to go outside and get a drink. They accepted, and went through the big Halstead street gate, where several policemen were watching, and also some union pickets, scanning sharply those who passed in and out. Jurgis and his companions went south on Halstead street, past the hotel, and then suddenly half a dozen men started across the street toward them and proceeded to argue with them concerning the error of their ways. As the arguments were not taken in the proper spirit, they went on to threats; and suddenly one of them jerked off the hat of one of the four and flung it over the fence. The man started after it, and then, as a cry of "Scab!" was raised, and a dozen people came running out of saloons and doorways, a second man's heart failed him and he followed. Jurgis and the fourth staid long enough to give themselves the satisfaction of a quick exchange of blows, and then they, too, took to their heels and fled back of the hotel and into the yards again. Meantime, of course, policemen were coming on a run, and as a crowd gathered other police got excited and sent in a riot-call. Jurgis knew nothing of this, but went back to "Packers' Avenue," and in front of the "Central Time Station" he saw one of his companions, breathless and wild with excitement, narrating to an ever-growing throng how the four had been attacked and surrounded by a howling mob, and had been nearly torn to pieces; how bricks had been hurled and knives and revolvers flourished; how the speaker himself had escaped by knocking down several men, but his companions had been caught and were being murdered; how the police had charged with drawn clubs—and so on. While Jurgis stood listening to this, and smiling cynically, several dapper young men stood by with note-books in their hands, and took it down, and it was not more than two hours later that Jurgis saw newsboys running about with armfuls of newspapers, printed in red and black letters six inches high: *"Violence in the Yards! Strike Breakers Surrounded by Frenzied Mob"* If he had been able to buy all of the newspapers of the United States the next morning, he might have discovered that his beer-hunting exploit was being perused by some two or three score millions of people; and had served as a text for editorials in all the staid and solemn business men's newspapers, warning the leaders of the unions that by such tactics they were forfeiting the good-will with which "public opinion" had been disposed to regard them.

Jurgis was to see more of this as time passed. For the present, his work being over, he was free to ride into the city, by a railroad direct from the yards, or else to spend the night in a room where cots had been laid in rows. He chose the latter, but to his regret, for all night long gangs of strike-breakers kept arriving. As very few of the better class of workingmen could be got for such work, these specimens of the new American hero contained an assortment of the criminals and thugs of the city, besides negroes and the lowest types of foreigners—Greeks, Roumanians, Sicilians and Slovaks. In the morning Jurgis met several he had seen in the Bridewell, and in the dives and brothels he had frequented with Jack Duane. They had been attracted more by the prospect of disorder than by the big wages; most of them had brought a bottle or two with them, and they were not deterred from smoking, either by the placards on the walls, or by the total absence of fire-escapes in the building. They made the night hideous with singing and carousing, and only went to sleep when the time came for them to get up to work.

In the morning, before Jurgis had finished his breakfast, "Pat" Murphy ordered him to one of the superintendents, who questioned him as to his experience in the work of the killing-floor. His heart began to thump with excitement, for he divined instantly that his hour had come—that he was to be a boss!

Some of the foremen were union members, and many who were not had gone out with the men. The packers had made extraordinary efforts to retain them—to one man they had offered a bonus of five hundred dollars and a contract at fifty dollars a week for five years. It was in the killing department that they had been left most in the lurch, and precisely here that they could least afford it; the smoking and canning and salting of meat might wait, and all the by-products might be wasted—but the fresh meats must be had, or the restaurants and hotels and brown-stone houses would feel the pinch, and then "public opinion" would take a startling turn.

An opportunity such as this would not come twice to a man; and Jurgis seized it. Yes, he knew the work, the whole of it, and he could teach it to others. But if he took the job and gave satisfaction he would expect to keep it—they would not turn him off at the end of the strike? To which the superintendent replied that he might safely trust Anderson's for that—they proposed to teach these unions a lesson, and most of all, those foremen who had gone back on them. Jurgis would receive five dollars a day during the strike, and twenty-five a week after it was settled.

So our friend got a pair of "slaughter-pen" boots and "jeans" and flung himself at his task. It was a weird sight, there on the killing-floor—a throng of stupid black negroes, and foreigners who could not understand a word that was said to them, mixed with palefaced, hollow-chested book-keepers and clerks, half-fainting for the tropical heat and sickening stench of fresh blood —and all struggling to dress a dozen or two of cattle in the same place where, twenty four hours ago, the old "killing-gang" had been speeding, with their marvelous precision turning out four hundred carcasses every hour!

The negroes and the "toughs" from the levee did not want to work, and every few minutes they would feel obliged to retire and recuperate. In a couple of days Anderson & Company had electric fans up to cool off some of the rooms for them, and even couches for them to rest on; meantime they could go out and find a shady corner and take a "snooze," and as there was no place for any one in particular, and no system, it might be hours before their boss discovered them. As for the poor office-employees, they did their best, moved to it by terror; thirty of them had been "fired" in a bunch that first morning for refusing to serve, besides a number of women-clerks and typewriters, who had declined to act as waitresses.

It was such a force as this that Jurgis was set to organize and teach. He did his best, flying here and there, placing them in rows and showing them the tricks—where to break the neck, and how to slit the hide, and how to split the breastbone. Jurgis had never given an order in his life before, but he had taken enough of them to know, and he soon fell into the spirit of it, and roared and stormed like any old stager. He had not the most tractable pupils, however. "See hyar, boss," a big black "buck" would begin, "ef you doan' like de way Ah does dis job you kin git somebody else to do it; 'cause Ah doan' stay to take no orders from nobody. Ah doan'—" and so on, while the crowd would gather and listen and stare. After the first meal nearly all the steel knives had been missing, and now every negro had one, ground to a fine point, hidden in his boots.

There was no bringing order out of this chaos, Jurgis soon discovered; and he fell in with the spirit of the thing—there was no reason why he should wear himself out with shouting. If hides and guts were slashed and rendered useless, there was no way of tracing it to anyone, and if a man lay off and forgot to come back there was nothing to be gained by seeking him, for all the rest would quit in the meantime. Everything went, during the strike, and the packers paid—before long Jurgis found that the custom of resting had suggested to some alert minds the possibility of registering at more than one place and earning more than one five dollars a day. When he caught a man at this he "fired" him, but it chanced to be in a quiet corner, and the man tendered him a ten dollar bill and a wink, and he took them. Of course, before long this custom spread, and Jurgis was soon making quite a good income from it.

In the face of handicaps such as these the packers counted themselves lucky if they could kill off the cattle that had been crippled in transit, and the hogs that had developed disease. Frequently, in the course of a two or three days' trip in hot weather and without water some hog would develop cholera, and die; and as the hog is the most ferocious cannibal among animals, the rest would attack him before he had ceased kicking, and when the car was opened there would be nothing of him left but the bones. If all the hogs in this car-load were not killed at once, they would soon be down with the dread disease, and then their flesh would defy even the chemistry of Packingtown to make it palatable. It was the same with cattle that were gored and dying, or were limping with broken bones stuck through their flesh—they must be killed, even if brokers and buyers and superintendents had to take off their coats and help drive and cut and skin them. And meantime, all over the country, agents of the packers were gathering men; they were placarding all the cities of the Middle West, and were gathering gangs of negroes in the country districts of the far South, promising them five dollars a day and board, and being careful not to mention there was a strike. Already car-loads of them were on the way, with special rates from the railroads, and all traffic ordered out of the road. Many towns and cities were taking advantage of the chance to clear out their jails and work-houses—in Detroit the magistrates would release every man who agreed to leave town within twenty-four hours, and agents of the packers were in the court-rooms to take them to Chicago!—And meantime trainloads of supplies were coming in for their accommodation, including wagon-loads of beer and whiskey, so that they might not be tempted to go outside; likewise all the available prostitutes of the city and the vicinity were hired to serve as cooks and waitresses. They hired thirty young girls in Cincinnati to "pack fruit," and when they arrived, put them at work canning corned-beef, and put cots for them to sleep in a public hallway, through which the men passed. As the gangs came in day and night, under the escort of squads of police, they stowed them away in unused workrooms and storerooms, and in the car-sheds, crowded so closely together that the cots touched. In some places they would use the same room for eating and sleeping, and at night the men would put their cots upon the tables, to keep away from the swarm of rats.

But with all their best efforts, and the boasting statements with which they filled the papers, the packers were completely demoralized. The strike had come before they expected it; and none of them had been prepared for anything like the show of strength the unions had developed—some of them had believed there would be no strike at all, if the unions' bluff were called. Now they found that ninety per cent of the men had walked out; and they faced the task of completely remaking their labor force—and with the price of meat up thirty per cent, and the public clamoring for a settlement.

Six hours after the strike had been ordered they had made an offer to submit the whole question at issue to arbitration. They knew that it was too late for the offer to be accepted, but it gave them and the papers a chance to declare that the strikers had rejected such an offer. They had continued it for a day or two, but the unions had refused to submit the question of a wage-reduction for the unskilled men, and negotiations had been broken off. Later, however, a threat of nineteen unions not yet involved had led them to renew the offer to arbitrate the whole matter; and at the end of ten days the unions accepted it, and the strike was called off. It was agreed that all the men were to be re-employed within forty-five days, and that there was to be "no discrimination against union men."

That was on July 21st, and in the afternoon some of the packers began paying off the strike-breakers, many of whom were glad to quit without a hint from the paymasters. An attempt was made to take about three hundred negroes out by the Halstead street cars, under the escort of an equal number of police, and when the strikers divined the plan a howling mob of about four thousand gathered. The motormen of the cars refused to stop, until finally the police drove a patrol-wagon onto the track, and then, when half a dozen cars had been gathered, the terrified negroes dashed aboard, most of them flinging themselves down upon the floor of the cars, piled three deep. When they started off there were showers of missiles, and for two miles the street was filled with a jeering crowd.

This was an anxious time for Jurgis. He was willing to risk taking care of himself in any fight; but if the men were taken back "without discrimination" he would lose his present place. He sought out the superintendent, who smiled grimly and bade him "wait and see." Anderson's strike-breakers were not leaving.

Whether or not the "settlement" was simply a trick of the packers to gain time, or whether they really expected to break the strike and cripple the unions by the plan, cannot be said; but that night there went out from the office of Anderson & Company a telegram to all the big packing-centres: "Employ no union leaders." And in the morning, when the twenty thousand men thronged into the yards, with their dinner-pails and working clothes, Jurgis stood near the door of the hog-trimming room, where he had worked before the strike, and saw a throng of eager men, with a score or two of policemen watching them, and saw a superintendent come out and walk down the line and pick out man after man that pleased him; and one after another came, and there were some men up near the head of the line who were never picked, and they were union stewards and delegates and the men Jurgis had heard making speeches at the meetings. Each time, of course, there were louder murmurings and angrier looks. And it was the same all over the Anderson works and the same at Smith's; in the car-shops, out of five hundred men only six were taken back. Over where the cattle-butchers were waiting, Jurgis heard shouts and saw a crowd, and he hurried there. One big butcher, who was president of the Packing Trades Council, had been passed over five times, and the men were wild with rage; they had appointed a committee of three to go in and see the superintendent, and the committee had made three attempts, and each time the police had clubbed them back from the door. Then there were yells and hoots, continuing until at last the superintendent came to the door. "We all go back or none of us do!" cried a hundred voices.

And the other shook his fist at them. "You went out of here like cattle," he shouted, "and you'll come back like cattle!"

And instantly the big butcher president leaped upon a pile of stones and yelled: "It's off, boys. We'll all of us quit again!" And so the cattle-butchers declared a second strike on the spot; and gathering their members from the other plants, where the same trick had been played, they marched down Packer's Avenue, which was thronged with a dense mass of workers, cheering wildly. Men who had already got to work on the killing-floor dropped their tools and joined them; and some galloped here and there on horse-back, shouting the tidings. Within half an hour the whole of Packingtown was on strike again, and beside itself with fury.

ANDERSON & Company, which had kept most of its strike-breakers, went on with its work after the second strike; but some of the other plants were left in a desperate plight, with half-dressed meat lying on their floors and rotting in the stifling midsummer heat. The discharged negroes were called back, and messages sent out to rush new hands; and at the same time the unions were telegraphing the call for a general strike of all the meat workers in the country, and holding mass-meetings denouncing the packers for their treachery.

There was quite a different tone in Packingtown after this—the place was a seething caldron of passion, and the "scab" who ventured into it fared badly. There were one or two of these incidents each day, the newspapers detailing each one with vehement denunciation. They always blamed it upon the unions—it was the inevitable consequences of the union propaganda, they said. Yet ten years before, when there were no unions in Packingtown, there was a strike, and national troops had to be called, and there were pitched battles fought at night, by the light of blazing freight-trains. The public was never reminded that Packingtown was always a centre of violence; that the people were ignorant, and that the work they were forced to do accustomed them to scenes of cruelty and to the shedding of blood. In "Whiskey Point," where there were a hundred saloons and one glue factory, there was always fighting, and always more of it in hot weather. Anyone who had taken the trouble to consult the station-house blotter would have found that there was less violence that summer than ever before—and this while twenty thousand men were out of work and with nothing to do all day but brood upon bitter wrongs. The public could not go there and see, and there was no one to tell it the truth, to picture the mighty battle the union leaders had to fight—to keep this huge army in rank, to keep it from straggling and pillaging, to cheer and encourage and guide a hundred thousand people, of a dozen different tongues, through six long weeks of hunger and disappointment and despair. When the union leaders were not at their headquarters, transacting business and attending to the distributing of supplies, they were riding about the district, exhorting and pleading with the men. They posted pickets at intervals, and when there was trouble they would be notified by telephone, and would ride to the scene to intercede. They pleaded with the men to work at home, to go fishing on the lake-front, to do anything but loaf on the corners. As only a minority of the strikers belonged to the unions, the officers could not always have their way; but with the help of the three thousand members of the girls' union, they put an absolute end to "can-rushing," and they all but spoiled the business of the saloons. They plastered the neighborhood with warnings; and early in August, at their monster parade, in which forty-thousand people took part, the girls gave out basketfuls of printed cards that read as follows:

WE WILL WIN

The eyes of the nation are upon us!
The cause of unionism is at stake!
We have raised wages 25 per cent, but manliness 50 per cent!
Let us stand firm for law and order!
We must win by fair means!

Perhaps none of these cards came under the eyes of the newspaper reporters; at any rate none of the papers printed them. Furthermore, as tending to show how the packers appreciated such efforts in the cause of peace, it should be added that of the girls who were conspicuous in the giving out of these cards, not one could get work in Packingtown when the strike was over.

There was violence by the unions, and there was some by the newspapers, and there was still more by the police. It was violence for the newspapers to declare, when the packers put up a bill-board fence, that they were constructing a stockade. It was violence for them to magnify every saloon-row and street-fight into a union riot. It was violence of the police, whenever such a fight occurred, to plunge into the midst of the crowd of the idle and curious, and club every head they saw, men and women and children, driving the panic-stricken people before them like sheep. It was violence of them to seize the first they laid hands on, until they had prisoners enough to fill their patrol-wagons; and it was violence for the mayor of the city to summon to his office and lecture a magistrate who failed to punish such prisoners to the satisfaction of the packers. It was violence to seize the president of the Teamsters' union and throw him into a cell for the offense of calling from the window of his office an order to a member of his own union. It was because of such things as these, and only because of them, that "disgraceful" riots took place; such as once when the police began clubbing union men who were trying to stop a fight between two drunken gamblers, and the people of Packingtown swarmed out of their houses, and there was a pitched battle, lasting an hour, between three thousand frenzied men and women and a hundred policemen, in which many of the former were badly hurt, and some of the latter would have been torn to pieces but for the exertions of union officials.

Meantime the packers had now set themselves definitely to the task of making a new labor force. A thousand or two of strike-breakers were brought in every night and distributed among the various plants. Some of them were experienced workers—butchers, salesmen and managers from the packers' branch-stores, and a few union men who had deserted from other cities; but the vast majority were "green" negroes from the cotton-districts of the far South, and they were herded into the packing-plants like sheep. There was a law forbidding the use of buildings as lodging-houses unless they were licensed for the purpose, and provided with proper windows, stairways and fire-escapes; now, in a "paint-room," reached only by an inclosed "chute," a room without a single window and only one door, one hundred men were crowded upon mattresses placed in a solid row upon the floor. Upon the third-story of the "hog-house" of Morton's was a store-room, without a window, into which they crowded seven hundred men, sleeping upon the bare springs of cots, and with a second shift to use them by day. When the clamor of the public led to an investigation into these conditions, and the mayor of the city was forced to order the enforcement of the law, the packers got a judge to issue an injunction forbidding him to do it.

And that was but a small part of the "violence" of the packers. The sanitary arrangements in the packing-houses had always been grossly inadequate; and now the corners of every room where meat was being prepared were reeking with the stench of human filth. The mayor was boasting that he had put an end to gambling and prize-fighting in the city; while here a swarm of professional gamblers had leagued themselves with the police to fleece the strike-breakers; and any night, in the big open space in front of Smith's, one might see brawny negroes stripped to the waist, and pounding each other for money, under the eyes of policemen, while a howling throng of three or four thousand surged about, men and women, young white girls from the country rubbing elbows with big buck negroes with daggers in their boots, while rows of woolly heads peered down from every window of the surrounding factories. The ancestors of these black people had been savages in Africa; and since then they had been chattel-slaves, or held down by a community ruled by the traditions of slavery. Now for the first time they were free—free to gratify every passion—free to wreck themselves. They were wanted to break a strike, and when it was broken they would be shipped away, and their present masters would never see them again. So whiskey and women were brought in by the car-load and sold to them, and hell was let loose in the yards. Every night there were stabbings and shootings, rape and murder stalking abroad—the packers had blank permits, which enabled them to ship dead bodies from the city without troubling the authorities. They lodged men and women on the same floor, and with the night there began a saturnalia of debauchery—scenes such as never before were witnessed in America, and never in the world since the days of Baal and Moloch. Along the platforms where the railroad-cars were loaded one could not pass for the bodies of men and women, black and white, sleeping together, and as the women were the dregs from the brothels of Chicago, and the men were for the most part ignorant country negroes, the nameless diseases of vice were soon rife—one company physician stated that he treated two hundred cases every week. And these men handled the food which was sent out to every corner of the civilized world—tin-cans which would infect the person who cut his hand upon them, meat that would be handled by millions of people, any one of whom, chancing to have an open sore upon his hands, might be made the victim of a loathsome disease that would cause his fingers or a part of his face to rot away and drop off.

The "Union Stock Yards" were never a pleasant place; but now they were not merely a collection of slaughter-houses—they were the camping place of an army of fifteen or twenty thousand of the lowest and most degraded of human beasts. All day long the blazing mid-summer sun beat down upon their square mile of abominations—upon tens of thousands of cattle crowded into pens whose wooden floors stank and steamed contagion, upon bare, blistering, cinder-strewn railroad-tracks, and huge blocks of dingy meat-factories, whose labyrinthine passages defied a breath of fresh air to penetrate them; and there were not merely rivers of hot blood and car-loads of moist flesh and the fetid, sickening stench of viscera, rendering-vats and soap-caldrons, glue-factories and fertilizer tanks that smelt like craters of hell—there were also tons of garbage festering in the sun, and the greasy laundry of the workers hung out in every hallway to dry. In the rooms where bread was being baked and food prepared would be great piles of lumpy mattresses, and grey blankets stiff with filth; and next door would be a windowless toilet-room that was an open sewer; and beyond this would be a meat storeroom with a litter of boxes and barrels, old ladders and trucks flung to one side, and an improvised dining-room with a dozen or two of long tables covered with oilcloth and black with flies. The floor would be slippery with tobacco-juice and scraps of food, and rats would scurry about it in broad daylight; there would not be a window in the place, only gas-jets burning dimly in a haze of tobacco smoke—and here four hundred men would crowd to feed at noon on an August day, clad in "jeans" and under-shirts, their faces dripping with sweat and their hands smeared with blood.

And then at night, when this throng would pour out into the streets to play! Fighting, gambling, drinking and carousing, cursing and screaming, laughing and singing, playing banjoes and dancing, black and white mingled together in the sordid democracy of vice. They were worked in the yards all seven days in the week, and they had their prize-fights and crap-games on Sunday nights just the same; and then around the corner one might see a bon-fire blazing, and an old, grey-headed negress, lean and witchlike, her hair flying wild, and her eyes blazing, now yelling and now chanting of the fires of perdition and the blood of the "Lamb," until men and women lay down upon the ground, moaning and screaming in convulsions of terror and remorse.

Such were the stock-yards during the strike; while the strikers watched in sullen despair, and the country clamored like a greedy child for its food, and the packers went grimly on their way, bringing order out of chaos, and breaking the opposition. Each day they had more workers, and could be more stern with those they had—could put them on piece-work, and threaten and dismiss them if they did not keep up the pace. Jurgis was now one of their agents in this process; and he could feel the change day by day, like the slow starting up of a heavy train. He had gotten used to being a master of men; and because of the stifling heat and the stench and the fact that he was a "scab" and knew it and despised himself, he was drinking and developing a villain-ous temper, and he stormed and cursed and raged at his men, and drove them until they were ready to drop with exhaustion.

Then one day late in August, a superintendent ran into the place and shouted to Jurgis and his men to drop their work and come. They followed him outside, to where, in the midst of a dense throng, they saw several two-horse trucks waiting, and three patrol-wagon loads of police. Jurgis and his men sprang upon one of the trucks, and the driver yelled to the crowd and they went thundering away at a gallop. Eleven steers had just escaped from the yards, it was said; the strikers had got hold of them, and now the wagons were going to the rescue, and there would be the chance of a scrap!

They went out at the Ashland Avenue gate, and started in the direction of the "dump." There was a yell as soon as they were sighted, men and women rushing out of houses and saloons as they galloped by. There were eight or ten policemen on the truck, however, and there was no disturbance until they came to a place where the street was blocked with a dense throng. Those on the flying truck yelled a warning and the crowd scattered pell-mell; then the rescue party saw one of the steers lying in its blood. There were a good many cattle-butchers at large in the neighborhood, with nothing much to do, and hungry children at home; so some one had knocked out the steer—and as a first-class man can kill and dress one in a couple of minutes, there were a good many steaks and roasts already missing from it. This was thieving, of course, and called for punishment—which the police proceeded to administer by leaping from the truck and darting into the throng, cracking at every head they saw. There were yells of rage and pain, and the terrified people fled into houses and stores, or scattered helter-skelter down the street. Jurgis and his gang joined in the sport, every man singling out his victim, striving to bring him to bay and "punch the daylights" out of him. If he fled into a house his pursuer would smash in the flimsy door with his shoulders, and follow him up the stairs, hitting everyone who came within reach, and finally dragging his squealing quarry from under a bed or pile of old clothes in a closet.

Jurgis and two policemen were chasing two men who ran into a bar-room. One of them took shelter behind the bar, and one of the policemen cornered him and proceeded to whack him over the back and shoulders until he lay down and gave a chance at his head. The other leaped a fence in the rear, balking the other policeman, who was fat; and as he came back, furious and cursing, a big Polish woman, the owner of the saloon, rushed in screaming, and he gave her a poke in the stomach that doubled her up on the floor. Meantime Jurgis, who was of a practical temper, was helping himself to the contents of a bottle on the bar; and the first policeman, having laid out his man, joined him in this, handing out several more bottles, and filling his pockets besides—and then, as he started to leave, cleaning off all the balance with a sweep of his club. The din of them crashing to the floor brought the fat Polish woman to her feet again, gasping with terror, and another member of the killing gang who had come in to share the fun crept up behind her and put his knee into her back and shut his hands over her eyes; and then he called to the policeman, who went back and broke open the cash drawer and filled his pockets with the contents. Then the three went outside and the man who was holding the woman gave her a shove that sent her spinning and dashed out himself. The gang having already boosted the carcass onto the truck, they set out at a trot, followed by screams and curses, and a shower of bricks and stones from unseen enemies. These bricks and stones, with the addition of a few imaginary pistol-shots, would figure in the accounts of the "riot" which would be sent out to a few thousand newspapers within an hour or two; but the episode of the cash-drawer would not be mentioned again, save in the heart-breaking legends of Packingtown. Certainly, at any rate, Jurgis did not mention it, for during the drive the policeman slipped into his hand two "cart-wheels" that had come out of the till.

It was late in the afternoon when they got back, and they dressed the remainder of the steer and a couple of others that had been killed, and then knocked off for the day. Jurgis went downtown to supper, with three friends who had been on the other truck, and they exchanged reminiscences on the way. Afterwards, they drifted into a roulette-parlor, and Jurgis, who was never lucky at gambling, dropped about fifteen dollars. To console himself, he had to drink a good deal, and he went back to Packingtown about two o'clock in the morning, very much the worse for his excursion. As he was going to the place where he slept he met a painted-cheeked woman in a greasy "kimona," and she put her arm about his waist to steady him. With no further formality than an inquiry as to terms, they turned into a dark room they were passing. Scarcely, however, had they taken two sips before another door opened, and a watchman entered, carrying a lantern.

"Who's there?" he called sharply.

Jurgis started to murmur some reply, but at the same instant the man raised his light, and it flashed in his face, and Jurgis recognized him; he stood stricken dumb, and his heart gave a leap like a mad thing. He caught his breath and a sudden trembling seized him. The man was Connor!

Connor, the boss! Connor, who had seduced his wife, who had sent him to prison, and wrecked his home, and ruined his life! It was Connor who stood there, staring, with the light flashing upon his hated face! Jurgis had thought of him often since coming back to Packingtown, but it had been as of something far off, that no longer concerned him. Now, however, as he saw him, alive and in the flesh, the same thing happened to him that had happened before; a flood of rage boiled up in him, a blind frenzy seized him—he flung himself at the man, and smote him between the eyes, and then, as he fell, seized him by the throat and began to pound his head upon the floor.

The woman had screamed in fright, and people came rushing in. The lantern had been upset and extinguished, and it was so dark they could not see a thing; but they could hear Jurgis panting, and hear the thumping of his victim's skull, and they rushed there and tried to pull him off. Precisely as before, Jurgis came away with a piece of his enemy's flesh between his teeth, and as before, he went on fighting with those who had interfered with him, until a policeman had come and beat him into insensibility.

So he spent the balance of the night in the stock-yards station-house. This time, however, he had money in his pocket, and when he came to his senses he could get something to drink, and also a messenger to take word of his plight to "Bush" Harper. Harper did not appear, however, until after Jurgis, feeling very weak and ill, had been haled into court and remanded at live hundred dollars' bail to await the result of his victim's injuries. Jurgis was wild about this, because, a different magistrate being now on the bench, he stated that he had never been arrested before, and that he had been attacked first—and if only some one had been there to speak a good word for him, he might have been let off at once.

But Harper explained that he had been down-town, and had not got the message. "What's happened to you?" he asked.

"I've been doing a fellow up," said Jurgis, "and I've got to get five hundred dollars' bail."

"I can arrange that all right," said the other. "It may cost you a few dollars, of course. But what was the trouble?"

"A man that did me a mean trick once," answered Jurgis.

"Who is he?"

"He's a boss in Smith's sausage-department—or used to be. His name's Connor."

And the other gave a start, "Connor!" he cried. "Not Phil Connor?"

"Yes," said Jurgis, "that's his name, I think. Why?"

"Good God!" exclaimed the other, "then you're in for it, old man! I can't help you!" "Not help me! Why not?" "Why, he's one of Cassidy's best men—he's a vice president of the War Whoop League, and they talked of sending him to the State Legislature! Phil Connor! Great heavens!"

Jurgis sat silent with dismay. "Why, he can send you to Joliet, if he wants to!" declared the other.

"Can't I have Cassidy get me off before he finds out about it?" asked Jurgis, at length.

"Cassidy's out of town," the other answered. "I don't even know where he is." (The boss of the stock-yards had gone into hiding—having found that it is not possible for a man even to pretend to serve two masters, when the masters are at open war.)

That was a pretty mess, indeed. Poor Jurgis sat half-dazed—his pull had run up against a bigger pull, and he was down and out! "But what am I going to do?" he asked, weakly.

"How should I know?" said the other. "I shouldn't even dare to get bail for you—why, I might ruin myself for life!"

Again there was silence. "Can't you do it," Jurgis asked, "and pretend that you didn't know who I'd hit?"

"But what good would that do you when you came to stand trial?" asked Harper. He sat buried in thought. "There's nothing—unless it's this: I could do as you say, and have your bail reduced; and then if you had the money you could pay it, and forfeit your bail and skip."

Jurgis did not understand this, until it was explained at length. "How much will it be?" he asked finally.

"I don't know," said the other. "How much do you own?"

"I've got about three hundred dollars saved," was the answer.

"Well," was Harper's reply. "I'm not sure, but I'll try and get you off for that. I'll take the risk for friendship's sake—I'd hate to see you sent to state's prison for a year or two."

So finally Jurgis ripped out his bank-book—which was sewed up in his trousers—and signed an order, which "Bush" Harper wrote, for all the money to be paid to him. Then the latter went and got it, and hurried to the court, and explained to the magistrate that Jurgis was a decent fellow and a friend of Cassidy's who had been attacked by a strike-breaker. So the bail was made three hundred dollars, and Harper went on it himself; he did not tell this to Jurgis, however—nor did he tell him that when the time for trial came it would be an easy matter for him to avoid the forfeiting of the bail and pocket the three hundred dollars as his reward for the risk of offending Tom Cassidy! All that he said, when he came with the bond, was that Jurgis was free, and that the best thing he could do was to get out of the neighborhood as quickly as possible; and poor Jurgis overwhelmed with gratitude and relief, took the dollar and fourteen cents that was left him on his bank-account, and put it with the two dollars and a quarter that was left from his last night's celebration, and boarded a street-car and got off at the other end of Chicago, an outcast and a tramp once more.

JURGIS had come into conflict with one of the creatures of the jungle whose power was greater than his own; and he had been worsted in the combat, beaten down and trampled upon, and left wounded and crippled, to drag himself away. He was literally crippled—as literally as any creature which has lost its claws, or been torn out of its shell; he had been shorn, at one cut, of all those mysterious weapons whereby he had been able to make a living easily, and to escape the consequences of his actions. He could no longer command a job when he wanted it; he could no longer steal with impunity —he must take his place in the common herd. Nay worse, he dared not mingle with the herd—he must hide by himself. He was one marked out for destruction. He could no longer frequent his old haunts. His old companions would betray him, for the sake of the influence they would gain thereby; and he would be made to suffer, not merely for the offense he had committed, but for others which would be laid at his door, just as had been done for some poor devil on the occasion of that "hold up" of the "country customer" by him and Duane.

And Jurgis labored under still another handicap since his fall. He had acquired new standards of living, and they were not easily to be altered. When he had been out of work before he had been content if he could sleep in a doorway or under a truck out of the rain, and if he could get fifteen cents a day for saloon lunches. But now he desired all sorts of other things, and suffered because he had to do without them. He must have a drink now and then, a drink for its own sake, and apart from the food that came with it. The craving for it was strong enough to master every other consideration—he would have it, though it were his last nickel, and he had to starve the balance of the day in consequence.

Jurgis became once more a besieger of factory gates. But never since he had been in Chicago had he stood less chance of getting a job than just then. For one thing, there was the economic crisis, the million or two of men who had been out of work in the spring and summer, and were not yet all back, by any means. Then there was the "Beef Strike," with seventy thousand men and women all over the country idle for a couple of months—twenty thousand in Chicago, and many of them now seeking work throughout the city. It did not remedy matters that a few days later the strike was given up and about half the strikers went back to work; for nearly every one taken on, there was a "scab" who gave up his job and fled from Packingtown. So the huge cesspool of vice and crime that the yards had been was drained into the city; the ten or fifteen thousand of "green" negroes, foreigners and criminals, gathered from all over the country, were turned loose to shift for themselves. Everywhere Jurgis went he kept meeting them, and he was in an agony of fear lest any one of them should know that he was "wanted." He would have left Chicago, save by the time he had realized his danger he was almost penniless; and the cold weather was coming, and the "hoboes" flocking into the city. It would be better to go to jail than be caught out in the country in the winter time.

At the end of about ten days Jurgis had only a few pennies left—and he had not yet found a job—not even a day's work at anything, not even a chance to carry a satchel. As before, when he had come out of the hospital, he was absolutely defenseless—bound hand and foot, and facing the grisly phantom of starvation. Raw, naked terror possessed him, a maddening passion that would never leave him, and that wore him down more quickly than the actual want of food. He was going to perish of hunger! The fiend reached out its scaly arms for him again—it touched him, its breath came into his face; and he would cry out for the horror of it, he would wake up in the night, shuddering, and bathed in perspiration, and start up and flee. He would walk, begging for work, until he was exhausted; he could not remain still—he would wander on, gaunt and haggard, gazing about him with restless eye, seeking, seeking for the chance that never came. Everywhere he went, from one end of the vast city to the other, there were hundreds of others like him; and everywhere the sight of plenty—and the merciless hand of authority waving them away. There is one kind of prison where the man is behind bars and everything that he desires is outside; and there is another kind where the things are behind the bars, and the man is outside.

When he was down to his last quarter Jurgis learned that before the bake-shops closed at night they sold out what was left at half price, and after that he would go and get two loaves of stale bread for a nickel, and break them up and stuff his pockets with them, munching a bit from time to time. He would not spend a penny save for this; and, after two or three days more, he even became sparing of the bread, and would stop and peer into the ash-barrels as he walked along the streets, and now and then rake out a bit of something, shake it free from dust, and count himself just so many minutes further from the end.

So, for several days he had been going about, ravenous all the time, and growing weaker and weaker; and then one morning he had a hideous experience, that almost broke his heart. He was passing down a street lined with warehouses and stacked with boxes and barrels. Before one of the buildings several empty trucks were lined up, loaded by men under the direction of a big Irishman, and Jurgis was already making for him, when he called: "Hey, there! Want a job?"

"Yes, sir!" Jurgis answered in a flash. "Get to work, then," said the man, and the other flung off his coat and started. But before he had time to touch one of the boxes he heard the boss's voice again: "Hey, come here!"

Jurgis turned and went toward the man, who was eyeing him narrowly, his hollow, sunken cheeks and his yellow skin. "Less see your arms," he said: and as Jurgis held out one, in perplexity, he caught it just below the elbow and squeezed it.

Then he dropped it, with an exclamation of disgust. "Faugh!" he said. "It's all skin! You can't lift anything!"

Jurgis's heart gave a throb of fright. "I can, sir," he cried. "Try me!"

"Get out!" said the other, turning away; and as Jurgis followed him, pleading, he turned, clenching his great fists. "Get the hell out of here!" he cried; and Jurgis stood dumbfounded, about half a minute—just long enough to see two other men come up on the run, and to see one of them set to work at his job. Then he picked up his coat and walked off.

It was all that he could do to keep from crying like a baby. He was lost! He was doomed! There was no hope for him! But then, with a sudden rush, his fear gave place to rage. He fell to cursing. He would come back thereafter dark, and he would do that scoundrel up, by God he'd show him whether his arms were "all skin" or not!

Then suddenly, at the corner, he came upon a green-grocery, with a tray full of cabbages in front of it. Jurgis gave one swift glance about him, and stooped and seized the biggest of them, and darted around the corner with it. There was a hue and cry, and a score of men and boys started in chase of him; but he came to an alley, and then to an other branching off from it and leading him into another street, where he fell into a walk, and slipped his cabbage under his coat and went off unsuspected in the crowd. When he had gotten a safe distance away he sat down and devoured half the cabbage raw, stowing the balance away in his pockets till the next day.

Just about this time one of the Chicago newspapers, which made a great fuss over the "common people," opened a "free-soup" kitchen for the benefit of the unemployed. Some people said that they did this for the sake of the advertising it gave them, and some others said that the motive which influenced them was a fear lest all their readers should be starved off; but whatever the motive, the soup was thick and hot, and there was a bowl for every man, all night long. When Jurgis heard of this, from a fellow "hobo," he vowed that he would have half a dozen bowls before morning; but, as it proved, he was lucky to get one, for there was a line of men two blocks long before the stand, and there was just as long a line when the place was finally closed up.

This depot was within the danger-line for Jurgis—in the "Levee" district, where he was known, but he went there, all the same, for he was desperate, and beginning to think of even the Bridewell as a place of refuge. So far the weather had been fair, and he had slept out every night in a vacant lot; but now there fell suddenly a shadow of the advancing winter, a chill wind, howling from the north, and a driving storm of rain. And that day Jurgis bought two drinks for the sake of the shelter, and at night he spent his last two pennies in a "stale-beer dive." Men drew off the old dregs of beer that lay in the barrels set outside of the saloons to be carted away, and, after they had doctored it with chemicals to make it "fizz," they sold it in horrible cellar dives for two cents a can, the purchase of a can including the privilege of sleeping the night through upon the floor, with a mass of degraded outcasts, men and women.

The next morning Jurgis went out again to beg for his life. But it was still raining, and people would not stop for anything he might say. He begged all day and got not a cent, and it was nearly dark before he could find anyone to listen to him. Then he saw an old lady with an umbrella and a bundle trying to get off a car, and under the very eyes of a policeman he rushed forward to help her to the sidewalk. As she paused to rest under an awning, he began his oft-repeated "hard-luck story."

The old lady wore spectacles and a straight-laced black dress, and eyed him like a hawk, sniffing at him suspiciously. But he had had nothing to drink all day, and the rain had washed the odor of the dive out of him. Not a word of the story he was telling her was true, but he had learned to do the work scientifically, and he looked hungry enough for any role.

"Every time I give a man money he goes to a saloon with it," said the old lady; to which he answered, breathlessly, "I never drink, ma'am—not a drop. My word of honor, ma'am. I'm an honest workingman—"

"Do you belong to the church?" inquired the other, severely.

"Yes, ma'am," said, Jurgis, with desperate seriousness, and striving to think of what church this victim might be a member. "I belong to the Meth'dis' church, ma'am, and to the Presbyterium, ma'am—"

"How do you belong to two churches?" she demanded.

"I don't know, ma'am," he answered, "but I do—that is, I've been in places where there was only one. That was when I lived in Missouri, where my home was burned down—"

"What town was that?" Jurgis named a town near which he had worked in the harvest-fields, and he saw that he had "landed." "I came from Missouri myself," said the old lady—"the western part, though."

"Yes, ma'am," said Jurgis. "And I haven't been able to get a mouthful all day, ma'am, and nobody will help me—"

"Will you go with me to get something to eat?" queried the other; to which he answered "Yes, ma'am," in a flash.

She took him to a cheap restaurant, and paid the proprietor a quarter, and told him to see that Jurgis had a dinner. And so he ate soup and bread, and boiled beef, and potatoes and beans. Then—the old lady having of course left—the proprietor told Jurgis to "git;" but he, having been sharp enough to look at the bill-of-fare, announced that he had corned beef and cabbage and pie and coffee still coming to him; and when the proprietor tried to bluster it out, he backed up against the wall and declared that he would wreck the place before he would leave without his rights. As several people in the restaurant had seen the quarter paid, the other had to give in, and so when Jurgis left it was with a skin stuffed as tight as a foot-ball.

Nor did good fortune come singly. When he came out of the restaurant, into the rain and the darkness, far down the street he saw red lights flaring and heard the thumping of a bass-drum. His heart gave a leap, and he made for the place on the run—he knew without the asking that it must be a political meeting.

Though a political campaign, alas, no longer meant to Jurgis what it had once meant, he knew that one was in full swing just now. Within five or six weeks the voters of the country would select a president; and that would mean at least one day of prosperity for all the outcasts and wretches of the city. They talked about it with eager expectation, and were duly appreciative of the advantages of living in a republic.

The campaign had so far been characterized by what the newspapers termed "apathy." For some reason or other the people refused to get excited over the struggle, and it was almost impossible to get them to come to meetings, or to make any noise when they did come. Those which had been held in Chicago so far had proven most dismal failures, and tonight, the speaker being no less a personage than a candidate for the vice presidency of the nation, the political managers had been trembling with anxiety—when a merciful Providence had sent this storm of cold rain; and now all it was necessary to do was to set off a few fireworks, and thump awhile on a drum outside of the hall, and all the homeless wretches from a mile around would pour in! And then on the morrow the newspapers would have a chance to report a tremendous ovation, and to add that it had been no "silk-stocking" audience, either, which proved that the high tariff sentiments of the distinguished candidate were pleasing to the wage-earners of the nation.

Jurgis found himself in a large hall, elaborately decorated with flags and bunting; and after the chairman had made his little speech, and the orator of the evening rose up, amid an uproar from the band, Jurgis was astonished to discover that he was none other than the famous and eloquent Senator Spareshanks, who had addressed the "Wendel Republican Association" at the stock yards, and helped to elect Tom Cassidy's ten-pin-setter to the Chicago Board of Alderman.

The sight of Senator Spareshanks almost brought the tears into Jurgis's eyes. What agony it was to him to look back upon those golden hours—the hours when he, too, had a place beneath the shadow of the plum-tree! When he, too, had been within the magic circle of the elect through whom the country is governed—when he had had a little bung in the campaign-barrel for his own! It was almost like a dream, he could scarcely believe that it was true. Sitting here, a forlorn and homeless wretch, without a single penny in his pockets, what a maddening thing it was to be suddenly confronted with the vision of last spring—to be reminded that this was another election in which the Republicans had the barrel, and that but for one hideous accident he as well as Senator Spareshanks, might have a hand in it.

The eloquent senator was explaining the system of Protection; an ingenious device whereby the workingman voted to enable the manufacturer to charge him higher prices, in order that the manufacturer might, in turn, pay him higher wages; thus taking his money out of his pocket with one hand, and putting a part of it back with the other. To the eloquent senator this unique arrangement had somehow become identified with the higher verities of the universe, and the tears came into his eyes and his voice shook with fervor as he spoke of it. It was because of this arrangement that Columbia was the gem of the ocean; and all her future triumphs, her power and good repute among the nations, depended upon the zeal and fidelity with which each citizen held up the hands of those who were toiling to maintain it against the forces of treason and disruption. The name of the heroic company was "the Grand Old Party"—

And here the band began to play, and Jurgis sat up with a violent start. Singular as it may seem, Jurgis was making a desperate effort to understand what the eloquent senator was saying—to comprehend the high destinies of the American republic, the astounding extent of her prosperity, the enormous expansion of her commerce, her future in the Pacific and in South America, and wherever else the oppressed were groaning. The reason for it was that he wanted to keep awake. He knew that if he allowed himself to fall asleep he would begin to snore loudly; and so he must listen—he must be thrilled, like everyone else. But he had eaten such a big dinner, and he was so exhausted, and the hall was so warm, and his seat was so comfortable! The eloquent senator's gaunt form began to grow dim and hazy, to rise up before him and dance about, with figures of exports and imports, and Chinese cotton-statistics and dragons; until suddenly the band struck up "Hail Columbia," and he sat erect.

But it was only to begin all over again. In ten minutes he was snoring once more. His neighbor gave him a savage poke in the ribs, and he sat up again and tried to look innocent; but then he was at it again, and men began to stare at him with annoyance and to call out with vexation. Finally one of them called a policeman, who came and grabbed Jurgis by the collar, and jerked him to his feet, bewildered and terrified. Some of the audience turned to see the commotion, and Senator Spareshanks faltered in his speech; but a voice shouted cheerily: "We're just firing a bum! Go ahead, old sport!" And so the crowd roared, and the senator smiled genially, and went on. And in a few seconds poor Jurgis found himself landed out in the rain with a kick and a string of curses.

He got into the shelter of a doorway and took stock of himself. He was not hurt, and he was not arrested—more than he had any right to expect. He swore at himself and his luck for awhile, and then turned his thoughts to practical maters. He had no money, and no place to sleep; he must try begging again.

He went out, hunching his shoulders together and shivering at the touch of the icy rain. Coming down the direct toward him was a lady, well dressed, and protected by an umbrella. He turned and walked beside her. "Please, ma'am," he began, "could you lend me the price of a night's lodging? I'm a poor workingman—"

Then suddenly he stopped short. By the light of a street-lamp he had caught sight of the lady's face. It was Alena Jasaitis!

Alena Jasaitis, who had been the belle of the wedding-feast! Who had looked so beautiful, and danced with such a queenly air, with Juozas Raczius, the teamster! Jurgis had only seen her once or twice afterwards, for Juozas had thrown her over for another girl, and Alena had gone away from Packingtown, no one knew where. And now he met her here!

She was as much surprised as he was. "Jurgis Rudkos!" she gasped. "And what in the world is the matter with you?"

"I—I've had hard luck," he stammered. "I'm out of work, and I've no home and no money. And you, Alena—are you married?" (He was looking at her fine clothes.)

"No," she answered, "I'm not married, but I've got a good place."

They stood staring at each other for a few moments. Finally Alena spoke. "Jurgis," she said, "I'd help you if I could, upon my word I would, but it just happens that I've come out without my purse, and I honestly haven't a penny with me. I can do something better for you, though—I can tell you how to get help. I can tell you where Marija is."

Jurgis gave a start. "Marija!"

"Yes" said Alena; "and she'll help you. She's got a place, and she's doing well, and she'll be glad to see you."

It was not much more than a year since Jurgis had left Packingtown, feeling like one escaped from jail; and it had been from Marija and Elzbieta that he was escaping! But now, at the mere mention of them, his whole being cried out with joy. He wanted to see them; he wanted to go home! They would help him—they would be kind to him. In a flash he had thought over the situation. He had a good excuse for running away—his grief at the death of his son; and also he had a good excuse for not returning—the fact that they had left Packingtown, and gone no one knew where. "All right," he said, "I'll go."

So she gave him a number on Clark street, and added: "There's no need to give you my address, because Marija knows it." And Jurgis set out, without further ado, and found a large brown-stone house of aristocratic appearance, and rang the basement bell. A young colored girl came to the door, opening it about an inch, and gazing at him suspiciously.

"What do you want?" she demanded.

"Does Marija Biarczynskas live here?" he inquired.

"I dunno," said the girl. "What you want wid her?"

"I want to see her," said he; "she's a relative of mine."

The girl hesitated a moment. Then she opened the door and said, "Come in." Jurgis came and stood in the hall, and she continued, "I'll go see. What's yo' name?"

"Tell her it's Jurgis," he answered, and the girl went up-stairs. She came back at the end of a minute or two, and replied: "Dey ain't no sich person here."

Jurgis's heart went down into his boots. "I was told this was where she lived!" he cried.

But the girl only shook her head. "De lady says dey ain't no sich person here," she said.

And he stood for a moment, hesitating, helpless with dismay. Then he turned to go to the door. At the same instant, however, there came a knock upon it, and the girl went to open it. Jurgis heard the shuffling of feet, and then heard her give a startled cry; and the next instant she sprang back, and past him, her eyes shining white with terror. She bounded up the stairway, screaming at the top of her lungs: *"Police! Police! We're pinched!"*

JURGIS stood for a second, bewildered. Then, seeing blue-coated forms rushing upon him, he sprang after the negress. Her cries had been the signal for a wild uproar above; the house was full of people, and as he entered the hallway he saw them rushing hither and thither, crying and screaming with alarm. There were men and women, the latter clad for the most part in wrappers, the former in all stages of *deshabille*. At one side Jurgis caught a glimpse of a big apartment with plush-covered chairs, and tables covered with trays and glasses. There were playing-cards scattered all over the floor—one of the tables had been upset and bottles of wine were rolling about, their contents running out upon the carpet. There was a young girl who had fainted, and two men who were supporting her; and there were a dozen others, rushing towards the front door.

Suddenly, however, there came a series of resounding blows upon it, causing the crowd to give back. At the same instant a stout woman, with painted cheeks and diamonds in her ears, came running down the stairs, panting breathlessly, "To the rear! Quick!" She led the way to a back staircase, Jurgis following with the throng; in the kitchen she pressed a spring, and a cupboard gave way and opened, disclosing a dark passageway. "Go in!" she cried, to the crowd, which now amounted to twenty or thirty, and they began to pass through. Scarcely had the last one disappeared, however, before there were cries from in front, and then the panic-stricken throng poured out again, exclaiming: "They're there, too! We're trapped!"

"Upstairs!" shouted the woman, and there was another rush of the mob, women and men cursing and screaming and fighting to be first. One flight, two, three—and then there was a ladder to the roof, with a throng packed at the foot of it, and one man at the top, straining and struggling to lift the trap-door. It was not to be stirred, however, and when the woman shouted up to unhook it, he answered: "It's already unhooked. There's somebody sitting on it!"

A moment later came a voice of authority from down-stairs: "You might as well quit, you people. We mean business, this time."

So the crowd subsided; and a few moments later several policemen came up, staring here and there, and leering at their victims. Of the latter the men were for the most part frightened and sheepish-looking. The women took it as a joke, as if they were used to it—though if they had been pale one could not have told, for the paint on their cheeks. One black-eyed young girl perched herself upon the top of the balustrade, and began to kick with her slippered foot at the helmets of the policemen, until one of them caught her by the ankle and pulled her down. On the floor below four or five other girls sat upon trunks in the hall, making fun of the procession which filed by them. They were noisy and hilarious, and had evidently been drinking; one of them, who wore a bright red kimona, shouted and cried in a voice that drowned out all the other sounds in the hall—and Jurgis took a glance at her, and then gave a start, and a cry: "Marija!"

She heard him, and glanced around; then she shrunk back and half sprang to her feet in her amazement. "Jurgis!" she gasped.

For a second or two they stood staring at each other. "How did you come here?" Marija panted.

"I came to see you," he answered.

"When?"

"Just now."

"But how did you know—who told you I was here?"

"Alena Jasaitis. I met her on the street."

Again there was a silence, while they gazed at each other. The rest of the crowd was watching them, and so Marija got up and came closer. "And you?" Jurgis asked. "You live here?"

"Yes," said Marija, "I live here."

Then suddenly came a hail from below: "Get your clothes on now, girls, and come along. You'd best begin, or you'll be sorry—it's raining outside."

"Br-r-r!" shivered someone, and the women got up and entered the various doors which lined the hallway.

"Come," said Marija, and took Jurgis into her room, which was a tiny place about eight by six, with a cot and a chair and a dressing-stand and some dresses hanging behind the door. There were clothes scattered about on the floor, and hopeless confusion everywhere—boxes of rouge and bottles of perfume mixed with hats and soiled dishes on the dresser, and a pair of slippers and a clock and a whiskey-bottle on a chair.

Marija had nothing on but a kimona and a pair of stockings; yet she proceeded to dress before Jurgis, and without even taking the trouble to close the door. He had by this time divined what sort of a place he was in; and he had seen a great deal of the world since he had left home, and was not easy to shock—and yet it gave him a painful start that Marija should do this. They had always been decent people at home, and it seemed to him that the memory of old times ought to have ruled her. But then he laughed at himself for a fool. What was he, to be pretending to decency!

"How long have you been living here?" he asked.

"Nearly a year," she answered.

"Why did you come?"

"I had to," she said; "I had to live. And I couldn't see the children starve."

"You were out of work?" he asked.

"I got sick," she replied, and after that I had no money. And Elzbieta was sick, too, and then little Stanislovas died—"

"Stanislovas dead!"

"Yes," said Marija, "I forgot. You didn't know about it."

"How did he die?"

"The rats killed him."

Jurgis gave a gasp. "Rats killed him!"

"Yes," said the other; she was bending over lacing her shoes as she spoke. "He was working in an oil-factory—at least he was hired by the men to get their beer. He used to carry cans on a long pole. And he'd drink a little out of each can, and one day he drank too much, and fell asleep in a corner, and got locked up in the place all night. When they found him the rats had killed him and eaten him nearly all up."

Jurgis sat, frozen with horror. Marija went on lacing up her shoes. There was a long silence.

Suddenly a big policeman came to the door. "Hurry up, there," he said.

"As quick as I can," said Marija, and she stood up and began putting on her corsets, with feverish haste.

"Are the rest of the people alive?" asked Jurgis, finally.

"Yes," she said.

"Where are they?"

"They live not far from here. They're all right now."

"They are working?" he inquired.

"Elzbieta is," said Marija, "when she can. I take care of them most of the time—I'm making plenty of money now."

Jurgis was silent for a moment. "Do they know you live here—how you live?" he asked.

"Elzbieta knows," answered Marija. "I couldn't lie to her. And maybe the children have found out by this time. It's nothing to be ashamed of—we can't help it."

Marija was standing in front of the glass fastening her dress. He sat staring at her. He could hardly believe that she was the same Marija he had known in the old days; she was so quiet—so hard! It struck fear to his heart.

Suddenly she gave a glance at him. "You look as if you had been having a tough time of it yourself," she said.

"I have," he answered. "I haven't a cent in my pockets and nothing to do."

"Where have you been?"

"All over. I've been hoboing it. Then I went back to the yards—just before the strike." He paused for a moment, hesitating. "I asked for you," he added. "I found you had gone away—no one knew where. Perhaps you think I did you a dirty trick going away as I did, Marija—"

"No," she answered. "I don't blame you. We never have—any of us. You stood it longer than most men would have. You did your best—the job was too much for us. She paused a moment then added: "We were too ignorant—that was the trouble. We didn't stand any chance. If I'd known what I know now we'd have won out."

"You'd have come here?" Jurgis asked.

"Yes," she answered, "but that's not what I meant. I meant—you—how differently you would have behaved—about Ona—if you'd only had some sense."

Jurgis was silent; he had never thought of that aspect of it.

"When people are starving," the other continued, "and they have anything with a price, they ought to sell it, I say. I guess you realize it now when it's too late. Ona could have taken care of us all in the beginning."

Marija spoke without emotion, as one who had come to regard things from the business point of view. "I—yes, I guess so," Jurgis answered, hesitatingly. He did not add that he had paid three hundred dollars, and a foreman's job, for the satisfaction of knocking down the boss a second time.

The policeman came to the door again just then. "Come on, now," he said. "Lively!"

"All right," said Marija, reaching for her hat, which was big enough to be a drum-major's, and full of ostrich feathers. She went out into the hall and Jurgis followed, the policeman remaining to look under the bed behind the door.

"What's going to come of this?" Jurgis asked, as they started down the steps.

"The raid, you mean? Oh, nothing—it happens to us every now and then. The madam's having some sort of time with the police; I don't know what it is, but maybe they'll come to terms before morning. Anyhow, they won't do anything to you. They always let the men off."

"Maybe so," he responded, "but not me—I'm afraid I'm in for it."

"How do you mean?"

"I'm wanted by the police," he said, lowering his voice, in spite of the fact that their conversation was in Lithuanian. "They'll send me up for a year or two."

"Hell!" said Marija. "That's too bad. I'll see if I can't get you off."

Downstairs, where the greater part of the prisoners were now massed, she sought out the stout personage with the diamond earrings and had a few whispered words with her. The latter then approached the police-sergeant who was in charge of the raid. "Billy," she said, pointing to Jurgis, "there's a fellow who came in to see his sister. He'd just got in the door when you knocked. You aren't taking hoboes, are you?"

The sergeant laughed as he looked at Jurgis. "Sorry," he said, "but the orders are everyone but the servants."

So Jurgis slunk in among the rest of the men, who kept dodging behind each other like sheep that have smelled a wolf. There were old men and young men, college boys and gray-beards old enough to be their grand-fathers; some of them wore evening-dress—there was no one among them save Jurgis who showed any signs of poverty.

When the round-up was completed, the doors were opened and the party marched out. Three patrol-wagons were drawn up at the curb, and the whole neighborhood had turned out to see the sport; there was much chaffing, and a universal craning of necks. The women stared about them with defiant eyes, or laughed and joked, while the men kept their heads bowed, and their hats pulled over their eyes. They were crowded into the patrol-wagons as if into street-cars, and then off they went amid a din of cheers. At the station-house Jurgis gave a Polish name and was put into a cell with half a dozen others; and while these sat and talked in whispers, he lay down in a corner and gave himself up to his thoughts.

Jurgis had looked into the deepest reaches of the jungle, and grown used to the sights in them. Yet when he had thought of all humanity as vile and hideous, he had somehow always excepted his own family, that he had loved; and now this sudden horrible discovery—Marija a whore, and Elzbieta and the children living off her shame! Jurgis might argue with himself all he chose, that he had done worse, and was a fool for caring—but still he could not get over the shock of that sudden unveiling, he could not help being sunk in grief because of it. The depths of him were troubled and shaken, memories were stirred in him that had been sleeping so long he had counted them dead. Memories of the old life—his old hopes and his old yearnings, his old dreams of decency and independence! He saw Ona again, he heard her gentle voice pleading with him. He saw little Antanas, whom he had meant to make a man. He saw his trembling old father, who had blessed them all with his wonderful love. He lived again through that day of horror when he had discovered Ona's shame—God, how he had suffered, what a madman he had been! How dreadful it had all seemed to him—and now, today, he had sat and listened, and half agreed when Marija told him he had been a fool! Yes—told him that he ought to have sold his wife's honor and lived by it!—And then there was Stanislovas and his awful fate—that brief story which Marija had narrated so calmly, with such dull indifference! The poor little fellow with his frost-bitten fingers and his terror of the snow—his wailing voice rang in Jurgis's ears, as he lay there in the darkness, until the sweat started on his forehead. Now and then he would quiver with a sudden spasm of horror, at the picture of little Stanislovas shut up in the deserted building and fighting for his life with the rats.

All these emotions had become strangers to the soul of Jurgis; it was so long since they had troubled him that he had ceased to think they might ever trouble him again. Helpless, trapped as he was, what good did they do him—why should he ever have allowed them to torment him? It had been the task of his life to fight them down, to crush them out of him; and never in his life would he have suffered this way again, save that they had caught him unawares, and overwhelmed him before he could protect himself. He heard the old voices of his soul, he saw its old ghosts beckoning to him, stretching out their arms to him; but they were far-off and shadowy, and the gulf between them was black and bottomless; they would fade away into the mists of the past and their voices would die, and never would he see or hear them—the last faint spark of manhood in his soul would flicker out.

AFTER BREAKFAST Jurgis was driven to the court, which was crowded with the prisoners and those who had come out of curiosity, or in the hope of recognizing one of the men and getting a case for blackmail. The men were called up first, and reprimanded in a bunch, and then dismissed; but Jurgis, to his terror, was called separately, as being a suspicious-looking case. It was in this very same court that he had been tried, that time when his sentence had been "suspended;" it was the same judge and the same clerk. The latter now stared at Jurgis, as if he half thought that he knew him; but the judge had no suspicions—just then his thoughts were upon a telephone-message he was expecting from a friend of the police-captain of the district, telling what disposition he should make of the case of "Polly" Simpson, as the "madam" of the house was known. Meantime, he listened to the story of how Jurgis had been looking for his sister, and advised him dryly to keep his sister in a better place; and then let him go, and proceeded to fine each of the girls five dollars, which fines were paid in a bunch from a wad of bills which Madam Polly extracted from her stocking.

Jurgis waited outside and walked home with Marija. The police had left the house, and already there were a few visitors; by evening the place would be running again, exactly as if nothing had happened. Meantime, Marija took Jurgis up-stairs to her room, and they sat and talked. By daylight, Jurgis was able to observe that the color on her cheeks was not the old natural one of abounding health; her complexion was in reality a parchment yellow, and there were black rings under her eyes.

"Have you been sick?" he asked.

"Sick?" she said. "Hell!" (Marija had learned to scatter her conversation with as many oaths as a longshoreman or a mule-driver.) "How can I ever be anything but sick, at this life?"

She fell silent for a moment, staring ahead of her gloomily, "It's morphine," she said, at last. "I seem to take more of it every day."

"What's that for?" he asked.

"It's the way of it; I don't know why. If it isn't that, it's drink. If the girls didn't booze they couldn't stand it any time at all. The madam would rather they took dope, of course, for that keeps them quiet—when they have had enough, they don't care what is done to them. She always gives it to them when they first come, and they learn to like it; or else they take it for headaches and such things, and get the habit that way. I've got it, I know; I've tried to quit, but I never will while I'm here."

"How long are you going to stay?" he asked.

"I don't know," she said. "Always, I guess. What else could I do?"

"Don't you save any money?"

"Save?" said Marija. "Good Lord, no! I get enough, I suppose, but it all goes. I get a half share, two dollars and a half for each customer, and sometimes I make twenty-five or thirty dollars a night, and you'd think I ought to save something out of that! But then I am charged for my room and my meals—and such prices as you never heard of; and then for extras, and drinks—for everything I get, and some I don't. My laundry bill is nearly twenty dollars each week alone—think of that! Yet what can I do? I either have to stand it or quit, and it would be the same anywhere else. It's all I can do to save the fifteen dollars I give Elzbieta each week, so the children can go to school."

Marija sat brooding in silence for a while; then, seeing that Jurgis was interested, she went on: "That's the way they keep the girls in these places—they let them run up debts, so they can't get away. A young girl comes from abroad, and she hasn't a friend to help her, and she doesn't know a word of English, and she gets into a place like this, and when she wants to go the madam shows her that she is a couple of hundred dollars in debt, and takes all her clothes away, and threatens to have her arrested if she doesn't stay and do as she's told. So she stays, and the longer she stays, the more in debt she gets. Often, too, they are girls that didn't know what they were coming to, that had hired out for house-work. Did you notice that little French girl with the yellow hair, that stood next to me in the court?"

Jurgis answered in the affirmative.

"Well, she came to America about a year ago. She was a store-clerk, and she hired herself to a man to be sent here to work in a factory. There were six of them, altogether, and they were brought to a house just down the street from here, and this girl was put into a room alone, and they gave her some dope in her food, and when she came to she found that she had been ruined. She cried, and screamed, and tore her hair, but she had nothing but a wrapper, and couldn't get away, and they kept her half insensible with drugs all the time, until she gave up. She never got outside of that place for ten months, and then they sent her away, because she didn't suit. I guess they'll put her out of here, too—she's getting to have crazy fits, from drinking absinthe. Only one of the girls that came out with her got away, and she jumped out of a second-story window one night. There was a great fuss about that—maybe you heard of it."

"I did," said Jurgis, "I heard of it afterwards." (It had happened in the place where he and Duane had taken refuge from their "country customer." The girl had become insane, fortunately for the police.) "I've seen something of that side of it myself," he added; "I knew a man who used to get forty dollars a head for girls he fetched from New York."

"There's lots of money in it," said Marija—"they bring them from all over. There are seventeen women in this place, and eleven different countries among them. In some places you might find even more. We have several French girls—I suppose it's because the madam speaks French herself. French girls are bad, too, worst of all, except for the Japanese. There's a place next door that's full of Japanese women. But I wouldn't live in a place where one of them was."

Marija paused for a moment or two, and then she added: "Most of the women here are pretty decent—you'd be surprised. I used to think that such women must be fiends; but fancy the idea that a woman would sell herself to ten or a dozen men in a day—every kind of man that comes, old or young, black or white—and do it because she liked to!"

"Some of them say they do," said the man.

"I know," said Marija; "they say anything. They're in, and they know they can't get out. And they dope themselves, and booze, and that helps them. But they didn't like it when they began—you'd find out it's just the same as it was with me—it's misery, always misery! There's a little Jewish girl here who used to run errands for a milliner, and got sick and lost her place. She was four days on the streets without a mouthful of food, and then she went to a place just around the corner and offered herself, and they made her give up her clothes before they would give her a bite to eat!"

"Do you know about Alena Jasaitis?" Marija asked, after a moment's silence.

"No," replied Jurgis; "is she—"

"Since last week," said the other. "She used to be a kept woman."

"I only had a few words with her," said Jurgis. "She seemed to be in a hurry to get away."

"She's very unhappy," Marija went on. "She takes it hard. She's so proud, you know—such a beauty, and she thought she wasn't like other girls. I suppose that people would say she fell because of badness. Maybe so; she sold herself for her teeth."

"Her teeth!"

"Yes—to save them. It was queer. After young Raczius threw her over, she began going with Higgins, her superintendent. He had no idea of marrying her, of course, and she knew it, but he gave her things and took her round, and I suppose she thought she could take care of herself. But then one day she had a bad toothache and went to the dentists, and he told her that all her teeth were decaying, and that if she didn't have them taken care of at once, she would lose them all. It would cost her nearly fifty dolars, he said, and Alena had always spent her money on herself, and hadn't a penny saved. She always dressed like a lady, you know—I suppose she thought she would make a better catch, and come out ahead in the end. But just then her brother fell ill, and she had to support the family; and so the dentist told her that the only thing to do would be to have all her teeth pulled out, and a set of false ones made. She could have that done for fourteen dollars, and he would be willing to trust her for that. Poor Alena nearly cried her eyes out. She had the toothache all the time, of course, but still she couldn't make up her mind. It would have disfigured her for life, you see. In the end she made a date with the dentist, but she couldn't get up the courage to keep it, and instead she went and told Higgins about it. He was very decent, and gave her the fifty dollars; only that night he took her to a hotel, and she hadn't the courage to refuse him. And soon after that she left Packingtown, and he kept her in a flat; but a couple of months ago he brought another girl there, and she wouldn't stand for that, and left him. Then she tried to find work, and when she couldn't she went out on the streets for herself. But the police caught her the first week—a woman can't do business alone here in Chicago, you know, for they charge her more than she can earn, so last week Alena went into a house around on Custom-House Place, and that will be the end of all her pride."

Marija sat for a minute or two, brooding somberly. "Tell me about yourself, Jurgis," she said, suddenly. "Where have you been?"

So he told her the long story of his adventures, since his flight from home; his life as a tramp, and his work in the freight-tunnels, and the accident; and then of "Jack Duane" and the Wheelers, of his political career in the stock-yards, and his downfall and subsequent failures. Marija listened with sympathy; it was easy to believe his tale of his late starvation, for his face showed it all. "You found me just in the nick of time," she said. "I'll stand by you—I'll help you till you can get some work."

"I don't like to let you—" he began.

"Why not? Because I'm here?"

"No, not that," he said. "But I went off and left you"—

"Nonsense!" said Marja. "Don't think about it. I don't blame you.—You must be hungry," she said, after a minute or two. "You stay here to lunch—I'll have something up in the room."

She pressed a button, and a colored woman came to the door and took her order. "It's nice to have somebody to wait on you," she observed, laughing, as she lay back on the bed.

As the prison breakfast had not been liberal, Jurgis had a good appetite, and they had a little feast together, talking meanwhile of Elzbieta and the children, and old times. Shortly before they were through there came another colored girl, with the message that the "Madam" wanted Marija—"Lithuanian Mary," as they called her here.

"That means you have to go," she said to Jurgis.

So he got up, and she gave him the new address of the family, a tenement over in the ghetto district. "You go there," she said. "They'll be glad to see you."

But Jurgis stood hesitating. "I—I don't like to," he said. "Honest, Marija, why don't you just give me a little money and let me look for work first?"

"What do you need with money?" was her reply. "All you want is something to eat and a place to sleep, isn't it?"

"Yes," he said, "but then I don't like to go there after I left them—and while I have nothing to do, and while you—you—"

"Go on!" said Marija, giving him a push. "What are you talking? I won't give you money," she added, as she followed him to the door, "because you'll drink it up, and do yourself harm. Here's a quarter for you now, and go along, and they'll be so glad to see you, you won't have time to feel ashamed. Good-bye!"

Jurgis went out and walked down the street to think it over. He changed his mind every five or ten minutes. First he would go and face it out, and then he wouldn't; he kept wandering, now a block towards the place, and now a block away from it. It was curious to him to look back upon this, as he did in after times, when he realized the importance of the issue that had been at stake. He decided that he would first try to get work, and so he put in the rest of the day wandering here and there among factories and warehouses without success. Then, when it was nearly dark, he concluded to go home, and set out; but he came to a restaurant, and went in and spent his quarter for a meal, and when he came out he changed his mind once more—the night was pleasant, and he would sleep somewhere outside, and put in the morrow hunting. So he started away again, only to begin hesitating and doubting once more—which was his state of mind when suddenly he chanced to look about him, and found that he was passing down the same street and past the same hall where he had listened to the political speech the night before. There was no red fire and no band now, but there was a sign out, announcing a meeting, and a stream of people pouring in through the entrance. In a flash it came over him that he might go in again, and sit down and rest while making up his mind what to do. There was no one taking tickets, so it must be another free show.

He entered. There were no decorations in the hall this time—only a big flag, a strange flag to Jurgis. There was quite a crowd upon the platform, and almost every seat in the hall was filled. He took one himself, as far in the rear as he could, and straightway forgot all about where he was. Would Elzbieta think that he had come to sponge off her, or would she understand that he meant to get to work again and do his share? Would she be decent to him, or would she scold him for having run away? If only he could get some sort of a job before he went—if that last fellow had only been willing to try him!

Then suddenly Jurgis looked up. A tremendous roar had burst from the throats of the crowd, which by this time had packed the hall to the very doors. Men and women were standing up, waving handkerchiefs, shouting, yelling. Evidently the speaker had arrived, thought Jurgis; how absurdly they were behaving. What were they expecting to get out of it anyhow—what had they to do with elections, with the governing of the country? Jurgis had been behind the scenes in politics.

He went back to his thoughts, with only one further fact to reckon with— that he was caught here. The hall was now filled to the doors; and after the meeting it would be too late for him to go home, so he would have to make the best of it outside, for that night. Perhaps it would be better to go home in the morning, anyway, for the children would be at school, and he and Elzbieta could have a quiet explanation. She always had been a reasonable person; and he really did mean to do right. He would manage to persuade her of it—and besides, Marija was willing, and Marija was furnishing the money. If Elzbieta were ugly he would tell her that, in so many words.

So Jurgis went on meditating; until finally, when he had been nearly two hours in the hall, there began to prepare itself a repetition of the dismal catastrophe of the night before. Speaking had been going on all the time, and the audience was clapping its hands and shouting, thrilling with excitement; and little by little the sounds were beginning to blur in Jurgis's ears, and his thoughts were beginning to run together, and his head to wobble and nod. He caught himself many times, as usual, and made desperate resolutions; but the hall was hot and close, and his long walk and his dinner were too much for him again—in the end his head sunk forward and he went to sleep.

And then someone nudged him, and he sat up with his old terrified start. He had been snoring again, of course. And now what? He fixed his eyes ahead of him with feverish intensity, staring at the platform as if nothing else ever had interested him, or ever could interest him all his life. He imagined the angry exclamations, the hostile glances; and he imagined the policeman striding towards him—reaching for his neck. Or was he to have one more chance? Were they going to let him alone this time? He sat trembling, waiting.

Then suddenly came a voice in his ear—a woman's voice, gentle and sweet: "If you would try to listen, comrade, perhaps you would be interested."

Jurgis was more startled by that than he would have been by the touch of a policeman. He still kept his eyes fixed ahead and did not stir; but his heart gave a great leap. Comrade! Who was it that called him comrade?

He waited, long, long; and at last, when he was sure that he was no longer watched, he stole a glance out of the corner of his eyes at the woman who sat beside him. She was young and beautiful; she wore fine clothes, and was what is called a "lady." And she called him "Comrade!"

He turned a little, carefully, so that he could see her better; then he began to watch her, fascinated. She had apparently forgotten all about him, and was looking towards the platform. A man was speaking there; Jurgis heard his voice vaguely, but all his thoughts were for this woman's face. A feeling of alarm stole over him as he stared at her. It made his flesh creep. What was the matter with her, what could be going on, to affect anyone like that? She sat like one turned to stone, her hands clenched tightly in her lap, so tightly that he could see the cords in them. There was a look of excitement upon her face, of tense effort, as of one struggling mightily, or witnessing a struggle. There was a faint quivering of her nostrils; and now and then she would moisten her lips with feverish haste. Her bosom rose and fell as she breathed, and her excitement seemed to mount higher and higher, and then to sink away again, like a boat tossing upon ocean surges. What was it? What was the matter? It must be something that the man was saying, up there on the platform. What sort of a man was he? And what sort of a meeting was this, anyhow. So all at once it occurred to Jurgis to look at the speaker.

32

IT WAS like coming suddenly upon some wild sight of nature—a mountain forest lashed by a tempest, a ship tossed about upon a stormy sea. Jurgis had an unpleasant sensation, a sense of confusion, of disorder, of wild and meaningless uproar. The man was tall and gaunt, as haggard as his auditor himself; a thin black beard covered half of his face, and one could see only two black hollows where the eyes were. He was speaking rapidly, in great excitement; he used many gestures—as he spoke he moved here and there upon the stage, as if he were reaching with his long arms to seize each person in his audience. His voice was deep, like an organ; it was some time, however, before Jurgis thought of the voice—he was too much occupied with his eyes to think of what the man was saying. But suddenly it seemed as if the speaker had begun pointing his finger at him, as if he had singled him out particularly for his remarks and so he became suddenly aware of the voice, trembling, vibrant with emotion, with pain and longing, with a burden of things unutterable, not to be compassed by words. To hear it was to be suddenly arrested, to be gripped, transfixed.

"You listen to these things," the man was saying, "and you say, 'Yes, they are true, but they have been that way always.' Or you say, 'Maybe it will come, but not in my time—it will not help me.' And so you return to your daily round of toil, you go back to be ground up for profits in the world-wide mill of economic might. To toil long hours for another's advantage; to live in mean and squalid homes, to work in dangerous and unhealthful places; to wrestle with the spectres of hunger and privation, to take your chances of accident, disease and death. And each day the struggle becomes fiercer, the pace more cruel; each day you have to toil a little harder, each day the iron hand of circumstance closes upon you a little tighter. Months pass, years maybe—and then you come again; and again I am here to plead with you, to know if want and misery have yet done their work with you, if injustice and oppression have yet opened your eyes! I shall still be waiting—there is nothing else that I can do. There is no wilderness where I can hide from these things; though I travel to the ends of the earth I find them there. I find the same accursed system whereby all the powers of humanity, all the fair and noble impulses of the spirit, the dreams of poets and the agonies of martyrs, are shackled and bound in the service of organized and predatory Greed! And, therefore, I cannot rest, I cannot be silent; therefore I cast aside comfort and happiness, health and good repute, and go out into the world and cry out the pain of my spirit; therefore, I am not to be silenced by poverty and sickness, not by hatred and obloquy, by threats and ridicule—not by prison and persecution, if they should come—not by any power that is upon the earth or above the earth, that was, or is, or ever can be created. If I fail tonight, I can only try tomorrow; knowing that the fault must be mine, knowing that if once the vision of my soul were spoken upon earth, if once the anguish of its defeat were uttered in human speech, it would break the stoutest barriers of prejudice, it would shake the most sluggish soul to action; it would abash the most cynical, it would terrify the most selfish; and the voice of mockery would be silenced, and fraud and falsehood would slink back into their dens, and the truth would stand forth alone! For I speak with the voice of the millions who are voiceless; of them that are oppressed and have no comforter; of the disinherited of life, for whom there is no respite and no deliverance, to whom the world is a prison, a dungeon of torture, a tomb! With the voice of the little child who toils tonight in a Southern cotton-mill, staggering with exhaustion, numb with agony, and knowing no hope but the grave! Of the mother who sews by candle-light in her tenement-garret, weary and weeping, smitten with the mortal hunger of her babes! Of the man who lies upon a bed of rags, wrestling in his last sickness and leaving his loved ones to perish! Of the young girl who, somewhere, at this moment, is walking the streets of this horrible city, beaten and starving, and making her choice between the brothel and the lake! With the voice of those, whoever and wherever they may be, who are caught beneath the wheels of the juggernaut of Greed! With the voice of humanity, calling for deliverance; of the everlasting soul of Man, arising from the dust—breaking its way out of its prison-house—rending the bands of oppression and ignorance—groping its way to the light!"

The speaker paused. There was an instant of silence, while men caught their breaths, and then like a single sound there, came a cry from a thousand people.—Through it all Jurgis sat still, motionless and rigid, his eyes fixed upon the speaker. He was trembling, smitten with wonder.

Suddenly the man raised his hands, and silence fell, and he began again, in a quieter voice.

"I am here tonight," he said, "to plead with you, whoever you may be, provided that you care about the truth; but most of all I plead with working-men, with those to whom the evils I have portrayed are not mere matters of sentiment, to be dallied and toyed with, and then perhaps put aside and forgotten—to whom they are the grim and relentless realities of the daily grind, the chains upon their limbs, the lash upon their backs, the iron in their souls! To you, workingmen! To you, the toilers, who have made this land, and have no voice in its councils! To you, whose lot it is to sow that others may reap, to labor and obey, and ask no more than the wages of a beast of burden, the food and shelter to keep you alive from day to day. It is to you that I come with my message of salvation; it is with you that I plead. I know how much it is to ask of you—I know, for I have been in your place, I have lived your life—there is no man before me here tonight who knows it better. I have known what it is to be a street-waif, a boot-black, living upon a crust of bread, and sleeping in cellar-stairways and under empty wagons. I have known what it is to dare and to aspire, to dream mighty dreams, and to see them perish—to see all the fair flowers of my spirit trampled into the mire by the wild beast powers of the world. I know what is the price that a working-man pays for knowledge—I have paid for it with food and sleep, with agony of body and mind—with health, almost with life itself; and so, when I come to you with a story of hope and freedom, with the vision of a new earth to be created, of a new labor to be dared. I am not surprised that I find you sordid and material, sluggish and incredulous. These are the obstacles that lie before; and that they do not tempt me to despair is simply because I know also the forces that drive behind—because I know the raging lash of poverty, the sting of contempt and mastership, 'the insolence of office and the spurns.' Because I feel sure that in the crowd that has come here tonight, no matter how many may be dull and heedless, no matter how many may have come out of idle curiosity, or in order to ridicule—there will be some one man whom pain and suffering have made desperate, whom some chance vision of wrong and horror has startled and shocked into attention and readiness; and to whom my words will come like a sudden flash of lightning to one who travels in darkness, revealing the way before him, the perils and the obstacles—solving all problems, making all difficulties clear! And the scales will fall from his eyes, the shackles will be torn from his limbs—he will leap up with a cry of thankfulness, and stride forth a free man at last! A man delivered from his self-created slavery! A man who will never more be trapped, whom no blandishments will cajole, whom no threats will ever frighten; who from tonight on will move forward and not backward, who will study and read and understand, who will gird on his sword and take his place in the army of his comrades and brothers! Who will carry the good tidings to others, as I have carried them to him—the priceless gift of liberty and light, that is neither mine nor his, but is the heritage of the soul of man! Workingmen, work-ingmen—comrades! Open your eyes and look about you! You have lived so long in the toil and heat that your senses are dulled, your souls are numbed—but realize once in your lives this world in which you dwell—tear off the rags of its customs and conventions—behold it as it is, in all its hideous nakedness! Realize it, *realize it!* Realize that out upon the plains of Manchuria tonight two hostile armies are facing each other—that now, while we are seated here, a million human beings may be hurled at each other's throats, striving with the fury of maniacs to tear each other to pieces! And this in the twentieth century—nineteen hundred years since the Prince of Peace came down to earth! Nineteen hundred years since his words were first preached as divine, and now two armies of men are rending and tearing each other like the wild beasts of the jungle! Philosophers have reasoned, prophets have denounced, poets have wept and pleaded—and still this hideous Monster roams at large! We have schools and colleges, newspapers and books—we have searched the heavens and the earth, we have weighed and probed and reasoned—and all to equip men to destroy each other! We call it War, and pass it by—but do not put me off with platitudes and conventions—come with me, come with me—realize it! See the bodies of men pierced by bullets, blown into pieces by bursting shells! Hear the crunching of the bayonet, plunged into human flesh; hear the groans and shrieks of agony; see the faces of men crazed by pain, turned into fiends of fury and hate! Put your hand upon that piece of flesh—it is hot and quivering—just now it was a part of a man! This blood is still steaming—it was driven by a human heart! Almighty God! and this goes on—it is systematic, organized, premeditated—and we know it, and read of it, and take it for granted—our papers tell of it, and the presses are not stopped—our churches know of it, and do not close their doors—the people behold it, and do not rise up in horror and revolution!

"Or perhaps Manchuria is too far away for you—come home with me then, come here to Chicago. Here in this city tonight ten thousand women are shut up in pens, and driven by hunger to sell their bodies. And we know it, we make it a jest! And these women are made in the image of your mothers, they may be your sisters, your daughters; the child whom you left at home tonight, whose laughing eyes will greet you in the morning—that fate may be waiting for her! Tonight in Chicago there are ten thousand men, homeless and wretched, willing to work and begging for a chance, yet starving, and fronting in terror the awful winter cold! Tonight in Chicago there are a hundred thou-sand children wearing out their strength and blasting their lives in the effort to earn their bread! There are a hundred thousand mothers who are living in misery and squalor, struggling to earn enough to feed their little ones! There are a hundred thousand old people, cast off and helpless, waiting for death to take them from their torments! There are a million people, men and women and children, who share the fate of the wage-slave—who toil every hour they can stand and see, for just enough to keep them alive; who are condemned till the end of their days to monotony and weariness, to hunger and misery, to heat and cold, to dirt and disease, to ignorance and drunkenness and vice! And then—and then! There are a thousand—ten thousand, maybe—who are the masters of these slaves, who profit by their toil. They do nothing to earn what they receive, they do not even have to come for it—it comes to them of itself, their only care is to get rid of it. They live in palaces, they riot in luxury and extravagance—such as no words can describe, as makes the imagination reel and stagger, makes the soul grow sick and faint. They spend hundreds of dollars for a pair of shoes, a handkerchief, a garter; they spend thousands and tens of thousands for gowns, and flowers, and dogs. They spend millions for horses and automobiles and yachts, for palaces and banquets, for little shiny stones with which to deck their bodies. Their life is a contest among them-selves for supremacy in ostentation and recklessness, in the destroying of useful and necessary things, in the wasting of the labor and the lives of their fellow creatures, the toil and anguish of the nations, the sweat and tears and blood of the human race! It is all theirs—it comes to them; just as all the springs pour into streamlets, and the streamlets into rivers, and the rivers into the ocean—so, automatically and inevitably, all the wealth of society comes to them. The farmer tills the soil, the miner digs in the earth, the weaver tends the loom, the mason carves the stone; the clever man invents, the shrewd man directs, the wise man studies, the inspired man sings; and all the result, the products of the labor of brain and muscle, are gathered into one stupendous stream and poured into their laps! The forest is cleared and the land settled and civilized; railroads spread over it, mighty cities arise upon it; machines are devised, industrial systems are organized—and all for them! The whole of society is in their grip, the whole labor of the world lies at their mercy —and like fierce wolves they rend and destroy, like ravening vultures they devour and tear! The whole achievement of man belongs to them, forever and beyond recall—do what it can, strive as it will, the human race lives for them and dies for them! They own not merely the labor of society, they own the governments. In nations like America, which were once democracies, and in which the people's will stood in their way, they have accomplished a revolution by bribery; and everywhere they use their raped and stolen power to intrench themselves in their privileges, to dig wider and deeper the channels through which the river of profits flows to them! And you, workingmen, workingmen! You have been brought up to it, you plod on like beasts of burden, thinking only of the day and its pain—yet is there a man among you who can believe that such a system will continue forever—is there a man here in this audience so hardened and debased that he dare rise up before me and say that he believes it can continue forever, that the product of the labor of society, the means of existence of the human race, will always belong to a few idlers and parasites, to be spent for the gratification of vanity and lust—to be spent for any purpose whatever, to be at the disposal of any individual will whatever—that somehow, somewhen, the labor of humanity will not belong to humanity, to be used for the purposes of humanity, to be controlled by the will of humanity? And if this is ever to be, how is it to be—what power is there that will bring it about? Will it be the task of your masters—will they write the charter of your liberties? Will they forge the sword of your deliverance—will they marshal the army and lead it to the fray? Will their wealth be spent for the purpose—will they build colleges and churches to teach you the way, will they print papers to herald your progress, organize political parties to guide and carry on the struggle? Can you not see that the task is your task—yours to dream, yours to resolve, yours to execute? That if ever it is carried out, it will be in the face of every obstacles that wealth and mastership can oppose—in the face of ridicule and slander, of hatred and persecution, of the bludgeon and the jail? By the force of your naked bosoms opposed to the rage of oppression! By the grim and bitter teaching of blind and merciless affliction; by the painful gropings of the untutored mind, by the feeble stammerings of the uncultured voice; by the sad and lonely hunger of the spirit— by seeking and striving and yearning, by heart-ache and despairing, by agony and sweat of blood! By money paid for with hunger, by knowledge stolen from sleep, by thoughts communicated under the shadow of the gallows! By a movement beginning in the far-off past—a thing obscure and unhonored, a thing easy to ridicule, easy to despise; a thing unlovely, wearing the aspect of vengeance and hate—but to you, the workingman, the wage-slave, calling with a voice insistent, imperious—with a voice that you cannot escape, wherever upon the earth you may be, with the voice of all your wrongs, the voice of all your desires, with the voice of your duty and your hope—of everything in the world that is worth while to you! The voice of the poor, demanding that poverty shall cease! The voice of the oppressed, pronouncing the doom of oppression! The voice of power, wrought out of suffering—of resolution, crushed out of weakness—of joy and beauty, born in the bottomless pit of anguish and despair! The voice of Labor, despised and outraged! A mighty giant, lying prostrate—mountainous, colossal, but blinded, ignorant of his strength. And now a dream of resistance haunts him, hope battling with fear; until suddenly he stirs, and a fetter snaps; and a thrill shoots through him, to the farthest ends of his huge body—and in a flash the dream becomes a resolution! He starts, he lifts himself! The bands are shattered, the burdens roll off him! He rises—towering gigantic! He springs to his feet—he shouts in his new-born exaultation—"

And the speaker's voice broke suddenly, with the stress of his feelings; he stood with his arms out-stretched, and the power of his vision seemed to lift him from the floor. The audience came to its feet with a yell; men waved their arms, laughing aloud in their excitement. And Jurgis was with them, he was shouting to tear his throat—shouting because he could not help it, because the stress of his feeling was more than he could bear. It was not merely the man's words, the torrent of his eloquence; it was his presence, it was his voice, a voice with strange intonations that rang through the chambers of the soul like the clanging of a bell—that gripped the listener like a mighty hand about his body, that shook him and startled him with sudden fright, with a sense of things not of earth, of mysteries never spoken before, of presences of awe and terror! There was an unfolding of vistas before one, a breaking of the ground beneath him, an upheaving, a stirring, a trembling; he felt himself suddenly a mere man no longer—there were powers within him undreamed of, there were demon forces contending, age-long wonders struggling to be born; and he sat oppressed with pain and joy, while a tingling stole down into his finger-tips, and his breath came hard and fast; until suddenly the tension broke, and he gasped like a man coming out of a nightmare, and bounded to his feet and shouted aloud.

The sentences of this man had been to Jurgis like the crashing of thunder in his soul. A flood of emotion surged up in him—all his old hopes and longings, his old griefs and rages and despairs; all that he had ever felt in his whole life seemed to come back to him at once, and with one new emotion, hardly to be described. That he should have suffered such oppressions and such horrors was bad enough; but that he should have been crushed and beaten by them, that he should have submitted, and forgotten, and lived in peace—ah, truly that was a thing not to be put into words, a thing not to be borne by a human creature, a thing of terror and madness! "What," asks the prophet, "is the murder of them that kill the body, to the murder of them that kill the soul?" And Jurgis was a man whose soul had been murdered, who had ceased to hope and to struggle—who had made terms with degradation and despair; and now, suddenly, in one awful convulsion, the black and hideous fact was made plain to him! There was a falling in of all the pillars of his soul, the sky seemed to split above him—and he stood there, with his clenched hands upraised, his eyes bloodshot, and the veins standing out purple in his face, roaring in the voice of a wild beast, frantic, incoherent, maniacal! And when he could shout no more he stood gasping, and whispering hoarsely to himself: "By God! By God! By God!"

The man had gone back to a seat upon the platform, and Jurgis realized that his speech was over. The applause continued for several minutes; and then some one started a song, and the crowd took it up, and the place shook with it. Jurgis had never heard it, and he could not make out the words, but the wild and wonderful spirit of it seized upon him—it was the Marseilleise! As stanza after stanza of it thundered forth, he sat with his hands clasped, trembling in every nerve. He had never been so stirred in his life—it was a miracle that had been wrought in him. He could not think at all, he was stunned; yet he knew that in the mighty upheaval that had taken place in his soul, a new man had been born. He had been torn out of the jaws of destruction, he had been delivered from the thraldom of despair; the whole world had been changed for him—he was free, he was free! Even if he were to suffer as he had before, even if he were to beg and starve, nothing would be the same to him. He would understand it, and bear it; he would no longer be the sport of circumstances, he would be a man, with a will and a purpose; he would have something to fight for, something to die for, if need be. Here were men who would show and help him; and he would have friends and allies, he would dwell in the sight of justice, and walk arm in arm with power!

The audience subsided again, and he sat back. The chairman of the meeting came forward and began to speak. His voice sounded thin and futile after the other's, and to Jurgis it seemed a profanation. Why should any one else speak, after that miraculous man—why should they not all sit in silence? The chairman was explaining that a collection would now be taken up to defray the expenses of the meeting, and for the benefit of the campaign-fund of the party. Jurgis heard, but he had not a penny to give, and so his thoughts went elsewhere again.

He kept his eyes fixed on the orator, who sat in an arm-chair, his head leaning on his hand and his attitude indicating exhaustion. But suddenly he stood up again, and Jurgis heard the chairman of the meeting saying that the speaker would now answer any questions which the audience might care to put to him. The man came forward, and some one—a woman—arose and asked about some opinion the speaker had expressed concerning Tolstoi. Jurgis had never heard of Tolstoi, and did not care anything about him. Why should anyone want to ask such questions, after an address like that? The thing was not to talk, but to do; the thing was to get hold of others and rouse them, to organize them and prepare for the fight! This Tolstoi was not altogether in agreement with the speaker, it seemed—then so much the worse for Tolstoi, and enough said about him!

But still the discussion went on, in ordinary conversational tones, and it brought Jurgis back to the every-day world. A few minutes ago he had felt like seizing the hand of the beautiful lady by his side, and kissing it; he had felt like flinging his arms about the neck of the man on the other side of him. And now he began to realize again that he was a "hobo"—that he was ragged and dirty, and smelt bad, and had no place to sleep that night!

And so, at last, when the meeting broke up, and the audience started to leave, poor Jurgis was in an agony of uncertainty. He had not thought of leaving—he had thought that the vision must last forever, that he had found comrades and brothers. But now he would go out, and the thing would fade away, and he would never be able to find it again! He sat in his seat frightened and wondering; but others in the same row wanted to get out, and so he had to stand up and move along. As he was swept down the aisle he looked from one person to another, wistfully; they were all excited, discussing the address—but there was nobody who offered to discuss it with him. He was near enough to the door to feel the night air, when desperation seized him. He knew nothing at all about that speech he had heard, not even the name of the orator; and he was to go away—no, no, it was preposterous—he must speak to some one, he must find that man himself and tell him. He would not despise him, tramp as he was!

So he stepped into an empty row of seats and watched, and when the crowd had thinned out he started towards the platform.

THE SPEAKER was gone; but there was a stage-door that stood open, with people passing in and out, and no one on guard. Jurgis summoned up his courage and went in and down a hall-way, and to the door of a room where many people were crowded. No one paid any attention to him, and he pushed in, and in a corner he saw the man he sought. The orator sat in a chair, with his shoulders sunk together and his eyes half closed; his face was ghastly pale, almost greenish in hue, and one arm lay limp at his side. A big man with spectacles on stood near him, and kept pushing back the crowd. "Stand away a little, please;" he would say. "Can't you see the comrade is worn out?"

So Jurgis stood, watching, while five or ten minutes passed. Now and then the man would look up, and address a word or two to those who were near him; and, at last, on one of these occasions, his glance rested on Jurgis. There seemed to be a slight hint of inquiry about it, and a sudden impulse seized the other. He stepped forward. "I wanted to thank you, sir!" he began, in breathless haste. "I could not go away without telling you how much—how glad I am I heard you. I—I didn't know anything about it all—"

The big man with the spectacles, who had moved away, came back at this moment. "The comrade is too tired to talk to anyone—" he began; but the other held up his hand.

"Wait," he said. "He has something to say to me." And then he looked into Jurgis's face. "You want to know more about Socialism?" he asked.

Jurgis started. "I—I—" he stammered. "Is it Socialism? I didn't know. I want to know about what you spoke of—I want to help. I have been through all that."

"Where do you live?" asked the other.

"I have no home," said Jurgis, "I am out of work."

"You are a foreigner, are you not?"

"Lithuanian, sir."

The man thought for a moment, and then turned to his friend. "Who is there, Walters?" he asked. "There is Ostrinski—but he is a Pole—"

"Ostrinski speaks Lithuanian," said the other.

"All right, then; would you mind seeing if he has gone yet?"

The other started away, and the speaker looked at Jurgis again. He had deep, black eyes, and a face full of gentleness and pain. "You must excuse me, comrade," he said. "I am just tired out—I have spoken every day for the last month. I will introduce you to someone who will be able to help you as well as I could—"

The messenger had had to go no further than the door; he came back, followed by a man whom he introduced to Jurgis as "Comrade Ostrinski." Comrade Ostrinski was a little man, scarcely up to Jurgis's shoulder, wizened and wrinkled, very ugly, and slightly lame. He had on a long-tailed black coat, worn green at the seams and the buttonholes. His eyes must have been weak, for he wore green spectacles, that gave him a grotesque appearance; but his hand-clasp was hearty, and he spoke in Lithuanian, which warmed Jurgis to him.

"You want to know about Socialism?" he said. "Surely. Let us go out and take a stroll, where we can be quiet and talk some." And so Jurgis bid farewell to the master wizard, and went out.

Ostrinski asked where he lived, offering to walk in that direction; and so Jurgis had to say once more that he was without a home. At the others request he told his story; how he had come to America, and what had happened to him in the stockyards, and how his family had been broken up, and how he had become a wanderer. So much the little man heard, and then he pressed Jurgis's arm tightly. "You have been through the mill, comrade!" he said. "We will make a fighter of you!"

Then Ostrinski in turn explained his circumstances. He would have asked Jurgis to his home—but he had only two rooms, and had no bed to offer. He would have given up his own bed, but his wife was ill. Later on, when he understood that otherwise Jurgis would have to sleep in a hallway, he offered him his kitchen-floor, a chance which the other was only too glad to accept. "Perhaps tomorrow we can do better," said Ostrinski. "We try not to let a comrade starve."

Ostrinski's home was in the "ghetto district," where he had two rooms in the basement of a tenement. There was a baby crying as they entered, and he closed the door leading into the bedroom. He had three young children, he explained, and a baby had just come. He drew up two chairs near the kitchen stove, adding that Jurgis must excuse the disorder of the place, since at such a time one's domestic arrangements were upset. Half of the kitchen was given up to a work-bench, which was piled with clothing, and Ostrinski explained that he was a "pants-finisher." He carried great bundles of clothing here to his home, where he and his wife worked on them. He had always made a living at it, but it was getting harder all the time, because his eyes were failing. What would come when they gave out he could not tell; there had been no saving anything—a man could barely keep alive by twelve or fourteen hours' work a day. The finishing of pants did not take much skill, and anybody could learn it, and so the pay was forever getting less. That was the competitive wage system; and if Jurgis wanted to understand Socialism, here was the place for him to begin—with what was called "the iron law of wages." Wages tended constantly to the lowest possible level; the workers were dependent upon a job to exist from day to day, and so they bid against each other, and no man could get more than the lowest man would consent to work for. That was the fundamental fact of life, from the point of view of the poor. By combination, unions and strikes, and so on, they could raise the level a little, but there was always the mass of the unorganized and unemployed, and it swept over them like a flood, and wages sank again; and thus the vast mass of the people were always in a life and death struggle with poverty. That was "competition," so far as it concerned the wage-earner, the man who had only his labor to sell. To those on top, the exploiters, it appeared very differently, of course; there were few of them, and they could combine and dominate, and their power would be unbreakable; and so they paid what they pleased for labor, and charged what they pleased for products, and the key to all the problems of the modern world was that combination of a monopoly price and a competitive wage. It was owing to this that all over the world two classes were forming, with an unbridged chasm between them—the capitalist class, with its enormous fortunes, and the proletariat, bound into slavery by unseen chains. The latter were a thousand to one in numbers, but they were ignorant and helpless, and they would remain at the mercy of their exploiters until they were organized—until they had become "class-conscious." That was a Socialist phrase; it meant that a workingman had come to perceive once and for all that the interests of his employer and his own were opposite; and then he would join the Socialist movement, and devote all his efforts to opening the eyes of others. It was a slow and weary work, but it would be done—it was like the movement of a glacier, once it was started it could never be stopped. Every Socialist did his share, and lived upon the vision of the "good time" coming—when the working-class should go to the polls and seize the powers of government, and put an end to private property in the means of production. No matter how poor a man was, or how much he suffered, he could never be really unhappy while he knew of that future; even if he did not live to see it himself, his children would, and, to a Socialist, the victory of his class was his victory. Also he had always the progress to encourage him. Here in Chicago, for instance, the movement was growing by leaps and bounds—Chicago was the industrial center of the country, and its working-men were years ahead of the rest of the country in "class-consciousness." Nowhere else were the unions so strong; but their organizations did the workers little good, for the employers were organized, also; and so the strikes generally failed, and as fast as the unions were broken up the men came over to the Socialists. It was a fine thing to see—one could feel the excitement in the very air, and even the "old party" papers were forced to admit that the Socialists were holding the most successful political meetings of the present campaign. There were half a dozen every night, and on Saturday night fifteen or twenty; the vote was going to be a record-breaker. It would set a mark, and break the conspiracy of silence of the capitalist press—they would have to discuss Socialism, and, even though they told lies about it, more people would begin to ask questions. So it was that the party made its progress, carrying the ground inch by inch, in the face of every obstacle.

Ostrinski explained the organization of the party, the machinery by which the proletariat was educating itself. There were "locals" in every big city and town, and they were being organized rapidly in the smaller places; a local had anywhere from six to a thousand members, and there were fourteen hundred of them in all, with a total of about twenty-five thousand members, who paid dues to support the organization. Then there were the state organizations, and above them the national, which had its headquarters in Chicago. "Local Cook County," as the city organization was called, had eighty branch locals, and it alone was spending several thousand dollars in the campaign. It published an English weekly, and a Bohemian, a German, and also there was a monthly published in Chicago, and a co-operative publishing house, that issued a million and a half of Socialist books and pamphlets every year. All this was the growth of the last few years—there had been almost nothing of it when Ostrinski first came to Chicago.

Ostrinski was a German Pole, about fifty years of age. He had lived in Silesia, a member of a despised and persecuted race, and had taken part in the proletarian movement in the early seventies, when Bismarck, having conquered France, had turned his policy of blood and iron upon the "International." Ostrinski himself had twice been in jail, but he had been young then, and had not cared. He had had more than his share of the fight, though, for just when Socialism had broken all its barriers and become the great political force of the empire, he had come to America, and begun all over again. In America everyone had laughed at the mere idea of Socialism then—in America all men were free. As if political liberty made wage-slavery any the more tolerable! said Ostrinski. He had understood, for himself, that Socialism would come more quickly in a free country than anywhere else, and when the comrades had sneered at the American working-man, saying that he had no idea save to get to be an employer himself, and turn upon his class, Ostrinski had always answered that when the country was once filled up, and the class-lines were drawn tightly, it would no longer be possible for the workingman to become a capitalist, and then they would find out the importance of free speech and free institutions to Socialism. Now that time had come, and the whole country was seething with agitation; so much so that it seemed to Ostrinski that America might really be the first of the nations to witness the industrial revolution.

The little tailor sat tilted back in his stiff kitchen chair, with his feet stretched out upon the empty stove. He spoke in low whispers, so as not to wake those in the next room. To Jurgis he seemed a scarcely less wonderful person than the speaker at the meeting; he was as poor as Jurgis himself had been, the lowest of the low, hunger-driven and miserable—and yet how much he knew, how much he had dared and achieved, what a hero he had been! There were others like him, too; thousands like him, and all of them working-men! The listener sat trembling, and lost in admiration; all this wonderful machinery of progress had been created by his fellows—he could not believe it, it seemed too good to be true.

That was always the way, said Ostrinski; when a man was first converted to Socialism he was like a crazy person—he could not understand how others could fail to see it, and he expected to convert all the world the first week. After a while he would realize how hard a task it was; and then it would be fortunate that other new hands kept coming, to keep him from settling down into a rut. Just now Jurgis would have plenty of chance to vent his excitement, for a presidential campaign was on, and everybody was talking politics. Ostrinski would take him to the next meeting of the branch-local, and introduce him, and he might join the party. All that one had to do was to sign a declaration that he renounced all connection with the old parties, and that he recognized the class-struggle as the fundamental fact of modern society. The dues were five cents a week, but anyone who could not afford this might be excused from paying. The Socialist party was the most democratic of political organizations—it was controlled absolutely by its own membership, with the freest use of the initiative and referendum, and the principle of the recall of officials. All of these things Ostrinski explained, as also the plan by which the party controlled its candidates who were elected to office. When they were nominated they placed their resignations in the hands of the party, for use at any time if they should prove false to Socialist principles.

You might say that there was really but one Socialist principle—that of "no compromise," which was the essence of the proletarian movement all over the world. When a Socialist was elected to office he voted with old party legislators for any measure that was likely to be of help to the working-class, but he never forgot that these concessions, whatever they might be, were trifles compared with the great purpose for which his party existed—the organizing of the working-class for the revolution. So the Socialists never made any sort of an alliance with capitalist parties, never "fused," or made a "deal," and never voted for capitalist candidates. This principle was the very life of Socialism, and so, of course, it was the thing which made the exploiters angriest; they were always trying to bribe or cajole or brow-beat the party into swerving from it, and though they always failed, they were always busy celebrating a success somewhere or other. For instance, it was the fact that the party in Germany was now more solidly class-conscious than it had ever been in its history before; yet it was the conventional lie, accepted by all the capitalist writers in America and England, that the German Socialists had abandoned the revolution, and became a party of political reform! This helped to take away from the American Socialists the prestige of the "three million party," and to make it easier to beguile the American workingman with futilities like free silver, municipal ownership, and "reform."

That, of course, was only one of a thousand ways in which they misrepresented Socialism, and against them all the Socialists had only one defense, to go out to the people and spread the truth by word of mouth. So far the rule in America had been that one Socialist made another Socialist once every two years. In 1888, when the party had first made nominations, it had cast two thousand votes; in 1896 it had cast thirty-two thousand, and in 1900 it had cast a hundred and twenty-six thousand. At the same rate it should cast half a million this year, two millions in 1908, and sweep the country in 1912 —though there were few Socialists who expected to succeed as quickly as that.

The Socialists were organized in every civilized nation; it was an international political party, the greatest the world had ever known. It numbered thirty millions of adherents, and it cast eight million votes. It had started its first newspaper in Japan, and elected its first deputy in Argentina; in France it named members of cabinets, and in Italy and Australia it held the balance of power and turned out ministries. In Germany, where its vote was more than a third of the total vote of the Empire, all other parties and powers had united to fight it. There was the Emperor—the warlord of the "mailed fist;" there was the mediaeval nobility and the descendants of the aristocracy of the army, whose officers beat and kicked and maimed the helpless soldiers; there was the bigoted seventeenth-century Protestant church, with its snuffy country parsons; there was the Roman Catholic church and the Jesuits; there was the bureaucracy, and the "reptile" press; and finally, there were the capitalists, the masters of them all. And in every country in Europe to which you went you found the same powers of darkness leagued together; and the wretched workers were jammed into slums and imprisoned in factories, or herded like sheep and sent out to the slaughter, to conquer new markets and new opportunities of profit for the masters. All this was frightful to see and understand—it was a sort of day-nightmare: the people burdened by poverty and ignorance, by race prejudice and religious bigotry, and crushed by a power such as this! Yet that was life—it was in this fiery furnace that the new civilization was being forged, it was in this agony that men were being brought together, and the dream of the Brotherhood of Man being made a reality. It would not do, Ostrinski explained. for the proletariat of one nation to achieve the victory; for that nation would be crushed by the military power of the others; and so the Socialist movement was a world movement, an organization of all mankind to establish liberty and fraternity, a party to which the rights of all men, white or black or red or yellow, were equally sacred. So the International Socialist movement was the new religion of humanity—or you might say it was the fulfillment of the old religion, since it was but the practical application of all the teachings of Christ.

Until long after midnight Jurgis sat lost in the conversation of his new acquaintance. It was a most wonderful experience to him—an almost supernatural experience. It was like encountering an inhabitant of the fourth dimension of space, a being who was free from all one's own limitations. For four years, now, Jurgis had been wandering and blundering in the depths of the Jungle; and here, suddenly, a hand reached down and seized him, and lifted him out of it, and set him upon a high mountain-top, from which he could survey it all—could see the paths from which he had wandered, the morasses into which he had stumbled, the hiding-places of the beasts of prey that had fallen upon him. There were his Packingtown experiences, for instance—what was there about Packingtown that Ostrinski could not explain! To Jurgis the packers had been equivalent to fate; Ostrinski showed him that they were the Beef Trust. They were a gigantic combination of capital, which had crushed all opposition, and overthrown the laws of the land, and was preying upon the people. Jurgis recollected how, when he had first come to Packingtown, he had stood and watched the hog-killing, and thought how cruel and savage it was, and come away congratulating himself that he was not a hog; now his new acquaintance showed him that a hog was just what he had been—one of the packers' hogs! Labor was their hog, and the public was their hog, and they themselves were the biggest hogs of all. They were business-men; and business was business. What they wanted from a hog was all the profits that could be got out of him; and that was what they wanted from the workingman, and that was what they wanted from the people. What the hog thought of it, and what he suffered, was not considered; and no more was it with the workingman, and no more was it with the purchaser of meat. That was true everywhere under capitalism, but it was especially true in Packingtown; there seemed to be something about the work of slaughtering that tended to ruthlessness and ferocity—it was literally the fact that in the methods of the packers a hundred human lives did not balance a penny of profit. When Jurgis had made himself familiar with the Socialist literature, as he would very quickly, he would get glimpses of the Beef Trust from all sorts of aspects, and he would find it everywhere the same; it was the incarnation of blind and insensate Greed, it was a monster devouring with a thousand mouths, trampling with a thousand hoofs; it was the Great Butcher, it was the spirit of Capitalism made flesh. Upon the ocean of commerce it sailed as a pirate-ship; it had hoisted the black flag and declared war upon civilization. Bribery and corruption, the overthrowing of laws and the defying of constitutions—these were its every-day methods. In Chicago the city government was simply one of its branch-offices; it stole billions of gallons of city water openly, it dictated to the courts the sentences of disorderly strikers, it forbade the mayor to enforce the building-laws against it. In the national capital it had power to prevent inspection of its products, and to falsify government reports; it violated the rebate laws, and when an investigation was threatened it burned its books and sent its criminal agents out of the country. In the commercial world it was a Juggernaut car; it wiped out thousands of businesses every year, it drove men to madness and suicide. It had forced the price of cattle so low as to destroy the stock-raising industry, an occupation upon which whole states existed. It had ruined thousands of butchers who had refused to handle its products. It divided the country into districts, and fixed the price of meat in all of them; it owned all the refrigerator cars, and levied an enormous tribute upon all poultry and eggs and fruit and vegetables. With the millions of dollars a week that poured in upon it, it was reaching out for the control of other interests, railroads and trolley lines, gas and electric-light franchises, the leather and the grain business of the whole country.

Ostrinski knew about these abuses through a Chicago editor whom he had met, and who was investigating them. The public was tremendously stirred up about them, for it affected its pocket-book directly. About the sufferings of the Packingtown employes, to whom the same slaughter-house methods were being applied, the public did not care anything—it read the capitalist papers, and was prejudiced against the workingmen. What would stir the public, however, was the realization of the third field in which the "Great Butcher" was at work—when it understood that he was dealing out, blindly and at random, a sudden and agonizing death to tens of thousands of human beings every year, through the sale of tainted and poisoned meats; when it understood that a man who took a particle of packing-house product into his stomach was simply playing a game of chance for his life. With the horrible and nauseating stuff that they put up in tins they had killed more American soldiers than all the bullets of the Spaniards in the last war; and with every carload they were shipping out tonight, they sent the death warrant of some poor helpless wretch in a hospital or a poorhouse or a convict-camp—not only in America, but all over the world, in the Panama ditches, and on the Manchurian battle-fields, and in the South African diamond-mines!

And then, as a contrast to this, Ostrinski went on to tell Jurgis how he had heard at Hull House Settlement a lecture by an Englishman, an expert upon sanitary science, who had been sent by the London Lancet to study the horrors of Packinstown. This man had described the model municipal slaughter-house of Berlin, where the governing power of an old time aristocracy put some slight check upon the crimes of commercialism. This slaughter-house killed for any one who brought animals to it, charging so much per head. It was built according to the latest scientific principles, light and airy, with concrete floors and no nooks or corners to hold dust and dirt; its walls and floors, every inch of them, were flushed every day with boiling water from a traveling machine pump; and from every animal that was killed there twelve samples were cut, which were examined by twelve different microscopes, and if the least sign of disease was found, the carcass was instantly destroyed. As the loss fell upon the owner, he was careful what he bought, and so the business of breeding diseased cattle had been wiped out. The difference between such a system as that and the one that prevailed in Chicago was, of course, simply the difference between civilization and savagery. Yet there was no hope of a national or a municipal slaughterhouse in America, with the packers in control in both the city and the nation. All that one could do was to teach the people, and to preach to them, and prepare them for the time when they were to seize the huge machine called the Beef Trust, and use it to produce food for human beings, and not to heap up fortunes for a band of murderers and pirates.

It was long after midnight when Jurgis lay down upon the floor of Ostrinski's kitchen; and yet it was an hour before he could get to sleep, for the glory of that joyful vision of the people of Packingtown marching in and taking possession of the Union Stock-yards!

JURGIS had breakfast with Ostrinski and his family, and then he went home to Elzbieta. He was no longer shy about it—when he went in, instead of saying all the things he had been planning to say, he started to tell Elzbieta about the revolution. At first she thought he was out of his mind, and it was hours before she could really feel certain that he was himself. When, however, she had satisfied herself that he was sane upon all subjects except politics she troubled herself no further about it. Jurgis was destined to find that Elzbieta's armor was absolutely imperious to Socialism. Her soul had been baked hard in the fire of adversity, and there was no altering it now, life to her was the hunt for daily bread, and ideas existed for her only as they bore upon that. All that interested her in regard to this new frenzy which had seized hold of her son-in-law was whether or not it had a tendency to make him sober and industrious; and when she found he intended to look for work and to contribute his share to the family fund, she gave him full rein to convince her of anything. A wonderfully wise little woman was Elzbieta; she could think as quickly as a hunted rabbit, and in half an hour she had chosen her life-attitude to the Socialist movement. She agreed in everything with Jurgis, except the need of his paying his dues; and she would even go to a meeting with him now and then, and sit and plan her next day's dinner amid the storm.

For a week after he became a convert Jurgis continued to wander about all day, looking for work; until at last he met with a strange fortune. He was passing one of Chicago's innumerable small hotels, and after some hesitation he concluded to go in. A man he took for the proprietor was standing in the lobby, and he went up to him and tackled him for a job.

"What can you do?" the man asked.

"Anything sir," said Jurgis; and added quickly: "I've been out of work for a long time, sir. I'm an honest man, and I'm strong and willing"—

The other was eyeing him narrowly. "Do you drink?" he asked.

"No, sir." said Jurgis.

"Well, I've been employing a man as a porter, and he drinks. I've discharged him seven times now, and I've about made up my mind that's enough. Would you be a porter?"

"Yes, sir."

"It's hard work. You'll have to clean floors and wash spittoons and fill lamps and handle trunks—"

"I'm willing, sir."

"All right. I'll pay you thirty a month and board, and you can begin now, if you feel like it. You can put on the other fellow's rig."

And so Jurgis fell to work and toiled like a Trojan till night. Then he went and told Elzbieta, and also, late as it was, he paid a visit to Ostrinski to tell him of his good fortune. Here he received a great surprise, for when he was describing the location of the hotel Ostrinski interrupted eagerly: "Not Hinds's!"

"Yes," said Jurgis, "that's the name."

To which the other replied: "Then you've got the best boss in Chicago —he's a state organizer of our party, and one of our best known speakers!"

So the next morning Jurgis went to his employer and told him; and the man seized him by the hand and shook it. "By Jove!" he cried, "that lets me out—I didn't sleep all last night because I had discharged a good Socialist!"

So, after that, Jurgis was known to his "boss" as "Comrade Jurgis," and in return he was expected to call him "Comrade Hinds." "Billy" Hinds, as he was known to his intimates, was a squat little man, with broad shoulders and a florid face, decorated with gray side-whiskers. He was the kindest-hearted man that ever lived, and the liveliest; he was inexhaustible in his enthusiasm, talking Socialism all day and all night. He was a great fellow to jolly along a crowd, and he would keep a meeting in an uproar; when once he got really waked up, the torrent of his eloquence could be compared with nothing save Niagara.

Billy Hinds had begun life as a blacksmith's helper, and had run away to join the Union army, where he had made his first acquaintance with "graft" in the shape of rotten muskets and shoddy blankets. To a musket that broke in a crisis he always attributed the death of his only brother, and upon worthless blankets he blamed all the agonies of his own old age. Whenever it rained, the rheumatism would get into his joints, and then he would screw up his face and mutter: "Capitalism, my boy. Capitalism! *'ecrasez I' Infame!'*"[1] He had one unfailing remedy for all the evils of this world, and he preached it to every one; no matter whether the person's trouble was failure in business, or dyspepsia, or a quarrelsome mother-in-law, a twinkle would come into his eyes and he would say: "You know what to do about it—vote the Socialist ticket!"

Billy Hinds had set out upon the trail of the Octopus as soon as the war was over. He had gone into business, and found himself in competition with the fortunes of those who had been stealing while he had been fighting; he had found the city government in the hands of such and the railroads in league with them, and honest business driven to the wall; and so he had put

---

1. "Hinds" is quoting Voltaire's famous comment regarding religious superstition, "Crush the infamous thing!"

all his savings into Chicago real estate, and set out single-handed to dam the river of graft. He had been a reform member of the city council, he had been a Greenbacker, a Labor Unionist, a Populist, a Bryanite—and after thirty years of fighting, the year 1896 had served to convince him that the power of concentrated wealth could never be controlled, but could only be destroyed. He had published a pamphlet about it, and set out to organize a party of his own, when a stray Socialist leaflet had revealed to him that others had been ahead of him. Now for eight years he had been fighting for the party, any-where, everywhere—whether it was a G. A. R.[2] reunion, or a hotel-keepers' convention, or an Afro-American business-men's banquet, or a Bible Society picnic, Billy Hinds would manage to get himself invited to explain the relations of Socialism to the subject in hand. After that he would start off upon a tour of his own, ending at some place between, New York and Oregon; and when he came back from there, he would go out to organize new locals for the state committee; and finally he would come home to rest—and would talk Socialism in Chicago. Hinds's hotel was a very hot-bed of the propaganda; all the employees were party men, and if they were not when they came, they were quite certain to be before they went away. The proprietor would get into a discussion with some one in the lobby, and, as the conversation grew animated, others would gather about to listen, until finally everyone in the place would be crowded into a group, and a regular debate would be under way. This went on every night—when Billy Hinds was not there to do it, his clerk did it, and when his clerk was away campaigning, the assistant attended to it, while Mrs. Hinds sat behind the desk and did the work. The clerk was an old crony of the proprietor's, an awkward, raw-boned giant of a man, with a lean, sallow face, a broad mouth, and whiskers under his chin, the very type and body of a prairie farmer. He had been that all his life—he had fought the railroads in Kansas for fifty years—a Granger, a Farmers' Alliance man, a "middle-of-the-road" Populist. Finally, Billy Hinds had revealed to him the wonderful idea of using the trusts instead of destroying them; and he had sold his farm and bought some tenements in Chicago. He went to collect the rent himself each month, and with every receipt went a Socialist tract, and a statement to the effect that, so long as the poor continued to vote to pay rent, he was in a position to put the money to better use than any capitalist.

That was Amos Struver; and then there was Harry Adams, the assistant clerk, a pale, scholarly-looking man, who came from Massachusetts, of Pilgrim stock. Adams had been a cotton-operative in Fall River, and the continued depression in the industry had worn him and his family out, and he had emigrated to South Carolina. In Massachusetts the percentage of white

---

2. Grand Army of the Republic, a fraternal organization of Union Civil War veterans.

illiteracy is eight-tenths of one per cent, while in South Carolina it is thirteen and six-tenths per cent; also in South Carolina there is a property quali-fication for voters—and for these and other reasons child-labor is the rule, and so the cotton mills were driving those of Massachusetts out of the business. Adams did not know this, he only knew that the Southern mills were running; but when he got there he found that if he was to live, all his family would have to work, and from six o'clock at night to six o'clock in the morning. So he had set to work to organize the mill-hands, after the fashion in Massachusetts, and had been discharged; but he had gotten other work, and stuck at it, and at last there had been a strike for shorter hours, and Harry Adams had attempted to address a street meeting, which was the end of him. In the states of the far South the labor of convicts is leased to contractors and when there are not convicts enough they have to be supplied. It is a favorite amusement of the authorities to go out hunting negroes—they will find a number of them playing craps in a hallway, or indulging in a poker-game on a Sunday night, and they will haul them up for "gambling," and send them for three or six months to a convict-camp, where the hours of labor are from dawn till dark, and a man who ventures to murmur is knocked over the head. Harry Adams was sent up by a judge who was a cousin of the mill-owner with whose business he had interfered; the life had nearly killed him, but he had been wise enough not to murmur, and at the end of his term he and his family had left the state of South Carolina—hell's backyard, as he called it. He had no money for car-fare, but it was harvest time, and they walked one day and worked the next, and so Adams got at last to Chicago, and joined the Socialist party. He was a studious man, reserved, and nothing of an orator; but he always had a pile of books under his desk in the hotel, and articles from his pen were beginning to attract attention in the party press.

Contrary to what one would have expected, all this radicalism did not hurt the hotel business; the radicals flocked to it, and the commercial travelers all found it diverting; of late, also, the hotel had become a favorite stopping place for western cattlemen. Now that the Beef Trust had adopted the trick of raising prices to induce enormous shipments of cattle, and then dropping them again and scooping in all they needed, a stock-raiser was very apt to find himself in Chicago without money enough to pay his freight bill; and so he had to go to a cheap hotel, and it was no drawback to him if there was an agitator talking in the lobby. These Western fellows were just "meat" for Billy Hinds—he would get a dozen of them around him and paint little pictures of the Beef Trust. Of course, it was not a week before he had heard Jurgis's story, and after that he would not have let his new porter go for the world. "See here," he would say, in the middle of an argument, "I've got a fellow right here in my place who's worked there and seen every bit of it!" And then Jurgis would drop his work, whatever it was, and come, and the other would say, "Comrade Jurgis, just tell these gentlemen what you saw in the stockyards." At first, this request caused poor Jurgis the most acute agony, and it was like pulling teeth to get him to talk; but gradually he found out what was wanted, and in the end he learned to stand up and speak his piece with enthusiasm. His employer would sit by and encourage him with exclamations and shakes of the head—when Jurgis would give the formula for "potted ham," or tell about the condemned hogs made into lard in another state, Billy Hinds would bang his knee and cry: "Do you think a man could make up a thing like that out of his head?"

And then the hotel-keeper would go on to show how the Socialists had the only real remedy for such evils, how they alone "meant business" with the Beef Trust. And when, in answer to this, the victim would say that the whole country was stirred up about the trust, that the newspapers were full of denunciations of it, and the government taking action against it, Billy Hinds had a knock-out blow all ready. "Yes," he would say, "all that is true—and what do you suppose is the reason for it? Are you foolish enough to believe that it is for the good of the public? There are other trusts in the country just as illegal and extortionate as the Beef Trust; there is the Coal Trust, that freezes the poor in winter—there is the Steel Trust, that doubles the price of every nail in your shoes—there is the Oil Trust, that keeps you from reading at night—and why do you suppose it is that all the fury of the press and the government is directed against the Beef Trust, and not against these?" And when to this the victim would reply that there was clamor enough over the Oil Trust, the other would continue: "Ten years ago Henry D. Lloyd told all the truth about the Standard Oil company in his 'Wealth versus Common-wealth;' and the book was bought up and allowed to die, and you can hardly get a copy of it. And now, at last, two magazines have the courage to tackle Standard Oil again, and what happened? The newspapers ridicule and vilify the authors, the churches defend the criminals, and the government —does nothing at all. And why is it so different with the Beef Trust."

Here the other would generally admit that he was "stuck;" and Billy Hinds would explain to him, and it was fun to see his eyes open. "If you were a Socialist," the hotel-keeper would say, "you would understand that the power which really governs the United States today is the Railroad Trust. It is the Railroad Trust that runs your state government, wherever you live, and that runs the United States senate. Often by direct ownership, and more often by a thousand subtle influences, it controls the press of this free republic; and, controlling the press, it controls public opinion, the churches, the schools, and the colleges. And all of the trusts that I have named are railroad trusts —save only the Beef Trust! The Beef Trust has defied the railroads—it is plundering them day by day through the Private Car; and so the public is aroused to fury, and the papers clamor for action, and the government goes on the warpath! The Steel Trust fixes the tariff laws of the country and robs us by wholesale, and nothing is done; the Coal Trust violates the law of Pennsylvania forbidding combinations between coal mines and railroads, and nothing is done; the same trust violates the rebate law in Colorado, and the self-confessed criminal sits in the president's cabinet and helps direct the attempt to put the packers in jail! And you poor common people watch and applaud the job, and think it's all done for you, and never dream that it is really the grand climax and culmination of the century-long battle of commercial competition—the final death-grapple between the chiefs of the Beef Trust and "Standard Oil," for the prize of the mastery and ownership of the United States of America! And the Beef Trust is winning, through its power to bleed the railroads; and the whole might of the United States government and of the press and public opinion of America, is being used in an attempt to reverse the victory!"

Such was the new home in which Jurgis lived and worked, and in which his education was completed. Perhaps you would imagine that he did not do much work there, but that would he a great mistake. He would have cut off one hand for Billy Hinds, and to keep Hinds's hotel a thing of beauty was his joy in life. That he had a score of Socialist arguments chasing through his brain in the meantime did not interfere with this; on the contrary, Jurgis scrubbed the spittoons and polished the banisters all the more vehemently because at the same time he was wrestling inwardly with an imaginary recalcitrant. It would be pleasant to record that he swore off drinking immediately, and all the rest of his bad habits with it; but that would hardly be exact. These revolutionists were not angels; they were men, and men who had come up from the social pit, and with the mire of it smeared over them. Some of them drank, and some of them swore, and some of them ate pie with their knives; there was only one difference between them and the rest of the populace— that they were men with a hope, with a cause to fight for and suffer for. There came times to Jurgis when the vision seemed far-off and pale, and a glass of beer loomed large in comparison; but if the glass led to another glass and too many glasses, he had something to spur him to remorse and resolution on the morrow. It was so evidently a wicked thing to spend one's pennies for drink, when the working-class was wandering in darkness, and waiting to be delivered, and when the price of a glass of beer would buy ten copies of a Socialist paper or fifty copies of a leaflet! And one could hand these out to the unregenerate, and then get drunk upon the thought of the good that was being accomplished. That was the way the movement had been made, and it was the only way it would progress; it availed nothing to know of it, without fighting for it—it was a thing for all, not for a few! A corollary of this proposition, of course, was that any one who refused to receive the new gospel was personally responsible for keeping Jurgis from his heart's desire;

and this, alas, made him somewhat impatient as a teacher, and somewhat uncomfort-able as an acquaintance. He met some neighbors with whom Elzbieta had made friends in her neighborhood, and he set out to make Socialists of them, and several times he all but got into a fight.

It was so painfully obvious to Jurgis! It was so incomprehensible how a man could fail to see it. Here were all the opportunities of the country, the land, and the buildings upon the land, the railroads, the mines, the factories, and the stores, all in the hands of a few private individuals, called capitalists, for whom the people were obliged to work for wages. The whole balance of what the people produced went to heap up the fortunes of these capitalists, to heap, and heap again, and yet again—and that in spite of the fact that they, and every one about them, lived in unthinkable luxury! And was it not plain that if the people stopped this ceaseless drain of "profits" there would be much more for all who worked? That was as plain as two and two makes four; and it was all there was to Socialism—the whole of it, absolutely the whole of it; and yet there were people who could not see it, who would argue about everything but that! They would tell you that the government could not manage things as economically as private individuals! They would repeat and repeat that, and think they were saying something! They could not see that "economical" management by masters meant simply that they, the people, were worked harder and ground closer and paid less! They—workingmen, wage-earners, servants, and menials, who had nothing but their work to sell, who had no hope of anything but a bare existence, and who were at the mercy of exploiters whose one thought was to get as much out of them as possible —they were taking an interest in the process, and were anxious lest it should not be done thoroughly enough! Was it not honestly a trial to listen to an argument such as that? To think of people who were unwilling to trust themselves to be free and equal dwellers in a house of which they were part owners, and preferred to be scullions and lackeys in a house that was managed "economically!"

That was hard—and yet there were things even worse. You would begin talking to some poor devil who had worked in one shop for the last thirty years, and had never been able to save a penny; who left home every morning at six o'clock, to go and tend a machine, and come back at night too tired to take his clothes off; who had never had a week's vacation in his life, had never traveled, never had an adventure, never learned anything, never hoped anything—and when you started to tell him about Socialism he would sniff and say: "I'm not interested in that—I'm an individualist!" And then he would go on to tell you that Socialism was "paternalism," and that if it ever had its way the world would stop progressing—because individual initiative would be destroyed. It was enough to make a mule laugh to hear arguments like that; and yet it was no laughing matter, as you found out—for how many millions of such poor deluded wretches there were, whose individualities had been so stunted by Capitalism that they no longer knew what individuality was, and were content to repeat a piece of stupid knavery that had been hatched in the secret councils of employers' associations, and passed along by subsidized college presidents and knavish politicians, by hireling newspaper editors and sleek society preachers! Only think of it—it was "Individualism" for tens of thousands of workingmen to gather together and obey the orders of a steel magnate, and produce hundreds of millions of dollars of wealth for him, and then let him give them libraries, and say who should manage them, and what books should be found in them; while for the men to take the industry and run it to suit themselves, and build their own libraries and run those to suit themselves—that was "Paternalism!" It was "Individualism" for political parties to be in the hands of corrupt and ignorant bosses, who were paid by big business-men to do their will, and to lead the people to the polls like sheep to the slaughter-pen; and when the people got up and started a party of their own, and paid its expenses and ran it to suit themselves—that was "Paternalism!" Sometimes the agony of such things as this was more than Jurgis could bear—his impotence in the face of such oppression as this. He longed for a million voices, that he might yell it into the ears of all the stupid fools at once—"No, Socialism is not paternalism! Capitalism is paternalism! It's doing as you're told and asking no questions, it's begging for work, and taking what's offered you, and being taught your place! Socialism is freedom and independence; it's owning your own job and being your own boss, it's working when you please and where you please, it's plenty and opportunity—it's everything that you want in the world and that your masters are trying to keep from you!"

And yet Jurgis was only at the beginning of his trials. He had yet to find out the newspapers, and the spurns that patient merit had to take from them. About a week after Jurgis got his job there came off the great "Hinds-Winslow Debate"—and when our friend read the accounts of this that were published in the Chicago papers, there was murder in his heart.

Dr. Oliver Winslow was a Baptist clergyman, whose church was just around the corner from the hotel; and the giving out of Socialist tracts during the campaign had moved him to a sermon denouncing Socialism as a menace to civilization. Straightway, of course, Billy Hinds and his cronies had gotten up a polite little letter challenging the gentleman to a debate. The letter was persuasively worded, in the name of fair play and free opinion; and it arrived on Saturday morning, and the clergyman mailed a refusal on Saturday afternoon—but on Sunday morning he discovered that the Socialists had printed their challenge and were giving it out in front of his church, so he wrote a second letter, accepting. Now, a month or so later, the debate came off, and it was a great event. The neighborhood had been placarded with advertisements of it, and all the clergyman's congregation had come, and likewise all of Billy Hinds's. Jurgis sat right up in front, and as it was the first time he had ever heard his employer on the platform, he all but jumped out of his skin with glee. Billy Hinds had a way of beating with one arm as he rushed on to his climaxes; and he would work up the crowd—he would lift them—lift them—till they leaped to their feet with yells of delight! Then he would spread out his arms with an imperious gesture, for applause had been barred, to save time; and they would sink back, and he would rush on again. The way he strode up and down the platform and romped away with the clergyman was a sight to see; there may have been some who thought him not quite respectful—but then Socialism is the working-class battle for life, and it cannot always consider an individual's feelings.

The clergyman had spoken about the man who had worked and saved and accumulated a little capital, and upon his "right" to the interest it would bring him. Billy Hinds's reply convulsed the crowd—"Dr. Winslow seems to think that the first dollar is a male dollar, and the second a female dollar, and that when the man puts them into the bank together they reproduce nickels and dimes, which by and by grow up to be dollars as big as their daddy! He doesn't understand that the thing he calls interest is wealth produced by another man and which the other man had taken from him!" And then the hotel-keeper went on to show how a person who could get ten thousand dollars, whether it was by saving it or stealing it, had an able-bodied man to work for him for the rest of his life. Day or night, that man would never stop; he would work in spite of sickness, of summer's heat or winter's cold, a blind and helpless slave of the owner of the ten thousand dollars! And there were tens upon tens of billions of such dollars—and those who were their slaves and worked for them were the wage-earners of the world!

The clergyman's speech had consisted mainly of two arguments—first, that the people could not manage the industries of the country properly; and, second, that Socialism would destroy individual enterprise. Said Billy Hinds: "I wouldn't really need to answer those two arguments—I could just tie them up by the tails and hang them over a clothes-line, and they would chew each other up like the Kilkenny cats!" And he went on to show how the second meant that we should stagnate because the government would be doing everything—and the first meant that there would be so much for us to do that we shouldn't be able to do it! The first simply meant that Dr. Winslow had failed to understand that Socialism implied, not merely the public ownership of the industrial machinery, but also its democratic administration. Our present idea of "government" was a tyrannical bureaucracy, the agent of the particular exploiting-class that was dominant at the time, but under Socialism the governing authorities would be like the board of directors of a club— indeed, the world would be exactly a big club, of which all men and women were free and equal members, and in the affairs of which all took part. So, of course, there might appear to be much force in the other argument, that there would be too much for the people to do, there is not public spirit enough, intelligence enough, said Dr. Winslow—"And of course there isn't!" cried Billy Hinds—"Who knows that better than the Socialists? If there were enough, we'd have Socialism; and since there isn't we have to fall to work to make it! We have to agitate and preach, we have to get the people together and organize them, we have to teach them, to make them read and study and think for themselves. We have to train men to write and edit, to speak and debate, to organize and to administer affairs. And what is all that but the people becoming capable of doing what the doctor says they aren't capable of doing at present? And why in heaven's name is he not helping us to make them capable—why, at least, does he not wish us God-speed, instead of calling us enemies of civilization? Why does he simply stand there and tell us that Socialism is an untried experiment—of course it is an untried experiment! So is the first attempt of the baby to get upon its feet—but is that any reason for strapping the little wretch down? Why, whenever newspapers discuss Socialism, do they always argue the question of dollars and cents, and fail to understand that Socialism is not merely a question of business, but a question of right and wrong; that the facts by which it is to be interpreted are not those of finance alone, but those of religion? Socialism is not an experiment in government; it is an act of will! It is a part of the perpetual miracle of the spirit, the coming into being of a thing that never was before, a thing created by the sovereign soul; it is the will of the evil man to do righteousness, the will of the perishing man to survive! It is the will of the working-class to put an end to exploitation, with all its accompaniments of luxury and poverty, of corruption, crime and war! It is not a thing that can be effected by an argument, or that can be comprehended by calculation—it is a gospel, a faith. When you, Christian ministers, meet a man who is a slave to drink, and who wishes to be free, you do not sit down with him and figure on the chances, you do not go to the statistics to find out if it is worth while; but you rouse him, you exhort him, you implore him to rise up and resolve, understanding that the power to be lies in the will to be, and that apart from the will there can be no power. Of course the man may fail; after all he may be too far gone for help; and so with Socialism—it may be that corruption has so far eaten into the fibre of our manhood, it may be that we are so dead to the call of freedom, that we shall fail in our efforts, and that the struggle of the disinherited for life will end only in chaos and ruin. If so, the fault will not be ours, who strove and did our best—it will lie at the door of those who mocked at us and despised us, who lied about us and misrepresented us, who sat by in idleness, while we toiled to deliver mankind!"

That was the climax of the debate; and so let it be imagined how Jurgis felt when he saw the papers the next day and discovered that though all of them had been notified, only one had reported the event, and that one under the heading: "Dr. Winslow Rebukes Socialism!" It represented the worthy doctor in the attitude of a school-master lecturing an unruly pupil; and it gave half a column of his arguments, while all that it had to say of Billy Hinds's effort was this one sentence: "To the argument of the clergyman that the govern-ment could not manage the industries of the country properly, his opponent replied by stating that to Socialists municipal ownership was not a question of finance, but of faith."

ONE OF the first things that Jurgis did when he got a job was to go and see Marija. She came down into the basement of the house to meet him, and he stood by the door with his hat in his hand, saying, "I've got work now, and so you can leave here."

But Marija only shook her head. No, she said, there was nothing for her to do and nobody to employ her. She could not keep her past a secret—girls had tried it, and they were always found out. Thousands of men came to this place, and sooner or later she would meet one of them. When a woman had once come to this, she never got out. "And, besides," Marija added, "I can't do anything, I'm no good—I take dope. What could you do with me?"

"Can't you stop?" Jurgis cried.

"No," she answered. "I'll never stop—I can't. What's the use of talking about it—I'll stay here till I die, I guess. It's all I'm fit for now." And that was all that he could get her to say—there was no use trying. When he told her he would not let Elzbieta take her money she answered indifferently: "Then it'll be wasted here—that's all." Her eyelids looked heavy and her face was red and swollen; he saw that he was annoying her, that she only wanted him to go away. So he went, disappointed and sad.

Poor Jurgis was not very happy in his home-life. Elzbieta was sick a good deal now, and the boys were wild and unruly, and very much the worse for their life upon the streets. But he stuck by the family nevertheless, for they reminded him of his old happiness; and when things went wrong he could solace himself with a plunge into the Socialist movement. Since his life had been caught up into the current of this mighty stream, things which had before been the whole of life to him now came to seem of relatively slight importance. His interests were elsewhere, in the world of ideas. His outward life became common-place and uninteresting—he was just a hotel-porter, and expected to remain one while he lived; but meantime in the realm of thought his life was a perpetual adventure. There was so much to know—so many wonders to be discovered!

Never, in all his life, did Jurgis forget one day when there came a telephone message from a friend of Harry Adams, asking him to bring Jurgis to see him that night; and Jurgis went, and met one of the great minds of the Socialist movement.

The invitation was from a man named Fisher, a young Chicago millionaire, who had given up his life to settlement-work and had a little home in the heart of the city's slums. He did not belong to the Socialist party, but he was in sympathy with it, and he had explained that he was to have as his guest that night the editor of a big eastern magazine, who wrote against Socialism, but really did not know what it was. It had occurred to Fisher that it might be a good idea to introduce the editor to some Socialists, and he suggested bringing Jurgis, with the idea of starting up the subject of the "Pure Food bill," in which the editor was interested.

The millionaire's home was a little two-story brick house, dingy and weather-beaten outside, but attractive within. The room that Jurgis saw was half-lined with books, and upon the walls were many pictures, dimly visible in the soft, yellow light; it was a cold, rainy night, so a log-fire was crackling in the open hearth. Seven or eight people were gathered about it when Adams and his friends arrived, and Jurgis saw to his dismay that three of them were ladies. He had never talked to people of this sort before, and he fell into an agony of embarrassment. He stood in the doorway clutching his hat tightly in his hands, and made a deep bow to each of the persons as he was introduced; then, when he was asked to have a seat, he took a chair in a dark corner, and sat down upon the edge of it, and wiped the perspiration off his forehead with his sleeve. He was terrified lest they should expect him to talk; but, as it chanced, he was let alone for nearly the whole time.

There was the host himself, a tall, athletic young man, clad in evening dress, as also was the editor, a dyspeptic-looking gentleman named Maynard. There was the former's frail young wife, and also an elderly lady, a Mrs. Miller, who taught kindergarten in the settlement, and a Miss Harkness, a beautiful girl with an intense and earnest face—a student of the great Standard Oil University. She only spoke once or twice while Jurgis was there—the rest of the time she sat by the table in the center of the room, resting her chin in her hands and drinking in the conversation. There were two other men, whom young Fisher had introduced to Jurgis as Mr. Lucas and Mr. Schliemann; he heard them address Adams as "Comrade," and so he knew that they were members of the party.

The one called Lucas was a mild and meek-looking little gentleman of clerical aspect; he had been an itinerant evangelist, it transpired, and he had seen the light and become a prophet of the new dispensation. At present he was on his way—as he phrased it—from San Francisco to Texas, by way of Maine; living like the apostles of old, upon hospitality, and preaching upon street-corners when there was no hall. The other was the man previously referred to, and he had been in the midst of a discussion with the editor when Adams and Jurgis came in; at the suggestion of the host they resumed it after the interruption, and Jurgis was soon sitting spellbound thinking that here was surely the strangest man that had ever lived in the world.

Nicholas Schliemann was a German Swede; a tall, gaunt person with hairy hands and bustling yellow beard. He was a university man, and had been a professor of philosophy—until, as he said, he had found that he was selling his character as well as his time. Also he was a violinist of a tremendous sort, but he would not sell his music, and instead had come to America, where he lived in a garret-room in this slum district. He made volcanic energy take the place of fire, and he studied the composition of food-stuffs, and knew exactly how many proteins and carbohydrates his body needed; by scientific chewing he said that he tripled the value of all he ate, and it cost him eleven cents a day. About the first of July he would leave Chicago for his vacation, on foot; and when he struck the harvest-fields he would set to work for two dollars and a half a day, and come home when he had another year's supply—a hundred and twenty-five dollars. That was the nearest approach to independence a man could make under capitalism, he explained; he would never marry—no man should allow himself to fall in love until after the revolution.

He sat in a big arm-chair, with his legs crossed, and his head so far in the shadow that one saw only two glowing lights, reflected from the fire on the hearth. He spoke simply, and utterly without emotion; with the manner of a teacher setting forth to a group of scholars an axiom in geometry, he would enunciate such propositions as made the hair of an ordinary person rise on end. And when the auditor had asserted his non-comprehension, he would proceed to elucidate by some new proposition, yet more appalling. To Jurgis the Herr Doctor Schliemann assumed the proportions of a thunder storm or an earthquake. And yet, strange as it might seem, there was a subtle bond between them, and Jurgis could follow him nearly all the time; he was carried over the difficult places in spite of himself, and went plunging away in mad career, a very Mazeppa-ride upon the wild horse Speculation.

Nicholas Schliemann was familiar with all the universe, and with man as a small part of it. He understood human institutions and blew them about like soap-bubbles. It was amazing that so much destructiveness could be contained in one human mind—his words were like a stream of burning acid, which frizzled to nothingness everywhere they touched. Was it government? The purpose of government was the guarding of property-rights, the perpetration of ancient force and modern fraud. Or was it marriage? Marriage and prostitution were two sides of one shield, the predatory man's exploitation of the sex-pleasure. The difference between them was negligible; marriage was leisure-class prostitution. If a woman had money she might dictate her own terms; equality, a life-contract, and the legitimacy—that is, the property-rights—of her children. If she had no money, she was a proletarian, and sold herself for an existence. Ethically considered, marriage was an act of poltroonery, like all other conventions, it was an attempt to obviate the soul. After the revolution, woman would be free, and she would not sell herself for a living; and with industrial equality, legitimacy would of course lose its meaning. With the abolition of menial slavery the family would go to pieces; machinery would take the place of the household drudge, and children would be reared co-operatively—which would mean that science would at last have something to say in the shaping of humanity. The greatest barrier to civilization at present was the home, and the chief task of the modern intelligence was the delivering of woman from herself.

And then the subject became Religion, which was the Arch-fiend's deadliest weapon. Government oppressed the body of the wage-slave, but religion oppressed his mind, and poisoned the stream of progress at its source. The workingman was to fix his hopes upon a future life, while his pockets were picked in this one; he was brought up to frugality, humility, obedience—all the pseudo-virtues of capitalism. Abroad, the destiny of civilization would be decided in one final death-struggle between the Red International and the Black, between Socialism and the Roman Catholic Church. Nor were things much better at home, for "the stygian midnight of American evangelicalism—"

And here the ex-preacher entered the field, and there was a lively debate. "Comrade" Lucas was not what is called an educated man; he knew only the Bible; but it was the Bible interpreted by real experience, and not merely learned by rote. What was the use, he asked, of confusing religion with men's perversions of it? That the church was in the hands of the merchants at the moment was obvious; but already there were signs of rebellion, and if Comrade Schliemann could come back a few years from now—

"Yes," said the other, "I have no doubt that in a hundred years the Vatican will be denying that it ever opposed Socialism, just as at present it denies that it ever tortured Galileo."

"I am not defending the Vatican," exclaimed Lucas, vehemently. "I am defending the word of God—which is one long cry of the human-spirit for deliverance from the sway of oppression. Take the twenty-fourth chapter of the Book of Job, which I am accustomed to quote in my addresses as 'the Bible upon the Beef Trust;' or take the words of Isaiah—or of the Master himself! Not the elegant prince with the golden crown and the fine linen of our debauched and vicious art, not the jewelled idol of our society churches —but the Jesus of the awful reality, the man of sorrow and pain, the outcast, despised of the world, who had nowhere to lay his head—"

"I will grant you Jesus," interrupted the other.

"Well, then," cried Lucas, "and why should Jesus have nothing to do with his church—why should his words and his life be of no authority among those who profess to adore him? Here is a man who was the world's first revolutionist, the true founder of the Socialist movement; a man whose whole being was one flame of hatred for wealth, and all that wealth stands for—for the pride of wealth, and the luxury of wealth, and the tyranny of wealth; who was himself a beggar and a tramp, a man of the people, an associate of saloon-keepers and women of the town; who again and again, in the most explicit language, denounced wealth and the holding of wealth: 'Lay not up for yourselves treasures on earth!'—'Sell that ye have and give alms!'— 'Blessed are ye poor, for yours is the Kingdom of Heaven!'— 'Woe unto you that are rich, for ye have received your consolation!'—'Verily, I say unto you that a rich man shall hardly enter into the Kingdom of Heaven!' Who denounced in unmeasured terms the exploiters of his own time: 'Woe unto you, scribes and pharisees, hypocrites'—'Woe unto you also, you lawyers'— 'Ye serpents, ye generation of vipers, how can ye escape the damnation of hell?' Who drove out the business-men and brokers from the temple with a whip! Who was crucified—think of it—for an incendiary and a disturber of the social order! And this man they have made into the high-priest of property and smug respectability, a divine sanction of all the horrors and abominations of modern commercial civilization! Jewelled images are made of him, sensual priests burn incense to him, and modern pirates of industry bring their dollars, wrung from the toil of helpless women and children, and build temples to him, and sit in cushioned seats and listen to his teachings expounded by doctors of dusty divinity!—"

"Bravo!" cried Schliemann, laughing. But Lucas was in full career—he had talked this subject every day for five years, and had never yet let himself be stopped. "This Jesus of Nazareth!" he cried. "This class-conscious workingman! This union carpenter! This agitator, law-breaker, firebrand, anarchist! He, the sovereign lord and master of a world which grinds the bodies and souls of human beings into dollars—if he could come into the world this day and see the things that men have made in his name, would it not blast his soul with horror? Would he not go mad at the sight of it, he the Prince of Mercy and Love! That dreadful night when he lay in the Garden of Gethsemane and writhed in agony until he sweat blood—do you think that he saw anything worse than he might see tonight upon the plains of Manchuria, where men march out with a jewelled image of Him before them, to do wholesale murder for the benefit of foul monsters of sensuality and cruelty? Do you not know that if he were in St. Petersburg now, he would take the whip with which he drove out the bankers from his temple—"

Here the speaker paused an instant for breath.

"No, comrade," said the other, drily, "for he was a practical man, and he would take pretty little imitation-lemons, such as are now being shipped into Russia, handy for carrying in the pockets, and strong enough to blow a whole temple out of sight."

Lucas waited until the company had stopped laughing over this; then he began again: "But look at it from the point of view of practical politics, comrade. Here is a historical figure whom all men reverence and love, whom some regard as divine; who was one of us—who lived our life, and taught our doctrine. And now shall we leave him in the hands of his enemies—shall we allow them to stifle and stultify his example? We have his words, which no one can deny; and shall we not quote them to the people, and prove to them what he was, and what he taught, and what he did: No, no—a thousand times no!—we shall use his authority to turn out the knaves and sluggards from his ministry, and we shall yet rouse the people to vengeance and resolution!—"

Lucas paused again; and the other stretched out his hand to a paper on the table. "Here, comrade," he said, with a laugh. "There is a place for you to begin. A bishop whose wife has just been robbed of fifty thousand dollars worth of diamonds! And a most unctuous and oily of bishops! An eminent and scholarly bishop! A philanthropist and friend of labor bishop—a Civic Federation decoy-duck for the chloroforming of the wage-workingman!"

To this little passage at arms the rest of the company sat as spectators. But now Mr. Maynard, the editor, took occasion to remark, somewhat naively, that he had always understood that Socialists had a cut-and-dried program for the future of civilization; whereas here were two active members of the party, who, from what he could make out, were agreed about nothing at all. Would the two, for his enlightenment, try to ascertain just what they had in common, and why they belonged to the same party? This resulted, after much debating, in the formulating of two carefully-worded propositions: First, that a Socialist believes in the common ownership and democratic management of the means of producing the necessities of life; and, second, that a Socialist believes that the means by which this is to be brought about is a class-conscious political organization of the wage-earners. Thus far they were at one; but no farther. To Lucas, the religious zealot, the Co-operative Commonwealth was the New Jerusalem, the Kingdom of Heaven, which is "within you," the reign of peace and good will towards men. He regarded with abhorrence the ideas of the other—to whom Socialism was simply a necessary step towards a far-distant goal, a step to be tolerated with impatience. Schliemann called himself a "philosophical anarchist;" and he explained that an anarchist was one who believed that the end of human existence was the free development of every personality, unrestricted by laws save those of its own being. Since the same kind of match would light everyone's fire and the same shaped loaf of bread would fill every one's stomach, it would be perfectly feasible to submit industry to the control of a majority vote. There was only one earth, and the quantity of material things was limited. Of intellectual and moral things, on the other hand, there was no limit, and one could have more without another's having less; hence "Communism in material production, anarchism in intellectual," was a formula of the best modern proletarian thought. As soon as the birth-agony was over, and the wounds of society had been healed, there would be established a simple system whereby each man was credited with his labor and debited with his purchases; and after that the processes of production, exchange and consumption would go on automatically, and without our being conscious of them, any more than a man is conscious of the beating of his heart. And then, explained Schliemann, society would break up into independent, self-governing communities of mutually congenial persons; examples of such at present being clubs, churches and political parties. After the revolution, all the intellectual, artistic and spiritual activities of men would be cared for by such "free associations;" romantic novelists would be supported by those who liked to read romantic novels, and impressionist painters would be supported by those who liked to look at impressionist pictures; and the same with preachers and scientists, editors and actors and musicians. If any one wanted to work or paint or pray, and could find no one to maintain him, he could support himself by working part of the time. That was the case at present, the only difference being that the competitive wage-system compelled a man to work all the time to live, while, after the abolition of privilege and exploitation, any one would be able to support himself by an hour's work a day. Also the artist's audience of the present was a small minority of people, all debased and vulgarized by the effort it had cost them to win in the commercial battle; of the intellectual and artistic activities which would result when the whole of mankind was set free from the nightmare of competition, we could at present form no conception whatever.

The editor requested to know upon what ground Dr. Schliemann asserted that it might be possible for a society to exist upon an hour's toil by each of its members.

"Just what," answered the other, "would be the productive capacity of society if the present resources of science were utilized, we have no means of ascertaining; but we may be sure it would exceed anything that would sound reasonable to minds inured to the ferocious barbarisms of Capitalism. After the triumph of the international proletariat, war would of course be inconceivable; and who can figure the cost of war to humanity—not merely the value of the lives and the material that it destroys, not merely the cost of keeping millions of men in idleness, of arming and equipping them for battle and parade—but the drain upon the vital energies of society by the war-attitude and the war-terror, the brutality and ignorance, the drunkenness, prostitution and crime it entails, the industrial impotence and the moral deadness? Do you think that it would be too much to say that two hours of the working time of every efficient member of a community goes to feed the red fiend of war?"

And then Schliemann went on to outline some of the wastes of competition; the losses of industrial warfare; the ceaseless worry and friction; the vices such as drink, for instance, the use of which had nearly doubled in twenty years, as a consequence of the intensification of the economic struggle; the idle and unproductive members of the community, the frivolous rich and the pauperized poor; the law and the whole machinery of repression; the wastes of social ostentation, the milliners and tailors, the hairdressers, dancing masters, chefs and lackeys. "You understand," he said, "that in a society dominated by the fact of commercial competition, money is necessarily the test of prowess, and wastefulness the sole criterion of power. So we have, at the present moment, a society with, say thirty per cent of the population occupied in producing useless articles, and one per cent occupied in destroying them. And this is not all for the servants and panders of the parasites are also parasites, the milliner and the jewellers and the lackeys have also to be supported by the useful members of the community. And bear in mind also that this monstrous disease affects not merely the idlers and their menials, its poison penetrates the whole social body. Beneath the hundred thousand women of the elite are a million middle-class women, miserable because they are not of the elite, and trying to appear of it in public; and beneath them, in turn, are five million farmers wives reading 'fashion papers' and trimming bonnets, and shop-girls and serving maids selling themselves into brothels for cheap jewelry and imitation sealskin robes. And then consider that, added to this competition in display, you have, like oil on the flames, a whole system of competition in selling! You have manufacturers contriving tens of thousands of catch-penny devices, store keepers displaying them, and newspapers and magazines filled up with advertisements of them!"

"And don't forget the wastes of fraud," put in young Fisher, at this point.

"When one comes to the ultra-modern profession of advertising," said the other—"the science of persuading people to buy what they do not want—he is in the very center of the ghastly charnel-house of capitalist destructiveness, and he scarcely knows which of a dozen horrors to point out first. But consider the waste in time and energy incidental to making ten thousand varieties of a thing for purposes of ostentation and snobbishness, where one variety would do for use! Consider all the waste incidental to the manufacture of cheap qualities of goods, of goods made to sell and deceive the ignorant; consider the wastes of adulteration—the shoddy clothing, the cotton blankets, the unstable tenements, the ground cork life preservers, the adulterated milk, the analine soda-water, the potato-flour sausages—"

"And consider the moral aspects of these things," put in the ex-preacher.

"Precisely," said Schliemann; "the low knavery and the ferocious cruelty incidental to them, the plotting and the lying and the bribing, the blustering and bragging, the screaming egotism the hurrying and worrying. Of course imitation and adulteration are the essence of competition—they are but another form of the phase to buy in the cheapest market and sell in the dearest. A government official has stated that the nation suffers a loss of a billion and a quarter dollars a year through adulterated foods; which means, of course not only materials wasted that might have been useful outside of the human stomach, but doctors and nurses for people who would otherwise have been well, and undertakers for the whole human race ten or twenty years before the proper time. Then again consider the waste of time and energy required to sell these things in a dozen stores where one would do. There are a million or two of business firms in the country, and five or ten times as many clerks; and consider the handling and rehandling, the accounting and reaccounting, the planning and worrying, the balancing of petty profit and loss. Consider the whole machinery of the civil law, made necessary by these processes; the libraries of ponderous tomes, the courts and juries to interpret them, the lawyers studying to circumvent them, the pettifogging and chicanery, the hatreds and lies! Consider the wastes incidental to the blind and haphazard production of commodities—the factories closed, the workers idle, the goods spoiling in storage; consider the activities of the stock-manipulator, the paralyzing of whole industries, the over-stimulation of others, for speculative purposes; the assignments and bank-failures, the crises and panics, the deserted towns and the starving populations! Consider the energies wasted in the seeking of markets, the sterile trades, such as drummer, solicitor, bill-poster, advertising-agent. Consider the wastes incidental to the crowding into cities, made necessary by competition and by monopoly railroad-rates; consider the slums, the bad air, the disease and the waste of vital energies; consider the office-buildings, the waste of time and material in the piling of story upon story, and the burrowing underground! Then take the whole business of insurance, the enormous mass of administrative and clerical labor it involves, and all utter waste—"

"I do not follow that," said the editor.

"The Co-operative Commonwealth is a universal automatic insurance-company and savings-bank for all its members. Capital being the property of all, injury to it is shared by all and made up by all. The bank is the universal government credit-account, the ledger in which every individual's earnings and spendings are balanced. There is also a universal government bulletin, in which are listed and precisely described everything which the commonwealth has for sale. As no one makes any profit by the sale, there is no longer any stimulus to extravagance and no misrepresentation; no cheating, no adulteration or imitation, no bribery, or 'grafting.'"

"How is the price of an article determined?"

"The price is the labor it has cost to make and deliver it, and it is determined by the first principles of arithmetic. The million workers in the nation's wheat-fields have worked a hundred days each, and the total product of the labor is a billion bushels, so the value of a bushel of wheat is the hundredth part of a farm labor-day. If we employ an arbitrary symbol, and pay, say five dollars a day for farm-work, then the cost of a bushel of wheat is fifty cents."

"You say 'for farm-work,'" said Mr. Maynard. "Then labor is not to be paid alike?"

"Manifestly not, since some work is easy and some hard, and we should have millions of rural mail-carriers and no coal-miners. Of course the wages may be left the same, and the hours varied; one or the other will have to be varied continually, according as a greater or less number of workers is needed in any particular industry. That is precisely what is done at present, except that the transfer of the workers is accomplished blindly and imperfectly, by rumors and advertisements, instead of instantly and completely, by a universal government bulletin."

"How about those occupations in which time is difficult to calculate? What is the labor cost of a book?"

"Obviously it is the labor cost of the paper, printing and binding of it—about a fifth of its present cost."

"And the author?"

"I have already said that the state could not control intellectual production. The state might say that it had taken a year to write the book, and the author might say it had taken thirty. Goethe said that every bon mot of his had cost a purse of gold. What I outline here is a national, or, rather international, system for the providing of the material needs of men. Since a man has intellectual needs also, he will work longer, earn more, and provide for them to his own taste and in his own way. I live on the same earth as the majority, I wear the same kind of shoes and sleep in the same kind of bed; but I do not think the same kind of thoughts, and do not wish to pay for such thinkers as the majority selects. I wish such things to be left to free effort, as at present. If people want to listen to a certain preacher, they get together and contribute what they please, and pay for a church, and support the preacher, and then listen to him; I, who do not want to listen to him, stay away, and it costs me nothing. In the same way there are magazines about Egyptian coins, and Catholic saints, and flying machines, and athletic records, and I know nothing about any of them. On the other hand, if wage-slavery were abolished, and I could earn some spare money without paying tribute to an exploiting capitalist, then there would be a magazine for the purpose of interpreting and popularizing the gospel of Friedrich Nietzsche, the prophet of Evolution, and also of Horace Fletcher, the inventor of the noble science of clean eating; and incidentally, perhaps, for the discouraging of long skirts, and the scientific breeding of men and women, and the establishing of divorce by mutual consent."

Dr. Schliemann paused for a moment. "That was a lecture," he said with a laugh, "and yet I am only begun!"

"What else is there?" asked Maynard.

"I have named some of the negative wastes of competition," answered the other. "I have hardly mentioned the positive economics of co-operation. Allowing five to a family, there are fifteen million families in this country; and at least ten million of these live separately, the domestic drudge being either the wife, or a wage-slave. Now set aside the modern system of pneumatic house-cleaning, and the economies of co-operative cooking, and consider just one single item, the washing of dishes. Surely it is moderate to say that the dish-washing for a family of five takes half an hour a day; with ten hours as a day's work, it takes, therefore, half a million able-bodied persons—mostly women—to do the dish-washing of the country. And note that this is most filthy and deadening and brutalizing work; that it is a cause of anaemia, nervousness, ugliness and ill-temper; of prostitution, suicide and insanity; of drunken husbands and degenerate children—for all of which things the community has naturally to pay. And now consider that in each of my little free communities there would be a machine which would wash and dry the dishes, and do it, not merely to the eye and the touch, but scientifically—sterilizing them—and do it at a saving of all of the drudgery and nine-tenths of the time! All of these things you may find in the books of Mrs. Oilman; and then take Kropotkin's "Fields, Factories and Workshops," and read about the new science of agriculture, which has been built up in the last ten years; by which, with made soils and intensive culture, a gardener can raise ten or twelve crops in a season, and two hundred tons of vegetables upon a single acre; by which the population of the whole globe could be supported on the soil now cultivated in the United States alone! It is impossible to apply such methods now, owing to the ignorance and poverty of our scattered farming population; but imagine the problem of providing the food supply of our nation once taken in hand systematically and rationally, by scientists. All the poor and rocky land set apart for a national timber-reserve, in which our children play, and our young men hunt, and our poets dwell! The most favorable climate and soil for each product selected; the exact requirements of the community known, and the acreage figured accordingly; the most improved machinery employed, under the direction of expert agricultural chemists! I was brought up on a farm, and I know the awful deadliness of farm-work; and I like to picture it all as it will be after the revolution. To picture the great potato-planting machine, drawn by four horses, or an electric motor, plowing the furrow, cutting and dropping and covering the potatoes, and planting a score of acres a day! To picture the great potato-digging machine, run by electricity, perhaps, and moving across a thousand-acre field, scooping up earth and potatoes, and dropping the latter into sacks! To see every other kind of vegetable and fruit handled in the same way—apples and oranges picked by machinery, cows milked by electricity—things which are already done, as you may know. To picture the harvest-fields of the future, to which millions of happy men and women come for a summer holiday, brought by special trains, the exactly needful number to each place? And to contrast all this with our present agonizing system of independent small farming—a stunted, haggard, ignorant man, mated with a yellow, lean and sad-eyed drudge, and toiling from four o'clock in the morning until nine at night, working the children as soon as they are able to walk, scratching the soil with his primitive tools, and shut out from all knowledge and hope, from all the benefits of science and invention, and all the joys of the spirit—held to a bare existence by competition in labor, and boasting of his freedom because he is too blind to see his chains!"

Dr. Schliemann paused a moment and then continued: "And now place beside this fact of an unlimited food-supply, the newest discovery of physiologists, that most of the ills of the human system are due to over-feeding. It has been demonstrated by Dr. Chittenden that the quantity of food needed by the body is about four-tenths of that previously considered essential by all authorities. Also, it has been proven that meat is unnecessary as a food; and meat is obviously more difficult to produce than vegetable food, less pleasant to prepare and handle, and more likely to be unclean; but what of that, so long as it tickles the palate more strongly?"

"How would Socialism change that?" asked Miss Harkness, quickly. It was the first time she had spoken since Jurgis came.

"So long as we have wage-slavery," answered Schliemann, "it matters not in the least how debasing and repulsive a task may be, it is easy to find people to perform it. But just as soon as labor is set free, then the price of such work will begin to rise. So one by one the old, dingy and unsanitary factories will come down—it will be cheaper to build new; and so the steamships will be provided with stoking-machinery, and so the dangerous trades will be made safe, or substitutes will be found for their products. In exactly the same way, as the citizens of our Industrial Republic become refined, year by year the cost of slaughter-house products will increase; until eventually those who want to eat meat will have to do their own killing—and how long do you think the custom would survive then? To go on to another item—one of the necessary accompaniments of capitalism in a democracy is political corruption; and one of the consequences of civic administration by ignorant and vicious politicians is that typhoid, an absolutely preventable disease, kills thirty-three per hundred thousand of our population every year. The well-to-do citizen reads magazines, and flatters himself that he dodges the peril by drinking pure spring water—and he drinks it out of a glass which has been washed and rinsed in city water! Again, there is tuberculosis, a disease which could be stamped out in a generation if we cared to do it, by the isolation of the worst cases and the education of the rest; and yet we continue to allow them to go among us, spitting in our cars and on our streets, sentencing one in every ten of us to death! And the rich man flatters himself that he does not ride in the street-cars—and then his wife goes to a store and buys a dress that was made in a sweat-shop, and a few weeks later his only child dies of scarlet fever, and his preacher tells him it was an act of Providence—as indeed it was. It was just a little Socialist lecture, delivered after the cold and impersonal fashion of Mother Nature; a demonstration of equality and human brotherhood to one who ridiculed and denied it! At present, of course, the majority of human beings are not human beings at all; they are machines for the creating of wealth for others, and they are penned up in filthy houses and left to rot and stew in misery. The conditions of their life make them ill faster than all the doctors in the world could heal them; and so, of course, they remain as centers of contagion, more or less poisoning the lives of all of us, and making happiness impossible for even the most selfish. I am sure it would be no exaggeration to say that all the medical and surgical discoveries that science can make in the future will be of infinitely less importance than the application of the knowledge we already possess, when the disinherited of the earth have established their right to a human existence."

Here the Herr Doctor concluded and relapsed into silence. Jurgis had noticed that the beautiful young girl who sat by the centre-table was watching him, with something of the same look that Jurgis himself had worn when he first discovered Socialism, and later on, when the group broke up, he heard Mrs. Fisher say to her, in a low voice, "I wonder if Mr. Maynard will still write the same things about Socialism," to which she answered, "I don't know—but if he does I shall know that he is a knave."

36

THE IMPRESSION which Jurgis got most keenly during these first weeks of his acquaintance with Socialism was of the boundlessness of the subject, and of his own overwhelming ignorance. Its moral appeal he was as fitted to judge as any man; but so far as its intellectual content was concerned, every difficulty which he conquered only revealed to him a dozen more. There was nothing for him to do but stick to it, however. He had to convert others, and could not remain ignorant forever.

He acquired the reading habit. He would carry in his pocket a tract or a pamphlet which some one had loaned him, and whenever he had an idle moment during the day he would read a paragraph and then think about it while he worked. Also he read the newspapers, and asked questions about them. One of the other porters at Hinds's was a sharp little Irishman, who knew everything that Jurgis wanted to know; and while they were busy he would explain to him the geography of America and its organization, its constitution, its laws, and its history; also he gave Jurgis a clear idea of the business system of the country, the great railroads and corporations, and who owned them, and the labor unions, and the big strikes, and the men who had led them. Then at night, when he could get off, Jurgis would attend the Socialist meetings. During the campaign one was not dependent upon the street-corner affairs, where the weather and the quality of the orator were equally uncertain. There were hall meetings every night, and he could hear speakers of national prominence. These discussed the political situation from every point of view, and all that troubled Jurgis was the impossibility of carrying off but a small part of the treasures they offered him. There was a man who was known in the party as the "Little Giant."[1] The Lord had used up so much material in the making of his head that there had not been enough to complete his legs; but he got about on the platform, and when he shook his raven whiskers the pillars of Capitalism rocked. The chairman of the evening, a man named Hinrichs, chanced to be long and lean, and the orator took him to illustrate the machinations of the enemy. "They tell you," said he, "that Socialists wish to abolish private property—that they wish us to divide up and own everything in common. Now, the truth is that not only do the Socialists contend for the right to own things, but their principal objection to

---

1. "The Little Giant" is probably Walter Thomas Mills. He fits the physical description, was well known to Sinclair, and is referred to in Eugene Debs' correspondence as "the little professor." Mills was the author of *The Struggle for Existence,* which also fits the description.

the present system is that under it most people are unable to own anything. Here are Comrade Hinrichs and I, who wear pants; and imagine us owning our pants in common! Do you think that Hinrichs would stay in a party that wanted him to go round in my pants? Not collective ownership of pants, but collective ownership of the means of producing pants, is the object of the Socialist party!"

Then there came a young author,[2] who had been a street boy in San Francisco—a salmon-fisher, an oyster-pirate, a longshoreman, a sailor. He had tramped the country and been sent to jail; he had lived in the White-chapel slums, he had been to the Klondike in search of gold. All these things he pictured in his books, and because he was a man of genius he forced the world to hear him. Now he was famous, but wherever he went he still preached the gospel of the poor.

And then there was one known as the "millionaire Socialist."[3] He had made a fortune in business, and spent nearly all of it in building up a monthly magazine which the postoffice department had tried to suppress, and had driven to Canada. He was a simple, quiet-mannered man, whom you would have taken for anything in the world but a Socialist agitator. Yet he had been a candidate of the party in England and in Australia, in British Columbia, California and New York.

There was a world-wide process of economic evolution, and he exhibited its laws and methods; he spoke simply and informally—he could not understand why anyone should get excited about it. Life was a struggle for existence, and the strong overcame the weak, and in turn were overcome by the strongest. Those who lost in the struggle were generally exterminated; but now and then they had been known to save themselves by combination —which was a new and higher kind of strength. It was so that the gregarious animals had overcome the predaceous; it was so, in human history, that the people had mastered the kings. The workers were simply the citizens of industry, and the Socialist movement was the expression of their will to survive. The inevitability of the revolution depended upon this fact, that they had no choice but to unite or be exterminated; this fact, grim and inexorable, depended upon no human will; it was the law of the economic process. The editor could show the details of it, with the most marvelous precision; how the irresistible tendency of the wealth of society to concentrate resulted in the slow elimination of the wage-worker. His existence depended upon his ability to find a job; and the job depended upon the master's ability to make profits;

---

2. This refers to Jack London.

3. The "millionaire socialist" is Gaylord Wilshire, publisher of *Wilshire's Magazine*. It's likely that Wilshire's magazine first introduced Sinclair to socialism, and the two men eventually became good friends.

and as the wealth concentrated, the markets necessarily grew scarcer. Of course, if the rich had spent all their income, consumption would have kept pace with production; but they could not do it—modern machinery, driven by steam and electricity, enabled one worker to produce a hundred times what he had formerly produced by hand, and when a man's income was fifty million dollars a year, he had to "save" it, whether he would or not. What he actually did was to reinvest it—that is, he used it to build new machinery, and to produce new wealth, which was reinvested in turn—and so on forever. Was it not obvious that this process of piling up and piling up could not go on without end. That some day capital would be over-produced, and interest —profits—would fail? That there would be more goods than could be sold, and that the factories would be closed and the workers left to starve? Of the imminence of the crisis the sign was the trust. The trust was necessary, because there were too many goods produced, because competitive selling no longer furnished profits. The trust monopoly was thus no diabolical invention, it was an economic necessity; and there could be no possible restoration of competition—the next change could only be from private to public monopoly. The productive machinery would be thrown open, and goods would be produced, no longer for the masters, but for the workers, and so consumption would balance production forever.

And then came the evening of the great meeting of the campaign, when Jurgis heard the two standard-bearers of his party. Ten years before there had been in Chicago a strike of a hundred and fifty thousand railroad employees, and thugs had been hired by the railroads to commit violence, and give a pretext to the President of the United States to send troops and break the strike, by flinging the officers of the union into jail without trial. When the president of the union came out of his cell he came out a Socialist; and now for just ten years he had been traveling up and down the United States, standing face to face with the people, and pleading with them for justice. In that long period there was scarce a workingman in the country who had not heard him; and now, tonight, in Chicago, where he had been crushed and ruined, the representatives of ninety-five labor unions sat upon the platform with him, and over forty of them had brought their union-banners for a sign. They were grouped in masses of color above the stage, and behind them all waved the standard of the revolution, the blood-red symbol of Brotherhood. The great auditorium was packed with a mob of four thousand workingmen, and when their leaders came upon the stage they rose and shouted—shouted!

He was a man of electric presence, tall and gaunt, with a face worn thin by struggle and suffering. The fury of outraged manhood gleamed in it—and the tears of suffering little children pleaded in his voice. He was represented in the papers as a man of violence, but he had the tenderness of a woman. "God was feeling mighty good when he made him," wrote James Whitcomb

Riley, "and he didn't have anything else to do all day." "He has ten hopes to your one hope," wrote another poet who loved him. "He has ten loves to your one love."[4]

When he spoke he paced the stage restlessly; he was lithe and eager, like a panther. He leaned over, reaching out for his audience; he pointed into their souls with an insistent finger. His voice was husky from much speaking, but the hall was as still as death, and everyone heard him. He spoke the language of workingmen—he pointed them the way. He showed the two political parties "two wings of the same bird of prey!" The people were allowed to choose between their candidates, and both of them were controlled, and all their nominations were dictated, by the same power. The people attended political meetings, of either party, and the hall was paid for, and the speakers were hired, out of the same purse. The Republican convention had nominated for vice president a railroad director and millionaire, and the Democratic convention had nominated a capitalist, the owner of a large part of the state of West Virginia, a coal-baron, who does not permit the men in his employ to organize. In his biography you will note that in his youth he was a slave-driver; and he is yet—he has simply exchanged a small number of black slaves for a large number of white ones. And if any of my audience are in this gentleman's class, let them vote for him! I shall be quite satisfied when all the capitalists vote for their candidates and all the workingmen vote for theirs."

The ex-president of the United States had recently published his version of the Chicago strike in a big Eastern magazine, and his victim had written a reply, which the magazine had refused to print. It had appeared in a Socialist weekly, of which three-quarters of a million copies had been sold; they were giving it out at this meeting, and Jurgis took a copy home with him and read it through. And so he became acquainted with the "Appeal to Reason."[5]

About twelve years previously a Colorado real estate speculator[6] had made up his mind that it was wrong to gamble in the necessities of life of human beings; and he had retired and begun the publication of a Socialist weekly. There had come a time when he had to set his own type, but he had held on and won out, and now his paper was an institution. It used a car-load of paper every week, and the mail-trains would be hours loading up at the depot of the

---

4. This refers to the most beloved figure in American socialism, Eugene V. Debs, who, in addition to being a five-time Socialist Party candidate for president, was imprisoned by the federal government for his opposition to World War I.

5. In the years prior to World War I, *Appeal to Reason* was the largest-circulation periodical in the world.

6. Julius A. Wayland.

little Kansas town.[7] It was a four-page weekly, which sold for less than half a cent a copy; its regular subscription list was over a quarter of a million, and its editions averaged four hundred thousand each week, and now and then touched the million mark. It went to every country town and cross-roads post office in America, and sometimes a single copy of it was read and re-read by a dozen people.

The "Appeal" was a "propaganda" paper. It had a manner all its own—it was full of ginger and spice, of Western slang and hustle. It collected news of the doings of the "plutes," and served it up for the benefit of the "American working-mule." It would have columns of the deadly parallel—the million dollars' worth of diamonds, or the fancy pet poodle-establishment of a society dame, beside the fate of Mrs. Murphy, of San Francisco, who had starved to death on the streets, or of John Robinson, just out of the hospital, who had hung himself in New York because he could not find work. It collected all the stories of graft and misery from the daily press, and made little pungent paragraphs out of them. "Three banks of Bungtown, South Dakota, failed, and more savings of the workers swallowed up!" "The mayor of Sandy Creek, Oklahoma, has skipped with a hundred thousand dollars of the public funds. That's the kind of rulers the old partyites give you!" "The president of the Florida Flying Machine company is in jail for bigamy. He was a prominent opponent of Socialism, which he said would break up the home!" The Appeal had what it called its "Army," about thirty thousand of the faithful, who did things for it; and it was always exhorting the Army to keep its dander up, and occasionally encouraging it with a prize competition, for anything from a gold watch to a steam yacht or an eighty-acre farm. It published its circulation-statement every week, with the "ons" and the "offs" from each state; and it would be exultant or mournful, according to circum-stances. Its office-helpers were all known to the "Army" by quaint titles— "Inky Ike," "the Baldheaded Man," "the Redheaded Girl," "the Bulldog," the "Office Goat" and "the One Hoss." There was an "Army Column," in which notable events were recorded, after such a fashion as this: "There was a moment's sudden silence, broken only by the rumble of the press. Then the Army Editor shouted: 'There it comes—get under cover!' Through the window came a huge projectile; the Sporting Editor, used to thinking quickly, scurried to the bomb-proof, followed quickly by all save the Religious Editor, who stood rooted to the spot, saying his prayers. Then it

---

7. Girard Kansas, which in addition to being the headquarters of *Appeal to Reason* was also the home of the Haldeman-Julius Company, the most prolific publisher of radical materials in U.S. history. During its existence, 1919–1951—it effectively collapsed with the death of its publisher, E. Haldeman-Julius, in 1951—it published over 2500 books and pamphlets, with a total press run likely exceeding 100,000,000 copies; one estimate places the total press run at half a billion.

landed, and the building shook like a battle-ship above an exploding torpedo. One hundred and sixty yearlies, from Comrade Smith, of Kalamazoo, Michigan."

But sometimes, again, the Appeal would be desperately serious. It sent a correspondent to Colorado, and printed pages describing the overthrow of American institutions in that state. In a certain city of the country it had over forty of its "Army" in the headquarters of the Telegraph Trust, and no message of importance to Socialists ever went through that city that a copy of it did not go to the Appeal. It would print great broadsides during the campaign; one copy that came to Jurgis was a manifesto addressed to striking workingmen, of which nearly a million copies had been distributed in the industrial centers, wherever the employers' associations had been carrying out their "open shop" program. "You have lost the strike!" it was headed. "And now what are you going to do about it?" It was what is called an "incendiary" appeal—it was written by a man into whose soul the iron had entered. When this edition appeared, twenty thousand copies were sent to the Stockyards district; and they were taken out and stowed away in the rear of a little cigar-store, and every evening, and on Sundays, the members of the Packingtown locals would get armfuls and distribute them on the streets and in the houses. The people of Packingtown had lost their strike, if ever a people had, and so they read these papers gladly, and twenty thousand were hardly enough to go around.

This was a work at which Jurgis would have tried to help, but he did not dare, for fear of Phil Connor and the police. Indeed, Billy Hinds was always urging him to be careful how he took part in the Socialist activities, because of the harm it might do the party to have one of its workers arrested for a crime. But Jurgis was reckless and impatient, and though he said that he had no idea of going near the Stockyards, the fact was that he was burning up with a desire to do just that. After all, Packingtown was his home; and now, about election time, when the yards were seething with agitation, and every report told of new gains by the party, it was hard for him not to be able to go out and see with his own eyes—it was hard for him not to be able to undo the work which he had done the previous spring, when he had served as a henchman of Tom Cassidy.

And a week or so before election day this impatience boiled over—there came a temptation which Jurgis simply could not resist!

The Democratic party had been for a long time a party of radicalism, and now that it had sold out to the trusts the politicians were at a loss for something to say to the people. In particular was this true of Packingtown, where the Socialists were literally having their own way, and Tom Cassidy and the Cook County machine were at their wits' end for an "issue". Almost at the wind-up of the struggle they bethought themselves of an appeal to race-prejudice; for the strike had been won by southern negroes, thousands of whom had stayed on since the trouble—and now it occurred to Cassidy that if he were to bring in an old-time "fire-eater", he would have somebody to whom the people of the district would listen.

There was a South Carolina politician known as the "Pitchfork Senator"; a gentleman who tore off his coat when he talked to workingmen, and damned and swore like a Hessian. And now one morning all Packingtown woke up to read that this famous orator was coming to pay it a visit! That same day a member of the Stockyards local came down to Billy Hinds's with the news, and the two, with Struver and Adams, locked themselves up for an hour or two and devised a counter-stroke. Two days later the people of the district found a new proclamation, posted everywhere underneath the other, and beginning: "Workingmen of Chicago, don't let them fool you! So long as white workingmen fight negro workingmen, the capitalists will own both!"

And then, when the day of the meeting came, as the men came home from their work, they found thousands of little green cards being mysteriously circulated. This was a work at which the Socialists had to be careful, for it was unlawful to distribute printed matter on the streets, and though a Y. M. C. A. or Methodist church meeting might be so announced, and nothing said, the police would recollect the law whenever they caught a Socialist breaking it. But nobody was caught this time, and before night every workingman in the yards had read a series of

QUESTIONS FOR THE PITCHFORK SENATOR!

1. What did you or your party ever do for the working class?
2. What makes you think that the shooting, hanging, and burning of Southern black workers, which you advise, will keep negroes from taking the jobs of Northern white workingmen?
3. If the working class owned the mills, mines, factories and machines with which wealth is produced, would they need to fight each other for jobs?
4. Who is putting up for the Democratic campaign fund from which your expenses are paid? Laborers or capitalists? If the latter, for whom are you talking? Whose "nigger" are you, anyhow?

When that meeting was called to order, Jurgis was there—wild horses could not have kept him away. Also there were about two thousand of the Stockyards workers, nearly half of them Socialists, and prepared to give the honorable senator the time of his life.

He had not talked two minutes before they got after him. He was denouncing the Republican candidate for favoring "race equality", and a man who sat just in front of Jurgis got up and asked the senator why the Democratic party had nominated a capitalist judge and a millionaire mine-owner. The senator was disconcerted for a moment, and tried to go on; but the man would have an answer, and the audience backed him up by hoots and yells. So the other explained that the ticket did not suit him perfectly, but that he had to make the best of it; and when the crowd laughed at this, he got angry, exclaiming: "If you were living in hell, wouldn't you be glad to get into purgatory for a while!" To which a voice replied: "We don't want hell or purgatory, either!" And when the senator inquired, "What do you want, then?" the whole building rang with the reply: "Socialism! Socialism!"

The unhappy orator had plainly not been warned; he did not seem even to know what Socialism was, and he started again to talk about "equality" and "amalgamation". When the crowd kept badgering him, he yelled in a rage: "I can't answer you down there. Come up here and face me!" And so one man got out into the aisle and propounded the problem: "If the negroes are the cause of all the workingmen's troubles, do they own the Southern cotton mills?"

"Of course they don't," answered the speaker, missing the point.

"And then, why is it that children six and eight years of age are compelled to work in them at night?" asked the other.

This put the senator in a corner again. and finally he confessed that this was a new problem to the South, and that he didn't know what would be done about it. Then someone inquired about the report that the Democratic nominee, while judge of the supreme court of New York, had declared the eight-hour law unconstitutional. The senator admitted that he didn't know about that, either. "I don't know everything," he said, with an attempt to be genial; to which a woman who rose up in front made answer: "You don't seem to know anything, Senator."

And again, when the uproar over this had subsided, the senator set out to show that it was the negroes who had broken the strike. They had done it once, and they would do it twice, he said—and then the same woman demanded: "Wouldn't they do just the same if a Democrat were president?"

It was fully a minute before the crowd stopped laughing over that. The senator was red in the face and he tried to reply, and they had it hot and heavy for a minute or two. Finally, however, he threw up his hands and cried: "I can face any man, but, my God, I'm not used to arguing with women!" The laughter over this would have cleared the atmosphere in any meeting less determined; but when it ceased, the woman was still there. She kept shaking her finger at the speaker—she would have answers, and the audience was behind her, backing up every word. She insisted upon being told what good it would do the Packingtown unions to elect a Democratic president. The senator could not tell her; he could not seem to realize just what he had struck, and finally he cried: "But if you vote for a Republican, how will that help you?" To which a woman replied: "We're not going to vote for a Republican!" "Then in the name of the Almighty, who are you going to vote for?" cried the other. And in a flash the audience was on its feet again, yelling altogether: "A Socialist! A Socialist!"

The Pitchfork Senator stood listening to the chorus. Then he demanded, in perplexity: "What do you Socialists want, anyhow?" Needless to say that proved a fruitful question; there were a dozen people anxious to tell him, and finally he chose one and they had an argument, winding up with a little speech by the Socialist.

"And do you expect to accomplish all these things this election?" the senator inquired; and when the other had answered, "No," he said: "Then you want the workingmen here to throw away their votes?"

The man denied that, but the other came at him again: "You do! You do!" he cried. "Don't you want the workingmen to vote for what they know they can't get?" "Well, Senator," retorted the other, "which is better, to vote for what you want and can't get, or to vote for what you don't want and get it?"

But even then the senator had courage to try again. He came back to the point again. The workingman must not throw his vote away! "But, Senator," asked the man, "why should the capitalists all be so anxious to save the workingman's vote? If it is to the workingman's interests to vote the Democratic ticket, why do the capitalists contribute millions of dollars to keep him from voting any other?" "They don't! They don't," cried the senator; to which the man demanded: "Then you deny that your campaign fund was made up by capitalists?" "I do," said the senator—and instantly the woman, his Nemesis, was upon her feet again, crying: "But, senator, you admitted just now that you had a millionaire mine-owner on your ticket; and didn't he do what he promised?"

There was a furious scrimmage over this point. The woman was ready with instances of where money had come from in previous campaigns. And then, presently, the argument came round to where the money went to—and at this point a new personage entered the debate. The senator was engaged in denying vehemently that the Democratic campaign-funds were used to bribe voters; and a dozen men were on their feet, shouting for a hearing—until finally one of them prevailed by sheer power of lung, and stood in the middle of the aisle, his hair rumpled, his eyes shining, his clenched fists upraised. It was Jurgis.

It was Jurgis, crazy with excitement. He had forgotten everything in the ardor of his fight; he stood there and faced the whole crowd. The word was concerning the character of Democratic politicians; and Jurgis had captured the meeting by yelling: "Dey are t'ieves! Dey are all dam t'eves!" Jurgis had his peculiarities of pronunciation, which have not been reproduced here; he could not round the letters "th", and he still called himself a "Lit-ua-nian".

"I have been dere myself!" he rushed on, when he had finally gained the ear of the crowd. "I have seen it wit' my own eyes. I have done it wit' my own hands!" And then he proceeded to tell them about it, all the details. "I lived here in the Stockyards once!" he cried—"I helped sell out the people! I have known Tom Cassidy! Every god damn cent dat feller has he gits from de packers, and den he goes an' elects Republicans—anybody—anything, he don't care—so it's his man. An' when de strike comes he runs away and hides! And now de people begin to wake up, an' he says he's goin' out of politics! He buys him a house in Hyde Park—he pays a hundred t'ousan' dollars for it! Who pays for dat house, you t'ink? I tells you stockyard men—"

And then suddenly Jurgis gave a gasp, and stopped. He stood for a moment, exactly as he was, as if hewed of stone; his jaw fell loose, and a deadly pallor spread over his face. The audience thought that it was embarrassment, and cheered and shouted, "Go on!" to encourage him. But Jurgis did not go on, and so someone else got up and began to shout at the senator, and in a few seconds the fight had rolled past. As for Jurgis, he still stood motionless, with a cold chill creeping down his back, and a deadly terror clutching his heart. He kept gazing, as if he were hypnotized, at a certain spot in the crowd to the right of the platform, where for one brief instant he had seen a face peering out at him—the face of his one enemy in the world—"Phil" Connor, the boss!

Jurgis was slow of thought, and never did his slowness cost him more than now. For a full minute he stood there—looking for the face again, and wondering if he had really seen it—before he turned and made a break for the door.

The aisle was packed half way up, so that he had to elbow his way, and he had scarcely got out of the door and into the corridor, when he heard the voice of Connor, at one side: "Hey, there! Stop that man! Stop him!"

Instantly, of course, the place was in an uproar. Jurgis buried himself into the crowd and started to fight his way out. When men tried to seize him he struck out, and was soon striking at everything he saw. He was within sight of the open door, and freedom, when suddenly he saw a policeman plunging toward him, club in hand; somebody grabbed him by the coat-tails, and he lunged at the man and floored him, and then the club swung at his head, and he ducked just in the nick of time. The next instant—knowing the police—he flung his hands into the air and shouted: "I give up! I give up!"

And so, in a second or two more, it was all over; the policeman had collared him, and another had reached him on the other side, and Connor, the henchman of Cassidy, had arrived and given his orders: "There's a warrant out for that man—run him in!"

CONCLUSION

IT WAS election day—when the long campaign was over, and the whole country seemed to stand still and hold its breath, awaiting the issue. Jurgis was out on a thousand dollar's bail, which his employer had furnished, and he and the rest of the staff of Hinds's hotel hardly waited to finish their dinner before they hurried off to the big hall which the party had hired for the evening.

Already there were people waiting there, and already the telegraph instrument on the stage had begun clicking off the returns. When the final accounts were made up, the Socialist vote proved to be about four hundred and thirty thousand—an increase of something like three hundred and fifty per cent in four years. And that was doing well; but the Socialists were dependent for their early returns upon messages from the locals, and naturally those locals which had been most successful were the ones which felt most like reporting; and so that night every one in the hall believed that the vote was going to be six, or seven, or eight hundred thousand. Just such an incredible increase had actually been made in Chicago, and in the state; the vote of the city had been 6,700 in 1900, and now it was 47,000; that of Illinois had been 9,600, and now it was 69,000. So, as the evening waxed, and the crowd piled in, the meeting was a sight to be seen. Bulletins would be read, and the people would shout themselves hoarse; and then someone would make a speech, and there would be more shouting; and then silence and more bulletins. There would come messages from the secretaries of neighboring states, reporting their achievements; in four years the vote of Indiana had gone from 2,300 to 12,000; that of Wisconsin from 7,000 to 28,000; that of Ohio from 4,800 to 36,000. And then, later on, came reports from the Far West, which was the most American part of the country, and accordingly the part in which the Socialist movement was the strongest. Washington had gone from 2,000 to 10,000. Oregon from 1,500 to 7,600, California from 7,600 to 30,000. There were telegrams to the national office from enthusiastic individuals in little towns which had made amazing and unprecedented increases in a single year: Benedict, Kansas, from 26 to 260; Henderson, Kentucky, 19 to 111; Holland, Michigan, 14 to 208; Cleo, Oklahoma, 0 to 104; Martin's Ferry, Ohio, 0 to 296—and many more of the same kind. There were literally hundreds of such towns; there would be reports from half a dozen of them in a single batch of telegrams. And the men who read the dispatches off to the audience were old campaigners, who had been to the places and helped to make the vote, and could make appropriate comments. Quincy, Illinois, had gone from 189 to 831—that was where the mayor had arrested a Socialist speaker! Crawford county, Kansas, had gone from 285 to 1,975, that was the home of the Appeal to Reason. Battle Creek, Michigan, had gone from 4,261 to 10,184; that was the answer of labor to the Citizens' Industrial Association.

And then there were official returns from the various precincts and wards of Chicago itself—the vote of Chicago had gone from 14,000 to 47,000 in two years. Whether it was a factory district or one of the "silk-stocking" wards seemed to make no particular difference in the increase; but one of the things which surprised the party leaders most was the tremendous vote that came rolling in from the Stockyards. Packingtown comprises three wards of the city, and the Socialist vote in the spring of 1903 had been five hundred, and in the fall of the same year, sixteen hundred. Now, only a year later, it was over sixty-three hundred—and the Democratic vote only eighty-eight hundred! There were other wards in which the Democratic vote had been actually surpassed; and in two districts, one of them including part of the Stockyards, members of the state legislature had been elected—the first Socialists ever chosen to state offices in Illinois. Thus Chicago now led the country; and what was more important, the size of the vote would entitle the party to hold primaries—and as the primary officials would be paid by the city, and would, of course, turn their pay over to the party, the city of Chicago would be made to contribute about five thousand dollars a year to the campaign fund!

So spoke an orator upon the platform; and two thousand pairs of eyes were fixed upon him, and two thousand voices were cheering his every sentence. This man had been the head of the city's relief bureau in the stockyards, until the sight of misery and corruption had made him sick. He was young, hungry-looking, full of fire. As he swung his long arms and beat up the crowd, to Jurgis he seemed the very spirit of the revolution. "Organize! Organize! Organize!"—that was his cry. He was afraid of this tremendous vote, which his party had not expected, and which it had not earned. "These men are not Socialists," he cried—"they do not know what Socialism is. They have voted because they wished to protest, and there was no other way to do it. But they are ready to learn, if you are ready to teach them. This election will pass, and the excitement will die, and people will forget about it; and if you forget about it too, if you sink back and rest upon your oars, we shall lose this vote that we have polled today, and our enemies will laugh us to scorn. It rests with you to take your resolution—to take it now, in the flush of victory, and stand by it; to find these men who have voted for us, and bring them to our meetings and give them our literature and organize them and bind them to us! We shall not find all our campaigns as easy as this one, and you must not be discouraged if the tide recedes. Everywhere in the country the old-party politicians are studying this vote, and setting their sails by it; and no where will they be quicker or more cunning than here in our own city. Fifty thousand Socialist votes in Chicago means a municipal-ownership Democracy in the spring! And they will fool the voters once more—they will poll the biggest vote in their history, and all the powers of plunder and corruption will be swept into office on the tide! But whatever they may do when they get in, there is one thing they will not do, and that will be the thing for which they were elected.

They will not give the people of our city municipal ownership—they will not mean to do it, they will not try to do it; what they will do is give our party in Chicago the greatest opportunity that has ever come to Socialism in America! We shall have the sham reformers self-stultified and self-convicted! We shall have the radical Democracy left without a lie with which to cover its nakedness! We shall have our people without a party that can even promise to carry out its will! And then will begin the rush that will never be checked, the tide that will never turn till it has reached its flood—that will be irresistible, overwhelming—the rallying of the outraged workingmen of Chicago to the standard of the revolution! And we shall organize them, we shall drill them, we shall marshal them for the victory! We shall bear down all opposition, we shall drive everything before us—and Chicago will be ours! *Chicago will be ours!!* CHICAGO WILL BE OURS!"

All of which was at one o'clock on the morning of the day after election; and at one o'clock of the afternoon of the same day Jurgis was handcuffed to a detective, and on his way to serve a two years' sentence in state's prison for assault with intent to kill.